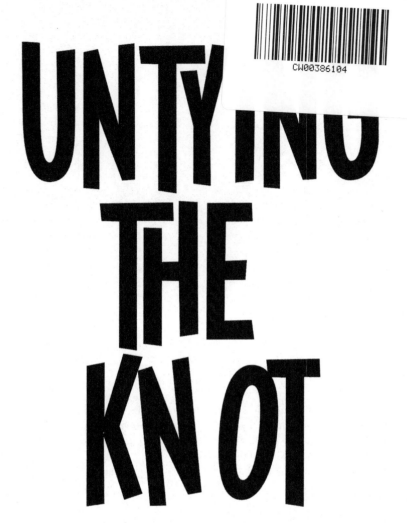

# UNTYING THE KNOT

USA TODAY BESTSELLING AUTHOR

# MEGHAN QUINN

Published by Hot-Lanta Publishing, LLC

Copyright 2022

Cover Design By: RBA Designs

# Prologue

## MYLA

"How does my hair look?" Nichole asks as she pushes the short blonde locks behind her ear.

"Still fresh, still curled, but don't put it behind your ear," I whisper.

"Are you sure?"

"Positive."

"Breath?" She blows in my face.

I take a large sniff—because that's what best friends are for—and say, "Smells like nothing."

"Good." She tugs on the hem of her black dress. "I thought those nachos we had at the bar were going to make me have cheese breath."

"Cheese breath is nowhere to be found."

"Thank God." She glances up the stairs of the townhome and then back at me. "He's cute, right?"

"Uh, he's more than cute," I answer. "He's hot."

"Yeah, okay. I wasn't sure if I was making it up in my head. But he's hot. His jawline is incredible."

"And his shoulders are broad," I answer. "And even though his shirt is loose, you can tell he has muscles."

"Lots of muscles, and what are we a fan of?" Nichole asks.

"Men with muscles," I answer with a fist pump.

"And this place is pretty nice." Nichole glances around. "I mean, it screams bachelor pad, but we've seen worse."

"Totally. At least beer cans aren't being used as decorations."

"Just stupid sports flags," Nichole says, gesturing to the large Phoenix Studmuffins flag pinned to the stark white wall.

One couch, one enormous TV mounted on the wall with loose cords, brown carpet that's seen better days, and a single four-by-six picture of two guys hanging next to the TV, their arms wrapped around each other in a "bro hug." There's not much to the space, not even a dining table where a dining table should be. It's just empty.

"Do you think they like the Studmuffins?" I ask. "That flag is very large. They're obviously fans of the Triple-A team."

"How do you know it's Triple-A?" Nichole asks. "You don't watch baseball."

"I waited a table that just came from a game." I shrug. "Either way, I wonder if they're actually fans or if it's more of an ironic thing. You know, like . . . they got it for free, and now it's the only decoration they have besides the four-by-six frame that's made for a side table, not a wall."

Nichole taps her chin. "Hmm, well, the guy . . . God, what's his name again?"

"Banner," I say with a roll of my eyes.

Out of the two of us, Nichole likes to sleep around, and I have no problem with that. *Get it in while you can* is what I say, but we're a package deal. Not as in threesome potential, but as in I have no shame in waiting for Nichole to get done with her business so we can walk out together, hand in hand.

"Oh right, Banner. Anyway, he seems more ironic than anything. The flowers on his button-up shirt scream ironic."

"I could see that," I answer just as the stairs creak.

"Oh God, he's coming." Nichole flashes her teeth at me. "Anything in them?"

"Nope, you're good."

"And breath is fine still?"

"It didn't change in the past three minutes."

She opens her mouth and closes it. Opens and closes. "How's my range, you know, in case I need to slip anything in my mouth tonight?"

I chuckle. "Looking a little stiff, but I'm sure he'll be stiff as well."

"Ha, good one."

"Hey," Banner says from the doorway of the living room. "Uh, you want to head up?" He gestures toward the stairs with his thumb. When we arrived, he asked for a minute—most likely to clean his room, make his bed, you know, make things comfortable—so we took a seat, but it looks like planned sexual intercourse is about to commence.

"Yeah, sure," Nichole says nonchalantly as she stands.

Eyes on me, Banner asks, "Are you just going to . . . sit there?"

"Don't mind if I do," I say as I lean back on the couch and cross one leg over the other.

"You don't want to go home or anything?" he asks, looking far too confused.

"Nope, I'm good. I'll just wait for Nichole. The couch is comfy, and if you can just direct me to the remote, I'll drown out the inevitable moans."

"Uh, yeah," he says as he walks over to the TV and removes the remote Velcroed to the side of it. Huh, they don't have a dining room table, but they have the wherewithal to Velcro the TV remote so it doesn't get lost. What kind of household is this?

He tosses the remote, and I do a fine job of not even coming close to catching it. It hits me in the arm instead.

"Ooof, that will leave a mark," I say. Rubbing my arm, I ask, "I'm going to assume what's yours is mine in this scenario?"

"What?" he asks, his brow furrowed. The patience in this one is wearing thin. Bet he didn't expect to bring home a hot date . . . and a squatter, but here we are.

"Am I free to roam about the cabin? You know, eat and drink what's available? I mean, my friend will be offering you one hell of an orgasm tonight—she's already done mouth stretches."

Nichole smiles brightly. "I did."

"So am I free to make myself at home?"

"Oh, yeah . . . sure," he answers and then looks at Nichole. "You did mouth stretches?"

"Always come prepared is my motto."

I stand from the couch and walk over to them. I place my hand on Banner's arm and say, "She's very bendy. Have fun." I give his arm a squeeze and then offer Nichole a thumbs-up. "Muscles are popping."

"Oh, yay." She takes his hand and pulls him up the stairs as I head to the kitchen.

Surprisingly more open than I expected, the kitchen is shrouded by dark oak cabinets, tan speckled countertops, and one window that looks out into what I'm going to assume is a backyard. Can't quite tell since it's past eleven at night. Not a single dish in the sink, the counters are shockingly clean, which means either they don't cook or they can actually clean up after themselves, and there are only two appliances in the kitchen. A coffee pot—nothing fancy, something you can buy at Target for twenty dollars on sale or snag for fifteen on Black Friday—and the most enormous toaster oven I've ever seen.

I walk up to it and pull down the hatch. "What does this hold? A whole loaf of bread at the same time? My God, where do you buy something like this?" I then try the fridge. "Would you look at that? Fruit and veggies." I bend down and push around Tupperware with precut vegetables. "This is real Tupperware. That's impressive. Ooo, a Capri Sun." I snag a fruit punch and then shut the fridge door. "Food, where is the food?"

I open a few empty cabinets, which makes me think they really don't cook here since there's nothing to cook with, and then I stumble across some food.

"What do we have here?" I push past boxes of oatmeal, protein bars—hmm, maple donut, wasn't sure anyone liked that flavor—and tubs of protein powder. "Typical," I mutter. Normally, I'm a healthy-ish person who can appreciate a solid tub of whey protein, but not after a sweaty night of drinking and dancing in a bar. I need some snacking food.

I move to another cabinet, and then another, and another but come up short. Hoping I can find something in the freezer, I whip that open as well, wishing for an ice cream bar of some sort but only find rotten bananas and ice packs.

"What kind of household is this?" Groaning, I go back to the fridge, snag the Tupperware full of grapes—plucked from the vine—and head back into the living room, where I sit on the couch and turn on the TV. I go straight to TBS, knowing there will be sitcom reruns, and to my delight, it's *The Big Bang Theory*. "Oh Sheldon, you crazy fuck," I say as I pop open the grapes and start inhaling them one at a time.

I'm in the middle of poking my straw through the hole in the Capri Sun when the front door opens and shuts. Locks are engaged, shoes are kicked off, and a bag of some sort slams to the floor before a man appears in the living room entryway.

Well, would you look at that? *Hello*, sir.

Tall, broad with brown hair, a man stands in front of me sporting a pair of baggy sweatpants and a plain black T-shirt. His long fingers twitch at his sides as his sculpted shoulders set back when he realizes he's not alone. Hiding under a

Studmuffins hat is a piercing set of blue eyes that carry confusion as he looks me up and down.

"Who the hell are you?" he asks.

I toss a grape in my mouth and answer, "A guest to this residence. Who the hell are you?"

"The renter of this residence," he responds.

"Ah, well . . . it would help guests greatly if you offer them more variety of snacks when they come over. Protein bars and grapes aren't going to cut it."

He glances around, clearly looking for any indication of what the hell is going on, and then turns back toward me. "Who are you here with? Banner?"

"Why yes, I am, technically." I hold my finger up to my mouth and say, "Now, shush. You're interrupting my show."

He glances at the TV and then back at me again. "Where the hell is Banner?"

"God, you with the questions." I roll my eyes. "He's upstairs with my best friend having sex."

"And you're down here, eating grapes and watching a show?"

"Yes, that's precisely what's happening. Good job stating the obvious."

He pulls on the back of his neck and shakes his head. "I don't have the fucking patience right now to deal with this."

"Good, then you can leave me to my show." With another shake, he heads up the stairs when I say, "Uh, dude . . . man, guy."

"Ryot," he says.

"What's that now?"

"My name is Ryot."

"Oh, that's an interesting one. Okay then, parents attempting to make you popular straight out of the womb. Anyway, do you happen to have a blanket? There's a swift breeze coming from the window, and I'd rather not catch a chill while sitting here."

"No, I don't," he answers.

"You don't have one single blanket?"

"Not for you to use," he answers again. This time, he starts walking up the stairs.

"Sheesh, what kind of host are you?"

"I'm not. You shouldn't be here." And before I can respond, he's out of earshot.

Well, he's fucking rude.

It's not like I asked for a homemade turkey dinner. I'm just looking for an ounce of comfort here.

Comfort I now need to find myself.

I glance around the downstairs and wonder if there's a blanket in a closet somewhere but realize that if he doesn't have even a single piece of junk food in the house, he's not going to have a spare quilt from a kooky aunt just rolled up waiting to be used.

Urgh, that's annoying.

A chill races up my spine as the air conditioner kicks on. This is not going to do.

I consider slipping my body under the couch cushions, but sure, their countertops might be clean, but who knows what has happened on this couch?

Do I ask for a spare sweatshirt?

Not sure *Ryot* would be partial to sparing his warm-weather garments, and if I've learned anything in the past, never disrupt Nichole while she's with a man—that's how I found out she's so bendy.

Hmm . . . I glance down at the cushion again . . . maybe I could unzip it and slip my body inside?

No.

Nope.

Not going to happen. People fart on couches, so there are farts in these threads and I just won't do it.

I sigh and lean back on the couch just as my eyes connect with the flag.

Huh.

You know . . .

That quite possibly could work.

I set my grapes and Capri Sun down and stand to examine the flag. It looks to be at least six feet long. A nylon material won't replace the warm cocoon of a wool sweater, but beggars can't be choosers.

This will have to do.

I examine how it's hung up and notice that it's held on the wall by Velcro as well. What is with these guys? Have they never heard of Command strips?

Either way, I give the flag a solid yank, listen to the sweet sound of Velcro tearing apart from its long-lost lover, and then bundle it up as I bring it to the couch.

Oh yes, I can already tell this was a good choice. I snuggle in close to my Studmuffin flag, grab my Tupperware of grapes and my Capri Sun, and sit back and relax.

There, now this is living.

⌷══════╌

"MYLA . . . MYLA, WAKE UP."

"Two more minutes, Dad," I murmur into my pillow.

"Myla, it's Nichole. Wake up." She shakes my shoulder, startling me out of a haze.

"Huh? What?" I ask, my eyes peeping open to find Nichole standing in front of me, her hair a mess and razor burn peppered along her face. "What's happening?"

"Time to go, Myla."

"Go where?" In my sleepy haze, I assess my surroundings. Where the hell am I?

"Home." Nichole tugs at the fabric wrapped around my body. "What are you doing with this?"

"With what?" I attempt to sit up, but I'm wrapped like a burrito, making it next to impossible. I shift to the left, then to the right, loosening the confines around me. That's when I notice the lettering, the scratchy fabric . . . and the damp feeling on my stomach. Oh God.

Nichole's one-night stand.

Feeling cold.

The flag . . .

"Dear Jesus, did I . . . did I wet myself?" I ask.

"What? Myla, please tell me that's not true."

Let's pray it's not.

"I don't normally wet myself," I say as Nichole helps lift me and then unravels me from the flag.

"What are you doing wrapped in this?"

"That Ryot guy wouldn't give me a blanket."

"You met Banner's brother?" Nichole asks as she strips me of the flag, revealing an empty Capri Sun pouch resting on my "wet spot." Both of us heave a sigh of relief. Well, that is a gift. Peeing faculties are still intact.

"Ryot is Banner's brother? Wow, they look nothing alike." I stand, and a few grapes fall to the ground.

"Where the hell were those stashed away?"

"Can't be sure." I take the flag from Nichole and bring it over to the wall. "Help me with this. If anything, we are tidy house guests."

We reach up to the Velcro but aren't quite tall enough to reach the top.

"Let's just fold it like a blanket," Nichole suggests.

"No, I got this." I stand under the Velcro on the wall, line up my hand with the Velcro on the flag, and then leap into the air and slap one side of the flag to the wall. Victorious, I do the other side and then step back to admire my work.

"It's crooked," Nichole says.

"Yeah, and it didn't have that Capri Sun wet spot on it either, or the grapes. But hey, at least we hung it."

"We sure did." We offer each other a high five and then head out the door.

"Diner?" Nichole asks.

"Where else would we perform the walk of shame?"

We call an Uber to take us to our favorite corner diner where the late-night partiers convene and try to remember what indiscretions they participated in the night before. We are avid diners on the weekend.

Once in our seats and our food's on the way—thanks to being well known by the waitstaff—Nichole pulls out her phone and starts searching through Instagram while I slip an electrolyte tablet from my purse and into my water.

"So how was he?" I ask.

"Easily the best orgasm of my life," Nichole says.

"Ooo, really?"

"Oh yeah. I'm surprised you didn't hear me."

"I was in a grape coma." I fiddle with the paper from my straw. "But I'm glad you had your pipes cleaned."

"God, don't say that." We both chuckle, and then . . . "Oh shit."

"What?" I ask.

Smiling, she turns her phone toward me. On the screen is a picture of the crooked flag posted by a Ryot.Bisley.Balls. In the comments, it reads: *To the girl who used my flag as a blanket and napkin last night, I hope you were comfortable.*

"Wow, talk about passive-aggressive," I say as I pull my phone out of my purse and look him up on Instagram.

"What are you doing?" Nichole asks.

"Responding . . . obviously." As I type, I talk out loud. "I was quite comfortable, thanks. P.S. Invest in some snacks."

"You're horrible." Nichole laughs.

I just shrug right as my phone vibrates with a notification.

"Ew," I say.

"What?"

"Ryot.Bisley.Balls followed me."

"Really?" She chuckles some more. "Did he respond to your comment?"

"No, just followed. What kind of psychopath does that?"

"Ryot.Bisley.Balls, apparently. So are you going to follow him back?"

"You have to know the answer to that." I roll my eyes and then click the blue follow button next to his name. "Obviously, I would. Nothing revs my engine like a solid passive-aggressive male with no decency toward house guests."

"Cheers to that."

# Chapter One

## MYLA

### *Twelve years later . . .*

I drum my fingers on the dining room table while staring at the clock on the stove I've made several meals on—meals that have felt empty and lifeless. Just sustenance to fill my stomach. Not a meal that made me feel like I was cooking for my man, in *our* home, to preserve a connection at the end of the day.

Nope, because that would require my husband to show up for dinner.

The third night this week I made dinner and ate alone.

The third night I received a text saying he was on his way, only for him to tell me he'd be delayed.

The eighth week in a row where I've felt invisible.

Do I think he's cheating on me? Not even a freaking chance.

Do I think he's so consumed with his new job that he's completely forgotten about me? Abso-fucking-lutely.

It was never like this before.

Before he retired from baseball, life was simple. When he wasn't playing, he was playing with me. Taking me out on dates, paying attention, and making up for the moments when the game took him away.

But now . . . it's almost as if I don't exist, and I can't quite understand what's changed so much over the past few months that's driven him to be this consumed by work.

Just then, my phone buzzes on the table. I glance down to see a text from Nola, Ryot's sister.

**Nola:** *Umm, excuse me, but Ryot sent me pictures of your pool. Why haven't you sent me anything yet?*

Because even though it's nice, I don't have much in me to be excited about it.

**Myla:** *Been super busy, sorry. You'll have to visit and try it out for yourself.*

I go to set my phone down, but she texts back right away.

**Nola:** *Don't tempt me. As soon as it starts becoming frigid in Maine again, I will be snowbirding to your place.*

Normally, texting with Nola turns into full-on conversations because that's how much we get along, but I just don't have it in me.

I sigh, and I'm about to take his plate into the kitchen when I hear the garage door open, signaling his arrival.

I check the text he sent earlier when he told me he'd be ten minutes late. I then look at the time now. More like fifty-three minutes late.

The garage door opens, and in walks my incredibly charming, handsome, and very late husband.

When he spots me at the dining room table, alone with his plate of food, his expression morphs into an apology.

"Babe, fuck, I'm so sorry." He sets his wallet, phone, and keys down on the kitchen counter and comes straight to me.

Wearing a three-piece navy-blue suit with a black button-up shirt underneath, he approaches with just enough swagger to remind me why I fell in love with him in the first place. With his kind, caring light-blue eyes, the scruff on his cheek that has rubbed against my fair skin, and the bulging muscles that strain the threads of his clothes—he's everything a fantasy could dream up. I only wish that fantasy was still the man I fell in love with.

He rests one of his hands on the back of my chair and leans toward me. He lifts my chin and looks me in the eyes when he says, "I'm really fucking sorry, Myla." *I've lost count how many times I've heard that over the last few months.*

"Thank you for apologizing," I answer as I stand and move around him. He grips my wrist gently, halting my retreat.

"Tell me about your day."

I look up at him and say, "I'm exhausted, Ryot. I'm going to go take a bath. Your dinner is cold, so warm it up if you want."

I snatch my wrist away and head up to our bedroom and into the master bathroom.

We're currently renting since we just moved out here a few months ago, and the house we're renting is nothing I would have chosen for us. It's a typical coastal-style house with an open floor plan, generic finishings, and expensive taste that lacks taste. From the marble bathroom, to the chandelier above the master bed, it's all too gaudy for me, which of course makes me hate this current state of living even more.

I throw on the bathtub jets and toss a bath bomb into the shallow water. As it foams with purples and pinks—a present from Ryot—I strip down and then brush my hair out only to pin it to the top of my head so it doesn't get wet. When the tub is ready, I shut off the faucet, keep the jets moving, and then slip in.

My body instantly relaxes as I soak all the way up to my neck.

With nothing to do, I flick at the bubbles on the top of the water and wonder—what the hell am I going to do with my life?

I'm not happy. Quite depressed, actually. Before we moved to California, I had a job, a social life, and purpose. But here, I feel like I'm just . . . I'm just Ryot's wife. And although I do take pride in marrying the man, I know I need more than this. I need him to listen to me and see me like he used to. I've told him how I feel, how sad I feel, how I need him to listen to me, but . . . he just hasn't.

I hear a pair of shoes hit the floor as I look up toward the bathroom entrance to find Ryot undressing. His suit jacket is off, his vest is gaping, and he's working on the last buttons of his dress shirt. His tan, carved skin peeks through, and even though I'm angry with him, I can't help but stare at my husband.

Since he left baseball, he hasn't given up on his routine, and sure, it might annoy me at times—why can't the man just eat a donut—but he looks amazing. Sexy. Irresistible.

"Thank you for dinner, babe."

"You ate that quick."

"I was starving." He sheds out of his dress shirt, and my eyes fall on his impeccable chest. He removes the watch I got him a few Christmases ago and sets it on the bathroom countertop next to his cologne that smells like absolute sin. When he turns back toward me, he says, "I'm sorry I let you down tonight. I know an apology means nothing, and my actions speak louder, but I need you to know I truly am sorry."

I can't look at him out of fear I might cry, so I play with the bubbles. "Thanks."

"Want to tell me what you did today?" he asks as he takes a seat on the side of the tub.

Since he seems focused, I say, "Not much. Went for a long

walk around the neighborhood. Went grocery shopping, did the laundry." I shrug. "Worked on some mock designs of a hotel lobby for fun. I have this idea—"

"I saw one of those mammoth dogs on my run this morning," he says, making me wonder if he actually listened all the way to the end of my answer or was already absorbed in his own day again.

He leans forward and lifts my chin so he can press a soft kiss to my lips.

And because I can't seem to keep myself away from him, I sink into his mouth as he slips his hand behind my head and filters into my hair.

Our kiss grows heavier, stronger, and more intense with every breath. Before I know what's happening, I'm rising from the water and undoing his pants.

He slips out of them and pulls me from the tub then lays me on the bath rug, where he spreads my legs and slips his delicious cock inside me.

I cling to him like he's a lifesaver, helping me stay afloat, yet . . . he's also the thing drowning me.

And with every pulse of his hips, I think to myself, why doesn't he see me like he used to?

Why can't he be the man I once knew and fell in love with?

Why can't our life be like it used to be several months ago when we were the only things that mattered in each other's lives?

Why can't I see myself lasting here even when I once thought Ryot's love was all I needed to feel complete?

⌶⎓⌶

RYOT

*Four weeks later . . .*

"WHAT THE HELL is wrong with you, Myla?" I shout as I shut the garage door behind me and toss my keys on the kitchen counter.

"Wrong with me?" she asks, spinning around to face me. Her piercing blue eyes slice right through me. "If you don't know the answer to that question, then I can't help you." She takes off toward the stairs.

I follow.

"I don't know the fucking answer. I can't read your goddamn mind."

Fresh from my good friend JP's engagement party, where I had to deal with her cold shoulder and tight-lipped attitude, followed by a magnificent display of the silent treatment in the car, I've just about had it.

Myla pauses at the top of the stairs and says, "Then I can't help you." She spins back around and heads into our bedroom.

I'm going to have a fucking coronary.

Charging up the rest of the stairs, I plow into the bedroom, where Myla is slipping off her dress. "Uh, excuse me, a little privacy, please?"

Through a clenched jaw, I say, "You're my goddamn wife. There is no such thing as privacy."

"What rulebook are you reading? Peeping Tom, Edition One?"

"Enough with the sarcasm, Myla." I tug on my hair, my patience nonexistent at this point. "Just tell me what the fuck I did that has put you in this shit mood."

"Like I said, if you don't know——"

I grip her wrist and spin her toward me. Only in her bra and underwear, her body presses against mine. I wrap my arm around her waist.

"Now, Myla, we can do this the hard way or the easy way."

She rolls her eyes. "What are you going to do, Ryot? Fuck it out of me? Pretty sure we've figured out that sex doesn't get us anywhere in our arguments."

Realizing this might be more serious than I first assumed, which was some way I've annoyed her again, I say, "Then tell me what I can do. Tell me what the hell is going on so I can fix it."

"Why do you even care?" she asks as she presses her hand against my chest and attempts to get away.

"Why do I care? Uh, because you're my goddamn wife, because I love you, and because I don't want to live in this constant state of anger that we've been living in. Hell, Myla, it's been a month of this cold shoulder bullshit." Off and on. More angry days than not.

"You're exaggerating."

"I'm not. Ever since we moved out to California, you haven't been yourself."

"Oh, so this is my fault?" Her expression morphs into disbelief. "Are you really going to blame me?"

"No, Jesus. I'm just trying to have a conversation."

She pushes away from me and steps toward the bathroom. "Yeah, well, communication has never been our strong suit, now, has it?"

"Because you won't fucking talk to me," I say. "You won't communicate with me. You just shut down. And when I do try to have a conversation, you turn everything into sex."

"Haven't heard you complain about the orgasms," she says as she strips out of her bra and underwear, leaving her completely naked.

Yeah, I'd never complain about the orgasms because our sex life has always been fucking incredible. So if she wants to fuck, I'm naked in seconds.

From the hook near her vanity, she grabs her short silk robe and slips it on.

While she starts her nighttime routine of putting her hair in a bun secured by a silk scrunchie and washing her face, I move toward the doorframe and lean on the wood, watching her.

In a soft, steady voice, I say, "Just tell me what I fucking did, Myla. I don't want to fight with you."

Her shoulders roll in, and she drops her hands to the counter as she uses the mirror to look at me. Her eyes are tired with bags resting under them. Her face is thinner than normal, and so is her body. Normally curvy, with delicious thighs that I love gripping on to, she seems more . . . fragile and, right now, there's only intense animosity. Toward me. "Do I look happy, Ryot?"

"No," I answer honestly. "You don't."

Something isn't right. This isn't just a fight. There seems to be something deeper happening.

"Because I'm not." She turns now to face me and leans against the counter, her posture no longer snide but defeated, as if she can't take this back and forth anymore, and she's throwing up the white flag. "I haven't been happy for a while."

I swallow hard. I've noticed a change, but I thought that maybe she was taking a second to adjust to our new house, our new life.

"Happy with me?" I ask.

"Happy with my life," she says with a sigh.

"What does that mean?" My heart trembles in my chest.

"I haven't been happy for months now, and I thought . . ." She pauses, her voice catching in her throat. "I thought that maybe it would get better. That we would get better. But we're not."

"What are you talking about?" I ask, my throat growing tight. "Babe, we've been fine. We made love this morning."

"No, we fucked, Ryot. Fucking has never been an issue

20

between us. But fucking isn't going to make me happy. You can fuck me all you want, but at the end of the day, it won't put a smile on my face."

"Then what will?"

"A healthy marriage, and that's not what we have." Pulse thundering, I try to steady my shaking legs. "We are anything but healthy." Her head drops forward as she grips the counter behind her. That ominous, doomsday feeling falls over me. She's avoiding eye contact with me. The air around us stills as the tension grows thick and muddy. She quietly says, "I want a divorce."

The room spins around me in slow motion, squeezing the air from my lungs in one fell swoop, leaving me gasping.

"What . . . what did you just say?" I can barely hear my own voice over the hammering of my heart. My mind whirls, trips, tumbles, and struggles to comprehend the words that came out of her mouth. There's no way.

Did she really say divorce? She couldn't have . . . right?

When her gaze lifts to mine, her mouth thins, and with no expression in her eyes, she repeats, "I want a divorce." She opens one of her vanity drawers and pulls out a yellow envelope and sets it on the countertop.

"What the fuck is that?"

Still dead in her eyes, she says, "Divorce papers. I had them drawn up last week. I'm asking for absolutely nothing. I don't want your money—"

"Our fucking money," I say.

"It's your money, Ryot. You're the one who played in the Major Leagues, and you're the one who cashed in on the endorsements, so that's your money, not mine. And I'm not about to sit here and argue with you about it. I don't fucking want it. All I ask is to keep my car and half of the sale from the house in Chicago since I'm the one who did the renovations."

"Hold the fuck on for a second," I say, trying to wrap my head around all of this. "You want a divorce?"

"Yes. Everything is done. You just need your lawyer to look it over and then sign it." *Everything is* done? *When did she start?*

"The fuck I will," I say, moving closer to her. "I'm not about to sign divorce papers without knowing where all this is coming from. I love you, Myla——"

"Don't, Ryot. Don't say that shit when you don't mean it."

"Of course I mean it!" I shout. "Don't fucking tell me how I feel."

"If you loved me, then we wouldn't be in this mess."

"Maybe if you talked to me——"

"I did," she yells. "Several times, Ryot. You haven't been paying attention. You've been so focused on life after baseball and how you can satisfy your drive to be successful. Meanwhile, you've forgotten about me. You've forgotten about *our* life. You've forgotten your promises, and no amount of communication will take away the bitterness I have toward you for that." She pushes off the sink and blows past me.

"Myla, wait——"

"Sign the papers, Ryot. End this for us, so we can both move on."

And then she's out of the bedroom and halfway out of my life.

———

"WOW, YOU LOOK LIKE ABSOLUTE SHIT," Banner says as he sits across from me at Café Lola with coffees in hand for both of us.

After Myla retreated from the bathroom, I tried to coax her to talk to me, but she shut down once again. Last night was the first time we *chose* to sleep apart since we were married. When I woke up this morning, the divorce papers were on her pillow with a note that said, "Sign them today."

I tossed them to the floor and told Banner to meet me in half an hour.

With my thumb and index finger, I rub my tension-filled brow. "Myla asked for a divorce last night."

Cup midway to his mouth, Banner pauses. "What the actual fuck? Is this some sort of prank?"

"Why the hell would I joke about this?" I slouch in my chair.

"Fuck, I don't know. Why?"

I slowly shake my head.

*You haven't been paying attention. You've been so focused on life after baseball and how you can satisfy your drive to be successful. Meanwhile, you've forgotten about me. You've forgotten about our life. You've forgotten your promises, and no amount of communication will take away the bitterness I have toward you for that.*

"She wouldn't talk about it. All I really know is that she's very unhappy and has been for a while. She gave me the divorce papers and then slept in the guest room." *Loneliest night of my life.*

"Jesus. I'm sorry, man. Are you going to sign—"

"No," I shout and then quiet my voice when I'm snapped back into reality. There are people around us. I don't need them listening in on my private conversation. "I don't want a divorce." A divorce would fucking break me. Losing Myla would break me.

"Did you tell her that?"

"I mean, I think I made it pretty clear. I tried to tell her I loved her, and she immediately shot me down."

"Dude." Banner rubs the back of his neck. "Fuck. I did not see this coming."

"I had no fucking clue either. What do I do?" I ask. "I knew she was acting weird, but a divorce? That's the last thing I expected. Have I really been that busy, that blind to the situation?"

"I don't know, man . . . maybe . . ." Banner shrugs just as I spot someone approaching us.

"Did the meeting start without me, boys?"

Penn Cutler.

One of my best friends and former teammates and the reason I came up with the idea of The Jock Report. It's the reason we moved to California and probably why I've been so blind to what's been going on with my home life.

Just to splash you with some quick backstory—boring I know, but it's needed—Penn and I played with the Chicago Bobbies a few years back. I tore my rotator cuff and couldn't recover despite my many attempts, and Penn . . . well, his haunted past drove him off the pitcher's mound. A former alcoholic who attended rehab during the off-season, he was picked apart by the media, season after season. One bad game and they assumed he was back to drinking. It got to the point where the Bobbies couldn't manage the press anymore, so Penn cut ties with them before they could cut ties with him. And that was how his career ended.

It was so fucking unfair to be pushed out of his sport for a past that he cleaned up, so I came up with the idea of The Jock Report, a social media website run by the athletes where they have their own voice, can tell their own stories, and can interact with fans. It's been a billion-dollar idea, and with the help of my brainiac brother and investment from Cane Enterprises, we've been able to shoot up to the top-selling app in the world. Together, Penn, Banner, and I moved to Los Angeles, where we opened an office and now manage over fifty employees. This all happened within a few months. Yeah, that fucking fast.

Turning to Banner, I say, "You invited him?"

"I thought it was a business meeting," Banner says while cringing.

Penn pulls out a chair, then spins it around so he's sitting on it backward. "What's going on?"

Sighing heavily, I say, "Please don't make a big fucking deal about this . . ."

"Why not?" Banner asks. "It's a huge fucking deal."

"What's a big deal?" Penn looks back and forth between us.

Pushing my hair, I say, "Myla asked for a divorce last night."

Penn's brow creases. "No, she fucking didn't."

"Yes, she did," I reply before lifting my coffee to my lips. "She had papers drawn up and everything."

"Why the hell does she want a divorce?"

Banner pipes up, "She's not happy."

"Well, yeah, I could have told you that. She hasn't been herself for a while. That quick wit of hers has faded, but I just assumed she was going through something. A divorce? Has she talked to you about it at all?"

"No," I answer while setting my coffee back down. "This came out of nowhere. She was acting weird last night, very cold, and I called her out on it when we got home. That's when she laid into me." I scrub my hand over my face. "Fuck, I don't know how to handle this with all the other shit right now. The business taking off at a rapid rate, the move . . . JP's goddamn wedding, which is now in three weeks. I don't know what to fucking do." *I can't lose her, but is it right to hold her back from happiness if she's so unhappy with me?* "I mean . . . do I sign?"

"Do you want to sign?" Banner asks.

"No, but . . . I don't want to force her to be with me either. Especially if she's not happy."

"So you're just going to give up?" Penn asks. "Dude, we're talking about Myla here."

Yeah . . . Myla . . .

The girl who captured me the moment she commented on my Instagram post.

The girl with the most unique sense of humor.

The girl who has made me feel whole, as if before I met

her I was missing something in my life. She came along and changed everything.

"I don't know what to do. She's shut down. I could see it in her eyes last night. She had the same look when her dad passed away and she broke up with me. She's not open to solving problems. She just wants out, an escape."

Banner pulls on his hair. "How did you win her back after she broke up with you? I can't remember how that all went down."

"She had to attend a meeting with her mom and dad's lawyer alone, so she asked me to pretend we were still together until after," I answer. "But I made a last-ditch effort to show her that she didn't need to lose me just because she lost her dad. She kissed me in the car after the meeting, and I knew we'd be okay."

"And you think this situation is similar?" Banner asks.

"Slightly, but this time, I truly don't understand where this is coming from. I don't know what triggered this or caused this line of thinking, so I don't feel optimistic about fixing it."

"Well, you gotta try, man," Penn says. "This is your forever girl." He pauses as if an idea has struck him. "You know, JP's wedding is in three weeks. Why don't you treat that event like what happened with the reading of the will?"

"What do you mean?" I ask.

He shifts on his chair and says, "Tell her you will give her the divorce—"

"But I don't want a divorce."

"I understand that. But she's going to be angry with you if you don't go along with what she wants, which will put her on the defensive. So maybe if you tell her you're going to grant her wishes, she'll be more receptive to your idea."

"And what exactly is my idea?" I ask.

"Tell her you will give her what she wants, but in exchange, she needs to pretend to be with you for JP's wedding because you don't want to stir up drama for your friend before they get married. I'm sure she'll say yes, so then that buys you some time. You can be there for her and hopefully get to the root of the problem while she 'pretends' to help you by staying married."

"Hey, that's a pretty good idea," Banner says, perking up. "Shit, you should be glad I invited him."

I hate to admit it, but Banner is right. It's not that bad of an idea.

I scratch the side of my face. "But that's three weeks. I don't think she'll buy it."

"That's why you need to act like you're giving her what she wants," Penn says. "Don't pressure her, don't try to win her back, but rather . . . observe. Learn. Figure out how you can fix this."

"Yes," Banner adds while lightly knocking the table. "She lowers her defenses when she doesn't feel threatened. If she believes you're giving her what she wants, if you're indifferent to the whole thing, then hopefully, she'll relax and open up a bit more. You know that's how she works, man. Think about her past. She's scarred from people leaving her life constantly —from her parents' marriage, and from being bullied most of her childhood. She doesn't process her feelings normally, so if you back off and let her believe you're giving her what she wants, then maybe she'll concede something, and you'll get to the root of the problem."

I think it over and know Banner is right. Her troubled past has bitten me in the ass several times throughout our life together. I've been more than happy to work through it with her, but I've only been able to navigate through it once I get her to open up. This is no exception, though the stakes are much higher. I can't lose Myla. I love her. She's my whole world.

"So what does this have to do with the wedding?" I ask.

Penn places his phone on the table and pulls up his drawing app. He makes a line across the screen and then puts an X at the end. "This is the wedding week." He makes a slash on the other end. "This is you, now." He makes two marks between. "This is the time you get her to think you don't care anymore. She wants a divorce, fine, here's the divorce." He circles the X. "And this is the time when you 'fake' being a happy couple still. This is when you make your move. This is when you show her how good you are together, how much you appreciate her. This is when you woo her and take all the things you observed over the past two weeks and lay it down." Banner slow claps.

"This is brilliant." No. It's horrible. Why the hell would I try to convince my wife that I don't love her anymore? Wouldn't that be the final nail in the coffin that is our marriage? And hurt Myla even more than I have done?

"You don't think it's a bit extreme? Shouldn't I just be able to talk to her about this?"

"This is Myla we're talking about," Banner says. "She doesn't operate on the same wavelength as others. When she's hurt, she feels that hurt down to her bones. You might want to solve this like two mature adults looking for a solution, but Myla doesn't work like that."

Penn swats my shoulder. "And who's to say this is actually what she wants? This could be a knee-jerk reaction."

"Divorce is a bit extreme for a knee-jerk reaction," I say. "She might be walking to the beat of her own drum, but she wouldn't do anything this harsh just for the hell of it."

"Which is why this plan will work." Penn taps his phone.

"I don't know." I waver back and forth.

"What do you have to lose?" Banner asks. "Your wife? Well, man, you're already halfway there."

"Trust me, this will work," Penn says with unbridled confidence.

I lean back in my chair and let out a large sigh. It's frightening that I'm even considering this plan, given the absurdity of it, but then again, I don't think I have many options.

They're right. If I tell her I'll give her a divorce, she won't be so defensive.

She may be more open to talking to me when she's not defensive.

When she's open to talking, that's when I'll figure out what's going on.

This should work . . . right?

Only one way to find out.

"Okay . . . I'll do it."

"Thatta boy." Penn slaps me on the shoulder. "Aren't you excited? You have a plan."

"Yeah, maybe . . ." I twist my coffee cup. "But . . ." I sigh. "I'm fucking pissed."

"Oh, wasn't expecting that," Banner says as he props his arm on the table. "Why are you pissed?"

"Because." I look up at both of them. "Out of everything Myla and I have been through, rather than trying to save our marriage, she's throwing it away." She's thought about this for a long time if she's already seen a lawyer, discussed the split of assets, and had the papers drawn up. *As if I mean nothing to her at all.* "This is how she wants to end it?" I shake my head. "It's fucking bullshit."

Banner winces. "Yeah, good idea, get that out now because I don't think going back to the house with that sort of attitude will help the situation."

Grumbling to myself, I stand from my chair. "I'm out."

"Wait, why? You're still angry. Sit down and work through it."

"It's only going to make me angrier. I just need to get this conversation with Myla over with and then go from there."

Penn steadies his hand against my stomach, stopping me from my retreat. "Dude, I think it's in your best interest to just take a second. I know you're hurt and frustrated, and this doesn't seem fair. I'm sure this plan is not how you want to handle things, but this could give you the time you need to fix things. So just sit down and talk out the feelings. You don't want to do something stupid when you get back home . . . like piss her off even more."

"Too late for that," I say as I push past Penn and head out to my car.

## Chapter Two

RYOT

*Eleven years ago . . .*

"Dude, you didn't dress up." Banner looks me up and down.

"That's what you're going to say to me? Not great game, nice job hitting two home runs? And that diving play at third, that was epic?"

Banner rolls his eyes. "Yeah, great job on the field. You're a real magician with a ball. Now tell me why the fuck you didn't dress up when you knew you were coming to a costume party at the bar?"

"Halloween in May is dumb," I say as I take a seat next to him at the bar.

"It's their play on Christmas in July, Halloween in May. Now all the slutty nurses won't freeze to death. It's brilliant if you ask me."

"No one asked you," I say as I steal Banner's full beer.

Banner turns toward me, one arm resting on the bar top. "Care to explain why you're acting like a dick?"

"I'm tired. The last thing I want to do is go to a costume party for a fake Halloween in May, but since you asked, I'm here."

Banner pokes at the corner of my lip and tilts it upward. "You're here, but I'll need you here with a smile."

"You're asking too much," I say just as someone bumps into my shoulder, causing my beer to slosh over the sides of the pint glass and all down my hand. "Jesus," I say as I spin around to find . . . well, two slutty nurses.

"Oops, did we bump into you?" one of the girls asks.

"Yeah, you did."

"Nichole?" Banner says, looking over my shoulder.

"Oh hey . . . uh, Brandon."

I snort as Banner's smile droops. "It's Banner."

"Oh right." She steps up between us now. Wearing a white shirtdress, she has the top few buttons undone, showing off cleavage that is propped up by a red bra. "Banner, the best sex of my life, still to date." She pulls the other girl forward. "You remember my friend, Myla, right?"

I twist just in time to see the grape girl who ruined my flag next to Nichole. And holy fucking shit is she hot.

Sure, when I came home from my game and found her on my couch drinking a Capri Sun and eating my grapes, I thought she was pretty, but I was too clouded by my irritation to really take note. When I saw that she commented on my post the next day, I checked out her profile, which didn't show much of her. Actually, her account has been dedicated to taking up-close pictures of her drinks—my Capri Sun being featured. It was such an odd account, so I decided to follow it, never expecting her to follow me back.

I considered asking her what was with the pictures of drinks but moved on quickly.

Now that she's here, in this getup, I'm thinking maybe I should have asked her about the drinks, because fuck. Her tits nearly kiss her chin, and her hair is pulled up but with tendrils cascading down and framing her face. Her nurse's shirt-dress falls to her upper thighs, thighs so goddamn thick my mouth waters, and she's wearing the brightest red lipstick I've ever seen. A red so bright, I wonder what it would look like all over my body.

"Yes, I remember Myla. You're the one who used our flag as a blanket," I coolly say.

Myla raises her hand cutely. "Guilty." Then she turns to me and asks, "Invest in any snacks yet?"

"Not so much," I answer.

She shakes her head in disappointment. "You disappoint me."

"Are you girls hungry?" Banner asks. "We can grab a table upstairs and get something to eat."

"I don't have my wallet," Myla says. "It didn't fit in my cleavage."

"I have exactly twenty-nine dollars," Nichole says. "That's what fits in mine."

"We got you," Banner says. "Our treat."

"Well then, don't mind if I do." Myla sweeps her hand in front of her. "Lead the way, kind sirs."

Banner hops off his chair and nods toward the stairs at me, indicating that I'm a part of this too. Grumbling to myself, I take my pint glass in my beer-covered hand and follow them up the stairs to the dining area of the bar, which I wouldn't really call a dining area. Booths are lined along the perimeter while high-top tables fill in the middle. It's shrouded with people decked out in costumes—a few superheroes, sexy devils, sexy maids, sexy just insert a noun here, and a dedication to the costume T-Rex in the far corner—leaving me looking like the odd one out.

"Find a seat if you can," the hostess says as we approach. "We're pretty cramped."

I glance around the crowded space, my irritation already revving from having to be here, but now that we're in a spot where people are elbow to elbow, I want nothing more than to go home.

"Oh look, there's a table for two over there in the corner," Banner says.

"And one to the right," Nichole adds.

Silence falls between us, and I know what's going to happen next. It doesn't take a rocket scientist to figure out the math.

"So, uh, why don't you take Maya to the right?" Banner starts.

"It's Myla," she says. "But I won't hold it against you."

"Shit, sorry."

"No offense taken. I know how this goes. You'll dine with my friend here, work up the sexual tension until you can't take it anymore, and probably meet up in the bathroom for release while I get wined and dined by your cranky brother who doesn't know how to properly stock the cabinets with snacks. Not a problem." And with that, she loops her arm through mine and drags me toward the table to the right while saying over her shoulder, "Let me know when you're done."

When we reach the table, Myla releases my arm to sit at the two-person high-top table. Completely unsure how I got into this situation—it happened so fast—I take a seat across from her, where I get a straight shot down her cleavage.

Jesus.

"Don't worry, I'm not going to break the bank for you." She grabs one of the menus resting between the salt and pepper shaker and scans it. "I might just order some broccoli. Do you like broccoli? I can order two sides of it. Hmm, I wonder if they have peanut butter. Have you ever tried peanut butter on your broccoli before? It might sound gross, but it's actually quite good."

"Uh, no. I haven't."

"I would like to say that I'm shocked, but given your barren kitchen and confession to not investing in snacks, I'm not shocked at all."

I pluck a menu for myself. "You know, you don't have to do this. I have no problem eating alone or just leaving, for that matter."

"And what, leave me here to fend for myself?" She shakes her head. "No way."

"I'm sure any man in this bar would be more than happy to offer you a free meal."

"Yeah, but that free meal comes with strings attached. At least with you, I know you're doing this for your brother, and you'll cash in on a favor from him later down the road. Therefore, it's your brother who owes you, not me." She looks up from her menu and offers me a large smile. "See how that works?"

Oddly, yes.

I turn back to the menu and browse the selection. Nothing speaks to me other than the family-sized nachos, so I ask Myla, "Do you want to split the nachos with me?"

"Hmm." She taps her chin. "You know, I think I could eat some nachos right now. But we'll need extra jalapeños because I like it spicy."

"Fine." I slip the menu back into its spot and then lean my arms on the table, trying to look anywhere but at her breasts . . . or her lips.

"Why aren't you dressed up?" she asks, her eyes scanning me so intensely that I nearly feel naked.

"Not really someone who dresses up."

"Ah, I see. You're too cool for it."

"No, I just don't see the point in dressing up."

"The point is to draw attention," she says. "For instance,

do you really think I would be earning myself a free meal tonight if my friend and I weren't showing off an ungodly amount of cleavage? Probably not. We would have been looked over for some other sexy nurse costume. But, because we are trying to suckle at the teat of our early twenties and use the lack of gravitational pull on our breasts, we decided to dress up. Look where it's gotten us. Nichole will get another great orgasm from your brother, and I get to sit here with you —albeit less than ideal company—and get a free meal out of it."

Who the hell is this girl? I don't think I've ever met anyone who truly lived their life by the motto, "I give zero fucks."

"Hey, sorry about the wait," our server says as she stands next to our table. She glances at Myla and says, "Oh damn, girl, your boobs look amazing."

Myla grips them and then does this side-by-side shuffle with them that has my eyes nearly bugging out. "Thank you," she says. "Can you believe I got this bra at Target?"

"No way."

"Yup." She tucks her loose strands of hair behind her ear. "Best purchase I've made in a while. And I'm already getting my money's worth with a free meal from this guy." She thumbs toward me.

"She's not getting a free meal because of the bra," I defend, not wanting to come off as a creep.

"Keep telling yourself that." The server winks, then asks, "What can I get you two?"

"We're going to get the nachos. I was going to get broccoli, but since I'm not paying, I don't want to press my luck, you know? And water is good for me. I'm sure my grumpy friend across the table will need another beer to get him through the night. And from the looks of it, your IPA is on tap. Am I right?"

"Yes," I answer, hating that she can peg me so well.

"Great. I'll be back with drinks and food."

When the server is out of earshot, I say, "It wasn't the boobs."

"Yes, I know, but you're not complaining about them, are you?"

Not really. Not sure any red-blooded, straight male would complain about them.

She takes a napkin and blots at them. Not sure why, but I shamelessly watch her.

Has it really been that long since I've been with someone? Yeah . . . it has been. Spring training ate up most of my time, and when I wasn't called up to the Majors this season, I've been working even harder in the weight room and batting cages so that when I do get a chance, I'm ready.

I couldn't even tell you the last pair of tits I saw.

The server plops our drinks on the table and takes off again without a word. Myla reaches into her shirt to the right and pulls out her phone. Jesus, that was there the whole time? I was too distracted by the cleavage that I didn't even notice.

She holds her phone in front of her drink, and I watch her take a picture.

"Is that for your Instagram?"

"Of course," she says as she taps away on her phone. "Got to keep my followers satisfied with content."

"But it's water," I say.

"So?" she asks. "I don't complain about your incessant need to show videos of you batting. We get it. You can hit a ball."

"You realize hitting a baseball is one of the hardest things to do in sports?"

"Shall I throw you a parade?" she asks right before she glances up and smirks. "Ooo, I can feel the steam of your anger from all the way over here. Chill, dude. I'm just joking. But seriously, don't hate on my pictures. I have an avid following . . . including you. Which, by the way, I meant to ask, why did you follow me?"

I shrug. "I don't know. It was a year ago."

That's a lie. I know why I followed her. She intrigued me. I threw up a passive-aggressive post, she commented as if it was nothing, and I was surprised. Also, the drinks thing was weird. She got me interested.

"Why did you follow me?" I ask in return.

"In case you threw any more shade my way. A girl has to defend herself."

"When she uses unsuspecting people's wall décor as a throw blanket, then I guess so."

She lifts her water to her lips and says, "You and I both know that flag is anything but décor. And what's with the Velcro?"

"What do you mean?"

"Do you have stock in it or something? Who hangs wall décor"—she uses air quotes—"with Velcro. If anything, you would use tacks, or perhaps Command strips."

"Aren't Command strips just a fancy alternative to Velcro?"

"No," she answers and leaves it at that, even though I'm pretty sure it is.

"Well, we had Velcro, so that's what we used."

"Odd." She sets her water glass down and props her chin on her palm, her boobs nearly exploding out of her shirt now. "Tell me, Ryot Bisley Balls, do you still have the flag hanging up?"

Of course she would call me my Instagram name. I'm surprised it took her this long.

I take a swig of my beer because I know she's about to rain down upon me with insults when I tell her the truth. "Yeah, I do."

"And let me guess, it's still crooked from when I slapped it back up on the wall."

"Yup." I take another sip of my beer.

"I knew it." She smirks. "And here you are, complaining about it on Instagram. All for show."

"If you're not garnering some sort of reaction from followers, what are you really doing?"

"Uh-huh, and precisely what interaction are you garnering from your hitting videos?" She taps the table, waiting for an answer.

"Compliments." I twist my pint glass on the table, not wanting to see that smirk of hers again.

"Oh, Bisley Balls, what a sad, sad life you lead."

Just then, the server drops off our nachos and a side of broccoli. With a wink at Myla, she says, "The broccoli is on me. We can't let this penny-pincher stop you from hitting your vegetable intake for the day."

"You are a true blessing in my life," Myla says while clutching her chest.

As the server walks away, I say, "I'm not a penny-pincher. I would have splurged on the broccoli."

"Sure, big guy, let's just see how you tip, huh?" Myla says with a smile at the server.

—————

"THE SEX HAS COMMENCED," Myla says as she wipes her mouth with a napkin.

I don't think I've ever seen someone—man or woman—take down a plate of nachos as Myla just did. She just shoveled it in, one chip right after the other, and anytime I even remotely came close to a jalapeño, she slapped my hand away and growled. It was unbelievable . . . and hot.

"What do you mean the sex has commenced?" I ask as I pick at the broccoli Myla demanded I needed after she ate her bowl.

"Nichole and your brother. She just texted me that the giraffe is headed to the barn."

"Is that code?"

"What do you think, genius?" She reaches for my beer—again, this started after she began to growl—and she takes a long pull.

. What an odd combination in a woman. She's gorgeous, that's unmistakable. Her eyes, highlighted by her long lashes, would penetrate any soul with how beautifully blue they are. There's a cute slope to her nose that I don't think I've ever noticed on a person before, and her jawline cuts right to those plump, red lips. And then match that with her curves, her plump ass, and those tits, and she's a total knockout. Stunning, but her personality . . . fuck, it does not match her looks. It's not what I'd expect if I saw her walking down the street. She's brash, unperturbed, and free. She doesn't seem to care what anyone thinks of her, says what's on her mind, and holds absolutely nothing back. I realized this when she told me my left pec looked bigger than my right.

And for some insane, asinine, completely fucked reason, it turns me on.

She turns me on.

Her mouth.

Her brain.

Her quick wit.

Her no-holds-barred attitude.

I'm attracted to it.

"Have you ever had sex in a public restroom?" she asks, breaking the silence and pulling me from my irritating thoughts.

"No. Have you?"

"Attempted it, but the guy ended up slipping and dunking his butt in the toilet. He left unsatisfied and with swamp ass. I gave him my thong as a parting gift. I think he sold it on some underwear website because I saw one very similar to mine."

"What are you talking about? Underwear website?"

"Oh yeah, pervs pay big money for used underwear. I've sold a few items here and there."

"What?" I feel my eyes pop out of my sockets. Jesus, I'm not an innocent man by any means, I've done my fair share of obscure things, but selling used underwear? That's a new one for me.

"Oh yeah, once I made over one thousand dollars and scored a stalker through the website, so I called it quits. The money is great and all, but I have some level of dignity, you know? Now I just have an Only Fans account for my feet. Helps supplement my server income while I'm in school."

"Wait, you're serious."

"Yeah. I just upload a picture daily to satisfy the customers and move on with my life."

I pause. Is she joking with me? From what little I know about her, it doesn't seem like this would be a joke, but then again, I'm sure she's just waiting to tell me what an idiot I am for believing her. So I decide to ask questions.

"Are you in these pictures?"

"Why, you interested?"

Christ, I should have seen that coming.

"No. I don't have a foot fetish."

She squeezes her boobs together even more and says, "No, just a boob one, right?"

*Fuck.*

*Yes.*

I rest my hand on the bar-top table. "Any straight man has a boob fetish."

"I once went out with a guy who was more interested in my belly button."

"Where the hell are you meeting these people?"

"Oh, you know, while tagging along on Nichole's ventures." She smiles, her eyes looking me up and down.

"I'm not one of them," I say quickly.

"How do I know that? You could seem pretty normal, but then inwardly have a real freaky side to you. Is that the case?"

"I don't know," I answer. "I don't fantasize over feet or belly buttons, if that's what you're asking."

"Okay, but have you ever spanked a woman?"

"Yes," I answer, which perks her up.

"Really?" she drawls. "Ooo, tell me more. Have you ever tied someone up?"

"Just hands," I answer.

"Giving her free range with her legs, that's fair."

"No, I just wanted to control how far I spread her."

Myla sits tall now as her mouth falls open slightly.

Ha!

Looks like I found a way to finally stun her.

Eyes on me, she reaches for her newly filled water glass. Pulling an ice cube out, she brings it to her chest, where she rubs it across her tan skin.

Well, fuck . . . me.

My eyes travel with the ice cube, watching it run over each breast, the water slipping down between the two plump mounds and into the valley I desperately want to explore. And in seconds, with my eyes watching her and her breath picking up, the tension between us grows.

"How many times in one night have you made a woman come?" She continues to move the ice cube around, and I continue to follow it.

Licking my lips, I say, "Too many to count, but my bare minimum is at least two before you leave my bed."

"How kind of you."

"I tend to be generous."

"I see." She gulps. "And, uh, would you say you're at least nine inches?"

Smiling to myself, knowing the tables have turned, I say, "Why, you interested?"

I expect her to be flustered, to maybe lie and say no, but

that's not what happens. Nope, that confidence of hers just pours right out. "If you're at least nine inches, then yes, I am."

"High standards."

"I know what feels good, so I only settle for the best."

"I am the best," I say, now leaning both arms on the table so I'm closer. "I know how to edge out a woman, bring her to the precipice of an orgasm, only to make her wait, and wait . . . and wait." She sighs. "Until she can't take the pressure, the buildup, anymore and I allow her to come. I know how to use my tongue, how to make you shiver from my touch, how to make you beg for my dick, and how to create such desperation in your mind that I'm the only man you will ever think about again."

She wets her lips and then drags her finger along my hand. "I see. And how do I know you're telling the truth?"

"Just ask your friend," I say as I spot Nichole heading toward our table. "It runs in the family."

I hop off my chair, grab my wallet, and throw some cash down just as Nichole reaches the table. Her lipstick is smeared across her cheeks, her neck is reddened from beard burn, and her hair is sticking out in all different directions. But there's a satisfied smile.

"God," Nichole says as she rests her hand on the table. "I don't think I'll be able to walk home."

Myla glances back at me, and I just wiggle my brows before walking away, feeling completely and utterly justified. Now that was satisfying.

# Chapter Three

MYLA

***Present day* . . .**

"Myla, where are you?" Ryot calls out as the garage door slams behind him.

"Right here," I say as I poke my head up from the couch.

"Oh." His eyes scan me, and I can see him processing, trying to figure me out. It's what he's done from the very first day I met him. I'm a puzzle he's constantly trying to solve. Sometimes he figures it out, and sometimes he throws in the towel and gives up. And lately? Lately, I think he's forgotten I existed. At least in his plans for the future. I don't think I exist in those. "I need to talk to you."

"Ryot, I don't want to get into this," I say as I lie back down on the couch and clutch the throw pillow that's propped my head up.

"Don't worry, we won't be getting into much," he says, his voice distant and edgy. A voice I've only heard him use maybe a few times since we've been together.

He sits on a chair across from the couch and rests his arms on his legs. When our eyes connect, I see . . . nothing. No emotion. He's completely expressionless. I'm not looking to hurt him or for him to be hurt. I'm not that type of person. Just because you've hurt me doesn't mean that I'm going to retaliate.

"I'm not signing the papers . . ." he starts, which of course makes me sit up. Before I can say anything, he holds his hand out to stop me. "Yet," he finishes.

"What do you mean you're not signing them yet?"

"I have a stipulation." He rubs his hands together, and I can see he's thought about this. That's Ryot, though. He always puts thought into his big decisions, even if it doesn't include me.

I cross my arms. "Okay, what's your stipulation?"

"JP and Kelsey are getting married in three weeks. We are obviously invited to the wedding, and I don't want to stir any drama before or during their wedding, so I'm proposing that you go to the wedding with me, pretend everything is fucking great between us, and then after that, we go our separate ways. I'll sign the papers, and you can do whatever the hell you want."

"You want me to go to the wedding and act like everything is fine? How is that helpful to you?"

"It's not for me, Myla," he says through clenched teeth. "It's for my friend who has done a lot for me. If you don't show up to the wedding, they'll wonder why. I don't want to pull the attention away from them. So if you agree to act like everything is fine, then I'll sign your papers, no questions asked, and give you what you want."

"And what do we do until the wedding?"

"Whatever the hell we want," he answers. "If you want

me to sleep in the guest room, I'll sleep in the guest room. If you want me to find my own place, I can do that too. I'll be discreet about it, but when we're here, at home, we don't need to act like everything is fine. We can even lay out ground rules and become roommates who don't talk. I don't give a fuck. I just need you to go to the wedding with me, and then after that, you can do whatever the hell you want with your life, Myla."

"You don't have to sound so rude about it," I say.

"Oh, I'm sorry, did you want me to roll out the red carpet and pamper you while I told you my plan? Should I try again?"

"Now you're being a dick."

"Yeah, well, excuse me if I'm handling this differently than you. Not all of us can give zero fucks about life."

"Okay, I can see we're not going to be civil about this."

"Being civil would have included you talking about this with me. It would mean trying to work it out, but I can see that's not even on the table as an option. So yeah, I'm going to be fucking bitter, I might very well be a dick, and if I'm frustrated, it's because of you." Venom drips from his voice, and his brows are narrowed as anger seeps from every pore on his body.

"I've tried talking to you, Ryot, and you haven't listened. So I'm done. There's nothing more I can give you."

Frustrated, he pushes his hand through his hair. "Just tell me if you'll do the wedding, and then I'll leave you alone."

Even though I want to move on with my life, I know what Ryot says is right. If we separate now, attention will be stolen away from JP and Kelsey. I don't know them well at all, but I do know that I'm not an asshole, and I wouldn't want to steal the attention from anyone on their special day. Despite wanting to end this mental purgatory that I've been in, I know it's the right thing to do.

"It doesn't seem fair of you to ask me to do this. Pretend to be your wife when we're not together."

"I'm not asking you to solve world fucking hunger, Myla. I'm asking you to just act like you can be around me for a week."

"A week?" I ask, my voice rising. "Why a whole week?"

"Because it's a whole thing in Napa." He pinches his brow in frustration. "Listen, if you don't do this, I'm not signing."

"Are you threatening me?"

"I don't know what else to do." He holds his arms out. "You sprung this on me out of nowhere. So yeah, maybe I am threatening you."

"That's how it always is, right, Ryot? You do what it takes to get your way?" I stand and toss the throw pillow on the couch.

"Care to explain to me what your hidden message is with that statement?"

"I'm good," I say as I move toward the fridge to grab a La Croix. "But since I want a divorce, looks like I'll be attending your friend's wedding, smile and all."

"Good," he says as he rises from the chair.

"A thank you wouldn't hurt."

"You want me to thank you? After you threw a divorce at me last night without discussion, just a pen and a tab of where to sign? Yeah, no such luck, Myla." He moves by me toward the pantry, where I'm sure he'll grab one of his godforsaken protein bars.

But as he passes, I catch a whiff of his cologne, and for a moment, and only a moment, the smell reminds me of the man I fell in love with. The man who wasn't driven by proving himself but who simply lived life to his fullest. The man who took me into his arms when I needed him the most and showed me how much I mattered. How much he truly loves me.

And that makes me sad.

Because even though I'm angry and feel like I'll never come first in his life, I still love him.

I still very much care for him.

And I don't think those feelings will ever leave me. But the bitterness that has evolved, the resentment, is clouding my strong feelings and reminding me why I asked for a divorce. Either way, it's going to take a lot of healing and a lot of patience to get over someone like Ryot Bisley. For a few years, even though he was busy playing baseball, I knew I was his world. *Well, I shared it with baseball.* But I used to feel treasured. And lately, all I've felt is . . . invisible. *I don't want to live like that anymore.*

When he leaves the pantry—protein bar in hand—he asks, "Do you want me to sleep in the guest room?"

I pop open my La Croix and shake my head. "I've already moved my stuff in there."

"Why doesn't that surprise me? Acting without discussing."

"I've learned from the best," I say, giving him a sardonic smile.

"Whatever, Myla. Just tell me how I can stay out of your way."

"Interesting you want my opinion now. Where was that several months ago?"

He turns to face me. "The passive-aggressive comments aren't necessary."

"But they're fun."

"You know two can play at this game, right?"

"What game?" I ask.

He motions between us. "This bitterness, this resentment. You might be angry with me from months ago, but I'm angry with you now, fucking pissed off," he growls. "So we can either live peacefully or make each other's lives a living hell. Take your pick."

Moving past him, I bump him with my shoulder. *Live peace-*

*fully or make each other's lives a living hell. That sounds kinda fun.*
"Just stay out of my way."

And then I head to the first-floor guest room where I collapse onto my bed. I weep into my pillow because I'm at a loss. This . . . this is supposed to make me feel better. This separation is supposed to solve the problem, so why do I feel significantly worse?

⸻

"HE SORT OF HAS THE right to be angry," Nichole says while sucking an olive off her martini stick as I talk to her on Face-Time for our "happy hour." She still lives in Chicago, and when I moved, we made a pact to meet up regularly for happy hour despite being hundreds of miles apart.

"What?" I ask in outrage. "How does he have any right to be angry?"

"Uh, he had no idea you wanted a divorce, and then bam, papers. Any person has the right to be angry about that."

"I haven't been happy for months, so this should not be a surprise."

"But have you talked to him about it?" Nichole asks.

"Yes," I nearly shout. "I have. Several times and every single conversation has been interrupted. He's blown me off, or he flat out hasn't listened. One time, we had a date scheduled to talk about our life and what we want, and he skipped out on that for a meeting with the Cane brothers. It's not like I'm some heroine in a movie who breaks up with someone because of miscommunication. I've tried several times to have open and honest conversations. I've told him I'm not happy. I told him I didn't want to move to California. He hasn't listened. Ever since he retired from baseball, he's been on this weird campaign to prove himself, and I don't get it. He has several world championship wins to his name, so why does he need more? Why does he feel the need to prove himself?" My eyes well up with tears, and that's when Nichole sets her drink down and leans closer to the phone.

"Do you want me to come out there? I can help you pack, take your mind off things, and maybe go out and have some fun?"

"No," I say, wiping my nose. "I know you're busy with work."

"I just hired an intern and planned on passing some work her way. Plus, I recently finished up a big web design project so I'm only working on minor things right now. I have time."

"You know he'll hate it if you come out here."

"Pshhh, why? I'm a delight."

"You always get me in trouble with men."

She chuckles. "Well, good thing you're getting a divorce, huh?" With a wink, she opens her computer and starts tapping away. "I'm going to book a flight. I have some things to finalize, but this weekend, I'll be there. It will be like old times—you and me, prowling the town."

"I don't want to prowl," I say as I snuggle into my pillow, forgetting all about the seltzer water with a splash of cranberry juice that I poured myself. "I still love him, Nichole, even if he did hurt me."

"Well then, you can watch me prowl. Maybe take some pointers for when you are ready to make a move."

"Doubt that will be anytime soon," I mutter. Underneath his selfishness and self-centeredness, I know he's a good man. A great man, actually. The best. *I just haven't seen that man for a long time, and, it seems, no begging or conversation will bring him back.*

"Either way, I'm coming to visit, and if you want, I will act as the big spoon at night."

"Not necessary." I crack a smile.

"Ooh, see, there's a glimpse of my bestie. Just wait. When I get out there, I'm going to turn that frown upside down."

"I don't think I want to be cheered up," I say, feeling like the weight of the world rests on my shoulders. "I think I just want to be sad." We said vows to each other. Vows to love and cherish each other until death parts us. And I'm just so sad that those vows now mean nothing.

"Then I'll be sad with you." Growing serious, she says, "Myla, I know how much Ryot means to you. I know he's the love of your life and the one who broke past the many barriers you've erected over time. And I know how much this decision has weighed on you, so trust me when I say I will be there for you in whatever capacity you need. Just give this girl a few days."

"Thank you, Nichole. That means a lot to me."

"I know. I love you."

"Love you, too." I sigh.

# Chapter Four

*Eleven years ago...*

**DrinkWithMe:** *Bisley Balls, I see that you posted another picture of your batting. Riveting.*

**Ryot.Bisley.Balls:** *Sliding into my DMs? I'm surprised it took you this long.*

**DrinkWithMe:** *More like stomping into your DMs with a PSA. You keep reposting the same video. If you want to grow your audience, you really must push past your comfort zone.*

**Ryot.Bisley.Balls:** *This coming from the girl who posted a glass of orange juice this morning with the comment: no pulp.*

**DrinkWithMe:** *And I have twelve thousand likes and over two hundred comments. Just checking your post \*licks finger, flips paper over on clipboard\* and ah, yes, it says that you have eight comments and fifty likes. Soo . . . I think one of us is doing something right.*

**Ryot.Bisley.Balls:** *So do you want me to start posting my drinks?*

**DrinkWithMe:** *Uh, dude, try to be original. I know it might be difficult, but desperation for likes doesn't look good on you.*

*Ryot.Bisley.Balls:* I'm not desperate for likes. The only reason I even thought about it is because you keep harping on me.

*DrinkWithMe:* Are you calling me a nagging wife?

*Ryot.Bisley.Balls:* Wife? Isn't that stretching it a bit far?

*DrinkWithMe:* I don't know. I've slept over at your house. You paid for my meal. You told me all about how you like to spread legs. We're practically married at this point.

*Ryot.Bisley.Balls:* Hell, has the dating circuit really changed that much since I've been out of it? Didn't know I could marry that quickly with two interactions.

*DrinkWithMe:* Oh yeah, real hook, line, and sinker out there. One date = engaged. Second date = old married couple. Welcome to the world of sexual social engagements.

*Ryot.Bisley.Balls:* Eh, I think I'll crawl back into my hole. Thanks.

*DrinkWithMe:* Have you really not dated anyone in a while?

*Ryot.Bisley.Balls:* Let's just say dinner with you the other night was the closest thing I had to a date in about a year. And that wasn't a date, that was . . . hell, I don't know what that was.

*DrinkWithMe:* I don't know. You left me satisfied and wanting more.

*Ryot.Bisley.Balls:* Then you must be easy to please.

*DrinkWithMe:* If only.

---

DRINKWITHME: So . . . what is this game of baseball you play?

*Ryot.Bisley.Balls:* Never heard of it?

*DrinkWithMe:* Sports have never tickled my tits. Now balls, on the other hand . . . hey-o!

*Ryot.Bisley.Balls:* Tickled your tits, huh? What exactly does that? Besides balls of course.

*DrinkWithMe:* Glad you asked. Three things in particular: tongues, fingers, and peanut butter.

**Ryot.Bisley.Balls:** *Do tongues and peanut butter ever come into play together?*

**DrinkWithMe:** *Only once and it was an absolute disaster. The guy gagged from peanut butter mouth, dry-heaved, and I ended up running across the house, raccoon tail butt plug dangling out my ass as I grabbed him water.*

**Ryot.Bisley.Balls:** *Can we discuss the raccoon tail butt plug?*

**DrinkWithMe:** *The guy was a bit of a freak. It lasted a month. After the peanut butter fiasco, we called it quits. I returned the butt plug and went on my way.*

**Ryot.Bisley.Balls:** *Now that's what you should be taking pictures of . . . butt plugs.*

**DrinkWithMe:** *Yeah, so I can have pervs like you sliding into my DMs daily? No, thank you. I get enough of that by selling pics of my feet.*

**Ryot.Bisley.Balls:** *As I recall, YOU were the one that slid into MY DMs.*

**DrinkWithMe:** *For education, not because I wanted to. I think it will do you a great deal of service to remember that.*

---

RYOT.BISLEY.BALLS: *Hey, did you see my post today? *Wiggles eyebrows**

**DrinkWithMe:** *You know, I have better things to do with my life than hound your Instagram profile.*

**Ryot.Bisley.Balls:** *Could have fooled me.*

**DrinkWithMe:** *Feeling spicy today, I see.*

**Ryot.Bisley.Balls:** *Just trying to keep up with you. Now go check my feed.*

**DrinkWithMe:** *A photo of you lifting weights. Is that supposed to impress me?*

**Ryot.Bisley.Balls:** *Do you see the muscles? Isn't that what people call a thirst trap?*

**DrinkWithMe:** *Ahh, I see what's going on. You're trying to garner an audience by sexualizing yourself.*

**Ryot.Bisley.Balls:** *Do you think it's working?*

**DrinkWithMe:** *Well, I stared at it for longer than I care to admit.*

**Ryot.Bisley.Balls:** *Then my job here is done.*

———

DRINKWITHME: *I heard some women talking about you today at the restaurant I work at. One of them claimed that you were going home with her tonight after she flashed you her boobs while you were on the field. So I have two questions. Did someone flash their boobs at you? And did you take her home? An immediate response is required.*

**Ryot.Bisley.Balls:** *If someone did flash me their tits, I didn't notice. I'm currently alone in my townhome while Banner is out at the bars. If anyone is bringing someone home, it's him.*

**DrinkWithMe:** *Oh, that's a huge letdown. I was hoping for a good story. That girl was all talk.*

**Ryot.Bisley.Balls:** *Yeah, I'm disappointed too. Seems like, in her fantasy, it could have been a good night.*

**DrinkWithMe:** *So why aren't you out at the bar with Banner?*

**Ryot.Bisley.Balls:** *Tired as shit.*

**DrinkWithMe:** *Because of the baseball?*

**Ryot.Bisley.Balls:** *Yeah, because of \*the\* baseball. I'm vying for a spot in the Majors right now, so I'm pushing myself harder than ever before. Don't really have time for hanging out at the bar.*

**DrinkWithMe:** *Majors being . . .*

**Ryot.Bisley.Balls:** *Professional. Major League. The Studmuffins are the Triple-A team for the Chicago Bobbies. I was hoping to make the roster after spring training, but unfortunately, I didn't. They noticed me, though. Right now, the third baseman for the Bobbies has been there for a few years. He's pretty good but on the older side.*

**DrinkWithMe:** *So what you're saying is you're one pulled hamstring away from going pro?*

***Ryot.Bisley.Balls:*** *Yeah, pretty much.*
***DrinkWithMe:*** *Then I shall hope for tight hamstrings.*
***Ryot.Bisley.Balls:*** *That might be the nicest thing you've ever said to me.*
***DrinkWithMe:*** *You're making me soft.*
***Ryot.Bisley.Balls:*** *Good thing YOU'RE not making ME soft.*
***DrinkWithMe:*** *Would you look at us . . . things are starting to get frisky.*

———

DRINKWITHME: *Thoughts on phone sex. Have you done it?*
***Ryot.Bisley.Balls:*** *I have not. Haven't really had a girlfriend or someone who I would do that with in my life. But not against it. I know some guys on the team do it with their girlfriends.*
***DrinkWithMe:*** *Poor, lonely Bisley Balls. No one to have phone sex with.*
***Ryot.Bisley.Balls:*** *Have you had phone sex?*
***DrinkWithMe:*** *Once. The guy came when I whispered out a moan. He was into ASMR.*
***Ryot.Bisley.Balls:*** *Why do you have such a fascinating life?*
***DrinkWithMe:*** *I've been around, Bisley. I have life experience.*
***Ryot.Bisley.Balls:*** *You do. Makes me think I'm not life-ing properly.*
***DrinkWithMe:*** *You are. You're just on a different path than others. I'm sure when you get to where you want to be, there will be opportunities to help you "life" hard.*
***Ryot.Bisley.Balls:*** *You're being nice to me.*
***DrinkWithMe:*** *I think it's this beer I've been nursing while lying on my bed . . . naked.*
***Ryot.Bisley.Balls:*** *Naked, huh? Care to share a picture of that?*
***DrinkWithMe:*** *Sounds intriguing, possibly something I could see myself doing, but not quite sure you're ready for a free show. Not sure you earned it yet.*

**Ryot.Bisley.Balls:** *I think you're right. Those tits are worth way more than a conversation in your DMs.*

**DrinkWithMe:** *Ooo, you're making me all hot with your nice-boy charm. Tell me something else.*

**Ryot.Bisley.Balls:** *I was taught how to wipe the outer edge of the toilet bowl before I put the toilet seat down.*

**DrinkWithMe:** *Oh God, that's hot. More. Tell me more.*

**Ryot.Bisley.Balls:** *I thoroughly scrub my balls every day and manscape so when a woman goes down on me, she has the cleanest cock to suck on.*

**DrinkWithMe:** *A true gentleman. Mmm . . . give me one more.*

**Ryot.Bisley.Balls:** *I always let the woman come first.*

**DrinkWithMe:** *That . . . you . . . do.*

---

RYOT.BISLEY.BALLS: *I overheard one of the guys on my team talking about this Only Fans account that he follows because he loves the girl's feet. I nearly choked on my protein bar.*

**DrinkWithMe:** *Oh, a local customer. I wonder if it's me. Feet With Me is my name on Only Fans. You should ask him if that's the one he likes.*

**Ryot.Bisley.Balls:** *Not gonna do that. I don't want him thinking I'm into feet like him. The dude is weird. I don't want to bond over foot porn. Also . . . Feet With Me? That's not very original.*

**DrinkWithMe:** *It's all about the branding. \*eye roll\* Honestly, Granddad, it's as if you're not in your twenties when you say things like that.*

**Ryot.Bisley.Balls:** *I barely know how to post on social media, let alone know anything about branding. Now, if you want to talk about the different spins on a baseball, that I can talk about.*

**DrinkWithMe:** *Hurry, go post another thirst trap before I get bored with you.*

**Ryot.Bisley.Balls:** *Your wish is my command . . .*

⊏⊐

DRINKWITHME: *So, uh . . . are those abs real?*
**Ryot.Bisley.Balls:** *LOL! Saw my picture today, did ya?*
**DrinkWithMe:** *Happened to come across it. Liked that subtle hint of abs as you lifted your shirt to dry off your forehead. Could have used the towel draped over your shoulder, but who am I to complain?*
**Ryot.Bisley.Balls:** *Got shit from the guys for posting it.*
**DrinkWithMe:** *Well, you're getting nothing but praise from me. Job well done, sir.*
**Ryot.Bisley.Balls:** *It was all for you.*
**DrinkWithMe:** *Lies!*
**Ryot.Bisley.Balls:** *Nope. I thought to myself, what kind of post would make DrinkWithMe so thirsty that she'd post a picture of the drink that cooled her down?*
**DrinkWithMe:** *Well, job well done because I have a strawberry cooler in my hand, and I'm about to settle down for a photo shoot. Maybe I'll include my lips in this picture . . . sucking on the straw.*
**Ryot.Bisley.Balls:** *Why did that just make my dick stir?*
**DrinkWithMe:** *Because you apparently never have sex, that's why.*
**Ryot.Bisley.Balls:** *Might have to figure out something for tonight, especially if you post a picture of those hot lips.*
**DrinkWithMe:** *Okay, okay . . . the flirting has picked up. I see what you're doing.*
**Ryot.Bisley.Balls:** *I posted a picture of my abs today, meant for you. I'd say the flirting has most definitely picked up.*
**DrinkWithMe:** *\*cracks knuckles\* Then I need to up my game.*

⊏⊐

DRINKWITHME: *I saw you today.*
**Ryot.Bisley.Balls:** *Really? Where?*
**DrinkWithMe:** *In my dreams . . .*
**Ryot.Bisley.Balls:** *It's now my turn to roll my eyes.*

**DrinkWithMe:** *Oh . . . so you don't want to hear about what we were doing?*

**Ryot.Bisley.Balls:** *Wait now, I didn't say that. We were actually doing things?*

**DrinkWithMe:** *Naughty things. Legit had an orgasm in my dream. It was hot.*

**Ryot.Bisley.Balls:** *Damn, that is hot. What were we doing?*

**DrinkWithMe:** *I was giving you a lap dance. You were hard, and I rode that ridge until I came.*

**Ryot.Bisley.Balls:** *Have you, uh, given many lap dances?*

**DrinkWithMe:** *I was a stripper for two hours once in my life. It was for some frat party. I was paid one thousand dollars. I kept my clothes on but just went around and rolled on men's laps. Easiest money I ever earned, but that was the only time I truly gave a lap dance. Anything else has just been more of a dry hump with a guy. Ever get a lap dance yourself?*

**Ryot.Bisley.Balls:** *Still trying to comprehend the whole stripper thing . . . yet your clothes stayed on?*

**DrinkWithMe:** *Well, I was wearing a thong and a red tank top that was wet. You couldn't see anything, but it was hot enough that the guys were pleased. I bought my class books with the money.*

**Ryot.Bisley.Balls:** *Why am I jealous?*

**DrinkWithMe:** *Because you think I'm hot. I get it. I would be jealous too if you told me you were stripping in front of women. I would want that bean pole of yours swaying in my face. But don't avoid the question. Have you ever gotten a lap dance?*

**Ryot.Bisley.Balls:** *Yeah. I've been to a few strip clubs, but nothing too intense. Just got a bit hard and that was it.*

**DrinkWithMe:** *I find that so freaking sexy. I would love to watch you get a lap dance by another woman. I bet you're controlled and hold in how you're feeling by biting on your lower lip.*

**Ryot.Bisley.Balls:** *That would never happen, getting a lap dance by another woman while you were watching.*

**DrinkWithMe:** *Why not? That doesn't intrigue you?*

**Ryot.Bisley.Balls:** *What would intrigue me is \*you\* straddling* *my lap, making me hard as I gripped your ass while you played with those sexy tits of yours.*

**DrinkWithMe:** *You're right, that is hotter. Would you suck on them if I offered them to you?*

**Ryot.Bisley.Balls:** *You wouldn't be able to stop me.*

**DrinkWithMe:** *Well . . . now I'm going to go have some fun with my vibrator. Thanks. Good night, Bisley.*

**Ryot.Bisley.Balls:** *Wait, that's it? Ugh, you're killing me, Myla.*

**DrinkWithMe:** *Yup, were you expecting me to help you get off? Have an imagination, Bisley. Go forth and jack off while finishing the fantasy. XOXO*

**Ryot.Bisley.Balls:** *But I want to finish the fantasy with you.*

---

DRINKWITHME: *I saw you on the television today. Looks like someone got a houser.*

**Ryot.Bisley.Balls:** *LOL, not a houser . . . a homer, as in a home run.*

**DrinkWithMe:** *Huh, completely butchered that.*

**Ryot.Bisley.Balls:** *It made me laugh.*

**DrinkWithMe:** *Are you happy? Celebrating? Suckling down a protein bar?*

**Ryot.Bisley.Balls:** *I'm actually out with Banner. He's talking to some girl while I'm nursing a Coke Zero.*

**DrinkWithMe:** *Where are you at, Bisley?*

**Ryot.Bisley.Balls:** *The Benchwarmer.*

**DrinkWithMe:** *Looks like our stars are crossing once again.*

---

# RYOT

"AS I LIVE AND BREATHE, Bisley Balls," I hear Myla say as she approaches from behind.

I turn just in time to catch her checking out my backside before her eyes meet mine. Fuck, it's been too fucking long since I've seen her, and this is a stark reminder of just how gorgeous she is. Teasing each other in our DMs over the past few weeks has been fun and helped me relax and not be so tense at the plate. But after the past couple of days, the tension has peaked, and now I'm so fucking horny. Seeing her has spiked that desire to get her naked in my bed.

"How did you ever find me?" I ask, a smile tugging at my lips as I check her out.

Sexy nurse costume long gone, she's now in a pair of fraying cutoffs and a crop top that shows off an inch of her stomach. Her hair is draped over her shoulders in soft waves. Her shorts and crop top accentuate her waist and chest. She truly knows how to play with her curves and make every man in this goddamn bar turn their head. Thank fuck she's talking to me.

"How did I find you? Well, fate of course," she says as she leans against the bar next to me.

I turn toward her and ask, "Can I get you something to drink?"

"I would love that." She grips her throat. "I'm completely parched."

"Well, we can't have that." I lean over the bar and grab the bartender's attention. "Could I have another Coke Zero for the lady?"

"Sure," he answers and fills up a glass right in front of us before sliding it closer.

I thank him and then hand her the drink. She glances at it and then asks, "What the hell is this?"

"A drink. You never specified what you wanted."

"There's no alcohol in this."

"Yeah, there's no alcohol in mine either."

She sips from the straw and asks, "Is this your version of fun?"

"Yeah. Have a problem with it? Because you didn't have to come find me."

"It's not like I wanted to. I just had this overwhelming sense that you were in need of entertainment." She glances at our drinks. "Clearly, I was right. Now come with me." She grabs my hand and pulls me through the bustling crowd, past a few fans at the bar, and then toward the back where there's a foosball table set up. She spins one of the poles and asks, "Have you ever foos-ed around?"

"Lame attempt at a joke." I chuckle.

"Says the guy who's laughing." She sets her drink down on the edge and then picks up a soccer ball from one of the goals. "Get ready to have your ass annihilated."

"Are you good?" I ask, setting my drink down as well and getting into position.

"Not even a little. But confidence wins games."

"Oh yeah, didn't know that."

She taps the side of her head. "Stick with me, Bisley. I know a thing or two." Then she drops the ball and starts spinning her poles, distracting me so much that I don't realize the ball is sailing toward my goal until it clunks to the bottom. "Fuck, yes!" She pumps her arm into the air. "God, my nipples are hard."

Because I'm a man, I glance down at her tits and see that her nipples are, in fact, hard.

When she catches me staring, she just smirks. "Get a good look?"

"Not nearly enough."

"Feel free to stare all you want while I destroy you at this game." She drops the ball and automatically starts spinning the poles, acting like a madwoman.

This time, I focus, and even though she's giving it her best effort, I block three of her shots, shoot the ball past her players, and then snap it into her goal.

"Ooo, that feels good," I say as I reach for my drink and bring it to my lips.

"You know, I would never have guessed you to be a gloater, but here we are."

"And I pegged you for a sore loser, so guess I was right on that."

She reaches for the ball. "Prepare for total domination."

While I still have my drink in hand, she drops the ball, flicks her wrist, and scores. With a shimmy in my direction, her tits flying at me in the best way, she says, "Need some cleavage to cry on?"

"You're something else." I shake my head in humor.

She presses her hand to her chest. "Why, thank you."

I reach for the ball just as my phone buzzes in my pocket. "Time out," I say as I pull my phone out. When I see my agent, Roark's, name on the screen, I say to Myla, "Hey, give me a second."

"Sure." She smiles and reaches for her drink as I step into a corner of the bar.

"Hey, Roark, what's up?"

"Ryot, lad, how's it goin'?" His heavy Irish lilt falls through the line.

"Good. Did you see the home run tonight?"

"I did. So did the Bobbies." My ears perk up. My skin prickles. "Jones tore a muscle in his back tonight diving for a ball, so they're calling you up."

"Wait, what?" I ask. My heart's beating so rapidly I can barely breathe.

"It's your time, Ryot. You're going pro."

"Holy fucking shit," I breathe into the phone. "Dude, you're not kidding me? This is for real?"

"So real that you need to be on a red-eye tonight at eleven."

I quickly glance at my phone to see the time. "That's in three hours."

"Yeah, so get packing."

"Holy shit." I grip my hair. "You're fucking serious. This is happening?"

"This is happening, man."

"Fuck, okay. I need . . . shit, I need to call my brother and pack."

"Let me know if you need anything. I'm arranging housing for you as well as transportation. I'll message you the details."

"Thanks, Roark. Fuck, okay, I gotta go."

"Talk soon. Cheers."

We both hang up the phone, and I quickly dial Banner's number. I pace the three-by-three space and pull on the short strands of my hair while I wait for Banner to pick up. After four rings, he answers, "This better be good."

"They fucking called me up, man," I say as my throat grows tight.

There's silence, and then, "Fuck, are you serious?"

"Yes. I have a red-eye flight in three hours. I'm going to head back to the house now and pack. Dude, you're coming, right?"

"You know I'll follow you wherever you go. That's the pact."

"Good, then it looks like we're headed to Chicago."

"Fuck yes, we are!" We both laugh. "Ryot?"

"Yeah?" I answer.

"I'm really fucking proud of you. Have you told Nola yet?" he asks, referring to our sister.

"Not yet, but I will."

"Okay, maybe we call her together while we pack. And then we can call Mom and Dad."

"Sounds good. Meet you at the house in twenty."

"On my way," he answers, and then we hang up. I head

back to the foosball table where Myla is waiting patiently. Wow, this could not have been worse timing.

"Everything okay?" she asks.

"Yeah, I, uh . . ." I scratch my chest. "I was called up."

The cutest crinkle pulls at her nose as confusion crosses her expression. "Called up to where? The bar? Heaven?" She presses her hand to her chest. "Has your time come to go through the Pearly Gates?"

Chuckling, I shake my head. "No, called up to the Majors. I'm headed to Chicago . . . tonight."

"Wow." Her eyes widen. "Really? That's amazing." She moves around the table and wraps her arms around my waist, pulling me into a tight hug. "Congratulations, Bisley Balls."

Caught off guard by her soft demeanor, I hug her back and say, "Thank you." But she doesn't let go. It's a long hug, a comforting hug, and I'm seeing a side of her I didn't think existed. She's been so brash, so outspoken, and so sarcastic that I wasn't aware there was a soft, caring side to her, and that's exactly what I'm feeling at this moment.

When she finally lets me go and takes a step back, she puts her hands in her pockets and glances up at me. "I'm assuming you need to go."

"Yeah. I have to pack and then head to the airport."

"Well . . ." She smirks. "I guess that ends our game. I can walk away a proud woman, knowing I just beat a Major League baseball player." With a wink, she walks away, but then she spins around and says, "See you around, Bisley Balls."

And before I can say another word, she's gone.

# Chapter Five

RYOT

*Present day . . .*

"How are you doing?" Nola asks, her voice sounding choppy from the poor reception.

"Let me guess, Banner called you?" I ask.

"He did. He was worried about you. Said you haven't been talking to him much. But don't worry, I didn't say anything to Mom and Dad."

Thank God for that.

Nola lives just outside of Port Snow, Maine, in Bright Harbor, where we grew up. She moved back a few years ago after a difficult breakup with her long-term boyfriend. She decided to restore our old childhood home after Mom and Dad moved into a more manageable cottage. After marrying the first boy who ever broke her heart, she's now living happily in her refurbished home with the love of her life.

Color me envious.

"So what's going on with Myla?"

I walk over to my bedroom door and shut it so my voice doesn't travel. "I don't know, Nola. She's dead set on divorcing me. We're not even sleeping in the same goddamn room. She had the papers drawn up and everything."

"Really?" she asks, sounding so sad.

Nola and Myla instantly connected the day they first met. Like long-lost sisters reuniting, they not only have so much in common, but they have a common goal to pick on Banner and me as much as humanly possible. Over the years, during holidays and vacations, they've had their fair share of jabs at us . . . and I've loved every goddamn second of it.

"Yeah, but I didn't sign them. I can't. Fuck, Nola, I can't even muster the strength to pick up a pen. I don't want a divorce. I love her."

"I know you do. I've never seen you happier than when you are with her. What happened?"

"I don't know." I press my palm to my eye. "I'm still trying to figure that out. It doesn't help that I'm so fucking mad that I could throw a chair through the wall at any given point."

"That doesn't sound healthy."

"It's not. I'm attempting to chill the hell out, but anytime I think about what's going on, there's this inner rage that I can't seem to tamp down."

"I guess that makes sense, though," she says. "You were blindsided, and you love her. You've worked hard in this relationship. Seeing it all tumble apart can't be easy."

"It's not," I reply. "But I do have a plan." Even if it might be a stupid plan, at least it's something.

"A plan?"

"Yeah, Penn and Banner helped me figure it all out."

"Penn and Banner?" she deadpans. "The two men who

wouldn't be able to have a steady relationship even if it smacked them in the head?"

"Yes, but it's an idea. The only idea I have."

"Uh-huh, let me hear it."

I explain the plan to her, including my approach for the wedding week, and once I'm done, she doesn't say anything. Not a word. To the point that I'm worried that she hung up or lost service.

"Hello? Nola, are you still there?"

"Yes, I'm here."

"So what do you think?" I roll back on my bed, pinching my brow, knowing exactly what she's going to say.

"Well, if my silence wasn't telling enough, I guess I have to say that's the stupidest plan I think I've ever heard."

Yeah, I know, but I'm also attached to the plan because it's helping me breathe. It's giving me minuscule hope.

"How so?" I ask, preparing myself for a lecture.

"For one, you're only going to piss her off even more. She's also already dead set on this divorce, so your mind trickery won't do anything other than reinforce her decision. And if you think a week away in a romantic location will solve all of your problems, you really are freaking delusional."

"Wow, tell me how you really feel."

"I'm just trying to bring everything into perspective for you, Ryot."

"Yeah, I get that, but Myla is so unreceptive to talking. I don't know any other way to reach her."

"But how have you approached her? Have you been angry?"

"Well, the night she told me, yeah, I was angry. How could I not be? And then the other night when I asked her to pretend to be my wife at the wedding, I was angry as well, but that's because I'm so fucking . . . ugh, I'm pissed. I can't seem to control it when I'm around her even though I need to."

"I know. I can't imagine what both of you are feeling right

now." Nola's calming voice eases some of the tension I've been feeling, but only some. "So you already asked her to do the wedding thing? Honestly, Ryot, why didn't you come to me in the beginning?"

"I don't know. I was embarrassed," I answer. "The last thing I want is to tell people that the love of my life wants to be rid of me. Doesn't feel too great."

"I can understand that, but you need to do some damage control."

"And how do you propose I go about doing that?"

"Well, being angry around her isn't one of them."

"Easier said than done," I say softly. "And I realize that she doesn't need my anger. I truly get that. She needs the man who can calmly talk to her and be her voice of reason like I have been in the past. But, Nola . . . I'm hurting here, and I'm having a really hard time controlling it."

"Perhaps taking a different approach might help."

"I'm listening."

"You need to talk this out, so go down to her room, knock on her door, and ask her if you can just have a simple conversation. See where her head's at. Tell her no pressure, but that you just want to know where you went wrong."

I scrape my fingers over my jaw. "That seems like it could work. Tell her I don't expect anything from her. I just want to know how I could be better."

"Exactly. See, aren't you glad I called you?"

"I'll be glad if it works."

"It will. Just watch. And try not to get angry, okay? I know you're sifting through a lot of emotions at the moment, but consider where Myla comes from. Remember her background. Anger is not going to help. Text me after your heart-to-heart, and we'll go from there."

"Okay, sure. Thanks, Nola."

"Any time."

We both hang up, and I set my phone down. A simple

conversation, that's all I need to have. It shouldn't be too hard. If I approach her without wanting to fix things between us, but to fix myself so I can be a better man, then she will be receptive. She's never had any problem harping on me about my faults. From the very beginning, she's always told me like it is, so this conversation should be very pleasing to her.

When I see her, I just need to remember not to let my emotions get the better of me.

I get up from my bed and head downstairs just as I hear voices in the kitchen. Two voices.

I pause on the stairs and listen closely.

I know that voice.

I've heard that voice many, many times.

"Okay, I say we start at the bar, grab some drinks and apps, and then see where the night takes us. Possibly the dance floor."

Yup. I know exactly who that is.

Fucking Nichole.

I have a serious love-hate relationship with the woman. I love that she's taken care of Myla over the years when I wasn't there for her. And I love that she had some one-night stands with my brother so I got to meet Myla, but I fucking hate the way she treats my relationship with Myla as if it's expendable.

There's no doubt that those divorce papers on my nightstand are a product of a conversation with Nichole.

So if she thinks for one goddamn second they're going out to the bars—where I know they will undoubtedly hit on men —then she is sadly mistaken. No way in fuck will I let my wife go out with Nichole.

No fucking way.

Anger surges.

My pulse screams through my veins.

And everything Nola told me is tossed right out the window as I descend the rest of the stairs and head straight to the kitchen, where I will be shutting down whatever plans they have for tonight.

———

## MYLA

I PICKED up Nichole an hour ago. While we drove home, Nichole listed off all the bars and clubs she wants to take me to. I just sat there quietly, nodding my head even though the last thing I really want to do is go out.

But that's why Nichole is here, to get me out of my funk.

Once we got back to the house, she picked out a dress for me to put on—a red number that I haven't worn in years— pulled my hair up into a tight bun, and did my makeup for me. Ryot has always made me feel sexy, but this outfit, this makeup, makes me feel sexy on my own. Like I don't need a man to boost my confidence, and that's sort of nice.

The only problem is, Nichole has it set in her mind that we're going to have "fun" and fun to me right now is eating ice cream in bed while bingeing Netflix. But I understand what she's trying to do. She's trying to shake me alive again, so I'm wearing this dress and listening to her plans for the evening.

"I think we start at Four, and then we move on from there. I heard they have great appetizers. Soft pretzels with beer dip? Yes, please."

"Sure, yeah, I went there—"

"Myla, a word," Ryot says from behind me, startling me. I didn't even hear him creep down the stairs.

"Oh, why hello there," Nichole says, waving her fingers at Ryot. "How's it going, Bisley?"

I catch Ryot flash his icy glare at Nichole before turning

back toward me. "Myla, I would like to speak to you in private."

"Not even a hello?" Nichole asks.

"Cut the shit, Nichole. You know the last thing I want to do is say hi to you."

"What a greeting. And here I thought we were friends."

"We were until you convinced Myla to break up with me after her father passed. Since then, you've been someone I've tolerated because I love my wife."

Nichole's face falls, and she's about to open her mouth to reply, but I move Ryot out of the kitchen and toward the guest bedroom, out of earshot. The last thing I need is a fight between them.

When the door is closed, I turn toward him and say, "Don't be rude to her. That was a while ago, and we've moved on."

"She might have, but I never did. What is she doing here anyway?"

"She thought I needed support."

"You, support?" he asks, his eyes blazing with fury. "How the fuck are you the one who needs support? I'm the one whose heart is being ripped out of his goddamn chest. I'm the one who was blindsided. I'm the one who thought everything was fine with this marriage." *And therein lies the problem. Ryot simply has no idea how desperately invisible I've felt for months. He's lost sight of me in his world. In us.* It's why my heart feels so utterly crushed. Why I've felt so alone.

"That's the problem, Ryot. It wasn't fine. Nothing was fine about this marriage."

"So you're just giving up and tossing in the towel? Are you going out with Nichole so she can attempt to hook you up with some random guy?"

No, not even close. I don't want to hook up with anyone, but I don't like his tone or assumption, so for some stupid reason, I don't deny it.

"I can do whatever the hell I want, Ryot." I try to move past him, but he stops me with his hand on my hip. His domineering body towers over me as he moves me against the wall where his other hand falls to the white surface, right next to my face.

"You're still my goddamn wife, Myla. That means you're mine." The hand gripping my hip tightens. "This body, it's mine. That sassy mind of yours is mine. And those rose-colored lips that have explored every inch of my body? They still belong to me." I stare up at him, ready to throw up my defenses, ready to tell him otherwise, but my body betrays me as my lungs pant for air, and my tongue wets my lips.

Ryot has always had control over my body. Not because he's stolen it or taken what was not given to him, but because I offered every part of myself to this man, and he's coddled it. He's held it close to his heart. Like I said, sex has never been an issue. Ever. And right now, I can feel that urge, that need, that want to be with him. To have him pin me to the bed on my stomach, lift my ass in the air, and drive into me with that delicious cock of his.

"You're thinking about it, aren't you?" he asks, the cockiness in his voice immediately irritating me.

"No." I look away, but he grips my chin and forces me to meet his intense glare.

"Yes, you fucking are." His fingers now fall to my jaw, where he tips my head back against the wall. "You're thinking about my cock and how delicious it feels thrusting in and out of you. You're thinking about the control, the command I have on you. Tell me I'm fucking wrong."

"It doesn't matter," I say, my hands pushing at his chest. Even though he's stronger than I am and would normally be unfazed by my push, he steps back, giving me space. "None of this matters."

"The fuck it doesn't," he says. "You're my wife. Therefore,

you're not permitted to even think about another man, not until those papers are signed."

"Permitted?" I fold my arms. "Where do you get off acting like you control me?"

"You took vows, Myla," he says in a low growl. "And until those vows are severed, you will respect them."

"Uh-huh, and would that apply to you as well?"

"They don't need to apply to me." He closes the space between us and, this time, takes both of my hands in his and pins them above my head. He leans in so his nose grazes my cheek. "I don't want anyone else. I don't need anyone else. It's you I think about. It's you I want in my goddamn bed. It's you I want wearing my ring." His lips skim my ear. "You're all I've ever wanted, Myla."

"Don't," I choke out. "Don't make this harder than it already is."

"Tell me you don't love me."

I shake my head. "No, because that would be a lie."

His lips brush against my cheek. "Tell me you don't want me."

"I don't . . . I don't want you."

"And that you can lie about?" he asks as his hand travels to the hem of my skirt and his fingers slip under the tight fabric. The calluses from many years of holding a bat drag over my sensitive skin as he smooths his hand all the way up to my hip, pulling the hem of the dress with it.

"I don't want to want you," I say.

"But you do."

"You can't . . ." I take a deep breath as his fingers toy with the strap of my thong. Jesus Christ, I shouldn't be allowing this. I should put an end to this, push past him, and go find Nichole, but for the life of me, I can't. And this is what has gotten me in trouble in the past, this raw need I have for the man. "You can't fix this with sex," I finally say as he pulls on the strap of my thong so it falls down my legs.

Fuck.

I kick it to the side and then spread myself wider for him.

*What is wrong with me?*

*Why am I letting this happen?*

Probably because I'm still desperate for him.

Because I know I'll never stop loving him despite our problems.

And this, this is one of the reasons. When he touches me, when he's this close, I feel guarded, protected, and comforted. And comfort is what I seek right now.

With his lips pressed to my ear, he whispers, "Are you wet?"

My head drops against the wall as I wiggle out of his pinned grasp and move my fingers between my legs. I drag them along my slick clit then bring them to his mouth, where he parts his lips and sucks them in.

His eyes remain on me as he sucks, as his tongue runs along my digits, lapping up every inch of them until I pull them away.

"Fuck," he moans right before licking his lips. "You still think I can't fix this with sex?"

"I know you can't," I answer, betrayed by the hitch in my voice.

"What if I tried? Would you let me?" he asks as his fingers trail along my inner thigh, his knuckle grazing my sensitive flesh.

Yes.

I would.

At this moment, with this blistering feeling of need pumping through me, I would. And I know I would hate myself after, just as I hated myself the morning we had sex before I gave him the divorce papers. It's next to impossible for me to deny him, especially when he's this close.

"Your silence tells me you would." He presses his fingers along my slit, briefly sliding across my clit.

Fuck. Me.

My brain screams at me, telling me to stop him.

But *I* grip his shoulders, looking for support as he swipes again.

And again.

And again.

"You love this," he says, leaning forward, his lips right next to mine. "I'm the only man who will make you feel this good. Who will make you come the way I can. I'm the only one who will ever understand your body the way you need." His thumb presses against my clit, and I moan loud enough for Nichole to probably hear me.

I'm surprised she hasn't come knocking on the door yet, looking for me.

"Tell me we can work on this, Myla."

My eyes fall to his as he pulls away, so our gazes lock. "Don't do that," I say to him, my throat tight as my body pulses with need. "Don't use sex to change my mind. That's not fair."

"None of this is fair." His thumb rubs my clit softer now, so soft that I almost don't feel him. "If this was fair, you would tell me how I could fix this."

"There's no fixing it." I tilt my pelvis, searching out his touch. "It's . . . it's over, Ryot."

He pauses, his hand stilling between my legs as the anger he exhibited only moments ago reappears. "Your drenched pussy tells me different."

"I might want your body, but that doesn't mean I want to be married to you anymore." *Because I think we're irrevocably broken. And that is the most devastating thing in the world to me.*

And that must be the proverbial cold bucket of water to him because he shoots away from me, his chest puffing with irritation.

"What are you doing?" I ask, my need to orgasm clouding my mind.

"Do you really think I'm going to finish you off after a comment like that?" he asks. "Fuck, Myla, you're killing me here."

"So what was that?" I ask. "You using my body to get what you want?"

"No." He looks away, and I know that's exactly what he was trying to do.

"That's messed up, Ryot. That's manipulative. That's you trying to get your way without putting in the actual work. And I'm done. I'm sick of it. You are no longer going to sit back and get your way, not anymore. I found my voice, and I'll be damned if you'll silence it." I bend down, pick up my thong, and reach for the door's handle just before he slaps his hand on the wood, keeping it shut.

"I have always lifted you up, Myla. With all of your endeavors. Always. Don't make me out to be a monster."

"Step away from the door," I say through clenched teeth. He's not a monster, but trying to manipulate me just then was not fucking okay.

To my surprise, he listens and moves away, but as I reach for the handle, he places his hand on it and says, "Do not fuck around on me. Understood? If you want to go out and meet men, fine, but at least give me the respect of waiting until after the papers are signed." He flings the door open and charges up the stairs without another word.

After a few beats, Nichole meets me in the doorway. "Should I assume we'll be staying in tonight?"

My eyes well up as I nod. "Yeah." Because Ryot is right, I would never disrespect him by fucking another man while I'm still married. *You can't do that to the man you love. Even if your soul feels so broken.*

# Chapter Six

RYOT

*Seven years ago* . . .

"This was not a good idea," I say as we finally make it to our reserved bar-top table. From the moment I entered the well-known Chicago pub that runs the best trivia nights in the city, it's been a goddamn parade. And sure, I'm grateful for all the love, especially since Bobbies fans can be so brutal if you're not performing, but I've been spotted several times. Not to mention the rival team to the Bobbies, the Rebels, also have rabid fans who are more than willing to bring you down in any way possible. I've heard a few comments from them as well.

Mostly, "Bisley, you suck!"

Now that I've gained popularity in the city and have a regular spot on the roster with the third-best batting average on the team, just falling short to Walker Rockwell and Knox Gentry, I'm well known throughout the city, which makes it very hard to do public things, like trivia night with Banner.

"It's fine." Banner takes a seat on one of the stools. "You just had to get in here. Now everything is normal." Banner stares at the menu, not noticing the hundreds of camera phones pointed at us.

"Dude, look around," I say through a smile. "Everyone is recording us."

"Well, then refrain from picking your nose, as you don't want to be caught doing that." He sets the drink menu down and smiles. "Seriously, just relax. It will be crazy for the first ten minutes, but once trivia night starts, everyone will be so focused on beating you that it won't matter."

"Thanks for that."

"You're welcome." He taps the drink menu. "They have that IPA you like. Are you going to drink tonight?"

"I'll have one," I say because I know Banner has planned this night to spend some time with me. With my schedule and his busy job coding apps, we haven't seen much of each other lately. When he asked me to go to trivia night with him, I knew I had to say yes.

"One drink? Living large, man," he teases.

Banner flags down a server, orders us each a drink and burgers with fries, and then picks up the laminated list of rules for trivia night.

"Have you done this before?" I ask.

"No, just heard about it from the guy down the hall."

"Which guy?" I ask. Banner and I share an apartment in the heart of Chicago. It's a two-bedroom with a decent living space. There are many people on our floor, and since Banner works from home, coding God knows what for companies, he has gotten to know our neighbors.

"Jetson."

"Jetson?" I ask. "That's his name?"

"Ehh, no, but he looks like George Jetson, so that's what I call him. I actually don't know his real name, but we talk in the elevator. He told me about trivia night here. Actually"—Banner perks his head up and looks around—"he might have come tonight. I saw him this morning and told him we were attending."

"Hey, are your other two teammates arriving soon?" a man with a long fire-red beard asks. He's sporting a backward hat and a plaid shirt and holding a mic in his hand that's turned off.

"Uh, what?" I ask. "It's just us." I motion to Banner.

"This is four-person trivia night."

"Oh, shit, really?" Banner asks. Then he leans toward me and whispers, "A minor detail Jetson left out."

"Are we able to play with two?" I ask.

"No, but don't worry, we have another pair who need a team as well, so we'll send them over here."

"Aces," Banner says with a thumbs-up, looking like a total dick. I know he's doing it in an ironic way, but he still looks stupid.

When the trivia host leaves, I turn to Banner. "Why don't we just find another place? We can just hang out and have a drink."

"No way, I ordered garlic tater tots. I'm not leaving until every one of them is in my belly."

"Okay then." I don't put up too much of a fight because Banner planned this, and I know he's been missing me. Playing professional baseball has definitely changed things. Don't get me wrong, I love it and wouldn't trade it for anything, but it's demanding. I'm either playing a night game, I'm out of town, or I'm training. It doesn't leave much time for brotherly bonding.

The server drops off our drinks, and just as I pick up mine to take a sip, the host comes back and says, "Here are your other two teammates. They've already picked a name for your team. Bisley's Balls."

A chill races up my spine as the host steps out of the way, and Myla steps forward with her friend Nichole.

What the actual fuck?

"Well, well, well, if it isn't Bisley Balls," she says with a large smile.

"Holy shit, Myla, what are you doing here?" I ask while I hop off my stool and step up to her. Unsure of what to do, I extend my hand out for a handshake but then also go in for a hug and end up poking her in the belly with my fingers. "Fuck, sorry," I say as she chuckles.

"What are you trying to do there, killer?" she asks.

"I don't know." I pull on my neck. "Didn't know if I should shake your hand or hug you, or . . . hell, I don't know."

"Let us show you how it's done," Nichole says right before she walks up to Banner, slips her hand to the back of his head, and gives him an open-mouthed kiss. Of course, my very single and horny brother receives her hello with open arms. When Nichole pulls away, she wets her lips and says, "We'll be heading to the bathroom later."

"You just tell me when, babe."

Seems like no time has been lost between them despite the few years that have gone by.

Still confused about why I'm seeing Myla, I ask again, "What are you doing here?"

"What do you mean? Trivia night of course."

"No, in Chicago," I say as Nichole takes a seat next to Banner and starts running her hand through his hair. Doubt there will be any brotherly time spent tonight now.

"Oh . . ." Myla pulls her stool toward mine and takes a seat. "I live here now."

"You . . . you live here?" I ask, shocked. I take a seat too. And just as she's done before, Myla steals my drink and starts sipping on it. "Did you just move?"

"No. I've been here for about a year now. Nichole got a job out here with a major tech company, and my parents live just north of Barrington now that they're retired from the Air Force, so I thought what the hell, I'll move too."

"Wait, so you've been here for a year, and you didn't think to message me?"

She just shrugs. "If our paths crossed, then they crossed." She smirks. "And looks like that happened." She sets my beer down, pulls out her phone, and takes a picture of it. "This is being listed as a beer belonging to a baller."

How can she act so casual? As if seeing me is just a normal, everyday thing? I know we didn't make any promises to each other, nor were we in any sort of relationship, but hell, I'm a little shook from seeing her.

After the thrill of being called up to the Majors and packing, I sat on my red-eye to Chicago thinking about how I'd bolted out of the bar and away from Myla before I could actually process it all. Guilt consumed me, and when I landed, I messaged her on Instagram and apologized for bolting. I told her if she was ever in Chicago to contact me.

She never wrote back.

And clearly, she never contacted me. Maybe she has a boyfriend?

I thought that she was mad, had moved on, or just didn't see the value in continuing our conversation. I still kept up with her drink pictures, and though I thought about her often, I never said anything because, well, I didn't want to badger her. She was in Phoenix, and I was in Chicago, so not much could be done.

But now that she's here . . .

She sets her phone down and looks up at me. Her beautiful eyes study what I can only imagine is a perplexed expression. "Why the scowl?" she asks, motioning to my forehead.

"I'm sorry." I shake my head, trying to rid myself of my

thoughts. "I'm just confused is all. I didn't expect to see you here."

"Aw." She places her hand on my thigh and leans forward. "Are you flustered?"

"A little." I chuckle.

"That's cute. Don't worry, I'll take it easy on you." She sips from my beer. "It's good to see you, though." Her eyes roam my body, mainly fixating on my chest. "Looks like those protein bars have been paying off."

For some stupid reason, I glance at my chest and then back up at her. "Uh, yeah. That and the strength and conditioning team for the Bobbies."

"Well, good on them. And you've been enjoying Chicago?"

"Yeah, as much as I've been able to enjoy it. Baseball has taken up a lot of my time, so I haven't really experienced the city as much as I've wanted. But what I have experienced, I've liked."

She leans her elbow on the table, those bright, brilliant eyes nearly cutting through me. How could I forget how fucking beautiful she is? "Has anyone ever told you, you need to loosen up?"

"Several people," I answer as I steal my beer for a sip, but then hand it back to her when I'm done.

"Maybe that's what you try to do tonight." She draws a circle over the back of my hand with her finger, and I willingly allow myself to revel in the way it makes me feel—turned on and wanting so much more. "Think you can have some fun with me?"

Uh, yeah . . . I think I can.

"Welcome to trivia night," the host says into the mic, which quiets the bar. "We have ten teams tonight, all vying for the coveted fifty-dollar gift card to the Cold Stone Creamery across the street."

The bar cheers as Myla says, "Fifty dollars' worth of

creamy creations . . ." She rubs her hands together. "You better be on your A game, Bisley. This girl wants some treats."

"No need to worry about me," I say as I glance toward Banner and Nichole, who seem to be heavy in conversation, and when I say conversation, I mean intimately touching each other. I hope they remember the four-person rule.

"What are your strengths in trivia?" Myla asks as she sips from our shared glass.

"Sports and history. What about you?"

In the most serious tone I've ever heard her use, she says, "Everything, Ryot. Everything would have been the best answer."

I chuckle. "Sorry. I meant everything."

She offers me a wink. "Good answer."

The host explains the rules.

Our burgers are dropped off, and I split mine with Myla.

And once we're set, the game begins.

⎯⎯

"RYOT, I swear to God, if you don't let me use my answer, I will scream."

"I don't think you're right."

"Well, guess what, I didn't ask you, Mr. Fact Checker, because I know you're wrong. One hundred percent you're wrong, and if you keep throwing up these half-assed answers, I'm not going to win that gift card to Cold Stone, and I'm going to lose my mind. So, erase your dumb answer and put down mine."

"You really think the answer is Tiger?"

"I know it is. Now write it," she snaps.

This is how it's been the entire time. Myla and I go back and forth with answers while Nichole and Banner whisper into each other's ears. Well, they're doing more than that. I actually witnessed Nichole's hand rubbing over Banner's jean-clad crotch, so I know it's only a matter of time before they take off.

Not wanting to argue anymore, I write down Tiger and hold up the whiteboard.

Once the time is up, the host for the night says, "Bisley's Balls, you're correct."

"For fuck's sake," I mutter while Myla claps excitedly.

She nudges me and says, "Have you learned your lesson yet?"

"Annoyingly so."

"We're going to take a ten-minute break before the finale," the host says. "Feel free to fill up on drinks."

"We're headed to the bar," Banner says. "Want anything?"

"I'm good," I answer. "Myla, do you want something?"

"We'll both take another beer, thanks." She winks and then turns toward me and rests her hand on my thigh. Our legs are touching because our stools are so close, and this entire time, even though we've been fighting over answers, she's been very intimate with her touches. "Okay, now, this finale, it's going to be worth all of the points. Are you going to argue with me or listen?"

"How about we have a healthy conversation over each answer? What if it's about baseball, and you don't know the answer?"

"If it's about baseball, you can write whatever you want." She pops a fry in her mouth.

"Aren't you generous?" I note.

"Very." She lifts a fry to my mouth, and I take a bite of it. "You know, this table of girls behind you has been staring at your back this entire time."

I don't turn to look at them. Instead, I keep my eyes on her. "Your point?"

"My point is you could go over there and make their dreams come true."

"Probably, but they're not who I want to talk to at the moment."

She smirks. "You flirting, Bisley?"

"Trying to pick up where we left off."

"And where was that exactly?" She taps her chin playfully.

"You don't remember? Oh, let me help. I think you were about to send me naked pictures . . ."

She tips her head back and laughs. "Is that how we left things? Hmm, I think I recall it a bit differently. I was owning you in foosball, just like I'm owning you in trivia. And then you took off for a flight."

"Hmm, I remember it differently."

"I'm sure you do." She rests her chin on her hand. "Tell me, Bisley, have you been seeing anyone?"

"No," I answer.

"Fucking anyone?"

Wanting to be transparent, I say, "Not recently, but yeah, I've fooled around with a few women."

"Anyone good?"

I shrug because no one truly blew my mind. It was just sex, nothing spectacular.

"Well, that's sad. A man like you." She moves her hand higher up my thigh. "All these muscles, you would think you'd be having ravenous sex every night."

"Haven't found the right person yet."

"You looking?"

"Not really, but if the right person came along, then I'd be willing to take that next step."

"And who exactly would be the right person?"

I tuck a strand of hair behind her ear before answering, "Someone with a smart mouth, a know-it-all attitude, who has no problem telling me like it is. Someone who makes me laugh, pushes me out of my comfort zone, and knows how to drive me crazy with one lick of their lips. Someone with fucking sexy thighs, an ass I could spend hours gripping, and tits that don't quit." She smirks. "You know . . . just the perfect girl."

"Hmm, seems like she would be a difficult one to find."

"Nah, I think she's a lot easier to find than you'd think."

"Bisley Balls, it seems you're trying to get into my pants."

I chuckle. "Just trying to let you know I'm interested."

"Coming on pretty quickly, don't you think? It's been a few years since we've seen each other. Don't you think we need to get reacquainted first?"

"Okay, tell me two things that have happened over the past few years. And I'll tell you two."

"You think two things is good enough?" she asks as her thigh rubs up against mine.

"It's a good start."

"Well, if you think so, then let's see." She cutely taps her chin. "Well, I've gained about fifteen pounds, so I'm not sure if that's a turnoff to you."

"Myla, I would fucking eat you right on this goddamn dirty-ass floor if you'd let me. Trust me, I've been fully turned on since the moment I saw you."

She smiles softly and then says, "Uh, I have zero aspirations in life at the moment. I'm just taking everything day by day. I had a job opportunity in early childhood education, which is what I got my degree in, but I turned it down because I didn't like the idea of being restricted to a regular job. I like the flexibility of being a server. Oh, and I now have over two thousand fans who like my feet, but I'm shutting down my Only Fans account soon because the demand is too high. And last year, when I moved to Chicago, a guy on the street tried to steal my purse, but I donkey-kicked him right in the penis. Two citizens helped me detain him until the police arrived. I know that's more than two things, but they kept coming. But I mentioned the no aspirations thing because I bet that's a big turnoff to someone like you."

"Not in the slightest," I say. "All I care about is that you're happy. And are you?"

"I am. Now tell me two things I need to know about you that happened during our hiatus."

I scratch the side of my jaw. "Well, I looked at your profile often, wondering if you'd ever post a picture of your face. I slammed my finger shut in a door at the stadium and was out ten games because I couldn't grip a bat. I once did this fundraiser for the firefighters here in Chicago and ended up accidentally setting a building on fire. Thankfully, they put it out very quickly. And despite being on the top of my game, I don't think I've truly smiled until tonight when I spotted you."

"That was more than two things." She draws a circle on my thigh while avoiding eye contact with me.

I place my fingers under her chin and lift her face until her eyes look into mine. "Yeah, because I wanted you to know I've never truly stopped thinking about you. Even though I might look like I'm happy from the outside, a part of me is not. I'm lonely. That's where you come in."

"Well." She smacks her lips together. "Seems as though you've also done some flexing since we've last seen each other because you sure as hell know how to say the right thing."

---

MYLA TWIRLS the gift card through her fingers while smiling at me. "Go ahead . . . say it."

Rolling my eyes, I set my third beer down—I know I said I'd only have one beer, but that changed quickly once Myla took off her sweater, leaving her in a low-cut tank top. Not to mention her ability to get me to focus on something other than baseball—my comfort zone. "You're not going to let me ever live this down, are you?"

She shakes her head. "Never."

Letting out a long, drawn-out sigh, I say, "Myla, you are easily the best competitor I've ever seen during a trivia night."

"Best and . . ."

"Prettiest," I answer.

Her smile stretches from ear to ear. "Ooo, I should have recorded that. Sounded like music to my ears."

Nichole and Banner left about twenty minutes ago. Thankfully, we thought to claim they went to the bathroom so we weren't disqualified. Not sure what Myla would have done if we weren't allowed to compete anymore, especially since we were so far ahead in points compared to the other teams.

"Care to get some ice cream with me—my treat—or do you have to go tuck yourself in?"

Technically, it's way past my preferred bedtime. I don't ever stay up past eleven, but here I am, sitting in a bar at eleven fifteen, thinking about getting ice cream.

"Is Cold Stone still open?" I ask.

She tucks her gift card in her cleavage and says, "Oh, you're so cute, Bisley. You thought I was going to let you use my gift card?" She shakes her head. "No, that's just for me. But there is a convenience store around the corner that sells Drumsticks, and I have a hankering for one." She hops off her stool. "You game?"

I should really get back to my apartment, but this evening has been about having fun. Hell, she looks so fucking good, standing there in her black jeans and black tank top with her sweater tied around her waist. I don't want to go "tuck myself in" just yet. I haven't seen this girl in four years. Sure, I've been out with, dated, and fucked other women, but a small part of me has always wondered what would happen if I messaged her again. Every time she made a new drink post, I thought about commenting. I thought about asking her how she was or if she ever considered visiting Chicago, but I held back because she's always seemed so aloof. Like a butterfly that could never be caught.

So now that she's standing in front of me, wanting to spend more time with me, I know exactly what my answer is.

"I would love some ice cream."

"Good answer," she says with a smile.

And then to my surprise, she takes my hand in hers and guides me out of the bar, her short frame leading the way. When we exit into the humid night air, she doesn't release my hand but rather leans in closer to me.

"Are you a Drumstick fan?" she asks.

"Yeah. Never can go wrong with a Drumstick."

"I would have assumed you were a strawberry shortcake kind of guy."

"Why would you assume that?" I ask her.

"You're not quite vanilla, definitely not commanding enough to be a chocolate lover, which leaves you as a strawberry shortcake."

I pause and face her. "If you're referring to how I fuck, then you've got me completely mislabeled. There's nothing strawberry shortcake about me."

Her eyes roam me again, more intensely this time. And when she's done, she says, "Yeah, maybe I am mislabeling you, but I guess I won't ever know." Then she starts moving forward again.

I fall in line with her strides and drape my arm over her shoulders. "Yeah, you probably won't," I say, just to see her reaction.

"Firsthand experience with you in the sack, yeah, I think I'll pass."

"Same," I say. "A night with you in my bed doesn't quite scream a good time."

"Not even close." She reaches up to my hand on her shoulder and links our fingers together. "Glad we established that. Would hate to put in all this time just to get back to your place and be bored out of my mind while you attempted to pelvic thrust in my direction."

"Yeah, saving ourselves a shit load of time." I pull her in closer so her side is right up against mine.

When we turn the corner, the convenience store comes into view. I open the door for her, and she goes straight to the freezer section where the individually wrapped ice creams are. We each grab a Drumstick, and when she goes to pay at the register, I say, "I can take care of it."

She holds her hand up to me. "No, this one is on me. I owe you after all." She pulls a five from her back pocket and tells the cashier to keep the change before picking up our ice creams and walking out of the store.

Across the street is a small park, so we make our way in that direction and find a bench to share. She hands me my ice cream and then unwraps hers.

"What's your favorite part of a Drumstick?" she asks.

"The bottom, obviously," I answer. "Where all the fudge has collected. Easily the best bite."

"Hmm, maybe you're not so bad after all, Bisley."

"Not so bad, huh? Was I a monster before this?"

"Borderline eel-man."

"Eel?" I laugh out loud as I drape my arm over the back of the bench while she turns toward me and sits cross-legged. "What kind of eel are we talking about? Because if it's an electric eel, then I'm game."

"Electric eel?" She lets out a large guffaw. "Ha! You wish. You're more like part eel, part salamander."

"Flattering," I reply, which makes her smirk. "So you've been here for a year and didn't bother to harp on me about my batting cage videos. What's that about?" I take a large bite of my Drumstick, the cold of the ice cream lighting up my mouth.

"I told you, if we crossed paths, then we did. I wasn't about to search you out."

"Why not?" I ask.

She shrugs. "Not really into forming attachments. I kind of let fate drive me forward at this point in my life."

"Okay, so what do you think about fate bringing you to the bar tonight and to my table to join my team?"

"I think fate was looking out for you."

"How so?" I ask.

She licks her ice cream, and I try not to watch closely as her tongue drags along the cold cream. "Well, you were surrounded by fans, and fans who hate you, so the stakes were high for you, and embarrassment was at risk. Fate brought me to you so you didn't fall flat on your face at trivia night in front of the raucous haters."

"I see. So basically, you're saying that fate brought us back together so you could save me."

She pats my leg. "Glad you see it that way."

"If that's the case, I should have bought you ice cream, not the other way around."

"Not true. I ate half of your burger and fries and stole your beer, so, yeah, I owed you. I might have been brought here tonight to resurrect your image, but I'm not blind to the fact that money is money, and I owed you a bit."

"You owe me nothing."

"Not how I see it." She bites into her cone, and a flake of chocolate falls to the corner of her mouth. Reaching out with my thumb, I snag it before sucking the chocolate into my mouth. "Smooth," she says with a wiggle of her brows.

"Maybe we're even now."

She shakes her head. "It's going to take a lot more than you dusting some chocolate off my mouth for us to be even after the performance I gave tonight. But it's really adorable that you're attempting to balance the playing field."

"I guess I'll take that as a compliment. So what have you been doing in Chicago?"

"Like job-wise?" she asks.

"Yeah. Or just in general."

"Well, when I left Phoenix, I didn't really have any attachments to jobs, so I found a waitressing one out here. It pays well, and I've just been enjoying life. Nichole and I go to a lot of concerts. We'll hang out down by the lake often, too. During the winter—even though it was frigid—we made the most of it and did some ice skating, went to some off-Broadway shows, and even took a short trip to San Diego, where I had the best tacos of my life."

"What kind of tacos?"

"Shrimp." She kisses her fingers. "Chef's kiss. Freaking delightful. Oh, and Nichole and I have been searching out the best place to get brunch around Chicago. Have you noticed my mimosa posts? Those are all from different brunch spots we've tried."

"I have noticed them. So did you find a good place?"

She bites into her cone and then says, "There's this rooftop restaurant downtown that moonlights as a nightclub, and I swear it's the best-kept secret. The brunch is phenomenal, the views are everything, and because it's also a nightclub, the breakfast drinks are a bit stronger than usual, which adds to the experience. It's called Bar Seventy."

"Oh, you know, Banner has been there a few times. He's told me about it."

"It's worth all the rage. You haven't been?"

I shake my head. "Not much time to do anything during the baseball season, especially in the morning. That's when I usually visit kids at the Children's Hospital."

She clutches her chest. "You do?"

"Yeah. There are a lot of Bobbies fans there, so when I don't have an early game, I try to visit as much as possible, or do whatever is on the list of charitable visits the Bobbies have created. And when I'm not doing that, I'm in the gym or in the cages, getting reps in."

"Baseball really is your life, isn't it?"

"It's been that way for a really long time," I answer as I lick up a drop of ice cream dripping down my cone.

"Do you ever wish you had a life outside of baseball?"

"All the time," I answer truthfully. "I miss out on a lot of things in life because I've been consumed by my goals. And there are times at night when I stare up at the ceiling, unable to sleep, wondering if it's all worth it, especially now hearing about your adventures. I can't remember the last time I took a vacation or focused on something other than my swing, my reps in the gym, or what I put into my body. Sometimes I just wish I could . . . relax."

"You can, you know." She takes a very small bite of her ice cream. "You can let loose, have fun, kind of like you did tonight."

"Yeah, I can." I look into her eyes and realize that I'm having fun right now because of her. When I reach the bottom of my cone, I show it to her. "You know, I'd be willing to offer you the best bite of the cone."

Her eyes fall to the fudge-filled triangle and then back up to my eyes. "What's the catch?"

"You find some time for me to take you out on a date."

Her teeth pull over her bottom lip before she takes another bite of her cone. "I don't really do relationships."

"I'm just talking a date. One date."

"One date where you fall madly in love with me. It's inevitable," she says confidently. "I can already see the intrigue and challenge in your eyes." She shakes her head. "Best we just leave this as is . . . running into each other randomly."

Yeah, I'm not sure that's what I want. Sure, fate might have brought us together and keeps reconnecting us, but I'm not interested in continuing to leave it up to fate. Not after seeing her again. Not after being around her energetic, sassy, zero-fucks attitude again. I like her and want to spend more time with her.

And after all the flirting tonight and from the past, I'm a

little confused by her answer. I would have sworn she wanted to start something just as much as I do.

"Why don't you date?" I ask.

"Do you want the short version or the long version?"

I pop the end of the cone in my mouth. "I have time, so give me the long version."

"Well, it's the classic tale of not wanting to live my life by example." She finishes her cone and then pulls her legs into her chest as she leans her side against the back of the bench. "My parents, even though they're still together, have an absolutely terrible relationship. I'm not sure they actually love each other anymore. I think they just stay together because it's easier than going through a divorce and everything that entails. Mom always followed Dad around from base to base even though she had a career of her own, and she began to resent him for it. She took it out on me. And I saw the ugly side of parenting, the ugly side of a relationship and marriage, and I want nothing to do with it."

"Wow, I'm sorry, Myla. I'm sure that couldn't have been an easy environment to grow up in."

"It is what it is," she says with a shrug, clearly not wanting to get into it.

"You do realize, though, that you're a different person than your parents, right?"

"Yes," she answers. "And I don't believe I'd make the same mistakes as my parents, but I'm also not well educated on how to be a good partner. I don't know what a healthy romantic relationship looks like, and I don't want to subject anyone to my drama. So I just don't bother."

I slowly nod. "I can understand that, but you might be missing out, you know?"

"Are you saying that because I turned you down?"

"Well, yes, you'd be missing out on an amazing date with me, but more than that, you're missing out on the opportunity to share the burden of your childhood with someone else. You know you don't have to carry that baggage by yourself. There are people out there willing to help you carry it. And the right person won't just carry it. They'll unpack it until there isn't much baggage left."

She hugs her legs tighter as she looks away. "No one wants to do that with me. Trust me." She sighs and drops her legs to the ground before standing. "Well, I should get back home. I'm sure you have an early-morning practice you have to get to."

She's distancing herself. It doesn't take an expert to realize what's going on. She opened herself up, allowed herself to be vulnerable, and now before she can be coaxed beyond her comfort zone, she's shutting down. That's okay because, even though this is the end of the evening, I know this isn't the end for me.

I stand as well and take her wrapper, then toss them in the trash before I meet back up with her. I loop my arm around her shoulders again, and she leans into me as I work our way back to the main road.

"Need a taxi?" I ask.

She shakes her head. "No. I live around the corner."

"Want me to walk you home?"

She glances up at me and smirks. "Although appealing, if you walked me home, I might be tempted to invite you up to my place, and I think you and I both know that's not a good idea."

I face her and take her hand in mine. "Yeah, because it would be boring, right?"

"Very, very boring. Wouldn't find satisfaction in any way."

"Not even a little." I smile at her and then bring her hand to my mouth. I place a light kiss across her knuckles and then step away. "So I guess I'll see you around?"

"Yeah." She takes a step back too. "I'll see you around."

And with one final wink, I turn away from her, hands stuffed in my pockets, and head back toward my apartment.

▭

# MYLA

"WHAT HAPPENED WITH BISLEY LAST NIGHT?" Nichole asks as she makes her way from her bedroom to the kitchen, dressed for her day, looking pristine with her makeup and hair done. She has a touch of pink to her lips today, which is her post-sex shade. I don't have to ask to know what happened last night. I'm just wondering how many times.

I'm sitting at the kitchen island, coffee in hand, feeling like I drank a liter of vodka when I know that's not the case at all. The hangover I'm experiencing is from spending a night with Ryot Bisley. He's like a drug. Each time I've seen him, I've felt drawn to him. And that's scary because I've never been drawn to anyone, nor have I ever—and I mean ever—opened up to someone like I did last night. The only one who knows about my parents is Nichole. So why I felt the need to reveal so much of myself to Ryot last night tells me there's something special about him.

"Nothing happened," I say as she pours herself a cup of coffee.

"What do you mean nothing happened?" she asks. "You were practically sitting on his lap last night."

"Nothing happened. We got ice cream, talked in the park, and then I called it a night."

"You did?" she asks, surprised. "This coming from the girl who has been drooling over the man's Instagram ever since he left Phoenix."

"I haven't been drooling over his Instagram," I say, even though I might have been.

"Okay." Nichole rolls her eyes. "What's the holdup? If he's

anything like his brother, you're going to want to ask him to spend the night." She sighs. "Trust me on this."

"Yeah, there's no doubt in my mind he would be amazing in bed."

"Okay, so what's the problem? You realize how crazy it is that we ran into them again, right?"

"Yes, I know."

"So . . ."

I groan and rest my head on the island as I mutter, "I like him, Nichole."

"Um . . . what was that?"

I lift my head and look her in the eyes. "I like him . . . *like* *him* like him."

"Oh." She pauses, letting my words sink in.

"Yeah, oh."

"Like, this isn't just carnal for you?"

I shake my head. "No, it's not. I feel drawn to him, like there's something special about Ryot that captures me. I can't pinpoint it, but it's there. I want to be close to him when he's near, and I just want to talk . . . talk about everything." I rub my eyes. "God, Nichole, I told him about my parents last night."

"Wait . . . what?" she asks. "Seriously?"

"Yes. He asked me out on a date, and I told him it probably wasn't a good idea. He asked why and for some reason beyond my comprehension, I told him the truth. It just came out of me. I didn't even second-guess it."

"How did he react?"

"The way I would expect him to—in the sweetest way possible. Told me I don't have to carry my baggage alone and that the right person would help me carry it, you know, the type of stuff you hear in romantic movies but never hear in real life." I groan and rest my head back down on the counter. "I don't need this right now."

"Don't need what?" Nichole asks.

"A crush," I answer.

"Ooooooo," Nichole coos, which just makes me want to bang my head against the counter. "My girl has a crush on a boy."

"Nichole, don't make this worse than it is. I'm already feeling weird about it and unsure how to navigate these feelings I really shouldn't be having."

"Why shouldn't you be having them? It's a natural thing to crush on a man who has been nothing but nice and sexy and fun."

"I don't have anything to offer him."

"I bet he thinks differently." She waggles her brows, which causes me to roll my eyes.

"You know what I mean. He seems like the forever type of man. From his baggage speech alone, I can tell he's into relationships. He's into dating and commitment. You know that scares the hell out of me, and I fear I'll hurt him if I go out with him. That's the last thing I want to do."

"So what are you going to do?" Nichole asks me. "Just never get involved with anyone?"

"You aren't involved with anyone," I point out.

"Because I'm not ready to settle down yet. I'm having fun, and nothing is wrong with that. And when the right man does come along, then yes, I will settle down, get married, and have kids, but I'm still young. I'm a free spirit. I love sex, and I will not stop because society's standards say I should be married at a certain age. But the difference between you and me is that I'm not avoiding relationships, and I'm not pushing men away out of fear of hurting them. I just know what I want right now. And that is fun. What do you want, Myla?"

"I don't know," I groan just as my phone dings on the countertop. I glance at the screen and see it's a message on my Instagram.

Nichole glances at my phone. "Is that him?"

"I'm thinking yeah." I pick up my phone and open the

app, where I find a message from Ryot.Bisley.Balls. I let out a large sigh. "Yup, it's him."

Nichole chuckles. "You picked the wrong brother. I got the player, and you got the sweetheart, relationship-prone one. Now you must decide what you're going to do about it."

She takes her coffee and heads back into her room, leaving me alone with my phone.

My thumb hovers over his name, and I consider swiping to the left to delete the message without even reading it. Despite my brain telling myself to do just that, I don't. I tap the message. Even though I know it's not right, I still want to see what he has to say.

**Ryot.Bisley.Balls:** *You know, I did some thinking last night after we said goodbye. I think you got the wrong impression of me, and I believe I need to prove you wrong.*

Don't message him back.

It will only lead to trouble.

It will lead to something I'm not ready for.

Yet . . . he's so playful, a breath of fresh air, an unexpected return to my life I didn't know I missed. Which is crazy, because we've only been around each other three times. That's it. Sure, we've messaged a lot, but that's it. So why does it feel like I know this man when I really don't? Why do I feel desperate to talk to him? To be around him?

My brain wavers between deleting and messaging him back.

This is the last thing I need. I still haven't figured out what I want to do with my life because I can't be a server forever. And that shows how far off I am from committing to a man in a relationship. I'm just not there yet.

Setting my phone down, I move away from it and into the kitchen, where I open the fridge and pull out a container of my overnight oats. The entire time, the message burns a hole in my brain. From the silverware drawer, I grab a spoon and take my pre-made peanut butter oats back to the island and have a seat. I stare at my phone.

My phone stares back at me.

*Don't, Myla. Don't answer the message.*

Don't even think about it.

It's a valiant effort, truly, but let's all be honest here. No way can I let that message go unanswered.

I pick my phone up and message him back.

**DrinkWithMe:** *What sort of impression do you think I have of you?*

Once I press send, I set the phone down and squeeze my eyes shut. God, what am I doing? Why am I entertaining this? I know where it's going to lead. There's no way we can just talk. There will be some sort of endgame, and that will probably be a date.

Am I ready for a date?

No.

Not even close.

I don't think I'm mentally prepared for anything past a fun night of flirting, which is all I've ever done with him.

My phone dings, and I pick it up so fast I nearly knock over my oats.

I open the app and click on his message.

**Ryot.Bisley.Balls:** *The whole boring in bed thing.*

**DrinkWithMe:** *Oh, well, is it not true?*

He types right away.

**Ryot.Bisley.Balls:** *No. Boring is not how I would describe it. More like . . . cries when he comes.*

I nearly spit out my mouthful as I laugh so loud that Nichole calls from her bedroom. "Not ready for dating, my ass."

"Shut up, Nichole," I call out.

# Chapter Seven

## MYLA

### *Present day . . .*

"Are you sure you want to do this?" Nichole asks as she hands me the last of the food from the kitchen fridge. *Am I sure? No, not at all. But I don't know what else to do.*

"Last night wasn't okay," I answer as I place the apples in the fruit bin. "I can't move out as I have nowhere to go yet, but I can draw a line in the sand, so to speak, to set stronger boundaries inside this house."

Nichole takes a seat on the stairs that lead from the garage to the kitchen. "Okay. I get that. What did he do? I know you were a mess, but a silent one, and that worried me."

It worried me too. I cried myself to sleep. *Again.*

Last night got out of hand. He used one of the best parts of our marriage as a weapon. He used our sex life to manipulate me. To control and seduce me. And if I gave in to him, if I fell back into our physical relationship, I'd probably feel demeaned. *That* would destroy something inside me and right now I feel too fragile. *I've had my share of feeling degraded.*

I can't go back there.

Not just for me.

But for him as well. I know Ryot is a better man than he is acting now, so I can't allow him to continue down this road.

"Last night . . . he pushed me too far. He knows my weakness. He knows that it's impossible for me to resist him, and he used that to his advantage."

"Probably because he still loves you and is mad about what's happening. Anger and love make you do stupid stuff, you know?" Yeah, I can attest to that.

"So because he loves me and is angry about the divorce, that should excuse his behavior? That should excuse the way he's treated me the past few months?"

"Nooooo," Nichole drags out. "But how is putting up rules in the house for him to follow going to make it better for the two of you? Taking the car away, moving the food to your own personal fridge? Do you think this will help?"

"No, but I'm not trying to solve anything here, Nichole. I'm grasping for any sort of control. I could move into a hotel or a short-term Airbnb. I know that. But I already feel so untethered here in LA. At least staying here for the next few weeks—around things that are somewhat familiar—will provide some solace. I have time to pack up my stuff and work out where I go next." Probably Chicago. "But because he won't sign the papers until after the wedding, I need boundaries. Without boundaries, without these rules, I don't think I'll mentally survive living here. I don't want to slip back into a lifestyle that wasn't healthy for either one of us." *I hate feeling so backed into a corner.*

She slowly nods. "I know, sweetie. But . . . I just hate to see it go down like this."

"It didn't have to," I say. "But he initiated this with what happened between us last night."

"So what you're saying is . . . in lack of a better term, this is war?"

I roll my eyes. "That seems a bit extreme."

"Taking his car away because you're the one who charges it is a bit extreme as well, don't you think?"

"Nichole," I groan. "Don't make me look like the bitch in this scenario."

"You're not." Nichole holds up her hands. "Not even a little. Your feelings are valid. The dismissal on his end has been seen and heard. I just want you to be prepared because, the moment he walks through the door and you throw down the gauntlet, you know he won't go down easy. He'll come out swinging, and you need to be ready for that. He's already started fighting back. Not to mention, there's clear intention behind his willingness to grant you a divorce so easily after the wedding. He's already in this battle. I think you might just be joining it."

"Trust me, I thought about this all night. If I put just enough distance between us, I can save what little pieces of my broken heart are left."

"By bringing fuel to the flame of this divorce war?"

"Better to be mad at each other than whatever the hell last night was. My battered heart can't take his mouth on me, his hands all over me, and the promise of the heat of his body."

She's silent for a moment.

If any two people in this world know me best, it's Nichole and Ryot. They know the uphill climb I've ascended my whole life. Nichole especially understands how meeting Ryot transformed my life. That uphill climb started to plateau. He carried the baggage I was carrying. *With and for me. As he promised.* He's been my comfort. My rock. My everything.

But also . . . my downfall.

He can so easily break me, so I need to keep my distance. I don't want to exit this marriage completely shattered.

"Well." Nichole stands and claps her hands together. "If this is a divorce gone completely wrong, might as well do it right."

"What do you mean by that?"

"If you want to make him mad to keep him as far away from breaking your heart again, then we have some work to do."

<hr>

## RYOT

I TEAR my AirPods out of my ears and set them on the kitchen counter as I try to catch my breath. After a sleepless night of tossing and turning and running my interaction with Myla over and over again, I decided to wake up early and get a long run in before the day got hot. I thought it would help my racing mind, but all it did was amp me up even more.

Do I believe Myla would go out last night and hook up with a man? No, but I'm also not blind to Nichole's influence either. I wasn't taking any chances, and sure, I didn't handle it well, but I couldn't stop myself. The moment I had her near me, it was like whenever I'm near her. I love this woman. And then she stuck her fingers in my mouth, letting me taste her arousal. I was gone. What comes naturally between us continued to happen. I wanted to make love to my wife.

And I regret not letting her come all over my fingers. Hell, I regret not pushing her onto the bed, yanking her skirt up, and pressing my mouth to her pussy where I would eat her out until she screamed my name.

I regret a lot of fucking things.

I open the fridge for the eggs to make some breakfast when I realize the fridge is empty besides a few yogurts I bought myself.

What the hell? There was food in here last night.

I shut the fridge door only to find Myla on the other side.

"Jesus," I say. "Where's all the food?"

"Oh, you mean the food I bought at the grocery store?" she asks, her arms folded, a tremble in her fingers.

"Yes, that food."

"It's in the garage fridge."

"Why is it in there?" I ask.

"Because that's my fridge."

"What?"

She props one hand on her hip as she leans against the counter. "Well, I had an epiphany last night." Her voice is shaky, but I sense an air of confidence too. "While I was making myself come in the shower after you left me hanging." Fuck. The image of her in the shower, fucking herself, feels like a full-on technicolor re-enactment in my head. "Are you paying attention?"

"Yes," I answer, my mind snapping back to her. "What was your epiphany?"

"Well, if you're going to have demands, then I think it's fair that I have mine as well."

"You think giving me the respect of not fucking another man while your name is still attached to me is a demand? That's just being courteous to your husband."

She glances away for a moment and then quietly says, "The fact that you even have to question the intention behind Nichole's presence here is insulting." Her eyes flick up to mine. "I would never cheat on you, Ryot."

Just like that, guilt consumes me because she's right.

She's shown me nothing but love and respect for our marriage.

An apology is on the tip of my tongue as she says, "Either

way. We have a couple weeks together before the wedding, and it might be best if we lay down some ground rules so we don't get in each other's way."

"Ground rules?" I ask. "Removing all the food from the fridge is your idea of ground rules?"

"It's food that I bought. Therefore, I believe it should be in my fridge. Also, if you noticed, the food in the pantry with the pink Post-it notes on them is mine. It's simple roommate protocol."

Oh hell. I move toward the pantry, switch on the light, and lo and behold, the shelves are covered in food with pink Post-it notes . . . even the baking flour.

And then her words hit me. Roommates?

I swing back around to look at her. "Roommates? I don't think so, Myla. You're still my wife."

She toes the ground, her confidence slipping in and out, and I can't quite pinpoint where her head is right now. Is this her way of getting back at me for last night? What is this wall she's erecting between us?

"Titles shouldn't mean much at this point, Ryot."

They mean something to me.

I exit the pantry, frustration starting to have a chokehold on me. "That's fine. I'll just order food." I grab my phone and open my DoorDash app, but it's asking me to sign in. "What's the username and password?"

"I changed that last night."

My eyes lift, and my brow raises in question. "What do you mean you changed it?"

"Well, it was my account, so I changed the password. You'll have to create your own account if you want to order food."

My nostrils flare, and I set my phone down. "Fine, I'll just have yogurt."

"Yeah, that's expired," she says just as I open the fridge. I grip the handle tightly and turn toward her.

"So is there no food in the house for me to eat?"

"Afraid not. But the store is open, so feel free to go shop for yourself. You know what a grocery store is, right?"

"Is this how it's going to be, Myla?" I ask, irritation creeping up the back of my neck.

Once again, she toes the ground. "Just trying to keep things neutral, so there are no misunderstandings."

Her words and actions scream "this is war," but her body language tells me she's hesitant to even be around me.

I should have known this wouldn't be easy. I just didn't think she'd take it to this level.

"Was this Nichole's idea?" I ask.

"She has nothing to do with this, so leave her out of it. I just want to make things fair, Ryot. You made that quite clear last night with your abuse of orgasms."

"All because I didn't want my wife fucking another man?" I ask. "Fucking sue me."

"No"—she steps up, anger in her voice—"because you know I love it when you fuck me. Because you know I can't resist you in that way. You took a vulnerable moment, and you took advantage of me."

"I fucked up, Myla. Okay? I should never have gone that far with you. I wanted to remind you who you belong to—"

"I didn't need the reminder. From the moment you first kissed me, I've been branded by your lips, rightfully yours. But not anymore."

"We sure as fuck belong to each other until those papers are signed," I yell, my irritation spiking before I can tamp it down. "Last night was a reminder."

"Well, I don't need it. I know exactly who you are to me. So now that we have that covered, let's talk about the house rules."

I lean against the counter and fold my arms over my chest. "Oh, this should be good."

From the kitchen junk drawer, she pulls out a piece of paper with a list of rules.

Holding it up for her to see, she starts listing off her demands with a touch more assertiveness. "The garage fridge is mine, and anything marked with a pink sticky note is mine. Don't eat my food. If you're hungry, go stock up on those protein bars you love so much."

"Fine." This entire thing is so stupid, as is her way to gain control of the situation. Just like last night was my way to gain some sort of semblance of control when I felt like I was spiraling. Was it the right thing to do? By no means, no, it was not. But I was afraid she might revert to how she and Nichole used to hang out before I came along.

"We'll split up the house so we aren't forced to be around each other. Therefore, the first floor is my space since the guest room is located there. Meaning, I get the living room. The kitchen is a neutral space. We are allowed in and out of this neutral space at our leisure. Food is the only thing off limits."

"But the living room is where the TV is located. And since you don't like TVs in the bedroom, how the hell am I supposed to watch my games?"

She turns, hiding the smirk playing on the corner of her lips. "Hmm, didn't think about that." Bullshit. "You might have to skip out on those sports games you like to watch so much."

"Baseball. You know what sports games I watch."

"Moving on," she says. "The pool is also a neutral zone since it's hot and we both enjoy a dip, but please note that the right side of the pool belongs to me and the left side belongs to you."

"I prefer the right," I say just out of spite.

"I know." She smiles. "That's why I took it. If you had taken the time to make the rules, then you could have chosen."

"I didn't know there would be rules."

"Yes, well, you don't know a lot of things when it comes to this marriage, so no surprise there." She checks something off on her list, ensuring that backhanded insult sinks in. In the back of my mind, I think . . . insult or truth? My pride is convincing me it's an insult. "As for the usage of vehicles. I'll be acquiring both."

"What?" I shout. "How the hell did you figure that?"

"Easily, I'm the one who regularly maintains them. I'm the one who takes them to get serviced, makes the payments on them, and ensures they're charged. Therefore, I will be acquiring both."

"Why the hell do you need two cars?"

"I don't. But it's the principle of the thing. I don't need all the food in the fridge, but hey, that's what happens when you piss me off and use sex as a weapon. It comes back to haunt you tenfold. Now, shall we discuss clothing?"

"You're not fucking taking my clothes."

"God, no." She shakes her head. "What on earth would I do with your clothes?"

"I don't know, Myla. What will you do with two cars?"

"Treat them as if they're my children and take them out every day so their tires don't get stiff, obviously." I roll my eyes. That sass of hers is on full display now that she's no longer nervous and on a roll. "Now, clothes. I've confiscated the latest batch of laundry that I just washed and folded for you. Since I put the time in to take care of them, they belong to me, but if you would like them back—which you might since your lucky running shorts are in there—you can repay me for my dirty work."

"Fine, how much? I have cash."

"I don't want your money."

Jesus Christ. "Then what do you want, Myla?"

"It's simple. You made it quite clear last night that there is one thing I want from you, one thing I can't seem to forget when it comes to you—and that's sex."

"You want me to fuck you for my clothes?"

"No, I don't want your dick—"

"That's bullshit."

"Just your mouth," she continues with returned hesitation. "If you want your clothes, then you make me come on your tongue." She glances away, clutching her paper tightly. "Until then, your clothes are mine, as well as the receipts to pick up your dry cleaning."

"What makes you think you're doing me a disservice here?"

Her long lashes lift as she says, "You don't think I know how hard and horny you get every time you go down on me? I know you. I know the way your body reacts when your tongue is buried between my legs. And I know the only way you'll be fully satisfied after making me come all over your mouth is if you flip me onto my stomach, pull my ass into the air, and fuck me bare."

I gulp because fuck, she's right.

"And I don't want your dick. I don't want anything to do with it. Just your mouth. So you can either get your clothes by giving me what I want, only to suffer from a serious case of blue balls, or you can start perusing your closet for a new pair of running shorts."

Jaw clenched, I grip the counter and say, "Is this satisfying to you? These rules? These restrictions?"

"Doesn't matter what they mean to me. It just matters that they're set in stone." Once again, she avoids eye contact with me, and it gives me pause.

She's in defense mode, and the only time she's like this is when she's so hurt she hides behind sarcasm. Scorn.

And fuck do I wish I knew *how* I hurt her.

Is she protecting her heart? From me?

Is she trying to erect a wall between us because I've hurt her so badly?

Or is she doing this out of pure spite? I can't tell.

Either way, I can't help the irritation pumping through me. She's making it impossible for me to reach her.

"Fine." I push off the counter and head toward the hallway to get ready for my day.

"Just a heads-up," she calls out. "I know you have a meeting today, but all of your suits are at the cleaners." I glance down at her as I'm halfway up the stairs.

"Do that on purpose, did you?"

"No, actually. It just worked out well for me." She tucks her hair behind her ears. "If you want the claim tickets, you know what you need to do."

Of course . . . give her my tongue.

As I stomp up the stairs, I run the conversation through my head. The pain in her eyes, the irritation, the anger building between us at such a rapid rate that I'm not sure there is any possibility of stopping it.

She dislikes me.

And right now, I think the sentiment is shared.

She's mad at me for what I've done in the past.

I'm mad about what she's doing now.

There's no Switzerland, no one to help us moderate the pain and frustration.

So rather than fix it . . . it's only building now.

---

RYOT: *Plans have changed. The battleground lines have been drawn.*

**Banner:** *What are you talking about?*

**Penn:** *Did we have plans today? Dude, I can't keep up with this schedule.*

**Nola:** *Why am I on a text thread with Penn?*

**Penn:** *Hey, Nola. Can you send me more of that pancake mix from that lobster place?*

**Nola:** *The Lobster Landing? No. You don't deserve any.*

**Penn:** *I told you I was sorry about the house paint comment. Okay? It was years ago. You're still holding it against me?*

**Nola:** *I will always hold that against you.*

**Ryot:** *Hey, hello! I'm the one who needs some help. Take up your vendettas with each other on another text thread.*

**Penn:** *Do you have a vendetta against me, Nola?*

**Nola:** *No, just a distaste for you in my mouth.*

**Banner:** *When has Penn ever been in your mouth?*

**Ryot:** *Jesus Christ.*

**Nola:** *NEVER!*

**Penn:** *Dude, I know I've fucked around, but never with your sister. Anyway, she's happily married.*

**Nola:** *Thanks for pointing out the obvious to my brothers.*

**Penn:** *Just trying to be a white knight is all . . . does that get me the pancake mix now?*

**Nola:** *NO!*

**Ryot:** *Enough with the pancake mix.*

**Banner:** *Would I be able to score some pancake mix? I didn't say anything shitty about the house paint you chose.*

**Nola:** *No, because you would just give it to Penn. I know how you work. No one is getting pancake mix.*

**Banner:** *What if I disassociate myself from Penn?*

**Penn:** *Dude!*

**Banner:** *Come on . . . it's the sacred pancake mix. You must understand the position I'm in.*

**Ryot:** *Can we please fucking focus! I'm being bamboozled by my wife, and I need some help.*

**Penn:** *He used bamboozled, must be serious.*

**Banner:** *Bamboozled is most definitely only used when serious.*

**Nola:** *Why am I part of this? You didn't listen to me last night, so clearly, I'm of no use to you.*

**Banner:** *What happened last night?*

**Nola:** *He lost his temper because Nichole is in town and basically told Myla she's not allowed to be with any men and then . . . he touched her.*

**Penn:** *Touched her as in . . . touched her?*

**Banner:** *Nichole's in town? Did she ask about me?*

**Ryot:** *I haven't spoken to her. We're really not on the best terms, in case you forgot about that.*

**Banner:** *I haven't. Still, let me know if she wants to hang.*

**Penn:** *The balls on this guy.*

**Banner:** *No shame.*

**Nola:** *Although this has been entertaining, I'm sort of interested in the bamboozlement.*

**Penn:** *Agreed. Lay it on us.*

**Ryot:** *You sure you don't want to talk about pancake mix?*

**Banner:** *Dude, we've moved on. Don't be dramatic.*

**Penn:** *Yeah, pancake mix is old news. Tell us how Myla is bamboozling you.*

**Ryot:** *So as Nola said, last night wasn't my best showing. I lost my temper and, well, did some stupid shit. She capitalized on that this morning. Let's just say she set ground rules. Took away my car—long story—and has made my life a nightmare. She has both cars, all the food, the TV, and my lucky running shorts.*

**Banner:** *Dear GOD! Not the shorts.*

**Penn:** *I think my taint just shriveled up.*

**Nola:** *Even I know the importance of the shorts.*

**Ryot:** *So I have no food, no transportation, no TV, no shorts, and I know there are some hidden things she's waiting to spring on me. The situation has just gone from surprised anger to designed pettiness.*

**Penn:** *Ah, so you're looking for help on how to retaliate. Am I reading you right?*

**Ryot:** *Precisely.*

**Nola:** *Why do I feel like this is not a good idea?*

**Banner:** *Because you're not understanding the situation. We have this all worked out. This was part of the plan anyway. She's just taking it up a notch.*

**Penn:** *Yes, exactly. This gives Ryot the leverage he needs.*

**Nola:** *You three are morons.*

**Banner:** *Don't you mean . . . geniuses?*

**Nola:** *No, I meant morons.*

**Ryot:** *Either way, I'm going to need your help, Nola. Are you in?*

**Nola:** *God, I hate you . . .*

**Penn:** *I think that's a yes!*

**Banner:** *Totally a yes.*

# Chapter Eight

RYOT

*Seven years ago . . .*

"Are you sure she's going to be here?" I ask Banner as I glance around the intimate baking class.

Yes, baking class.

Can you guess whose idea this was?

Banner's, that's who.

Since seeing Myla at the trivia night, I've been talking to her on Instagram, you know, like the start of every healthy relationship. And even though I've hinted toward taking her out—that's when she responds—she hasn't taken the bait. Because I'm a desperate man who apparently has no self-respect, I asked for Banner's help.

He contacted Nichole through Instagram—remember, healthy adults over here—and asked to meet up with her for coffee. That's when the planning happened. Apparently, Myla has been on a mission to try new things and attending a baking class is one of them.

The plan is for Myla and Nichole to come and then for Nichole and Banner to bail at the last minute—aka, go have sex somewhere—leaving me alone in the class with Myla.

See how that works?

Lame, but hey, I'll take what I can get.

"Yes, they'll be here. Now just chill, dude. You're starting to get sweaty."

"I'm not sweaty."

"I can see the beads of sweat on your upper lip."

"I'm not sweating," I say and then pick up a napkin and dab my upper lip, causing Banner to laugh.

"Oh, well, hello there," I hear a familiar voice say. "I didn't know you two were into baking."

Nichole. Right on time.

I turn around to find a smiling Nichole and a frowning Myla. Just as I suspected, she's not thrilled to see me. But hey, we can change that with some flirting.

"Wow, what are the odds?" Banner asks, his acting skills pure shit. "Never in a million years would I have imagined seeing you here."

Way to keep it chill, bro.

"Yeah, this is so unexpected." Nichole sighs and looks at her watch. "Gee, I can't believe I forgot about that thing I have to do. Right when we get here, too."

"Oh shit, I have a thing too." Banner pats my chest. "Sorry, bro, I have to bail, but hey, looks like Myla might need a partner."

Myla folds her arms at her chest. "Would you look at how that worked out? And so quickly too."

Yeah, they could have at least waited a minute before ditching us.

"Perfect if you ask me," Nichole says. "Okay, well, this has been fun. Looks like class is about to start, so we're just going to get out of your hair. You two have fun." Nichole presses a quick kiss on Myla's cheek. "Love you. Be nice."

And then without another word, Banner and Nichole take off together. Their job is done.

Now it's time to wipe that frown off Myla's face.

Hands in my pockets, I rock back on my heels. "Crazy how that all worked out."

She eyes me, those light-blue eyes carving me with sheer suspicion. "Yeah . . . crazy."

"But hey, we're here, might as well do some baking."

Head tilted to the side, she asks, "Don't you have practice or something?"

"Off day."

"Uh-huh, and you just so happen to like to bake on your off days?"

"Thought I would try something new. Is there something wrong with me baking?"

She shakes her head. "No, but I wouldn't have pegged you as someone who enjoys baking, you know, since last time I checked, you barely keep food in your pantry."

"I've changed my ways."

"Have you?" she asks with a tilt of her brow as she moves toward our kitchen setup. Ten individual counters in the classroom each have their own stove, oven, sink, mini fridge, and appliances as well as utensils.

"Yes, I have. I now make sure I have pretzels in my pantry at all times."

"Pretzels? Why is that a requirement?"

"I was reacquainted with them a while back, and now I always have them at my house."

"And how were you reacquainted with them?" She picks up a folded apron from the counter and drapes it over her head. I do the same.

"I like to eat them with a few of the guys before games.

We all sit in the cafeteria together, chat, and have fruit and pretzels."

She pauses as she's tying the string of her apron to look me in the eye. "That sounds so . . . elementary. Like you're sharing a snack in the schoolyard."

"We keep things simple."

"I guess I just thought you would be sucking down pre-game powder and pumping iron. But sitting around the table with fruit and pretzels? Well, that paints a new picture in my head of professional athletes."

I chuckle. "Is that a positive picture or a negative picture?"

"Positive," she says as I tie my apron. "I like that you're not some meathead jock, looking to break bats over your knees and whatnot."

"Never said I wasn't that guy either."

"Please." She shakes her head. "I don't believe it for a second. You're all mushy on the inside, aren't you?"

"No, hard as a rock."

She rolls her eyes. "Tell me this, when you're traveling for away games, how many women do you bring back to your hotel room?"

"Hundreds," I answer. "Sometimes ten at a time." *If only she knew I never take women back to my hotel. It's just not my thing.*

She smirks and props her hip against the table as the instructor walks into the room and starts setting up her station at the front. "Ten, huh? Wow, you must go through a box of condoms a night."

"I get paid so much, so I can afford all the condoms."

"Well, you learn something new every day, don't you? I figured you went back to the hotel after a game, takeout in hand, and turned on some sort of show you'd talk to the guys about later in the locker room. You know, just a bunch of guys gabbing about *Stranger Things*."

I chuckle and lean close. "You don't know how scary accurate that is. But instead of takeout, there are occasional nights when the boys and I go out to our favorite restaurants in each city. Then we go back to our rooms and watch *Stranger Things*."

"Ooo, so close to getting that right."

"Welcome to How to Bake with Beatrice," the instructor cuts through all the chatter. "I'm Beatrice, and I'll be your instructor. Who is ready to learn how to bake éclairs?"

Myla raises her hand and adds, "Woo," which of course draws attention toward us.

Because I don't want her to be alone, I fist-pump the air and say, "Éclairs, fuck yeah."

"Sir, please refrain from swearing . . . and shouting."

"Oh, sorry. Uh, éclairs, hooray!"

Myla snorts next to me, and when I glance at her and see that big, beautiful smile of hers, I know I'm doing something right.

---

"DON'T OPEN THE OVEN," I say as Myla reaches for the handle.

"But what if they're burning?"

"They're not burning. Just turn on the light if you're that concerned. If I learned one thing from my mom while she baked hundreds of cookies every year at Christmas, it's that you don't open the oven unless you have to, as it lets all the hot air out."

"Fine." She sits back down on one of the stools and drums her fingers on the counter.

Beatrice gave an unnecessarily long lecture about the history of éclairs that I nearly dozed off during and then a faster-than-life example on how to make them. I attempted to watch as best I could, but the lady was tossing ingredients around, making a show of just how quick she was that I barely understood a damn thing. Needless to say, I'm not super positive about these coming out well.

"Did you ever help your mom bake these hundreds of cookies?" Myla asks.

"Yes," I answer. "But I was more in charge of washing bowls, keeping the counters clean, and moving the cookies from the baking trays to the cooling racks."

Myla's nose scrunches up. "That doesn't sound very fun."

"It was for me," I answer. "I just liked spending time with my mom. Nola, my sister, would do the mixing, and Banner would get banished from the kitchen after ten minutes for being an instigator. He did it on purpose so he could go back to work on his computer."

"Are your parents still alive?"

I nod. "Yeah. They live in Maine in the same house we grew up in. An old Victorian with uneven floors, creaky stairs, and a multicolor exterior."

"Sounds like a dream. Were there ghosts in the house?"

"Dad will tell you no since he doesn't believe in paranormal activity. Mom will tell you yes. She believes there's an old couple who appreciates our family lives there."

"And where do you stand on the ghost front? Are you a believer?"

I press my hand to the countertop and smile. "Yeah, I am. But that's only because I swear they were fucking with me in the attic one day when I was in eighth grade. We kept the Christmas decorations up there, and I was attempting to hand Banner boxes, but the boxes kept moving on their own. I would hand one to him, then go back for another, and they were in a different spot. Banner said I was nuts, but I know what I saw. It was totally the ghosts."

"I could believe that as well. You seem like the kind of human spirits would be attracted to."

"How so?"

"Accepting of all is how I would describe you, even the deceased. So yeah, they would try to communicate with you."

"I'm assuming you're a believer."

"Eh, take it or leave it."

The timer dings and Myla hops out of her seat and squats down in front of the oven. She holds her hand to the sky. "Mitt me."

Chuckling, I slip an oven mitt on her hand. I watch as she carefully opens the oven and lets out a tiny squeal when she pulls the pastries out, then sets them on a trivet on the counter.

Golden-brown pastry logs are puffed and look delicious on the baking tray.

"Oh my God, look at what we did." She turns toward me. "Ryot, they look amazing."

"They do. We actually did it." She loops her arms around my waist, and I take that opportunity to drape my arms over her shoulders.

"Look at our little babies. Once mere ingredients, and now, they're all grown up and ripe for us to eat."

"Well, not quite. They have to cool, then we'll stuff them, and finally coat them in chocolate."

"Bet you can't wait to stuff them. Bet you're good at all kinds of stuffing."

I chuckle. "If only you had firsthand experience."

She sighs and then smiles up at me. "If only."

━━━

"I'M NERVOUS."

"Why are you nervous?" I ask Myla as we sit at our counter, each holding an éclair in hand. The filling was a breeze—a few blowouts, but that's okay—but the chocolate, that was a bit of a nightmare. We kept dropping the éclair into the bowl of melted chocolate and then squeezing the filling out. Yeah, there are a few mangled ones.

"Because what if they taste bad?"

"What if they taste good?"

"Great point." But she doesn't move to bring the éclair to her lips. "But if they taste bad, that's an omen."

"An omen for what?"

"That we don't have good chemistry."

I lower my éclair and give her an amused look. "Are you really going to base our chemistry off an éclair and not the fact that every time we're around each other, we have no problem holding a conversation?"

"I could hold a conversation with a paper clip if you asked me to," she says. "So yes, I'm basing our chemistry off an éclair."

"Wow, well then, if that's the case, I'd like to say that these smell like absolute heaven."

Her expression falls. "You have just relinquished your opinion."

I pause and then nod in agreement. "I accept the punishment."

With a smirk, she lifts the éclair and takes a large bite. And for some weird reason, as if this really matters, I wait on bated breath to see what she thinks. Just to see if her reaction is valid or not, I take a bite of my own as well. The chocolate combined with the cream center and the baked outside is fucking awesome on my tongue. If she says these are bad, I'll know she's a goddamn liar.

She chews.

I chew.

She swallows.

I swallow.

And then I watch her twist her lips to the side. "I don't know . . . they were sort of—"

"Don't even fucking lie. You know they're good."

That makes her smile. "Unfortunately, you're right. They are good."

"Why is that unfortunate? That means we have good chemistry, right?"

"Right, but I don't want good chemistry with you."

I'm about to shove the rest of the éclair in my mouth when I pause. "Why the hell not?"

"Because I told you, I don't do dating or anything like that, so the fact that we have good chemistry sadly puts a damper on my morals."

"Maybe this is the universe telling you to give me a chance. Besides, isn't it fate that we ended up at this class together?"

"No, I think that's meticulous planning behind the scenes to *force* that to happen."

"Either way," I say, brushing off her comment, "I think you should give us a chance."

"And then what? Date you? Aren't you busy with baseball? Don't you have a demanding schedule?"

"I do, but I also have a personal life. It's all about balance. I'm here at a baking class with you today, aren't I?"

"I guess so." She twists her lips to the side, giving it some thought. "But why me? Why are you so interested? It's not like I've blown steam up your ass like probably every other girl you've met. I don't toss you compliments you most likely receive daily from others around you. And I've done my very best to keep you at a DM distance only."

That she has, and it's been infuriating.

"Why you? Isn't it obvious? You put a smile on my face, Myla. I haven't been able to stop thinking about you ever since you curled up in my wall décor that one night."

"That was years ago. I'm pretty sure you stopped thinking about me at some point."

"Maybe here and there, but you were always in the back of my mind." I reach out and link our hands together. "Don't you want to see where this chemistry can lead?"

"No," she answers and then looks up at me through her eyelashes. "Maybe."

Hope springs in my chest from that one simple word.

Maybe.

There's a goddamn chance, which means I can't push her. I need to take today as a win and keep slowly gaining her trust.

"Okay, well, good to know." I smile, release her hand, and pick up another éclair.

"That's it? That's all you're going to say? Good to know?"

"Yup."

"What kind of game are you playing, Bisley?"

Game? The only person who would say that is someone insecure in relationships. And after the short conversation I had with her about her parents, I can guarantee you that question stems from the toxicity of the household she grew up in.

So I need to reassure her. She's delicate, fragile, and having spent more time with her, I can see the baggage she carries on her shoulders. Slowly and surely, I need to gently lift that off so she can be free. So she can enjoy life and take part in a relationship—something I know she wants when I look her in the eyes.

Taking a chance, I lightly cup her cheek. Keeping her eyes locked on mine, I say, "Myla, I can guarantee you one thing, the only game I play is baseball. Nothing else."

"How can I trust that?" she asks, her expression unsure.

"You're just going to have to get to know me to understand. That will take some time, time I'm willing to put in." I release her cheek and say, "Let's pack these up, and I'll walk you out."

———

RYOT.BISLEY.BALLS: *I feel comfortable telling you this. I've already eaten every éclair I took home.*

**DrinkWithMe:** *It's been two hours.*

***Ryot.Bisley.Balls:*** *I didn't say I was proud of what I've done, just that I'm comfortable telling you.*

***DrinkWithMe:*** *I would like to say I'm horrified by the volume of pastries you've consumed today, but I think your body needed it. Too many muscles.*

***Ryot.Bisley.Balls:*** *I don't think I've ever heard anyone complain about too many muscles before. And how would you know . . . unless you were checking out my Instagram feed?*

***DrinkWithMe:*** *The thirst traps might have caught my eye.*

***Ryot.Bisley.Balls:*** *If you want, I can send you your own personal thirst traps—and not like a dick pic or anything.*

***DrinkWithMe:*** *Why not? Send me a dick pic. Let me catch a glimpse of that peen.*

***Ryot.Bisley.Balls:*** *I'll send you a dick pic when you go out on a date with me.*

***DrinkWithMe:*** *Is that a promise?*

***Ryot.Bisley.Balls:*** *It could be. Let me think about it. I don't think I'm quite ready to ask you out yet.*

***DrinkWithMe:*** *Oh, I see. You have éclairs with me, and then you decide to play hard to get? Is that how this is going to work?*

***Ryot.Bisley.Balls:*** *No, when I had éclairs with you, I saw that I might have a chance at taking you out. But I won't pressure you. I'm trying to gain your trust first.*

***DrinkWithMe:*** *And how do you plan on doing that?*

***Ryot.Bisley.Balls:*** *You'll see.*

⊏⊐

RYOT.BISLEY.BALLS: *I want to send you something.*

***DrinkWithMe:*** *Is it a stripper?*

***Ryot.Bisley.Balls:*** *Do you like strippers?*

***DrinkWithMe:*** *I've had positive experiences with both males and females. I love a good rack in my face and a bouncing willy. Will accept both.*

***Ryot.Bisley.Balls:*** *I'll put it on the list of things I can* *send you.*

**DrinkWithMe:** *Aren't you a charmer?*

**Ryot.Bisley.Balls:** *But I do want to send you something, so I'm going to need an address.*

**DrinkWithMe:** *Hmm, not sure if you've earned it. Why don't I just meet you at a neutral location, and you can hand it to me there?*

**Ryot.Bisley.Balls:** *I would love to hand deliver it, but unfortunately, I'm in Miami right now.*

**DrinkWithMe:** *Playing the baseball?*

**Ryot.Bisley.Balls:** *Yes, playing \*the\* baseball. I have a game tonight.*

**DrinkWithMe:** *Think you're going to win?*

**Ryot.Bisley.Balls:** *Well, being that we're the number-one team in the country, I would say yes.*

**DrinkWithMe:** *Wait, really?*

**Ryot.Bisley.Balls:** *You really have no clue, do you?*

**DrinkWithMe:** *No clue about what? I don't follow sports, never been into them. I guess I don't have a clue about anything.*

**Ryot.Bisley.Balls:** *So you don't know that you're talking to the guy with the second-best batting average in the country as well?*

**DrinkWithMe:** *What's a batting average? Is that a sexual innuendo?*

**Ryot.Bisley.Balls:** *Christ. Just send me your address.*

———

DRINKWITHME: *I got a special delivery today.*

**Ryot.Bisley.Balls:** *And . . .*

**DrinkWithMe:** *Am I supposed to sleep with this?*

**Ryot.Bisley.Balls:** *Do you want to sleep with it?*

**DrinkWithMe:** *The nylon fabric does bring back old memories.*

**Ryot.Bisley.Balls:** *Well, I did send it to entice you.*

**DrinkWithMe:** *How is a Chicago Bobbies flag supposed to entice me?*

**Ryot.Bisley.Balls:** *A few ways. For one, it could remind you of* *how we first met.*

**DrinkWithMe:** *Nostalgia accomplished.*

**Ryot.Bisley.Balls:** *You could use it as a symbol of me and wrap it around yourself when you're missing me.*

**DrinkWithMe:** *Not quite missing you just yet, but maybe in the future. Continue.*

**Ryot.Bisley.Balls:** *And it gets cold in Chicago, so it could be an extra layer for those wintry days.*

**DrinkWithMe:** *I do find that appealing.*

**Ryot.Bisley.Balls:** *And finally, you could hang it up in your room, so whenever you look at it, you think of me, the guy with the second-best batting average in the country.*

**DrinkWithMe:** *Hmm, sounds interesting. If only you had sent Velcro with it . . .*

**Ryot.Bisley.Balls:** *Did you look in the package? It's there.*

**DrinkWithMe:** *Okay . . . I think you might have gotten me with the Velcro.*

**Ryot.Bisley.Balls:** *You're an odd one to please.*

---

DRINKWITHME: *So there's a billboard of you outside the restaurant I work at. Did you have them put it there on purpose? Also, your pants are tight. Very tight . . . that's a supreme rear end you have there, Bisley.*

**Ryot.Bisley.Balls:** *If I knew where you worked, then I would have asked them to put up three billboards, but fortunately for me, this was all by chance. Also, thank you for the butt compliment. I do a lot of squats.*

**DrinkWithMe:** *It shows.*

**Ryot.Bisley.Balls:** *I'm just going to act like your compliments don't faze me at all, even though I'm screaming inside.*

**DrinkWithMe:** *Why do I feel like more of the masculine one in this non-relationship?*

**Ryot.Bisley.Balls:** *Non-relationship? Is that what we're calling this?*

*DrinkWithMe: I think it has a nice ring to it. We're not friends, really . . . because frankly, if something were to ever occur between you and me, I don't want to be a friends-to-lovers cliché. And we're clearly not in a relationship, so . . . non-relationship it is.*

*Ryot.Bisley.Balls: What's wrong with friends to lovers? Some of the best love affairs start as friends.*

*DrinkWithMe: Name one.*

*Ryot.Bisley.Balls: Uh, I don't know . . . The Hangover.*

*DrinkWithMe: LOL! What? How is that friends to lovers?*

*Ryot.Bisley.Balls: At first, they didn't like Alan, but after quite the adventure, they loved him. See, friends to lovers.*

*DrinkWithMe: You need help.*

*Ryot.Bisley.Balls: Possibly.*

———

DRINKWITHME: *Is this how you're going to win me over? Gifts?*

*Ryot.Bisley.Balls: No, I'm going to win you over with my tongue, but we aren't quite there yet. Gifts are just a way to show you I'm thinking of you while I'm lying . . . all alone . . . in my hotel room. Do you like them?*

*DrinkWithMe: Probably the most decadent chocolate I've ever had in my mouth.*

*Ryot.Bisley.Balls: Vosges Chocolate is my favorite. Wasn't sure if you've had any since you've been in Chicago, but thought I'd give you a glimpse of what the city offers.*

*DrinkWithMe: The hazelnut almost made me orgasm.*

*Ryot.Bisley.Balls: Got you throbbing, did I?*

*DrinkWithMe: You did, which makes me realize that maybe I don't need a man at all. Maybe I just need Vosges.*

*Ryot.Bisley.Balls: Now, now, now, that was not the intention here.*

*DrinkWithMe: Yup, just me and my chocolates, that's all I need in life. Excuse me, I'm going to go climax now.*

*Ryot.Bisley.Balls: Well, that didn't go as planned.*

# Chapter Nine

MYLA

***Present day . . .***

"What is that heavenly smell?" I ask as I walk into the kitchen, fresh from a dip in the pool.

Update on the living conditions, in case you were wondering: tense.

That's the perfect word. It's been the word of the week, actually.

Just . . . tense.

And yes, I knew that would happen when I set the ground rules, but I'm not the only one shooting off icicles in this house.

Ryot has too.

And he's worked fast to create a better living environment for himself. A plethora of groceries were delivered this morning—I heard him talking to Banner on the phone about how to order them—he skimmed his side of the pool and put up a pool noodle barrier, and somehow, the man was able to get a TV installed in the pool area in a matter of twenty-four hours. See what money can do for you? He spent all morning watching highlight clips, but the moment I stepped out in my skimpiest bikini, he went back inside. I haven't seen him since, but then the sweet scent of baked goods beckoned me out of the pool.

When I look up, I find Ryot in the kitchen, shirtless in an apron, and hovering over a bowl of melted chocolate and dipping éclairs.

Oh mama, yes, please!

"You made éclairs?" I ask as I reach for one. "They look amazing—"

My hand is slapped away as a menacing expression meets my shocked one. "What the hell do you think you're doing?"

"Uh, grabbing an éclair."

"I see that. Did I invite you to my éclair party?"

"Is that what this is?" I look around at an empty kitchen. "A party? Doesn't seem like one."

"A party of one," he answers with a voice dipped heavy in spite. "And I don't think I did, so keep your sticky, clammy paws away from my delicious, puffy, and creamy éclairs."

Hand on my hip, I say, "Ah, I see what you're doing. This is your way of getting back at me for yesterday, isn't it?"

Seems like we're volleying the spite back and forth now. *And that, too, makes me sad. That we've come to this.*

"No idea what you're talking about," he says as he dips his last éclair into the melted chocolate and then rests it on a cooling rack.

"Uh-huh. Making my absolute favorite dessert the day after we had a rules talk has nothing to do with payback?"

"Let's just say I had a hankering," he says before taking the melted bowl of chocolate to the sink.

My eyes trail his muscular back all the way down to his . . .

"Oh my God, where are your pants?" I ask as I stare at his round, tight, sculpted ass.

Lord help me, he has the nicest backside. Even after retirement, he still stays in peak shape by running every morning and lifting weights, and man, does it show. His back has bulgy muscles everywhere, with two distinct muscles that protrude and connect with the curve of his ass and two dimples on either side. I've always been a fan.

"Didn't think I needed them," he answers while he cleans the bowl.

"What do you mean you didn't think you needed them? Nichole could see you." If Ryot knows anything, he knows I have a sweet spot for his backside.

"So?" he answers. "Wouldn't be the first time she's seen my ass. Remember, she caught me fucking you on the dining room table once?" It was a show for everyone.

"This is different."

He places the bowl on the drying rack and then turns back around. "Not really. This is my house too. Therefore, if I want to walk around in an apron and nothing else, then I will."

"I see, so if I want to walk around topless, that won't be a problem?"

"Do whatever your little maniacal heart desires."

As I said, I volley, and he volleys back.

I challenge, and he's waiting on the sidelines with revenge in his eyes and my name written all over it.

If this is our new normal, then I might as well play his little game. I reach behind me to the strings of my bikini top and tug on them until they're loose. With one swift pull, I'm topless. Resting the top on the counter, I say, "There, that's better."

He glances in my direction and then fully turns his head when he notices that my boobs are out, exposed. His tongue slides across his top teeth right before his jaw clenches, and he turns away.

"Nice day out, isn't it?" I lean against the counter, hands behind me, and thrust my breasts toward the air.

"Yup," he answers in a clipped tone, which makes me laugh. He moves toward the island where I'm stationed and where the éclairs are. "Is there a reason you're still in here?" His head is tilted down, not looking in my direction.

"Thought I'd soak up the smell of the éclairs since I can't have any. And since this is a neutral space, I'm allowed to be here. Why, do you have a problem with my naked breasts?"

He glances up, his eyes landing on my chest as he lifts an éclair to his mouth and takes a large bite. After chewing for a moment, he says, "You know I have no problem with your tits."

"Okay, just making sure." I turn and lean on the counter so my boobs are pressed together. "Wouldn't be fair if your ass was out and my tits weren't. A little tit for tootie, you know?"

He takes another bite of the éclair, but this time, he moans while chewing.

My eyes narrow.

"This fucking pudding. So creamy, fuck, I could lick at it . . . all . . . goddamn . . . day." And then he takes his tongue and slips it inside the éclair and then back out. In . . . and out.

In.

And.

Freaking out.

The motherfucker.

My body immediately heats from the base of my spine all the way up past my neck and to my ears. There are three things about this man I don't think I will ever get over. His ass, his tongue, and his dick.

And he knows it.

And he's using it to his advantage.

Sure, my tits are lethal, but they are no match for his tongue. Not even close.

"Too bad you can't have any," he says as he drags his tongue along the chocolate now.

"Yeah, a shame," I answer.

He sucks on the pudding now, making a slurping sound that makes my nipples hard. I imagine it's my clit he's sucking on, my nipples he's pinching between his fingers, and not that stupid pastry.

"Your face is flush. Anything bothering you?" he asks with a smirk.

I stare at him, my irritation ramping up. "You're an ass."

"I wasn't the one who started this. You were." He dips his fingers in his mouth where he sucks on them, making a *pop* noise when he drags them past his lips.

"Yeah . . . well . . ." My eyes fall to the éclair, then back up at him.

His eyes track mine.

I glance down again as he stands tall, realization hitting him.

"Don't you dare," he says right before I swipe an éclair off the cooling rack and bolt toward my room, squealing the whole time.

"Myla!" he shouts as he chases after me.

What a sight I'm sure we are. Me topless, sprinting for the shelter of my room, his apron flapping in the breeze as his ass hangs out the back, chasing after me, his powerful thighs closing the space between us.

"Ahhhhh," I scream as I'm feet away from my room, so close, yet I'm snagged around the waist by one powerful arm and pulled back into a strong, apron-covered chest.

"Drop the éclair."

"Never," I proclaim before I attempt to stuff it in my mouth. A large palm covers my face before I have a chance, and instead, I shove the éclair right into the back of his hand.

"Damn you," I mutter against his palm.

I drop the rest of the éclair to the floor and attempt to twist out of his grip as his arm skims the underside of my breasts.

"Let go of me, you buffoon."

"How the hell am I a buffoon?" he asks as he moves me up against the wall so my chest is pressing against the cold surface. "You're the one trying to steal pastries."

"Because you made them on purpose just to be spiteful."

He presses his large body against mine and leans his head forward as he speaks directly into my ear. "And what you did yesterday wasn't spiteful?"

"That was setting ground rules. A common occurrence when having to share a dwelling with another human being."

"What about removing your top? That's not evening the playing field because I wasn't wearing pants."

"Who bakes with their ass out? That's just unhygienic."

"Why don't you let me worry about me, and you worry about . . . you," he says as his thumb grazes the side of my breast.

"Don't you fucking dare," I say.

"Don't what?" he asks, and I can hear the smile in his voice.

"You realize how dysfunctional this is, right? You constantly attempting to turn me on?"

"Please, babe, I know you're turned on. You were turned on the moment you saw my ass."

Facts.

"Tell me, did it remind you of the time you had me on all fours on the couch, and you fucked me with a vibrator while sucking my cock?"

No, but it does now.

"Or the time you licked my taint for the first time?"

A spike of heat shoots up my spine.

"Or when you were in the pool that one time, and I was

getting out, only for you to stop me so you could suck me off from behind?"

Yeah, that's a core memory as well.

Clearing my throat, I answer, "Not quite. It reminds me of the time you were drunk in our backyard, tripped over a lounge chair, and face-planted in the grass, looking like a damn ostrich with his ass out." Between you and me, it was the most beautiful sight I had ever seen. Those meat cakes up in the air, his balls hanging out for me to see. The vibrator-sucking-his-cock night was fantasized by that moment.

"You're such a liar." He drags one hand across my stomach as his other hand glides along my side boob.

"I told you, don't," I say right before I spin around and come face to face with him. There's his tempting, seductive eyes, the feel of his hardening cock pressing against me, and those lips that I know can do the most euphoric damage to my body.

"Why do you hate me?" he asks, his voice sounding like it's full of gravel.

"Hate is a strong word."

"You don't love me," he says. "If you loved me, you'd be willing to give me another chance."

"I did give you another chance." I place my hands on his chest, ready to push him away. "I gave you three chances actually, but you just didn't listen."

"I listen to you, Myla."

"Do you?" I ask him with a tilt of my head. "Okay, so tell me, what classes have I been taking lately?"

His brow furrows. "Classes?" he asks. "You didn't tell me about any classes."

"Yes, I did," I say. "I told you about them when you took me out to that fancy seafood restaurant in Malibu. Your response was, 'do what makes you happy, babe,' and then you turned back to your emails." Hands still on his chest, I push him away and move toward my bedroom again.

"Myla, wait, I don't . . . I don't remember that."

"That's because you haven't been present since you hung up your cleats," I answer. My throat tightens, and before he can see me cry, I walk into my bedroom and shut the door behind me.

I have no idea where Nichole is. She probably met a guy at a coffee house, so I pull one of Ryot's Bobbies T-shirts from the basket of clothes I folded for him, slip it over my head, and then bury myself in my pillow where I cry.

I cry in frustration.

I cry in anger.

I cry because even though Ryot is the man I've always dreamed of, somewhere along the way, he lost himself and became the man I've always dreaded.

Careless.

Absent.

Indifferent.

But the worst part is when I see small glimpses of the man I fell in love with. Little windows into the past Ryot when he calls me babe, when he's playful with me, and when he's vulnerable like just now. *Those moments* remind me of the man who took his time to woo me into one single date.

But he's no longer that man.

He's crude, cunning, and power-hungry. And I don't like it.

After what feels like an hour of crying into my pillow, I lift as my door opens, praying it's not Ryot coming to talk. I hold my breath, but thankfully, it's just Nichole. She's holding a plate of éclairs with a Post-it note stuck to the top.

I wipe at my eyes. "What's that?" I ask.

"It was by the door," she says. "I'm assuming it's from your roommate upstairs."

She hands me the plate, and I pluck the Post-it note off the top. In pen, all it says is, "I'm sorry."

Shaking my head, I toss the note to the ground, place the éclairs on the nightstand, then lie back down on my pillow.

"Care to share what that's about?"

"Ryot realizing that maybe he's not as perfect as he likes to think he is."

"Something happen while I was gone?"

"Yeah, but I don't want to talk about it."

"Okay." She pauses. "Want to go for a walk? Or a drive? We can go down to the beach for the sunset, have dinner on a blanket, real romantic shit?"

I chuckle. "I don't know."

"Well, I do. You can't stay in this room when you're feeling like this. Let's get some fresh air, get you moving, *and* get you out of his shirt because I can't imagine that's helping the situation."

Tears well up in my eyes as I say, "I miss him, Nichole. I miss the old Ryot. The one who used to wake me up in the morning by pressing light kisses all over my face until my eyes opened. I miss the guy who would come home wearing a giant smile just because he saw me. I miss the man who would control me in bed, but then treat me like the most precious thing he'd ever held in his hands afterward. He'd scoop me up, take me to the shower, and wash me himself. He was gentle, caring, and loving. He's just . . . cold now."

"I know, sweetie." She lies down on the bed behind me and puts her arm around my waist. "I miss the old Ryot, too."

---

# RYOT

"DID you know Myla was taking classes?" I ask Banner as I let him in the house. After Nichole and Myla snuck out, I invited Banner over because . . . hell, I'm lonely.

"Classes? What kind of classes?"

Great question.

If only I knew.

"Not sure." I pull on the back of my neck. "Just classes."

"Uh, no, why would I know that?"

"I don't know," I say with a sigh as we head toward the backyard.

"Seems like something you should know. Oh hey, éclairs." Banner walks over to the counter, where I see the plate of éclairs I left in front of Myla's bedroom door. "Why is there a note on them that says 'no thank you'?"

"There is?" I step up next to Banner and take the note. "Fuck," I mutter.

"Uh-oh." He lifts an éclair to his mouth and takes a bite. "Am I guessing these were for Myla, but she didn't accept them the way you wanted her to?"

I lean against the counter and fold my arms over my chest. "I made them for myself after frustrations from yesterday, and when she tried to grab one, we got in a fight, and then she claimed I don't listen to her. I told her I did—"

"And I'm assuming this is where the classes come in."

"Yeah, she asked if I knew what classes she was taking. I didn't, so I gave her the éclairs as an apology, and apparently, she's rejected them."

"Brutal." He picks up another and heads to the back patio. "Dude, nice TV."

"Do you even care about what I just told you?"

"Yeah, but it's not like I can do anything about it." Banner takes a seat on the outdoor L-shaped couch. "All I can say is that it seems like the plan is working."

"What do you mean?" I ask, taking a seat as he picks up the remote and turns the TV on.

"I mean, isn't this what you wanted? To have her slip up here and there for you to learn things, so when it comes to the wedding, you're prepared and ready?"

I pause and then bring my leg up on the couch. "Huh, I guess that was the plan."

"So it worked. You got a nugget. She claimed you don't listen to her, she proved her point by the whole class thing, and now you just need to file that away as information learned and continue to move forward."

"Yeah, but she only said that to prove a point because she was mad."

"Exactly. When people are angry, they lower their defenses and try to make the other person feel bad by stating the truth. It's common in arguments. She let the truth slip when you fought the first night, when she handed you the papers, and just now. She fights with her emotions, not her brain. When she's calm and collected, she's guarded, and there's no way you're squeezing info out of that vault. So keep pushing her."

I guess I never thought about it that way.

It makes sense. She locks up her feelings, thanks to her abusive mom. But when she's upset, to her very soul upset, she lets her guard down, and that's when the true emotions come out.

"I just don't get why I've got to make her upset to gather information. Can't I just do nice things for her? Show her that I still love her?"

"That's all show, man." He stops on reruns of *Boy Meets World*. "Sure, you can offer her éclairs and bring her flowers and all that bullshit, but at the end of the day, that's not getting to the root of the problem, and the root of the problem is in her head. You need to crack that open the only way you know how—when she's emotional."

"I guess so," I mutter. "I don't like it, though." *I hate seeing her hurting. I promised her I'd never hurt her.*

"Yeah, well, going into this marriage, into this relationship, you knew she didn't function like everyone else. You knew she was carrying a lot of baggage, and you knew the struggles you'd face when it came to communication. As someone who has never been abused, who has never seen the back of a parent's hand, you can't comprehend how that individual is supposed to function. They have their own techniques, their own way of walking through this world so they're not reminded of the distrust they encountered. Is it dysfunctional? One hundred percent, but sometimes you simply meet someone at their own level to get them to open up. There's nothing wrong with that. It's called being an understanding human, even if you don't agree with their approach."

"I've always understood her, Banner. I've never once held her childhood, her past against her, but I've also felt like we've made strides toward better communication while being together."

"You have," he answers and finishes off his éclair. "But do you know what's interesting?" He licks his finger. "When people feel threatened and out of control, like they're spinning, not even the strongest humans can revert to new coping behaviors. They revert to the patterns of behavior they know best. And even though they're not handling their emotions appropriately, they're still managing, they're still breathing, and they're still walking along in this world."

I tug on my hair. "Yeah, you're right. And if I put myself in her shoes, she's told me time and time again that I've saved her from her thoughts, from her negative feelings. If I did something wrong, causing her to lose comfort previously found in me, that trust, she'd roll back to old habits. That means shutting down, and no amount of thoughtful gifts or actions will change her mind."

"Yup." He drapes his arm over the back of the couch. "It's why Nichole is out here, because she's a solid in Myla's life. She can count on her. She needs that right now." Banner glances in my direction. "So maybe be fucking nice to her."

Where the hell is that coming from?

My brow raises in question as I ask, "Is that for Myla's sake . . . or for yours?"

"Maybe a little of both." He smirks.

"Are you seeing her?"

"Nah, man. Just fooling around after Myla falls asleep. I drive over, we fuck in the car, and that's it."

"Wait, are you serious?"

"Yeah." He shrugs. "She's in town, so why not?"

"You're having sex in front of my neighbors?"

"Grow up. We're all adults. I'm sure if they were ever dick deep in Nichole's pussy, they'd understand." He turns back to the TV and says, "Now, do me a solid and fetch me another of those éclairs? If Myla doesn't want them, I have no problem devouring them for you."

# Chapter Ten

## MYLA

### *Seven years ago . . .*

***Ryot.Bisley.Balls:*** *Hey.*

***DrinkWithMe:*** *Hey? Is that your opening?*

***Ryot.Bisley.Balls:*** *Got you talking, didn't it?*

***DrinkWithMe:*** *Just because I'm so insulted by the simplicity.*

***Ryot.Bisley.Balls:*** *Sometimes simple is good. What are you doing?*

***DrinkWithMe:*** *Painting rocks.*

***Ryot.Bisley.Balls:*** *That's not what I expected you to say.*

***DrinkWithMe:*** *Oh sorry, let me change my answer . . . \*ahem\* Oh well, I'm so glad you asked because I'm just lounging on my bed, in my lingerie, trying to decide if my nipples are closer in shade to pink or to purple.*

**Ryot.Bisley.Balls:** *You know, I can always bring over my color wheel and put the wondering to rest.*

**DrinkWithMe:** *What a white knight you are.*

**Ryot.Bisley.Balls:** *I try. But hey, do you need help painting those rocks?*

**DrinkWithMe:** *What do you mean?*

**Ryot.Bisley.Balls:** *I got home last night from our two-week road trip and have the day off. I figured I would come by, and when I say come by, I mean I'm standing outside your apartment right now, so it would be pretty cool if you could let me in.*

I stare down at the message. He's here? Like . . . actually here?

A wave of uncertainty, nerves, and excitement hit me all at once.

After talking consistently for two weeks and receiving his little gifts—including chocolates and funny videos—he's actually here, in the flesh.

And I'm . . . oh God, I'm wearing nothing but an oversized shirt and a pair of underwear while sitting at the kitchen island, painting rocks.

*Knock. Knock.*

My eyes flash to the door.

"Myla, if you're there, open up. I look like a lurker."

"Uh," I shout. "Are you sure you want to come in?"

"Yes." He chuckles. "I promise, this isn't a date."

"It's not that," I say, dismounting my stool. "I'm just not looking up to par."

"I couldn't care less. Just open the door."

Of course, he wouldn't care. Why would he? He hasn't cared about any red flags I've sent his way, so why should this outfit be any different? Not that a shirt and underwear is a red flag per se. It's more of a way of seduction than anything.

Throwing in the towel, I walk over to the door and open it, only to have the wind knocked right out of me, because oh my God, I forgot how handsome he is.

Yeah, I might have stared at some of his thirst trap Instagram pictures over the past two weeks. And there was that day that I accidentally searched his name in Google and focused only on the images tab. Pictures online do no justice to the real thing.

Tanned skin, scruff lining his square jaw, and those brilliantly blue eyes of his that look happy to see me. Relieved.

He gives me a smooth once-over and then says, "I don't think there's anything wrong with your outfit." And then he steps forward, places his hand on my hip, and presses a quick kiss to the top of my head before making his way into my apartment.

So, uh . . . so we're just doing the old kiss the head thing now?

Okay, sure. It's not as though it made me melt like the Wicked Witch of the West or anything.

Just a normal kiss to the head that I can still feel, that is sending zaps of pleasure all the way down to the tips of my toes, that's all.

"Wait, so you're really painting rocks?" he asks, turning toward me, that smile of his so freaking adorable that I sigh from the sight of it.

"Yes, do you have a problem with rock painting?"

"No. I've never done it. Think you could spare one and let me try?"

I shrug. "If you must."

"Your generosity is awe-inspiring."

"I know." I smirk and then walk into the kitchen. "Can I get you anything to drink? I have water and apple juice, but I'd prefer you don't pick apple juice because I have just enough for tomorrow morning with my final piece of apple cinnamon coffee cake. I really don't want to lose the joy of experiencing the divine combination one more time."

His smile slowly spreads over his lips. "Water is good."

"Great choice," I answer as I fill up a glass for him. "Now, as for a snack, I do have more variety in that arena." I open my snack cabinet, and chip bags and cookie boxes come tumbling out. "You see, so many choices they just fall at your feet. So what would you like? We have cookies and chips and these okay-tasting vegetable crackers, and some Gushers, because I love a juicy squirt in my mouth, as well as these yogurt melt things made for babies, but Nichole oddly likes them. Oh!" I reach into the cabinet and pull out a bag. "And pretzels."

"Pretzels, babe. Pretzels all day, every day."

*Babe.*

Do not fangirl over the sound of him saying that.

DO. NOT!

I swallow back the surprising giddy behavior and ask, "Uh, do you want peanut butter to dip them in?"

"Do *you* want peanut butter to dip them in?"

"Obviously." I grab the peanut butter and scoop a large amount into a bowl and deposit it in front of Ryot as well as the pretzels.

Together, we each grab a pretzel and dip it in the peanut butter.

"Wow, okay, that shit is good." He grabs another pretzel and dips it. "Really fucking good."

"You can thank me with jars of peanut butter."

"On it." He turns toward me and says, "Okay, what kind of rock painting are we doing?"

I hand him a flat river rock the size of my palm. "I like to paint rocks to drop off at the Children's Hospital. They use them to decorate the plants around the hospital, as well as in the gardens and playground. They're supposed to bring color and joy, a reminder that the future is bright."

He studies me for a moment and asks, "Really? You're painting rocks for the Children's Hospital?"

"Yup. Keeps me busy, makes me feel like I'm doing something, and allows me to be creative."

"Are you a creative person at heart?"

I nod. "Always have been. Not much of an artist, but I'm great with colors. I have an eye for design, and I like keeping my hands busy with different crafts and projects."

"Like what?" he asks as he picks up a paintbrush and dips it into some orange paint that I have on a paper plate.

"Well, you see our coffee table?" He glances over his shoulder into the living room. "I made that."

"Really?" he asks, seeming impressed. "It looks expensive, like you got it from a fancy store."

"It's a Pottery Barn dupe. What should have cost me nine hundred dollars only cost me sixty-three dollars and thirty-three cents."

"Wow, that's impressive."

"You know how to say all the right things, Bisley."

"It's the truth. You impress me."

"Not sure how. It's not like I have the second-best batting time in the professional leagues."

He chuckles. "Second-best batting average in the Majors, and everyone is impressive in their own way."

"Okay, so tell me how I'm impressive?" While he decorates his rock with orange paint, I continue to snack on pretzels—dipped in peanut butter, of course.

"For one, you're painting rocks for the Children's Hospital on your day off. You are loyal, hold strong to your morals, look for the good in people, and don't take shit even from one of the most popular baseball players in Chicago."

"Doesn't seem impressive to me. Seems pretty average."

His hand connects with my chin, and he gently turns my head to look him in the eyes. "It's impressive, Myla. Not many people can say they hold strong to what they believe in, or that their loyalty is impenetrable. Very fucking impressive."

I will tell you something right now. When I woke up this morning and decided to paint rocks, the last thing I expected was for Ryot Bisley to sit across from me, taking time to help me see the value I offer to this crazy world.

But on top of that, with those dangerously handsome eyes of his, I never expected for my heart to flutter, my mind to whirl, and my soul to take charge—*and* that this would be the moment I start to fall for Ryot Bisley.

---

"OKAY, so where are you from again?" I ask as I cuddle up on the couch with Ryot only a few inches away from me. We painted three rocks together, ate half a bag of pretzels, and guzzled two glasses of water. An eventful afternoon if you ask me. And for some reason, after we cleaned up, I didn't want him to leave, so I asked if he wanted to stay for dinner. He said yes with one of his nipple-melting smiles, so we ordered Chinese for delivery.

"Bright Harbor, Maine. It's a small town on the coast. Have you ever seen those Lovemark movies, the Christmas ones that everyone raves about every year?"

"Uh, have I heard of them?" I raise my hand. "Avid watcher over here."

"Aw, then you would be happy to know, the neighboring town is Port Snow, where many Lovemark movies have been filmed. Sometimes, the filming has overflowed into Bright Harbor."

"Really?" I excitingly ask. "That's so cool. Have you ever seen them film there?"

"No, didn't happen until after I left. But my sister, Nola, and my parents have stood on the sidewalk while they've filmed."

"Nola, I love that name. So just two siblings? Nola and Banner?"

"Yup," he answers. "Nola is the oldest, Banner is the youngest, and I'm the dedicated middle child. And before you ask, no, I don't have any childhood complexes of growing up as the middle child. My parents were pretty cool about splitting up their time equally."

"And your parents still live in their original home you said."

"Yes. They were thinking about an old community where people their age live, but the thought of an old-person community village made them cringe."

"I can only imagine the kind of trouble that occurs in the village. I used to volunteer at a senior center in Phoenix, and if the thirteenth ever fell on a Friday, the staff knew the willies were coming out."

"What do you mean?" He laughs as his arm extends along the back of the couch. If he reached to the right, he could twirl my hair in his finger.

"I mean, the men would strip down naked, a few women would join them, and then they'd parade around the hall, warding off all evil with their nakedness."

"Fuck, are you serious?" He laughs.

"Yes. Some of them rode bikes around the center, and I'm going to tell you right now, once you see a pair of old man balls squished on a bicycle seat, you will never unsee it."

He shivers. "Can't imagine that sitting well in your mind."

I shake my head. "I can still see it. Like an aged snail attempting to come out of its shell."

"Ew, fuck." We both laugh.

But his laugh is hearty. It's very attractive, just like everything else about him.

"It seems you're close with Banner, since he moved with you."

"Very close. He's my best friend. He always said where I go, he would go, and that's how it's been ever since I moved out to Phoenix."

"Is there a reason?" I ask.

His fingers gently press along my shoulder, sending chills

all the way down my spine. "I think he feels safe around me. He had a different childhood than mine. I was the star athlete, and he was the computer nerd. He was picked on, teased, and got into a few fights at school because he's just . . . different. He has a different way of thinking, and I was the one who stuck by him. Defended him. Made sure no one touched him. He graduated early, because he's really fucking smart and, instead of going to college—there wasn't much he could learn that he hadn't already taught himself—he worked on coding. He worked twelve- to fourteen-hour days at times until he developed his first real app."

"What did it do?" I ask, totally unaware of how smart Banner is. I just assumed he played the hot nerd role with Nichole—the *best-sex-she'd-ever-had* hot nerd.

"Some banking exchange thing that a company in Japan bought from him." Ryot slowly draws a circle over my shoulder. "It meant he didn't have to get a nine-to-five job, which of course my parents were worried about when he moved out to Phoenix with me. For those first few years, he totally supported my ass because baseball players barely make enough to eat in the minor leagues."

"Wow, I had no idea. I guess I just assumed you got paid the same all around."

Ryot laughs and shakes his head. "No, not even close. It's why so many guys room with each other in the minors, because they can't afford to live alone. Thankfully, Banner was there for me."

"You're lucky to have him. I love your relationship."

"You would have loved it when we were kids. We weren't always as close as we are now. Before Banner started getting picked on, we constantly tried to get each other in trouble with our parents. It got to the point that whenever one of us did something, my parents grounded us both."

"Ooo, I bet that made you rethink your decisions."

"It did. That's how we became so close, because it was no longer us against each other, it was us against our parents."

"What about your sister?"

"She was always the goody two shoes. She's been a prime example of how to be the picture-perfect child growing up. Banner and I couldn't make it that easy on our parents, so we gave them a run for their money."

"Are you all close now?"

"Yes," he answers as his fingers play with some strands of my hair. "We get together for the holidays. I love Bright Harbor in the winter, and we keep in touch often. My parents, Nola, and Banner always plan a trip to one of my away games. They rent a house and stay in the city for a few days while attending my games. This year they went to Miami."

"I'm envious. I don't have siblings, and everything about my family is broken. I'm not sure we ever went on a family vacation. If we did, it was to a military base. Nothing special."

"That's sad," he says. "Is that why you've been to a few places with Nichole? Why you live so carefree? So you can experience life in a different way?"

I pause and tilt my head to the side. "You know, I never really thought about it that way. It makes sense. I've been more places with Nichole than I have with my parents, and any extra penny I make, I put to the side to continue those experiences."

"What's the favorite place that you've visited?"

"We went to Cancun a year or so ago, and it was so relaxing. We decided to make it a beach vacation. I had the best tan of my life, and while I was out and about at night, I'd also lay on a lounger in front of the ocean and just listen to the waves crash on the sand. It was the most peace I've felt in a long time. Not to mention, the coconut shrimp won my heart at that resort."

"I love coconut shrimp."

"Really? I wouldn't peg you for a coconut shrimp kind of guy."

"No?" he asks, brow raised as his fingers move along the back of my neck now. It's sending a deep, radiating chill down my spine, making me feel more alive than ever. "What kind of guy would you peg me as?"

Smirking, I answer, "The kind who orders chicken tendies at a seafood restaurant and calls them *chicken tendies*."

He lets out a laugh while shaking his head. "You got me all wrong, Myla."

"Do I?"

"Yeah, I would order fish sticks."

Now it's my turn to laugh. "With a gallon of tartar sauce, right?"

"What's a fish stick without tartar sauce?"

"Just like what's peanut butter without jelly?"

"See, you feel me." He wraps a piece of my hair around his finger and lightly twirls it, creating this warm sensation over my scalp and down my arms.

It feels so good. Like this is where he's supposed to be.

This is where I'm supposed to be.

I'm tempted to scoot closer, close enough that I could curl into his side, but if I did, where would that lead? What would he think? I like this guy so much and that freaks me out because I've never liked someone the way I like him. I've never found myself daydreaming about a guy before, or wishing that he would move in closer, or that he would lean over and press his lips to mine. Sure, I've kissed my fair share of guys. I'm not a kissing virgin. But this feels more like a *need* for him to kiss me. And I've never known *that*. Never wanted that.

And that's concerning because like I told him before, I don't think I'm mentally fit to have a relationship. I don't think I have it in me to be the kind of partner he probably needs.

"What's going on in that head?" he asks. "You went from smiling to worried."

I glance up, unaware that I was showing so much expression on my face. Of course he'd notice; he's a very observant man. "Uhhh, nothing," I lie.

"I see." He shifts. "I think you and I both know that's not the truth. But I could take this conversation two ways. I can either call you out on your bullshit answer and determine what just made your brow furrow, or I can respect your privacy and decide to skip over the momentary lapse in your beautiful smile. I'm good either way, I just need you to let me know what direction you want me to take this."

Who is this man?

He speaks his truth so effortlessly.

He doesn't play mind games.

He doesn't hide from the hard.

He just lays it all out on the table, and in all my years, I don't think I've ever seen anything like it. Definitely not from watching my parents' relationship. The closest person that I've seen so effortlessly truthful is Nichole. But even then, she hides things from me from time to time—like when she was diagnosed with breast cancer a few months ago. I only found out because she had to list me as a medical emergency contact before her surgery. Her reason for not telling me? She didn't want to worry me.

So excuse me while I blink a few times, trying to understand where this man comes from.

"You okay?" he asks.

"Yes, sorry. I'm just trying to process how honest you are. Not sure I've ever met someone like you."

"I'm just trying to be open with you, Myla." His eyes connect with mine, and his arm draped on the couch falls between us. His fingers tangle with mine until our palms are connected. His hands are rough, calloused, and worn. They look far too old for his young body, but they're large, thick, and sexy. "You told me you have baggage. I'm attempting to show you that you can trust me with that. I'm not here to play games. I'm not here to coax you into bed for one fucking hot night. I'm here because I like you, I want to get to know you more, and maybe, if you're ready one day, you'll let me take you out on a date, but I want to go at your pace. So yeah, I'm giving you the option on how to approach the somber mood you just fell into. I don't want to push you or make you uncomfortable. I want you to know that when you're around me, with me, you can rest on my shoulder, on my strength, on my courage, and any burden you might be carrying, I'll help you carry it as well."

I wet my lips, biding my time before I respond. My throat has grown tight from his speech because . . . I can see the sincerity in his proposition. I can feel it. It's so tempting to unload on someone else, to let them carry the nightmares, the worthless feelings I have of myself. But . . . he's too good. The best, actually, and all I'd do is drag him down. I know this.

On a deep breath, I say, "I appreciate your honesty, Ryot. I really do."

"Why do I feel like there's a 'but' attached to that sentence?"

"Because there is." I let go of his hand and turn so my back is against the couch, my eyes filling with tears. I can't possibly look at him when I say this. "I like you, Ryot, so much that it scares me. I know what I have to offer, and it's not much. I know the toll my past has taken on me and the negative thoughts I have in my head, the worthless thoughts I carry daily. And I don't deserve to take any of your strength or your courage because I would take too much. I would become reliant on that." I finally turn to face him. "You are big, Ryot. You have a life that you're building on, that you're creating, a great life that is only just beginning. Your dreams, your ambitions, they don't align with my trajectory in life. And what's going to end up happening is that I'll hurt you. I know it. I can feel it in my bones. And I don't want to do that. I don't want to hurt you, so . . . I think that it's best if we just stop talking to each other."

He doesn't answer right away as he continues to gaze at me. I can see his mind working, his brain attempting to figure out how to respond in the right way and not in a reactionary way.

After a few moments of silence, he leans forward on his thighs, and when he speaks, it's quiet. "I'm not sure I'm the guy you think I am." He clasps his hands in front of him. "I'm awkward, I'm unsure of myself on a daily basis. Hell, I went out with a girl once, and after that, sent her flowers once a day for a week. I don't know what the hell I'm doing when it comes to this shit. All I know is that I like you, that I'll be honest with you, and when or if you ever decide to let me into your world, I won't hurt you. I'll only protect you. I will always listen to you, acknowledge you, and hopefully, make you feel as special as I know you are."

After a large sigh, he stands from the couch just as there is a knock on the door.

Great, the food is here.

Without saying a word, he grabs the food for us and then sets it on the kitchen counter. He doesn't take a seat, and he doesn't start dishing it out. He just leaves it on the counter and then faces me.

Hands stuffed in his pockets, he looks up at me, those devastatingly handsome eyes penetrating my very soul. "I don't want to pressure you, Myla, so I'm going to give you your space as you asked. I want you to know, though, that I'm not mad at you. I'm not distancing from you. I'm just respecting you. And for the record, just in case I didn't make it clear enough, I like you too, Myla. A lot. You make me smile, you make me happy, you make me think, and you make me feel alive. If you're ever wondering what you bring to the table, it's *all* those things. In the world of baseball, we don't get much time to breathe, but you, you're my breath of fresh air." With a sad smile, he takes off toward the door and exits the apartment, leaving me in a puddle of emotions. And words. Lots of incredibly kind and thoughtful words. Words I never thought I'd hear directed at me.

*I like you too, Myla. A lot. You make me smile, you make me happy, you make me think, and you make me feel alive. If you're ever wondering what you bring to the table, it's all those things . . . you're my breath of fresh air.*

What the hell do I do with that? *Why the hell am I so messed up?*

---

## RYOT

"SHE MESSAGE?" Penn asks as he sits next to me in the locker room.

I shake my head and set my phone down. "No." Leaning back in my plush chair just in front of my locker, I say, "It's been three fucking weeks. I know I told her I'd give her space, but fuck, I thought that maybe she'd contact me by now."

"Dude, have you thought that maybe she's not the right person for you?" Penn asks as Walker approaches and sits on the other side of me.

A year ago, Walker and Penn never would have been seen within five feet of each other. A longtime rivalry between the two made locker room chats increasingly uncomfortable. But after a rough year, a lot of honesty, and Penn admitting he had a drinking problem and going to rehab, we're now able to sit peacefully in the locker room without them staring each other down. It was so weird. They were unstoppable on the diamond together. Penn as pitcher, Walker as catcher. Pure magic. Even though off the field was such a different story. Now, thank fuck, they're almost friends. *And* still unstoppable.

"Are you talking about Myla?" Walker asks as he picks up one of his cleats and adjusts the shoelaces.

"Yeah," I answer. "It's been three weeks. I just figured by this point, she would have contacted me. I even . . ." I rub my palm into my eye. "Hell, I even posted a video of me in the batting cages on Instagram, knowing she hates those videos, and it's been radio silence."

"I'm thinking she's not the right girl for him," Penn says. "I know she interests you, and you like her, but dude, you can't chase someone who doesn't want to be chased."

"I realize that, but I know she likes me. She told me she did, but she's just not letting herself like me. There's a difference, you know? With the time I've spent with her and the messages we've shared, I know there's something special between us, and I would hate to just give up on that."

"You might have to," Walker says. "It took me a long fucking time to get together with Kate, and as you know, I had to let her go at one point. If it's meant to be, then it will happen. But if you push it, you might push her away."

"I understand that, but my fear is that she's not going to ever come to me, that she's so in her head about not deserving a chance, that she'll just walk away."

Penn places his hand on my shoulder. "Then she walks away, man."

I let out a heavy sigh and kick my feet up on my locker.

But I don't want her to fucking walk away.

Hell, I thought I was so close when I went to her place. We talked for two weeks straight and joked around. I looked forward to her messages after my away games, and when I returned to Chicago, she was the first person I wanted to see. I took a chance and went to her place. And that chance was paying off, until . . . until she retreated, talking herself out of taking a chance on me.

"From his silence, I'm going to guess he's not good with that," Walker says.

"Yeah, I don't think he is," Penn agrees. "So best we prepare ourselves for what's to come."

"I'll be fine," I say as I stand from my chair. "I'm going to take a walk. I'll be back before we report to the field."

———

"ARE WE READY, BOYS?" Knox Gentry, our captain and shortstop, calls out as he warms up his arm with Carson Stone, our second baseman.

"Ready as we'll ever be," Dempsey says from where he's stretching on the ground.

"Head on right?" Knox asks me as I finish up my calisthenics. My arm is already warm, it's my legs and torso that are feeling a bit stiff, and I know why. Yesterday, I took my frustrations out in the weight room, and I'm paying for it now.

"Yeah, head's on right," I say as I line up near the foul line in the outfield and bend over to do some more stretching of my hamstrings, knowing damn well that someone in the stands is taking a picture of my ass this very moment.

"You sure? Because you don't seem like your normal self. It's crunch time, man."

"I know," I say while blowing out a heavy breath and stretching even further.

"Okay, if you need to talk, you know I'm here. I've been through my fair share of woman problems."

Yeah, you could say that. Knox is married to Emory, whom he met back in college, but their relationship was one hell of a roller coaster.

"Thanks. I'm just trying to focus on the game and then figure things out off the field."

Knox catches the long toss from Carson, who is now jogging in from all the way out in the center field. "Good. On the field, get the job done. Off the field, you let me know if you need to talk."

I give him a fist bump, grab my glove from the turf, and head to the stands where people are lined up, waiting for any interaction with the players. I make sure to interact with the fans because they spend enough money to come see us. It's the least that I can do. Recently, they've put up protective netting from foul pole to foul pole all along the backstop. It has limited our ability to sign things for the fans, but it was put up to protect them from foul balls. Oddly enough, the Bobbies staff gave us some training on how to sign balls through the small holes, so I quickly sign a few as well as take a few selfies, despite the netting, and then head toward the dugout.

As I approach the dugout, fans cheer, wave, and take pictures. I wave back, smile, and then I feel my heart stop as I spot a familiar face.

A familiar smirk.

A familiar pair of eyes that have captured my attention from the first moment I saw them.

Myla.

She's in the stands.

What the hell is she doing at the game?

# Chapter Eleven

## MYLA

### Present day . . .

**Myla:** *I wish you didn't have to leave.*
**Nichole:** *I know, but I have that appointment I can't miss. I'll try to find some time after the wedding to come visit you.*
**Myla:** *I should have gone with you.*
**Nichole:** *No, I told you it wasn't necessary. Just a routine checkup.*
**Myla:** *If it's routine, then why did you tell me it was really important?*
**Nichole:** *Let's not get into this right now, okay? Focus on you. Focus on getting through these next couple of weeks.*
**Myla:** *Just tell me, Nichole. Is the cancer back?*
**Nichole:** *As I said, worry about you right now. After the wedding, you and I will go somewhere fun. Maybe pick out your next project. That lake house up on Fox Lake could be perfect.*

**Myla:** *You're not answering the question.*

**Nichole:** *Because I don't know the answer. For now, let's not freak out. Let's focus on what we can control. And what we can control is the path you're going to create for yourself after all of this. You've been taking those design and woodworking classes, and you have the tools and the capital to have options. Why not pick out the house you want to renovate?*

**Myla:** *It's overwhelming, and my mind isn't focused.*

**Nichole:** *Then focus on one thing at a time. Where do you want to go when you're divorced? Are you moving back to Chicago? Are you going to find an old place to renovate? Are you staying in California?*

**Myla:** *I don't know. God, Nichole, I'm so messed up in the head because the mere thought of not being in the same state as Ryot makes me physically ill.*

**Nichole:** *Myla . . . I know I've been trying to be supportive, but do you think this is the answer? Divorce?*

**Myla:** *I don't know what else to do, Nichole. I really don't. I feel so hurt, so alone. I saw him more when he was playing baseball and gone almost every other week during the season than I've seen him after retirement.*

**Nichole:** *Then maybe you should talk to someone, a therapist.*

**Myla:** *I have. All she says is that I need to sort out my feelings.*

**Nichole:** *Well, I could have told you that.*

**Myla:** *Hence why I don't see her anymore. Anyway, I know you're probably tired, and I'm hungry, so I'm going to grab something to eat.*

**Nichole:** *Okay, love you.*

**Myla:** *Love you.*

I set my phone down on the table and toss my robe on over my bra and underwear because, even though I like messing with Ryot, I'm just not in the mood tonight. With my silk robe cinched tightly around my waist, I release my curled hair from the clip I had it in, fluff it a bit, and then head out toward the kitchen but stop immediately when I hear voices.

Has Ryot invited guests over?

Slowly, I approach the kitchen, and when I turn the corner

to not only see Ryot but JP Cane and his brother, Huxley, I freeze.

JP is the first to spot me. "Oh hey, Myla." He waves. "Ryot was just telling us about the éclairs he made for you." My eyes connect with Ryot, who has a pleading look on his face. Technically, I don't have to act like we're a happily married couple until the wedding, but that one look from Ryot is all it takes.

I tuck my hair behind my ear and smile. "They were some of the best éclairs he's made," I say quietly.

Ryot's shoulders visibly relax as he shifts in place, his hand gripping a tumbler tightly.

JP, completely oblivious to the tension, says, "Dude, then you need to make some of those for us."

Bringing the drink to his lips, Ryot says, "Nah, I only make those for my girl."

And that's a true statement. He's only ever made them for us, for me. He's never taken them to an event. He's never made them for company, just me and him, because that was something special between us.

"Well, I'll let you guys have your time," I say. "I was just going to grab something to snack on."

"Pizza will be here any second," Ryot says.

"Yeah, join us," Huxley adds, pushing off the counter. "I would love to get to know you better. I feel like we've barely spoken."

"Oh, I don't want to cut into whatever business you need to discuss."

"Nah, there's nothing too pressing. Plus, we can talk while we have dinner," JP says just as the doorbell rings.

"I'll, uh, I'll get that." Ryot sets his drink down on the counter. "Boys, why don't you head to the back patio and make yourselves comfortable? I put a cooler back there with drinks as well."

"Cool," JP says as he and his brother move to the back porch.

As Ryot approaches me, he says, "Can you have dinner with us? I didn't know they were coming over until ten minutes ago."

"A little warning would have been nice," I shoot back at him.

"I thought you were sleeping in your room. Hell, you've been holed up in there and I didn't even think you'd come out. I'm not entertaining in the dining room because I know that's your space."

"Are you trying to be sarcastic when you need me to pretend I'm in love with you?"

He pauses, his spine straightening as he turns toward me. Brows tilted down with a furious expression, he speaks through clenched teeth. "You *are* fucking in love with me. I don't care how much you try to hurt me with your denial. You do love me. So no, you're not going to have to pretend. You just have to act civilly as if you enjoy being around me."

"Well, that's not the case."

"That much is obvious."

He keeps pushing toward the door so he can grab the pizzas while I grab plates and napkins from the kitchen. Could I tell him to go fuck himself and not join his little meat parade in the backyard? Probably, but I also know we're in a battle of wills. And even though I would love nothing more than to grab a slice of pizza and go back to my room, I know that will only add fuel to his fire, and the last thing I need is for him to be pissed at me. Who knows what he'd do?

He brings the pizza into the kitchen, and when I turn to face him, he says, "No more than twenty minutes, then you can fake a headache and leave."

"Planned on it," I say with a sarcastic smile.

And then together, looking like the epitome of a happy marriage, we head to the patio with bright smiles on our faces and gracious host mentalities.

"I've never tried this place before," Huxley says as he grabs a slice of pepperoni pizza. "What's it called again?"

"Big Sal's," Ryot answers. "Myla found it. She loves looking up the best places to eat in a city. Big Sal's had huge reviews, and we hadn't been able to find a decent slice of pizza since being out here."

"This isn't deep-dish, though," JP points out. "Being that you came from Chicago, I would have assumed you were eating deep-dish."

"Deep-dish is good," I say. "But when Ryot took me to New York one year with him on an away trip, I spent my entire visit trying all the pizza I could. I became obsessed, and it set the bar higher for good pizza. So when we found Big Sal's, we haven't tried anywhere else."

"Did you go on a lot of away trips with Ryot?" Huxley asks.

"After we were married, I did. Up until then, I went when my work schedule allowed."

"Oh, what do you do?" JP asks. I should have known that was coming.

I hate this question. I hate it more than anything.

Because for some reason, our society has deemed it necessary to judge someone's self-worth off their career. And I really haven't had a career ever.

When I'm satisfied that everyone has pizza and a drink, I grab myself a slice of mushroom pizza just as Ryot pulls out the seat next to him. When I sit down, he rests his hand on my thigh. I quickly glance at him, but he doesn't even bother to act like this is anything but normal. And I guess it's normal for couples not fighting, not in the middle of a whirlwind of anger —*not divorcing*—but right now, it feels off. It feels off because his calloused palm is penetrating my icy exterior. He's been on the go for the past few months, and I'm not sure he's touched me like this in a while. It's confusing.

"Well, right now, I'm still figuring out the career thing," I say shyly because I'm sitting at a table with three men who have a clear-cut idea of their purpose. Two of them are billionaires, and Ryot is on the cusp. He's invested wisely, very wisely, and now with his new venture, The Jock Report, he's racking up the cash. "But before we got married, I was a server." I shrug and take a bite of my pizza.

To my surprise, Ryot says, "She's incredible at interior design and renovations. She has a clever eye for color, modern aesthetics, and mixing textiles."

Where the hell did that come from? He's never said anything like that. Then again, we are performing right now. Well, color me convinced because wow . . . it almost sounded like he meant it. And unfortunately, even if he didn't mean it, it still leaves a mark on me because it's something I wish I had heard from him more often.

"Really?" JP perks up. "I should get you to meet up with Kelsey. She's into organizing sustainably. I bet you two would hit it off. She's always looking for someone who's as into interior design as her."

"Oh yeah, that would be great," I say with a smile, even though I don't mean it. I have no intention of making friends, not when my future is up in the air.

Smoothing his hand over my thigh, Ryot continues the praise, "Myla's always had a philanthropic heart too. That's what she's focused on the most before and after we moved to California."

"That's great," Huxley says. "What organizations were you working with? We just started a non-profit under Cane Enterprises that JP oversees. We work with affordable housing in expensive cities. Starting in San Francisco, but we plan on expanding."

"Yeah, I think Ryot mentioned something about that. That's pretty great. I know the housing market has been insane lately with corporations coming in and taking over, so for you not to capitalize on it, but rather help others, you're changing lives."

"That's the plan," JP says while wiping his mouth. "So who did you work with?"

Ryot's thumb glides over my skin, momentarily distracting me as the soft touch shoots a rocket of lust straight up my leg. What's he doing? It's not like the guys can see under the table.

Clearing my throat, I attempt to focus on my answer, not on the way Ryot's touch is heating my body. "An organization in Chicago that helped families in desperate need of home makeovers for various reasons like needing wheelchair access, a deep cleaning, or just a fresh start. Renovate Chicago is the organization. It was so rewarding, and I loved it. But when we came out here, I had to pivot, so I'm still trying to figure out my next venture." I feel Ryot's eyes on mine as I answer. I can feel the questions forming on the tip of his tongue.

Having to leave Renovate Chicago is one of the primary causes of my bitterness, and why I'm so angry about moving to California. Because we weren't supposed to leave Chicago. We were supposed to stay there after Ryot retired. We were supposed to settle down and think about buying a lake house where we could relax. Even consider starting a family. I loved our house, our neighborhood, my work with Renovate Chicago, and the reasoning behind what I was doing. I was close to Nichole who—fuck—might be sick again. Everything was in Chicago. And after having to move from place to place to place with my Air Force parents, all I wanted to do was settle. I wanted a place I could call home.

That was the plan.

Until Ryot stole that by retiring earlier than he wanted.

"You should really have her meet up with Kelsey," Huxley says. "I bet they'd get along. Ryot was telling us it's been hard adjusting to California. Finding your tribe, so to speak."

My cheeks flush as I glance toward him. *For someone I feel so ignored by, it's unexpected to see how much he's talked about me.* "Yeah, you know how it is. Making friends with adults is hard."

"Isn't that the truth," JP says as he takes a large bite of his pizza.

"It's hard not to fall in love with Myla, though," Ryot says as his hand slides up higher on my thigh, kissing the opening of my robe. His fingers curl inwardly, and I catch myself gasping quietly from the feel of his strong hand. "Once she gets comfortable in her surroundings, there's no doubt she'll make friends. It's something she's so good at since she grew up in a military household."

"Oh really?" Huxley asks. "What branch of service?"

Ryot's pinky brushes up toward my underwear line, and I clamp my teeth over my lip, suppressing a moan.

"Air Force," he answers for me. "She's been all around the country. Illinois, Nebraska, Colorado, New Mexico, Ohio, and Arizona, which is where we met."

Can't believe he remembered all those states. I can barely keep up with where I've been.

"Ah, so you have experience moving," JP asks. "So this move must have been easy?"

Ryot's pinky is now stroking along the seam of my thong, not even bothering to be covert. My body is turning into a raging inferno, billowing heat in the pit of my stomach and then shooting through my veins. *What the fuck is he doing? I thought he'd stop this after the last time.*

"It was actually the hardest," I answer before Ryot can. And when I feel his gaze, I decide to light him up the way he's lighting me up, but for him . . . it will be different. "I was happy in Chicago, settled. You should have seen our house. Gorgeous. Once a mid-century modern near Lake Michigan, I spent time renovating it to keep the architecture of the era but add a modern twist. We had these expansive windows in the living room that allowed a brilliant amount of light in, even on Chicago's gloomiest days. Mature oak trees surrounded our parcel, almost making it feel like we were living in a forest in the middle of the city. But you know, duty calls, right? Ryot was presented with an opportunity he couldn't possibly refuse and took advantage of it, and here we are." I gesture toward the coastal-style house that we're now living in. It's beautiful, but it barely has any personality, and that just adds to the depression of our move.

JP exchanges glances with Huxley and then says, "Yeah, but hopefully, this is the last move for you."

"Chicago should have been the last one," I say just as Ryot squeezes my thigh, clearly not happy with my answers, but oh well. *You got us in this mess, so you deal with it.* I smile at the men, take a bite of my pizza, and chew.

I'm sure I'll hear about this later.

We spend the rest of the dinner eating our pizza, chatting about California and The Jock Report—of course, because that's all I ever hear about. The freaking Jock Report, the numbers on it, how it's the number-one trending app in the world, how it's already changed the world of sports . . . blah, blah, blah.

During the praise for my husband and his magnificent idea carried out by the genius expertise of his brother, Ryot scoots his chair closer to mine, drapes his arm over the back, and every so often, he twirls my hair around his finger like he used to do to steady my nerves. Probably trying to keep me simmering so I don't make another offhand comment about moving.

And do you know what I hate about his touch, about how he's twirling my hair, massaging my neck, keeping me so close as if to claim me in front of these other alpha men? It's that it feels so natural, so real, like in this small moment, nothing is wrong between us. But we all know playing pretend is not forever, and when this is over, I'll be thrust back into reality where we just don't seem to match up like we used to. Our goals are different, and our desires and needs are different. I might matter to him, but I don't matter the most. And that's the cold, hard truth. *Which breaks my heart. We were once so incredible together.*

While the men finish up their conversation, I pack up the leftover pizza, clear the plates, and then head back to my bedroom, where I open my computer and focus on the design I've been working on for one of my classes to get my mind off the way Ryot spoke about me with kind words and affirmations about my talents. That was a total mindfuck. I can't recall a time when he spoke so highly about that stuff. And I don't want you thinking that he's an asshole who never appreciated me, because he wasn't, we just . . . we never talked about those kinds of things around other people. Hearing him mention it to JP and Huxley was . . . weird, yet fulfilling, as if I've been waiting for that acknowledgment.

Not to mention, I needed to take a deep breath after sitting through a meal while he caressed my inner thigh and twirled my hair. It took me back to simpler times when we'd be resting on the couch together, watching mindless TV, and he'd have his hands on me in some way. It was his way of marking me, ensuring I was always with him.

After what seems like hours, my eyes feel blurry, so I decide to get ready for bed. Just as I shut my computer, there's a knock on my door. Knowing exactly who it is, probably ready to chastise me for my comment about moving, I mentally prepare myself for a fight. I answer the door to find Ryot on the other side, his hand gripping the edge of the doorframe. No longer in his jeans and a T-shirt, he's changed into a pair of shorts, and that's it. My eyes roam his chiseled torso, noticing how much more defined he's become. He's always been muscular, but I'm not sure if it's because I haven't been cooking for him, so he's just been eating protein bars. Either way, his stomach reads like a road map of strength, his abs like mini-islands all along his stomach.

"Can I help you?" I ask, finally pulling my gaze.

When his head lifts and his eyes focus on mine, he says, "I want my shorts."

"What?" I ask, confused.

His eyes narrow, his fingers curl around the wood, and through clenched teeth, he says, "My fucking shorts, I want them." And then before I know what's happening, he's lifting me up and depositing me on my bed.

"What are you doing?" I ask, confused but also turned on so fast that I feel my neck break out in sweat.

"My favorite running shorts. You told me the one way I can get my shorts back is with my mouth, so I'm getting them back."

With that proclamation, he tugs on the tie of my robe and parts it open, revealing my underwear and naked chest. My nipples are hard, pointing at the ceiling, ready for his touch. I watch as his eyes feast on me. White-hot hunger pulses through his pupils as he stands there, hands clenching at his sides, chest rising and falling. He looks like he's ready to burst, like he's been holding back for months and is now ready to be unleashed. It reminds me of the hunger I always saw in his eyes when he'd return from away games.

I'm not sure where this burst of need is coming from, if it's possibly from my compliance at dinner or that he truly wants his shorts, but either way, I can sense there won't be any stopping him until he gets what he wants.

And after a stressful night like tonight, one that was filled with confusion and intimate touches, and the thought that maybe . . . for a micro-second, I mattered, I'm wound up and ready to release the tension that's been twisting in my stomach.

With one swift tug, he pulls my thong down my legs and casts it aside. Then he pushes my legs apart, exposing me to his eyes that lazily soak me up.

"Am I allowed to play with your tits?" he asks.

*Yes.*

*I want you to suck on them. Squeeze them. Roll my nipples until I scream, the way you always do.*

But I also realize I'm in a situation where if I give in to his touch, to feeling all of him, I'm forfeiting my power, my control over what's transpiring between us. So even though I'm desperate for him to keep touching me tonight, to drive himself deep inside me until I feel like he's taken me back to Chicago, to when things were right, I know I can't give in. I know I'll want more. I'll want his kisses, his body, his soul, and I'm too emotionally weak to even consider going that far with him.

I should stop him right now, but there are two reasons I'm not.

I'm the one who started this, and I'll be damned if I don't finish it.

This is about control—about strength—and I might not have shown it in the past, but I'm showing it now.

And, secretly, deep down inside, past the bitterness and the hurt and the pain, I still want him. And granting myself this little taste, this tiny sample of the man I fell in love with, is necessary, especially after tonight's touches.

Keeping my chin held high, I answer him. "Your mouth on my pussy only, nothing else."

I watch carefully as the pride in his chest deflates and the excitement in his eyes fogs over. I know why. We've always felt the most connected in the bedroom. It's been a big part of our relationship. I don't want him to have that connection. I want him to miss it, just like I miss the man I married.

"If you want my mouth and mouth alone, then spread your legs farther," he says as he descends.

I fan out my legs so they can accommodate his broad shoulders, and then I lower my fingers so I'm spreading my pussy for him. I said tongue only, so that's what I'm going to get. He brings his mouth an inch away from my clit, his breath heavy on the sensitive skin.

"You said you didn't love me earlier," he whispers as I feel his words vibrate against my throbbing clit. "Yet as I stare at this fucking slick pussy, I wonder why the hell you're so wet already."

*Because I'll never stop wanting you.*

"No talking," I say, blocking out the internal dialogue that's making me want him even more. "Just make me come."

"That wasn't part of the deal," he says. "Tell me why you're wet, Myla."

"Why does it matter?"

"Because it's proving to me that you're a goddamn liar. That everything you're saying, you don't mean."

I lift, letting go of my grip, and rest on my elbows, staring down at him. "Excuse me? Are you really calling me a liar?"

"You say you don't love me, but it's clear that you do."

"You're assuming that because I'm turned on? Being wet has nothing to do with love and everything to do with wanting release. So don't try to pull this stunt about love because love isn't enough in this situation." I cover myself with my robe, pulling the sides closed, my irritation outweighing my lust. "Just take your shorts and leave. I don't need to deal with this inane questioning after tonight. After dealing with your constant touching, your attempt to turn me on."

"It worked," he says in such a cocky voice that it makes me want to scream.

Instead, I attempt to move off the bed, but he's quicker than I am, grips my hips, and pins them back against the bed, causing me to gasp.

In a tight tone, he says, "I'm not taking the shorts without giving you what you want. A deal is a deal, and I'm not about to back out."

"I don't want your mouth anymore," I say.

"Lies, so many fucking lies coming from that fuckable mouth of yours." His fingers dig into my skin the way he knows I like it. "Why are you lying so much, Myla? It makes me—fuck!" he shouts. "It makes me so goddamn mad because I see what we have. I know what we have. I saw how you acted tonight. Why are you fucking lying to me?"

"Because I don't want you to think that there is even a remote chance that we can work through this."

His eyes turn even darker, his brows more pronounced. Through clenched teeth, he says, "Well, good thing that's not why I'm here."

"Then why did you ask?"

"Just want to prove to you that I still turn you on, no matter what you say." His voice is empty, and I've known this man long enough to know what he's saying he doesn't mean. I can see he's in defense mode, and he's attempting to salvage his feelings.

That makes two of us.

I wet my lips and stare down at his hungry eyes. "You will always turn me on, Ryot, despite how much I wish you wouldn't."

His expression remains neutral, but I can tell that ounce of truth eases part of the anger he's feeling. His chest rises and falls as he stares at me, his gaze penetrating past the flimsy wall I've erected and right to my heart.

Those eyes have always been a window to his feelings, to his soul, and I can see that they're ragged, weary, run down. I feel the same way, like I can't keep up this fight. Like at any minute, we both might raise the white flag and surrender.

And as he lowers his head between my legs, his fingers spreading me, I realize that maybe tonight, he's the one throwing in the towel.

I should stop him.

I should just give him the shorts.

But after the emotional turmoil we've been through, I think this is what I need most.

His mouth.

And I think he needs my taste.

His eyes stay steady on mine as his ragged voice says, "This will be the last time I touch this cunt. Don't expect it again." And then his tongue swipes up and over my clit.

Between the feel of his tongue and his declaration of finality, I feel tears pluck at my eyes, even as a pleasurable hiss escapes me while I sink into the mattress.

If this is it, then I'm not going to waste the moment. *I'm not going to focus on the desperate grief I feel from Ryot's words either. They slay me.* No, *if this is it*, I'm going to take as much from it as I can.

My hands immediately go to my breasts, where I tease myself, slowly running circles around my nipples with the tips of my fingers, erecting them until they peak.

His mouth is hot, wild on me as he swipes continuously, pulsing against my clit, knowing exactly what I need when I need it and how I need it. It's always been like this. From the very start, he could read the needs of my body, the sounds coming out of my mouth, and translate them into his next move.

I shiver under his tongue. "Oh, fuck. Your taste. Missed this, baby," Ryot moans. *I've missed this too.*

With each swipe, I feel it deeper and deeper until my orgasm starts to build. A floating, rippling, out-of-this-world pleasure moves up my arms, up my legs. While he swipes, I tug at my nipples the way I know he likes. When I glance down, I catch him staring, watching my every move, so I let my teeth pull on my bottom lip as I arch my hips into his mouth.

The control he's had ever since he's come in here momentarily slips as he moans against my clit, the vibration setting me up for one of the best feelings of my life.

"Fuck," I moan as I move my pelvis again, aiding in the chase of release.

His tongue forms into a point, and knowing that I'm close, he performs short, quick flicks against my clit at a pace so rapid that I can't keep up with my fingers on my breasts, with my shallow breaths, with my ability to repress my orgasm until I can't take it anymore.

My body is greedy, needy, and ready to take everything he has to offer. My hands fall to either side of me, my chest rises and falls, and my legs spread even wider as I arch against his mouth.

"Oh God," I groan as I feel it, the beginning. A few more swipes, and I'm going to be gone. I'm so close, right on the edge.

Pulsing.

Wavering.

Hoping and praying he doesn't pull away.

And when he pauses, I nearly scream, but when I glance down, I watch him place a gentle kiss right on my clit before he pushes me over the edge, making me scream into the silence of our house.

His mouth continues to work against my clit, so fast, exactly where I need it that I feel like I'm coming forever until my body slowly falls from the high of my orgasm.

"Fuck," I whisper as I cover my face with my hands. When he stands up, I feel him move around the bed until he's right next to me.

He tugs on my hand, forcing me to look at him and the very large erection in his pants. When our eyes connect, I notice the anger is gone and in its place is a soft, desolate, and controlled voice. "Thank you for tonight, Myla. I love you. I always will." His appreciation never reaches his eyes or his beautiful smile but rather falls flat off the tip of his tongue before he moves away toward the door.

"Your shorts," I say to him, feeling desperate for him to stay.

"Drop them off. I need to take care of things." And then he leaves and heads up the stairs.

He's going to take care of things . . . I know exactly what that means.

And I don't know why, maybe because I still love him despite everything going on, maybe because I feel lost without him, but I want to hear. I want to listen to the moment he comes, knowing that this will be the last time we're semi-together.

I rise from the bed, tie my robe back up, and grab the laundry basket I folded for him before all of this went down, including the lucky shorts.

I take it up to what I used to call our room and notice the door is not fully shut. Then I hear the shower. He's going right to work. I sneak in and place the laundry basket on the bed before slipping in next to the opening of the bathroom. I lean against the wall and peer toward the shower where I spot his naked body immediately. He's hunched over, one arm propped against the marble tile, the other pumping his cock. His back muscles are tense, his ass is clenched, and his powerful legs hold him up.

I wet my lips as my eyes focus on his long, thick cock and how his hand is working over it. I've seen this pattern so many times. Watched him make himself come over and over again while on FaceTime when he was at an away game or when we were trying to make each other come by masturbating. He always gives himself two strokes, then rubs his thumb against the head, then back down. It's the motion that makes him come the hardest and fastest. And from his pace, he's right there.

I grip the wall, watch intently, and when I hear his first moan, my legs clamp together, ready for round two.

"Fuck me," he says, his hand flying faster now as his dick looks just about ready.

I want my mouth on his cock so bad. I want to be the one who makes him come. I want to be down on my knees, sucking him, creating the delicious moans that float up through his throat and vibrate against the tiles.

And I'm mad that I'm not.

I'm mad at him.

I'm mad we're in this position.

I'm mad that this is the last time I will hear him come.

I clench my teeth as tears start to well in my eyes.

I wish there was a way to fix this, to make it all better, but I know that's not a possibility. I've tried. I've attempted to focus his attention on us, but it hasn't worked. Nothing has worked.

"If you're going to watch, might as well make me come," he says, pulling me out of my thoughts. He faces me, beads of water cascading down every muscle. Then he turns off the shower and steps out onto the mat, his cock at full mast, his hand gripping the base.

"What are you doing?" I ask.

"Giving you what you want, a show." He leans against the closed shower door, dips his head back, and pumps hard on his length. Over and over again until his moans grow louder. His hisses pierce my very soul, and he's biting on his inner cheek, ready to explode.

I should leave.

I should not be watching this.

Yet, it's all I can do. I can't tear my eyes away.

"Fuck . . . ah fuck, Myla."

He gives himself two more strokes, and then he's coming, his body convulsing, his chest tightening only to expand with air as he takes his first breath after his orgasm.

When his laser-sharp eyes meet mine, he says, "Wish you were between my legs now?"

The audacity.

The arrogance.

And sure, he might be right, and he's saying that because it's written all over my face, but he doesn't have to make a point of it all.

It's the bitterness in him as well. The anger. The frustration.

It's not an excuse. It's the truth.

And I know exactly how he feels because I'm feeling it too.

There's so much animosity, so much that has gone wrong that even though I love this man, I can very well say that I hate him as well.

"No," I say, chin held high. "Glad I wasn't, actually."

"Fucking liar," he says once again as he moves back into the shower to clean himself up.

And he's right. I am a liar.

But a liar who is protecting her heart, protecting her health.

I make my way back to my room and take a seat on my bed, where I just stare at the wall, contemplating tonight. I feel so . . . destitute. *Should I move out now? For sanity's sake?*

Will I ever be able to leave this man?

Or the better question is, will this man ever leave my heart?

My emotions overwhelm me as I lie down on my bed and melt into my pillow, where I let out a sob. Nothing feels right. My mind is a complete mess. My heart is bruised and battered, duct-taped together and barely hanging on. I want him, I miss him, I love him. But he . . . he's forgotten about me. He's moved on to a life that doesn't involve me. He never asked, he never discussed, he just took. And I feel so powerless. So lost. So left behind that I'm not sure this consuming love I have for the man could ever make up for the way he's made me feel so . . . obsolete.

RYOT

AFTER A LONG, drawn-out shower where I spent too much time tasting Myla on my tongue, I brushed my teeth and got ready for bed. Naked, I slip under my covers and stare up at the ceiling, wondering what the hell I just did.

Probably something I shouldn't have. No, I know I shouldn't have, but if I'm honest, the pain I'm feeling is more about the words I said.

*"This will be the last time I touch this cunt. Don't expect it again."* And Myla's lack of response.

Agony slices through me because I can't see any way around this. Myla didn't protest. Just accepted my words. Accepted that we're over.

*She's done.*

*And I feel so empty.* And I have a feeling I'm going to feel this way for a fucking long time.

I grab my phone and shoot off a text.

**Ryot:** *Man, I fucked up. I just got a taste of her, and now, I don't think I can let her go. But I also don't think I can fix this. I'm angry. I'm mad at her. I'm mad at myself. I want her, but I don't like her, but fuck . . . I need her. I fucking hate this.*

When I set my phone down, I flop back on my bed and cover my face with my hands as I groan out in frustration.

Fuck!

My intention of going to her room was to give her what she wanted nights ago, my mouth. After what she did tonight, pretending to still be a happily married couple, I wanted to do something for her. Feels lame, but I was more than willing to give in to her demand because she helped me out when she could have told me to fuck off.

But seeing the hunger *and* hate in her eyes makes me feel unsettled. It's like this burning dagger is digging into my stomach, and I don't know how to stop the pain. I don't know how to end this miserable feeling. I don't know how to make things better. I don't know what she means about not hearing her. Fuck, I was complimenting her at dinner, and she seemed . . . shocked. Am I that much of an asshole that my praise surprised her?

For a moment, a brief second when my tongue was between her legs, it felt like everything was going to be okay. I know deep down that it's not. I'm on the verge of losing her. And I have no idea how to stop that from happening.

And I don't know how to stop this anger.

This bitterness.

This resentment I have for myself.

It's clouding me.

Torturing me.

Making me act out in ways I never would have before.

And for the life of me, I don't see an end to it all.

# Chapter Twelve

## MYLA

### *Seven years ago . . .*

"Oh God, he saw me," I say to Nichole, who is gripping my hand excitedly. "This was a bad idea. Why did we do this?"

"Because you can't stop thinking about him. Because I got free tickets, and it's about time you stop moping around the apartment and put yourself out there."

"Nichole, look around. Ryot is beloved by this city. Do you know how many Bisley shirts I saw as we walked in? He's way out of my league, way too nice, and I'm only going to bring him down. I can feel it. I will hurt him because I'm not mentally fit for a relationship." *She* made sure of that many years ago.

"And how long have you said that?" Nichole asks. *Probably*

montage of the Bobbies starts playing on the
ron. The fans around us erupt in cheers.

ou can tell I've never been to a baseball game because I
e no idea what's happening. "I think you've said that ever
since I've known you. Don't be that person, Myla."

"What person?" I ask as I clap reflexively because
everyone else is.

"The person who never shows any growth in their life, but
rather stays in their past, reliving the horrid lessons learned
from their childhood. You are so much better than that, and
it's about time you start showing it. You are so much better
than what your mother made you feel about yourself. And it's
about time you believe that. You have so much potential to be
anyone you want, any*thing* you want, Myla, but you're not
allowing that. Well, I'm sick of it."

Her voice is angry and irritated. Unlike anything I've
heard from her. It's startling.

"It's not that easy," I say as the Bobbies run out onto the
field to their spots. My eyes immediately fixate on Ryot, who
jogs out to third base. I notice his number, twenty-two, and I
wonder about the story behind it. Did he pick it out? Does it
have sentimental value to him?

"It's not easy because you're scared," Nichole says. "Are
you really going to let fear dictate your future? Or are you
going to face that fear head-on and see that there is another
side to life, Myla? A side where fear doesn't control your heart,
but rather opens it to new things?"

"I . . . don't know," I say.

"Excuse me? Miss?" I turn to my right, where a stadium
worker wearing a blue Bobbies polo and baseball cap stands.

"Yes?"

"Are you Myla Moore?"

"Uh, yeah, that would be me."

He nods. "This is for you."

He holds out an envelope, and I very shakily take it. "What is this?"

"Not sure. I was just told to hand it to you. Enjoy the game."

When he leaves, I turn to Nichole who has a huge smile on her face. "Did you do this?"

"Nope, I have no idea what it is, but based on the fact that your boy saw you in the stands, I'm sure he acted quickly to make something happen."

Confused, I peel open the envelope and find a Bobbies-themed blue and red lanyard attached to a VIP pass as well as a note. I crack open the card and read it out loud. "Miss Moore, please accept this VIP pass to locker room level after the game. Mr. Bisley will be waiting for you. Have any stadium worker direct you. Enjoy the game."

"Oooo, I knew he was good. But this is really freaking good." Nichole wraps her arm around my shoulder and squeezes me tight.

"Miss Moore?" the man says again. "I forgot to hand this to you as well." He holds out a Bobbies jersey, which Nichole takes for me and thanks him.

When she holds the jersey up, I immediately see Bisley across the back with the number twenty-two under it.

"Well, slap my ass. I think I went for the wrong brother." She takes the envelope from me and then hands over the jersey. "Put it on."

"What? Seriously?"

"Yes. Why wouldn't you?"

"I don't know, this all seems so—"

"Scary?" she asks.

"Yes, scary."

"Well, then, time to act like an adult and get over those fears." She helps me put on the jersey and then fluffs my hair over my shoulders right as the crowd stands and erupts in cheers.

Not knowing what the hell is going on, Nichole and I do the same. And then the Bobbies jog off the field.

"Wait, what's going on?" I ask.

"I think they got three outs," Nichole says.

I continue to clap as Ryot jogs toward the dugout, and when he reaches the top of the steps, he's only a few feet away from me. Under the brim of his hat, I catch those laser-sharp eyes as he says, "Looking fine, babe." And then he ducks into the dugout, disappearing out of sight.

"Oh fuck, someone needs to hose me down," Nichole says, waving her hand in front of her face.

Yeah . . . I think I need someone to hose me down as well.

<hr />

MYLA: *I'm freaking out. Players are starting to leave the hole thing.*

**Nichole:** *It's called a locker room, and be cool, okay?*

**Myla:** *I don't know what to say to him.*

**Nichole:** *We went over this. Just don't say anything at all. Enjoy the moment, and when he asks you on a date, SAY YES!*

**Myla:** *Are you sure this is the right move? Am I really ready for this?*

**Nichole:** *If his ass in those baseball pants didn't convince you, then I'm at a loss.*

**Myla:** *I stared at it anytime I had a chance.*

**Nichole:** *Shamelessly, I did too.*

"Hey." I hear his deep, sexy voice. When I look up from my phone, there he is, fresh from a shower, wearing a pair of dark jeans and a tight-fitted navy-blue T-shirt.

I brush my hair behind my ear, stick my phone in my purse, and on a deep breath, say, "Hey."

He holds his hand out to me and asks, "You coming with me?"

I glance at his large hand and then back up at him. This is it. There is no turning back. If I take his hand, that means I'm trying this, and I can't pull back from him again. If I don't take it, I'm making a statement that I don't think after everything I've been through with this man that I *can* make.

On a hope and a prayer that I can be normal for this man, I reach out and take his hand, which of course creates a breathtaking smile on his face.

"How have you been?" he asks as we walk down a long hallway.

"Um, pretty good. You? I mean that game, wow."

"Do you even know if we won?"

I chuckle, and the tension building in my chest eases. "I gathered that you won at the end from the cheering fans. Up until then it was a real nail-biter."

"We won ten to one."

"See, truly won by the skin of your teeth."

He chuckles. "Wow, I really need to spend some time educating you on my sport." He lifts our hand connection and then spins me around. "But damn, girl, you sure look good in my jersey."

Feeling even lighter, I tug on the fabric and say, "Oh, this old thing? I found it in a dumpster outside the stadium. Some girl tossed it, claiming her wild ways weren't working on Bisley. I thought I'd give it a try. Seems like it works just fine."

"It wasn't the jersey; it was the girl." He smirks and then pushes open the door to a gated-off parking lot. He guides me to a black SUV and unlocks it before pulling the passenger side door open. He helps me in because, if anything, the man is a gentleman. He then braces his hand on the door opening and dips his head so I can see him. "Do you want me to take you home?"

I swallow and realize this is him asking what's next. We're here at a crossroads again. Am I going to follow, or am I going to retreat?

I know my answer.

I shake my head. "No, I don't want to go home yet."

185

The smile that passes over his lips is so sexy that I might just croak right here, on his passenger side seat.

"Good answer." He brushes a strand of hair behind my ear and then asks, "Why did you come to the game, Myla?"

I turn toward him so my knees knock against his thighs. I reach out and tug on the hem of his shirt as I say, "Nichole got tickets from work, and I've been so desperate to see you that I thought, maybe even from far away, I could get my fill. I had no idea the tickets were right behind the dugout, and I had no idea that you would see me."

"If you were desperate to see me, why didn't you message me?"

"I was embarrassed," I admit. "I like you, but I don't want to hurt you. I'm not experienced when it comes to healthy relationships. And I know you said you would help me carry my baggage, but you shouldn't have to be weighed down by all of that."

"Good thing I lift weights then, huh?" He winks.

"I'm being serious, Ryot."

"And so am I. How about this? We take this one step at a time, okay? No pressure, no titles, just having fun and seeing where it takes us."

"That sounds doable."

"But . . ." he says, now resting his forehead on his arm as he stares down at me. "I ask two things from you."

"Okay, what are they?"

He holds up one finger and says, "Always be honest with me. No matter what you're feeling, you need to be honest if this is working for you or not. And two." He holds up a second finger. "We don't need a title, but I would like to be exclusive with you. I have no intention of going out with anyone else, and I would hope that you would feel the same way."

"I can barely gather myself to go out with you, let alone someone else, so no need to worry about that. And I've been honest with you thus far, so I can't see that changing."

"Good," he says. "So want to go get dessert with me?"

"What do you have in mind?"

All he does is wiggle his eyebrows and then shuts the door. I guess it's going to be a surprise.

▭

"YOU WERE RIGHT. Sharing a sundae was the right thing to do," I say as Ryot pulls out the sundae we ordered to go. In a take-out box big enough for an entrée, I'm not even sure we'll be able to finish it. After we grabbed the ice cream, Ryot took me to a public beach, pulled a blanket out of his trunk, and walked me to a spot where we have now commandeered a space for ourselves on the barely lit beach, with only a few lampposts providing light.

"They always have big servings there, and I swear they make it even bigger because they're fans."

"Ooo, do you go to many places that like the Bobbies?"

"Not on purpose. I go to places I like. Some of them boo me when I walk in because they're Rebels fans, but I take it as a compliment more than anything."

"I'm assuming you don't care for the attention from the way you seem so levelheaded," I say as he hands me a spoon and sets the ice cream between us.

I turn toward him, cross-legged, as he stretches out and uses his arm closest to me to prop himself up. "I don't seek it out, nor do I shy away from it. I want to ensure the fans know I appreciate them, so I wave if someone calls my name. If someone stops me, I take a selfie. If someone asks for an autograph, I sign it. And sure, I might have gotten to where I am because of hard work, but the fans play a big role in my confidence, so I owe them."

"Wow, you really are levelheaded. Any show boaters on your team?"

"Penn Cutler. He's a pitcher. I figured you wouldn't know that."

"Yeah, I barely know that you play third base."

He chuckles. "Well, Penn is big on showboating, and the fans eat him up for it. Helps that he's really fucking good."

"Did he pitch today?" I take another bite of this luscious butterscotch sundae and nearly melt from how good it is. I'm going to have to tell Nichole about this place.

"No, he pitched yesterday."

"Oh, does that mean he can't pitch today?"

He chuckles again and sighs. "Man, I'm going to have to give you a whole course on baseball, aren't I?"

"When I said I knew nothing, I meant it. I think today was the first time I sat through a whole game and paid attention. I followed the crowd. One guy behind me shouted fuck at one point, and I proceeded to shout fuck as well, thinking I was cheering with the Bobbies. Apparently, that was not the case. One of his players on the other team struck out."

"You rooting against us, Myla?" He mischievously grins.

"Not on purpose. I made up for it after when you scored. I did an old whoop whoop." I circle my fist in the air, causing him to laugh.

"A whoop whoop makes up for anything."

"That's what I thought."

⸻

"SO WHAT HAVE you been doing these last few weeks with me not bothering you?" he asks.

"Just working, saving my tips, and planning what I want to do with my life."

"Any thoughts?" he asks.

"Yeah, I have some," I say shyly.

We barely, and I mean barely, finished the ice cream. Ryot took care of the garbage, and then when I thought we were going to leave, he lay back on the blanket. He now has one hand propping up his head as he talks, distracting me with how his bicep pops against his shirtsleeve.

"Care to share?"

"Promise not to make fun of me?"

His brow furrows. "Why would I make fun of you?"

"Because I should have an idea at this point, and I don't. That's embarrassing."

"Says who? Pretty sure there isn't anything that says people need to have their life figured out by a certain age. My grandma Louise is the perfect example of that. She was an elementary school teacher for thirty years and then one day said she was going to start fishing lobster. And she did."

"What?" I laugh. "Isn't that arduous work?"

"She wouldn't bring in many, it was more of an after-retirement hobby, but she didn't know anything about lobster cages. She decided to learn, went out on her little boat, and she spent her days fishing for lobsters. To this day, I will always say she caught the best of the best, and boy, did she know how to cook them. She made this special butter sauce that melted in your mouth."

"I've never had lobster."

His eyes shoot open. "Wait, seriously?"

"Yeah. My mom never really thought I was special enough to spend money on lobster, and as an adult, I guess I've always been afraid to try it."

"Well, we're going to have to change that now, aren't we?"

"Any good seafood places around here?"

He shakes his head. "No, I'll have to take you to Maine. It's the only place to get lobster. I refuse to eat any other kind."

"Lobster snob, are we?"

"Yes."

"At least you're honest about it. So, Maine lobster, huh? What do you miss most about living there?"

"As you know, I grew up in a small town where everyone knew everyone and everything happening in each other's lives. It sometimes felt invasive, but when push came to shove, the town was there for you if you needed something. Also, Bright Harbor and Port Snow are magical during the holiday season. Twinkle lights as far as the eye can see, Christmas music playing all of the time, and little kiosks resurrected on each corner with homemade hot chocolate and cookies. Nothing beats it."

"I would love to see it one day."

"Where have you lived?"

"Everywhere," I say with a sigh. "Ohio, Arizona, Colorado, Nebraska, New Mexico, and here."

"Wow, that is everywhere. Which was your favorite?"

I think about that through the muddiness of my childhood. "Depends, Colorado was the prettiest, but I have the best memories when we were in New Mexico. That was before everything happened."

"Can I ask what you mean by everything?" he asks.

Nichole is really the only one that knows about my past. I haven't felt comfortable with anyone else to talk about this, but I don't know if it's the ice cream, the night, or probably the man stretched out in front of me, but I feel like I can trust him.

"My parents were both in the Air Force, I think I mentioned that. My dad was an engineer, and my mom was a therapist. Dad's role was seen as more important than Mom's, so my mom always had to follow him around. We moved from base to base because of him, and she had to put up with some lousy facilities because of it. She became bitter. He was gone a lot, promoted more, and my mom never got to prove herself the way she wanted to. She became bitter and took it out on me."

He sits up now, his brows turned down. "I know you've

mentioned this before, but what precisely do you mean that she took it out on you?"

"Started when I was eight," I say, my voice slightly shaking. "I forgot to do the dishes before I left for a friend's house. When I got home, my mom shoved my face into a sink of dirty dishwater. I was so shocked, I didn't know what to do. I swear, she almost drowned me. When she finally let me up for air, she told me not to do it again. I was so confused. I had no idea where the behavior came from. I mean, I had been spanked, and my mom had slapped me once, but that . . . that was extreme. And it only grew from that moment on. She saw me as weak and unsure, and she took advantage of it. The only time she wouldn't touch me was when Dad was around. But her jealousy of the relationship I had with Dad made the abuse worse. It wasn't until I was fifteen that I fought back and stood up for myself. By that time, we were in Arizona. I had three years left at home, I'd met Nichole, and I was planning my escape. But she knew how to track my moods, and when I was low, she took advantage of it. She knew when I felt worthless, and she made sure to cultivate that feeling."

"Holy shit, Myla." He takes my hand in his. "I know it's weird to ask, but are you okay?"

I shrug. "I've grown from it. I don't try to waste my time thinking about it because when I do, I turn into someone I don't like, someone who shelters herself from the world."

"I can understand that. Is that why you've sheltered yourself from me?"

I nod. "Yeah. It's hard for me to trust. It's hard for me to consider myself worthy enough. So yeah, that's been a main part of the holdup when it comes to us."

He brings my knuckles up to his mouth and lightly kisses them. "I'm so sorry you had to go through that. Did you ever tell your dad?" His compassion wraps around me, comforting me, showing me that maybe I am worthy.

I shake my head. "No, I was too scared what would

happen to me if I did tell my dad. So I just lied for her when he saw a bruise or a cut. You would think that would appease her, but it didn't. I want to believe my dad knew in a way because I saw their relationship deteriorate. My mom cheated on my dad, my dad cheated on my mom—at least that's what I heard during one fight. It was so toxic that I'm really glad I'm out of their house and don't have to deal with them anymore."

"Do you talk to them now?"

"Not my mom. I'll text my dad and call him on his birthday, but that's about it."

"Do you think you'll ever tell him?"

"Maybe. Not sure what the point would be at this time. And honestly, even if he didn't know and found out today, what would it change?"

"To help you heal," Ryot says in such a kind and understanding voice that it nearly makes me cry. And I never cry. I learned very quickly that crying was a weak thing to do. *Pathetic, groveling mouse. That's all you are. Pathetic. You'll never amount to anything. Especially as a crybaby.*

I blow out a heavy breath and glance toward Lake Michigan and the dark waves lapping at the beach. I haven't heard her voice saying those things for a while now. That's what even thinking about her does to me. "I shouldn't be on the verge of tears on our first date. Maybe we change the subject."

"You're considering this a date?" he asks, his voice playful, and I know he's trying to pull me out of the sadness that just eclipsed this conversation.

"Well, maybe half a date. There wasn't a full meal involved."

"Guess I need to impress you even more next time."

I reach out and press my hand to his chest. "You've already impressed me more than anyone ever has. No need to pull out all the stops."

"Yeah, well, with me, you get the full treatment, Myla."

⸺

"WHAT ARE YOU DOING?" I ask as Ryot reaches for his car door handle.

"Uh, going to walk you to your townhome."

I shake my head. "No, that's not necessary. We can just say bye here."

In a teasing tone, he asks, "You ashamed of me?"

"No, I just don't want to make a big thing of it."

He turns toward me, one arm draped over his steering wheel as he asks, "But how the hell am I supposed to romance you if I don't walk you to your door?"

"No need to romance me. You already have me hooked. It was infuriating trying to forget about you these past few weeks."

"Should I apologize for being unforgettable?"

I fold my arms and nod. "Yeah, you should. Ridiculous actually. A girl is trying to move on, and there you are, posting stupid batting videos, getting me all distracted."

"Ha!" He points his finger at me. "I knew you saw them."

I roll my eyes dramatically. "Of course I saw them. And I knew you posted those on purpose, just to get under my skin."

"Looks like it worked." His smile is so wide, so handsome, that it makes me want to kiss it right off him.

"It wasn't the video that made me miss you."

"No?" he asks, a question on his brow.

"No, it was not talking to you. It felt like when you left Phoenix, it was sort of like . . . *well, it was nice knowing that guy.* But when I came out here, and you were close, not talking to you about all the stupid shit you were posting or just joking around was sad. It made me feel even worse than I did before."

"Well"—he entwines our fingers—"no need to feel sad. You've got me now."

"Which means one thing," I say.

"What's that?"

"I'm going to have to learn baseball."

"I'll teach you. Trust me, you won't have to do it on your own."

I grin because he knows how to use my hot-button words. *Don't have to do it on my own.* I've had to do everything on my own for so long that I'm tired, and I'm ready to share the burden.

I glance at the time in the car. "It's getting late, I should go."

"Wait, before you leave." He pulls out his phone and hands it to me. "Give me your number. I like sending you DMs, but I'd rather be able to text and call you."

"Oh, yeah, that might be helpful." I take his phone and then lift my brow at him. "Are you really that guy who doesn't have a case for their phone?"

"These hands don't drop anything," he says, showing off his very large hands.

"Yeah, but you're now seeing me, and guess what, I'm a perpetual dropper."

"You can't be that bad."

I take out my cracked and nearly broken phone and show it to him. "This is a few months old."

His eyes widen before he scratches the side of his neck. "Uh . . . why don't I just enter your phone number in?"

I laugh and tap away on his phone, sending a text to myself. When I hand it back to him, I say, "I'll get you a pretty case for your phone."

"Why do I feel like it's going to be a picture of your face?"

"Because you're starting to understand me on a deeper level." I set my hands on my lap and say, "Okay, well, thanks for tonight. I had a lot of fun."

"Me too. I'm glad you came to the game. You made my fucking night."

All the joking diminishes as nerves bubble up inside me. I know what will happen next.

Isn't it obvious? This is the momentary pause before the big old moment. The moment everyone wonders about on a first date.

The kiss.

I have yet to do so, and a small part of me is worried if he will be a good kisser. A bigger part of me is worried that he will be the best first kiss of my life, and I know that once his lips press against mine, there will be no going back. Hands down, he will blow me away, and I will be forever attached to him. With one kiss, I am one hundred percent positive my life will change because he's so different than anyone I've ever met. He's patient and listens. He's funny, not to mention incredibly handsome. But the best part about him is he's not willing to give up on me. Despite the many times I've walked away, he hasn't given up. The only other person in my life who has done that is Nichole, which tells me he's a world above any man I've ever dated.

"You're nervous," he says, not as a question, more as an observation.

"Maybe." I roll my teeth over the corner of my lip.

"Why? It's just me."

"I know, that's the whole point. It's you, Ryot. And that terrifies me because I feel so attached to you already."

"Afraid I'm going to be a bad kisser?" he charmingly asks.

I shake my head. "No, I'm worried you're going to be the best kisser, and there will be no turning back for me."

He smirks and says, "Only one way to find out." He leans over the console and slips his hand to the back of my neck. He doesn't pull me close to him but rather anchors himself and waits for me to make the next move.

Eyes intent on me, he wets his lips and smiles. "Get over here, Myla."

The spark in his eye and the lightness in his voice ease the tension and help me lean forward. Our noses connect, our lips millimeters away as his fingers dig into my skin. My hand slides up his stony chest, to the side of his neck, and then up to his cheek as our eyes connect.

I make the smallest inhale of air right before he says, "Kiss me."

His voice sends a thrill of excitement up my spine, and like magnets drawn together, our mouths connect, collide, and mold. Sparks fly around me, shooting off like rockets ascending into the deep night sky, telling me exactly what I feared but also wanted—life will never be the same. Now that I've tasted him . . . it will never be the same.

He presses closer, his mouth open, controlling the kiss as I mirror his motions. I'm so unsure of myself, so overwhelmed, so entranced, that I have no other option but to follow him at this moment. And with every empty breath I take, I feel him grow closer and closer, giving me the air that I need to fill my lungs.

He twists his fingers in my hair, I dig my fingers into his neck.

His tongue swipes against my lower lip, I melt into his demands.

His teeth graze over my mouth, tugging, I let out the lightest moan.

"Fuck," he says, putting just an inch of space between us. "Myla, you can't moan like that."

"You made me," I answer right before he presses his lips to mine again.

His tongue swirls around mine, enticing me to want so much more.

I want his shirt off.

I want to explore his chest.

I want to see what this man is made of and then kiss every inch of him.

"You're ruining me," I say, my voice catching in my throat.

He pulls away again, his breathing heavy as a lazy smirk crosses over his lips. "Good, then I did my job tonight." He gives me one more chaste kiss, then faces his steering wheel and grips it tightly. "Now get out of here before I regret taking more before you're ready."

Trust me, I'm freaking ready.

More ready than I'm sure he even knows.

But I want this to be successful. I've never had a successful relationship, not one where I can look back and say that even though it didn't work out, it was a solid relationship. So I'm going to let him take the lead. I'm going to let him be in the driver's seat and relinquish control, something that's very hard for me to do.

"Okay." I open the door and move to get out, but not before he reaches across the console again, grabs me, and pulls me in for another soul-searing kiss.

Yup, I'll let him take all the control he wants if it's going to make me feel like this—so light—like there isn't a worry in my world. And even though I know that's not the case, if I spend more time with this man, I feel he will protect me from my biggest enemy. Myself.

# Chapter Thirteen

RYOT

*Present day* . . .

Have you ever felt like you were swirling around in a black hole with no way to get out? Where no matter how hard you attempt to think of a solution, there's nothing you can do? You're just floating further and further away?

That's how I've felt every goddamn second since JP and Huxley came over.

It wasn't planned. I was just as shocked as she was when they came over, and I was in desperation mode. I don't know what it is about those two men—because they're the nicest, most business-savvy but understanding men I've ever met— but I don't want to let them down. And I don't want them to see that I'm failing—failing at my marriage—especially since they take their relationships so seriously.

I'm still stunned that even though Myla's acted so ice cold since she asked for a divorce, she sat with us at dinner. And it was great until she started talking about the move.

The tension between us rose like an exploding volcano, and the boys picked up on it. They asked me if everything was okay. I just told them it's been a bit of an adjustment, but nothing to worry about.

And it all tumbled from there.

My frustrations, her frustrations.

Seeing through her lies about loving me, wanting me.

Tasting her.

Her watching. It's all so fucking confusing that I have no idea what I'm doing anymore, and I'm spiraling out of control.

Not to mention, since that night it's been a nightmare living with her.

Here's the thing with Myla you need to know—she doesn't handle her emotions well. She doesn't like to feel out of control or exposed in any way because it reminds her of her childhood. She keeps her guard up at all times.

The other night, when I was between her legs, she won't admit it, but she let down her guard, especially when she followed me to my room. And because she did that, now she's put up a fortress around her while shooting off bombs every chance she gets.

Meaning . . . she's trying to drive me fucking nuts.

She knows how to push my buttons, and she's doing exactly that. How, you ask? Simple, it's little, inconsequential things that in the grand scheme of life don't seem like a big deal, but when you know someone is doing it on purpose, it builds.

It mounts.

And boy, oh boy, am I at my fucking breaking point.

For instance, she keeps tilting the hung pictures around the house so they're crooked. Every time I pass one, something's off, and sure, I could walk away and not care . . . but fuck, I am not that man. I pull out the level and adjust the picture until it's perfectly back in place. It's to the point now that I carry my mini level in my back pocket while I walk around the house.

And laundry, if I don't take mine out of the washer right away and put it in the dryer, she pulls it out, sets the wet clothes on top of the dryer, and starts her own load. She doesn't grant me the courtesy of slipping my clothes into the dryer for me, so I end up having to wash my clothes again so they don't smell moldy. Infuriating—and yes, I know this is my fault. I've now set a timer on my phone, and when it goes off, I sprint up to the washer to make sure I don't waste any time putting my clothes in the dryer.

Not to mention the little things like walking around in her bikini, lying topless by the pool, or even parading around in a loose-fitting robe that does nothing to hide her sexy curves.

Don't even get me started about the batteries in my TV remote. Or how she is constantly moving my things around so they're out of place. Like my protein powder or my vitamins, or how she seems to only swim when I'm outside watching a game and blasts her music so loud I can't hear the announcers say a goddamn thing.

But that's fine because I'm the one who fucked up, right?

I deserve it all . . . right?

At least that's what I keep trying to tell myself so I don't fucking explode.

I slip my tie from around my neck and toss it on my bed. Banner picked me up and dropped me off today because I haven't bothered with transportation yet—you know, because she has my goddamn car. And what a fucking day. I woke up with a headache, and it's only gotten worse throughout the day as I sifted through mindless meetings, exciting, but boring-as-shit quarterly projections, which I know are required, and mind-numbing interviews of prospective employees. Apparently, I did a shit job of hiding my annoyance today because I got a lecture from Banner all the way back home about not showing my annoyance around the new employees. Because yeah, life might suck for me right now, but we're still on the cusp of a new venture, and I shouldn't be dragging it down with my personal life. He was right. Then he proceeded to tell me he's been working on something special that, if it goes through, will skyrocket The Jock Report to the next level. But because he didn't want to jinx it or get my hopes up, he refused to talk about it and offered me zero details.

None.

So he just slipped me right back into a bad mood.

Needless to say, I'm irritated and exhausted, and all I want to do is eat the steak and potatoes I picked up on the way home, drink a beer, and enjoy the Bobbies game. Harris is pitching tonight, and he's been on fire lately.

I don't want to deal with The Jock Report.

How I fucked up with Myla.

I quickly change into a pair of shorts and then pull out my phone and check my email once more. I was expecting an email from JP about a meeting with a merchandise vendor. My phone dings with incoming emails, and my inbox floods with over twenty.

The pounding of my head increases, becoming a constant throb at the forefront of my brain.

Power through. I search for an email from JP, and when I see it at the top, I open it. He hands me over an email for a guy he knows and tells me to contact him and tell him JP sent me over. Thankful that I have the Cane brothers to work with, I shoot an email over to James, the merchandise guy, with our general needs and my availability for a meeting. On a deep breath, I slip my phone into my pocket. Done for the day. How many times have I thought that only to be sidetracked by another call or several other emails? *The truth behind running your own company.*

Okay, beer, steak, and potatoes. My mouth waters at the thought of taking down one of my favorite steaks in Chicago, so I head downstairs and straight into the kitchen, where I find Myla standing with her back toward me in a thong bikini.

Fuck . . . me.

My headache has now turned into a full-on raging migraine.

Her bubbly ass is on full display, tan and perky. Her hair is down in waves, cascading over her shoulders, covering her bare back. Before she asked for a divorce, I would have slipped up behind her, tugged on the strings of her bikini bottoms, and pushed her over the counter so I could fuck her just the way we both like it. But now, I just have to deal with the fact that my wife with the finest fucking body I've ever seen is untouchable.

Keeping my eyes straight ahead, I walk toward where I left my take-out box only to stop mid-stride as Myla turns toward me, fork and knife in hand, half of my steak already gone.

My juicy, delicious, made-just-for-me steak with roasted seasoned potatoes and a side of horseradish sauce is being masticated by the one and only Myla Bisley.

"What . . ." I pinch the bridge of my nose. "What the hell are you doing?"

*Control your temper, man.*

Her eyes blink in confusion. "Eating the steak you brought me."

"Brought . . . brought you?" I ask. "What makes you think I brought that home for you?"

Her confusion morphs into defense as she straightens her shoulders. "Well, you left it on the counter and then retreated to your room. I just assumed you were done with it."

"Because I wanted to change out of my suit," I say, my voice rising.

"Oh, well, you should have put it in the fridge or something rather than leaving it in a neutral zone. I got you those blue Post-its for a reason."

"I didn't think I had to use one," I nearly shout.

She rears back and points her fork at her chest. "Are you really shouting at me right now? It was an innocent mistake." She shoves the to-go box toward me. "Here, eat it."

I shove it back at her. "I don't fucking want it now."

"From the drool in the corner of your mouth, I'm going to say you're a goddamn liar." She shoves the box back.

"I don't want this." I push it harder.

"Well, I don't want it now either," she says, shoving it harder than me.

"Ohhh, no, you're going to fucking finish what you started. Eat it, eat every last bit." I toss it at her now, the potatoes—the ones that are left—jiggle in the nearly empty to-go box.

"And watch you have the satisfaction of attempting to make me feel guilty? No way." She pushes the box toward me, but I stop her, gripping the other side.

Together, we push.

Our eyes simmer with rage, and our mouths curve in discontent.

Tempers rise.

Nostrils flare.

Necks become blotchy.

And then . . . the container puckers.

Bends.

It buckles . . . and before we can stop the inevitable, it pops up and out of our hands from the pressure of our pushing.

And in slow motion, the container flies into the air, steak and potatoes parachuting into the tension-thick air and falling to the floor with a loud, resonating splat.

"Wow, look what you did," she says, motioning to the food on the floor. "That was a perfectly good steak."

"I wouldn't know. I didn't get to have a bite," I snap through clenched teeth.

She holds the fork out to me. "Well, help yourself. Not sure the last time those floors were cleaned. Enjoy."

She turns and walks toward her bedroom, leaving me with the mess.

Head pounding, my stomach ripping with hunger, I pick up the steak, thinking that maybe it might be okay, but when I spot a long piece of hair sticking to it, I lose my appetite instantly. Fucking food waste only adds to the anger coursing through me.

I consider ordering something, but it's already late, so I go into the pantry where I grab a protein bar, a bag of Dot's pretzels, a banana with a blue Post-it note on it, and a beer. It's not steak and potatoes, but I try not to focus on that.

Arms full of food, I walk out to the patio, set everything down, and reach for my TV remote, only to realize it's not working.

"I'm going to fucking scream," I mutter as I rip the back case off and see that there are no batteries in it. "Myla!" I yell as I charge into the house.

Yup, I've lost all sense of decorum.

I'm trying to figure out what to do with her, how to approach her, how to go about fixing all that's been broken to avoid the divorce—which at this point, I might just hand her because I don't think there's any way I can override this—that I'm losing my goddamn mind.

I'm frustrated.

I'm irritated.

I'm horny as shit from how she prances around this house in barely any clothing. My hand is doing nothing to fix *that* problem.

And I'm just about at my breaking point.

"Myla," I yell again.

"What?" She pops out of her bedroom, topless, wearing only her bikini bottoms and holding . . .

Fucking.

Hell.

"What are you doing?" I ask.

She glances at the pink vibrator in her hand and then back at me. "What does it look like I'm doing?"

My hands fist at my side, my palm nearly imploding the remote in my hand.

"You . . . you can't walk around here topless," I say. It's the only thing I can think to say because I don't even know how to address the elephant in the room—that she's masturbating.

Not that I haven't done it way too fucking much lately, but she's never caught me in the act.

"You walk around here topless," she says, folding her arms and propping up her tits to the point that I can't stop staring at them.

"That's"—I lick my lips—"different."

"Uh, Ryot, my eyes are up here."

*I know.*

*I don't want to look at your eyes.*

Slowly, I drag my gaze away from her tits only to find her lips pursed, ready to fight. "Is that what you wanted to talk to me about? Being topless? Because I wasn't topless until I went back to my room to come."

Why am I here?

Why am I yelling?

And then it clicks. The batteries.

Very stiffly, I hold up my remote and say, "Stop taking the fucking batteries out of my remote."

"Who says I'm taking them?" She props one hand on her hip.

"Uh, me. Only two of us are in this house, and I wouldn't take them to drive myself crazy."

"Really, because it seems you're tilting the pictures crooked on purpose."

My jaw clenches tight.

My will is slipping.

She's fucking good at pushing buttons. I will give her that.

Really fucking good.

"But yeah, I took the batteries this time."

This time—insert eye roll.

"Why?" I ask. "Just to get on my goddamn nerves?"

"I have better things to do with my life than mess around with you, Ryot. Do you really think I'm going to spend the last three days together in this house before the wedding driving you crazy?"

"Yes," I shout. "I do. I think you're trying to drive me so fucking crazy that I want to be done with you after the wedding."

"I don't have enough time or energy to focus on petty things." The lies. I know why she's doing it. She's keeping me at an arm's length by pissing me off, and she's doing a hell of a job at it.

"Then why the fuck are you taking my batteries?" I hold the remote up in the air, shaking it as if that will help this conversation in any way.

"Because I needed them to masturbate, Ryot, if you need to know. I've been burning up batteries a lot lately. So excuse me for delighting in a round of orgasms. Not all of us can just stroke ourselves in the shower."

Nostrils flared.

Jaw so tight I think I might break a tooth.

And hands ready to rip open a fucking wall, I don't respond.

There is nothing to respond to.

So I stomp up to my room where I have a Costco-sized pack of batteries. I refill the remote. Walking back down the stairs, I hear the distant moaning of Myla combined with the buzzing sound of her vibrator.

Yup, she's really trying to break me.

And it's working.

I walk out on the patio, shut the door so I don't have to hear her when she comes, and turn on the TV to the Bobbies game. It's so late that I catch the eighth inning. The score is two to zero, the Bobbies are winning, and . . . holy fuck, Harris is still pitching.

I quickly pull out my phone and search the Bobbies game in my browser to look at the stats. Everything from a few minutes ago is quickly washed away as I glue myself to the television. Harris is . . . *gulp* he's pitching one hell of a game. Let's keep it at that.

I pop open my pretzels, too concerned with the game to even consider eating my protein bar, and I start munching, leaning forward on the couch.

History in the making.

Once the Bobbies get out of the inning untouched and head into the bottom of the eighth, I take a sip of my beer, but that's all I do. I don't move. I barely breathe because anything I say or do at this moment could jinx Harris. And I will be damned if I'm the one who . . . well, I will be damned, not going to say any more than that.

As the Bobbies step up to the plate, Myla opens the sliding glass door and walks outside with a towel.

"What the hell are you doing?" I ask her.

"Going for a swim in the heated pool," she answers, seeming almost bewildered.

"You can't be here," I say. "I need you to leave."

"What do you mean I can't be here. This is a neutral zone, Ryot."

"It's not that," I say, my eyes still on the TV. "It's the game, okay? It's important. Just go back to your room. It's almost over."

"It's really nice out and I want to take a dip in the pool. I'm not going to go back in the house. I need some fresh air."

"Myla, please, just go back into the house, and I'll call you out when it's done."

"What's the big deal? Is the pitcher throwing a perfect game or something?"

All the innards in my body seize and shrivel into dust as she mutters the words you should never fucking mutter. Throat dry, lips parched, unable to form the right words, I very slowly swivel my head to look at her.

And from my expression, she must understand what she just said. "Oh, that's the big deal? He's throwing a perfect game?"

"Stop," I squeak out. "Don't . . . don't say that."

"Say what? Perfect game?" She seems clueless, but is she really?

It's like a bullet to the chest, every time, whittling me down until nothing's left of me.

"Yes," I gulp.

"For God's sake, Ryot, you're so superstitious." She tucks her towel under her arm. "Me saying *perfect game* is not going to determine the results. He's either going to pitch a good game, or he's going to blow it in the end. But saying perfect game won't change that. Watch. Perfect game, perfect game, perfect game, he's throwing a perfect game . . . see, everything is fine."

Everything is *not* the same.

I have nothing to say.

I can't move.

And when she goes to the pool where she climbs in and splashes around, playing her music, all I can hear her say over and over again is "perfect game."

It's sounding off in my head as the Bobbies take the field in the top of the ninth.

It's in my head when Harris has two outs and two strikes on the last batter.

And it's in my head as Harris lets a home run go, ruining the entire fucking game.

⌐⊐

DO you know something Myla absolutely hates? Probably more than me at the moment?

Sports talk shows.

Any kind. On TV, the radio, and podcasts. She doesn't understand why people pick apart every little piece of a game. I tried explaining that it's not picking it apart, but that it's constructive analysis that helps further the listener's knowledge.

Yeah, she despises them.

I found this out early on in our relationship and invested in a good pair of headphones so she didn't have to listen to my multitude of podcasts that break down every single game to the nitty-gritty.

Well, guess who lost their headphones—on purpose?

This guy.

And guess who's blasting his favorite podcast while cooking his very own steak and potatoes? Me. I am.

Sure, this steak that I hand-picked from Whole Foods might not be as tender and juicy as the one from last night. And perhaps these purple fingerling potatoes that I thought were cute in the produce section won't have the same seasoning as the ones from last night, but they're better than a protein bar, pretzels, and a banana, and they will taste a lot like redemption.

"Oh my God!" Myla yells as she walks into the kitchen. "Can you turn the yammering down?"

"What's that?" I ask, holding up my spatula to my ear— making homemade pesto sauce while my potatoes crisp in the air fryer and my steak reverse sears in the oven. "I can't hear you."

"Because your stupid sports show is too loud," she shouts and then picks up my phone and puts it on pause. "Jesus, Ryot. Where are your headphones?"

"Misplaced them." I smile at her.

She folds her arms at her chest. "Did you, now?"

"Yeah, really upsetting. Anyway, I figured since you listen to your music on blast, I could do the same."

"Uh-huh, and what's that you're making?"

"Why does it matter? I'm not sharing with you."

"Why would I want to share with you when it smells like you're burning whatever you're making?"

"What? No, I'm not."

"Ryot, I could smell the burn from my bedroom. I had to open the windows."

"Jesus, you're dramatic," I say as I start to get slightly nervous that I am burning something.

I thought that was maybe the char for the reverse sear, or . . . am I doing a sear and cook? I don't fucking know at this point. I don't cook often anymore, so I've lost my touch.

"And there is no way that's pesto."

"Yes, it is," I defend.

"And your potatoes are overdone. They're probably shriveled up."

"What? You can't even see them." I move over to the air fryer and open the tray, where I find shriveled-up purple fingerling potatoes.

Son of a bitch.

But as if I'm going to give her the benefit of seeing me make a mistake.

After yesterday and her perfect game stunt, I can't see anything but red whenever she's around. I've pushed my mistakes to the back of my mind. I've pushed the divorce even further back. I'm in *Hunger Games*-type survival mode. I should

210

be figuring out a way to win her back. I should be offering her some of my shriveled potatoes and playing nice, but she's broken me.

There are at least five crooked picture frames that I can see.

I had to add more batteries to my remote this morning.

When I needed the car for a quick, quick moment to run to the store for more toilet paper—which she has mounds of in her room—she denied me the car. I had to bicycle to the corner store and bicycle back with toilet paper tucked under my arm. Do you understand the sort of catcalls I got from that adventure?

They weren't pretty!

I'm just trying to get to the wedding, to a point when I can take a deep breath and bring my attention back to what is important—figuring out how to save my marriage. We'll be on neutral ground, she can't fuck with me too much, and I can really focus on what it is that she needs from me—if anything.

Until then, I'm a rabid dog, fending for his life out in the wild, teeth snarling, hair sticking up, slightly mangy hindquarters. It's survival of the fittest, and I will not be torn down.

"How are those potatoes?" she asks, her hip bumped up against the counter.

"Crispy and perfect," I answer. "Just the way I like them."

I set the air fryer bin on a trivet and then go to the oven. When I open it up, a plume of smoke erupts, instantly setting off the smoke alarm.

"Told you, you were burning something," she yells over the ear-piercing beep.

"It's not burnt," I yell back as I toss the cast-iron pan on the stove and open all the windows around the kitchen and living room. With a piece of junk mail from the counter, I wave at the smoke, attempting to get it out of the house.

"Try a baking pan," she says as she hands me one. "That junk mail will do nothing for you."

I glance at the baking pan and then back at her, and because I'm stubborn and think I can do everything on my own when I'm apparently lost without this woman, I say, "This coupon offering roofing services is working perfectly fine. Thank you."

It's not.

The fire alarm screeches, my steak looks like roadkill, and my pesto is a funky shade of brown. The only good thing about this entire meal will probably be the freshly washed plate that I washed by hand because the rest of the dishes were in the dishwasher, and it was my turn to buy detergent, and I forgot.

Once the smoke is cleared out and the smoke detectors get their lives in check, I move back to the kitchen and pitifully plate my meal. I'll be straight with you. It looks like trash. But dammit, I'm going to eat every bit of it out of spite.

I adjust my potatoes on the plate so they don't look as shriveled, I take a chainsaw to my steak and cut it into medallions to make it more appealing, and then I drape my sauce over the steak for presentation, attempting to show off how green it is against the black of the steak. But . . . it's the color of a swamp. Not sure where I went wrong there.

Beer in hand and false pride in my chest, I take my plate out to the patio, where Myla is sitting and reading a book, and I take a seat. I press play on my podcast but keep it at a reasonable volume and then poise my fork and knife at my meal.

From across the table, Myla sets her book down and then lowers her sunglasses. "Looks positively five star over there."

"It is. It's really fucking good, so be jealous."

"Oh, I am. *So jealous*," she says as she watches me take my first bite.

Dear God, what is that flavor that just blasted my tongue? Tastes like . . . like burnt hair.

Did I burn hair while cooking?

I don't recall.

Either way, keep your face happy and pleasant.

Make moaning sounds.

Let her know what she's missing out on.

"Mmm, fuck is this deli"—is that a bone I just chewed?—"Delicious," I finish after I swallow.

Just then, the doorbell rings, and she gets up to answer it. When she's back in the house, I quickly search around my food for any burnt hair or bones, and when I come up short, I just realize it's my shit cooking that's the problem. I've been so fucking out of touch with life that I've completely forgotten how to act like a normal human.

I've always appreciated everything Myla has done for our marriage, especially with my demanding schedule. When it was break time, I would be sure to help cook, to pick things up at the store, to do something just as simple as rub her feet at night, but fuck, when did that stop?

When did I stop caring?

When did I become so detached from everyday life that I can't even cook myself a goddamn delicious meal?

Myla approaches while I hunch over my plate like I'm devouring this homemade delight as I watch her deposit a to-go bag from my favorite steakhouse, the very same one I went to yesterday.

"What's that?" I ask, my eyes zeroing in on what she pulls out.

"I couldn't get my mind off the steak that fell on the floor yesterday, so I ordered myself another one with potatoes and a side of lobster. And a cheesecake for dessert."

Goddammit, the cheesecake, like velvet satisfaction for the mouth.

"Well, enjoy. Bet it won't taste as good as mine." It actually pains me to lie through my teeth.

"Yeah, keep thinking that. Maybe it will help you choke down the swill on your plate."

I hate to admit it, but this is swill.

She takes a seat, pulls out her dinner, and then wafts her hand over it while taking a deep breath. "Oh, they have outdone themselves. And look at this butter for the lobster? So dreamy. Lobster on the West Coast really is supreme, don't you think?"

My eyes narrow because she knows exactly what I think about lobster that is from anywhere but Maine.

"Oh God, just look at this meat? I can't remember the last time I had this much meat in my mouth."

Boy, is she ripe today!

"Excuse me if I moan, but I'm going to suck the juice right out of this meat and enjoy this meal."

I stare at her.

At her exquisite meal.

At the low cut of her tank top that she's wearing sans bra.

And before I can stop myself, I mutter, "You're a rotten wench."

A chuckle pops out of her mouth right before she stuffs it with lobster. "Oh yeah," she says around her mouthful of seafood. "This is easily the best lobster I've ever had in my life. Hands down. No questions asked."

Yup . . . a fucking wench.

"RYOT," Myla shouts from the living room.

A large smile spreads across my face as I know exactly what this is about.

Let me give you some backstory first.

Over the years I've known Myla, she's been passionate about collecting one thing and one thing only: vinyl records. One year for her birthday, I bought her a Crosley record player and her top favorite records she's been wanting for years. Like ELO, Dolly Parton, even the record for White

Christmas—she has eclectic taste. These are her prized possessions. The one thing she would pull out of the house if there was ever a fire. Her sworn children.

No one is allowed to touch them besides her.

She lines them up in rainbow order because she thinks they're prettier that way, and every Friday, she pours herself a glass of wine, puts on a record, and then lies across the couch and just listens. Sometimes she designs at the same time, just for fun.

Guess what night it is?

Yup, Friday.

And guess what I did?

I think we'll just go downstairs and find out.

I fly down the stairs and stroll into the living room, looking none the wiser. "You beckoned?"

Standing in front of her record cabinet, *Singing in the Rain* record in one hand and *Journey* in the other, her eyes blaze like laser beams right at me.

"What did you do?" she asks.

"I didn't do anything," I say, feigning innocence just like she did with my batteries. I'm not an idiot. I know she keeps taking them.

"Don't play with me, Ryot. These are all mixed up. There is not one single record in the right case."

I know. I woke up in the middle of the night to do it. Even though I was dead tired, the thought of redemption really kept me going.

"That's so weird. I wonder how that happened." I scratch the back of my neck.

"You did it. That's how it happened."

"I don't remember doing that," I say. "You know"—I point at her—"maybe the same person who keeps stealing my remote batteries did it."

"This is not funny, Ryot. They could be scratched. They could be hurt." Her face falls before she crumples to the ground and starts panicking while pulling out her records and trying to carefully match them up.

Hell, maybe I went too far.

It's not like the crooked pictures on the wall are my prized possession.

"Hey, do you, uh, do you want some help?"

Her eyes snap up to me. "You've done enough."

Yeah, she doesn't want me around.

"Okay, well, I'll be outside watching the Bobbies versus Rebels game if you want any help."

She doesn't say anything, just keeps carefully working to put everything back in place. I shouldn't feel bad after all the hell I've been through, so why doesn't this feel right?

This was supposed to be redemption for her eating that beautiful steak in front of me last night—while I chewed my charred meat like gum until it felt like I wouldn't choke while swallowing. But it doesn't give me the kind of euphoric feeling I was looking for. It makes me feel like a dick.

Sighing, I take a seat on the couch outside, pick up my remote, and flip the TV on . . .

But nothing happens.

Fucking batteries!!!

Well, guess who doesn't feel bad about the records anymore?

———

"ANYONE THROWING A PERFECT GAME?" Myla asks as she walks out onto the patio with a blanket in hand.

"No," I mutter as I sip from my beer.

"Shame. I wouldn't want to jinx anything."

I snap my head in her direction and say, "You know damn well you're the reason Harris didn't have a perfect game."

"Yes, Ryot," she says sarcastically. "It was because of me. The universe heard me utter those words and then rained down its cosmic thunder onto Harris. It has nothing to do with the fact that he wasn't mentally stable enough to throw one last pitch, and he choked."

"You know damn well Harris never misses on his cutter."

"I don't actually, although I probably should. You had your annoying sports cast thing on loud enough this morning."

"Aw, did I wake you up?" I sarcastically pout.

"You disturbed my orgasm. By the way, thanks for the batteries."

My nostrils flare as I stare at her. "I'm going to start hiding my remote."

"That's fine. Do whatever makes you happy."

She takes a seat on the couch and crosses her legs. "What the hell are you doing?" I ask.

"This is a neutral space. Therefore, I'm taking a seat."

"Yeah, well, this TV is not neutral. It's mine."

She tilts her head to the side and says, "Aw, how cute. Do you want a Post-it note for it to remind me?"

"No, I just want to remind you that you're not allowed to watch my TV."

"I don't plan on it. I've watched enough baseball in my lifetime. I don't need to watch more. I'm just going to lay out here and scroll through Tik Tok until my eyes are blurry." She unfolds her blanket, fluffs it into the air and, as it settles over her, the image becomes clearer and causes my entire body to tense up.

"Why the fuck do you have that?" I ask her as I sit tall.

She glances at her blanket and then back at me. "Saw it in the store today, and it looked comfy. Why, do you want to use it?"

"The fuck I do," I say as I stare down at the Rebels logo plastered all over the blanket. She knows how I feel about the Rebels. In Chicago, you're either a Bobbie for life or a Rebel at heart. I'm going to tell you right now, I'm a goddamn

Bobbie for life. "You know, as a former Bobbies player, that shit doesn't belong in this household."

"Well, then"—she snuggles into the blanket—"good thing this household is broken because this is comfy."

Steam flies out of my ears as I barely, and I mean . . . barely hold it together.

⸺

"ARE YOU PACKING?" I ask as I walk up to Myla's open bedroom door. She's sitting on the unmade bed, typing away on her computer.

When she glances up from focusing on the screen, she asks, "Does it look like I'm packing?"

"You realize we leave tomorrow for Napa, right?"

"I'm well aware of your pressing schedule, Ryot."

"We leave at seven, so unless you plan on waking up early, there isn't enough time to pack."

She huffs. "Can you stop yammering? I need to finish this."

"You need to pack, Myla. It's past eleven."

"I'm more than aware what time it is."

"You're just doing this to drive me crazy, like last night with the blanket, with the batteries, and with the goddamn pictures. You know I like to be on time and orderly, and the fact that you haven't packed is just another way to get under my skin."

"Not everything is about you, Ryot." She keeps typing.

"Bullshit. You always forget something, always, packing early is what—"

"Ryot, please just shut up so I can finish this."

"What could possibly be that important right now?"

Her eyes shoot up to mine as she leans her back on her headboard. "What could be so important? Um, how about a paper I've been working on for my design class that includes not only my design work of an office lobby but the explanation about why I chose what I chose. Oh, and it's worth half of my grade and due by midnight. So, yeah, this is a little more important than packing, which if you must know, my bag is in the closet ready to go besides toiletries, which I will stash away in the morning."

Oh.

Well, fuck, don't I feel stupid.

Really stupid.

"Myla, I'm . . . I'm sorry."

"Just leave, Ryot."

But I don't, because I don't know anything about this class or this paper, or the design that she made for a lobby and that . . . that stings. I feel like I know this woman inside and out. I know why she's been driving me crazy—she's trying to push me away. She's trying to make it easier to walk when I sign the papers. Yet this is the first time in our relationship when it's clear that I don't know her at all.

I don't know the core of her.

These classes.

Her feelings.

How I've mishandled her hopes and dreams.

"Why didn't you tell me?" I ask, still standing there in the doorway.

She types away some more, clicks on her mouse, and then exhales as she closes her computer. She must have finished.

"Why didn't I tell you about my class? We went over this. I did tell you. You just weren't paying attention."

"Well, I'm paying attention now."

"It's too late," she says, hopping off the bed and walking toward her bathroom. I follow her as guilt tickles the back of my throat.

"So then tell me again. Tell me the truth about you."

She sardonically laughs. "The truth will hurt you too much."

She glances at me through the mirror, her reflection tired and worn down, just like mine. We've been at each other's throats for the past few days, and it's taken a toll on us. I'm not sure how we're going to survive Napa. Hell, right now, I can't see the point. The plan had been to use the three weeks to prompt her to talk to me. But there's been no communication. Just acts of . . . nastiness. Yes, we used to play around and do pranks like what's been going on of late. But nothing about my actions or Myla's has felt like pranks. It's been malicious. We're at the end of the rope. She's stayed quiet, I've stayed annoyed, and feelings have been hurt. I don't even feel like myself anymore. I feel bitter and resent the entire thing. I've lost track of the real reason behind what I'm trying to do . . . fix things with my wife. *Keep my marriage to the woman who has held my heart for the last seven years.*

So her truth might hurt me?

I guess we'll see about that.

"Try me," I say.

"Try you? You want the truth?"

I nod. "Yes, I want the truth."

"Okay." She pushes her shoulders back, ready to unleash on me as she turns around and leans against the counter. "We started falling apart months ago, and you've been too blind to see it. You say I love you, and yes, Ryot, that much is true. Even though I want to deny it, I might never stop loving you. But I've just felt so . . . disappointed. In you. With you. And slowly but surely, that's turned into resentment, and this might sting, but those feelings have turned into hate. I think I've hated you for a while now." *Shit. I was not expecting that. She's right. It does sting.* "You don't care about my dreams or goals, Ryot, and you haven't for a long time."

"That's not—"

"Do you want the truth, or do you want to argue?" she asks with a pointed look.

"The truth," I answer, swallowing hard.

"Then don't interrupt me and just listen."

Listen. That's what I've been waiting for, to listen to her talk. So even though this seems like it's going to hurt, this is what I've been waiting to understand—this deep-rooted hurt she's been carrying around. So I lean against the wall and do exactly what she wants, I listen.

"Many years ago, when we first started dating, you said something very validating to me. It was something like, 'I'll be honest with you, and when or if you ever decide to let me into your world, I won't hurt you. I'll only protect you. I will always listen to you, acknowledge you, and hopefully, make you feel as special as I know you are.' And for the most part of our marriage, I'd say you were successful at that.

"When you retired early from baseball, it was as if this cloud cast over you, and you turned into a different man. You might not have seen it, but I did. I went through the emotions with you. The resentment, the anger, the bitterness. At first, that was directed at the sport you'd been expelled from. But slowly your motives changed. You'd always played with your heart and gave back to the fans who'd helped your career. Appreciated them and the others in your world who were a part of that success. Suddenly you needed to prove something, and I don't even know to whom. Maybe yourself, maybe the fans, but you set yourself on a mission to prove to whoever was watching that you didn't need baseball to be successful. You looked straight ahead, plowed forward, and you walked over everyone to prove yourself . . . including me."

Her eyes well up with tears. She's no longer pulsing with anger, but more dripping with anguish.

"You were hell-bent on creating The Jock Report, and I understand the importance of it, don't get me wrong," she says with sincerity. "I saw what happened to Penn. I even saw the reports and negative press about you. No one, no matter their status, should ever be treated so unfairly by the media. But you never even consulted me, Ryot, your wife. You never once sat me down and said, 'hey, what if I work with Banner and Penn on starting this new app?' At first, I thought it was something to help you and Penn heal, and that was okay, but then it grew and grew. Before I knew what was happening, we were moving and creating a new life I never wanted. And the worst part is, you never asked. You just assumed it's what I wanted because it was with you."

She wipes at her eyes, pulling the tears away and then rubbing them on her shirt. Fuck, I did this to her. I made her this upset, and everything she's saying, it's . . . fuck, it's true. She's one hundred percent right. One hundred percent validated. I never asked her. *I plowed forward.*

"And the problem with assuming, Ryot, is that you took it upon yourself to figure out what was best for us, but what was best for us wasn't shutting me out. Nor was it walking all over me. This might sound selfish, but I've spent our whole relationship focusing on *your* dreams. And I was okay with that because we had an understanding, a promise: that after you retired, we'd focus on a goal together, just you and me." Tears are now flooding her cheeks, and there's no point stopping them. "But when is that going to happen, Ryot? When were you planning on bringing your goals and your dreams back to me, back to us?"

She takes a deep breath, and when her eyes connect with mine, I know I've lost her. Right here, at this moment, I've lost her. I've let her slip between my fingers. I've handled everything so poorly, so immaturely, and so selfishly.

With one final blow, she says, "And I've tried bringing it back to us. I planned a vacation at Jason Orson's cabin. I've planned date nights that you've canceled. I was even trying to tell you about the progress I've made with Renovate Chicago and the classes I've taken to make myself more valuable to our partnership. But it's all been pointless, because, during the pursuit of your dreams, you've completely forgotten about me. Abandoned me. Like my dad. You've invested in everything outside of our marriage and nothing *to* our marriage. And I just can't keep fighting for something only one of us wants."

She's right. I have no argument. *Fuck.*

Looking back over the past couple of months, if I really think hard, I can remember those canceled dates. I can remember the trip to the cabin when I spent most of it on the computer. My neglect is unmistakable. And I promised her I'd never do that. That I'd always ensure she felt heard. Her pain, her anger, is justified.

Needing to say something, I start, "Myla—"

She holds up her hand, stopping me. "Don't." She shakes her head. "I don't want to hear your sorrys or your reasoning, because it doesn't hold any weight. Whatever you say will be a reaction, not something that's been well-thought-out. So for both of us, don't apologize."

I push my hand through my hair and say, "Why didn't you tell me this earlier, when I asked?"

"Because I didn't want to hurt you," she answers. "Contrary to what you might think, I do care about you, Ryot, and I knew if I told you the truth, then you would be hurt, and I didn't want that."

"But not telling me the truth has only led to frustration and hurt anyway."

"I see that now," she says. "I guess there's no true way to break apart a love you thought would last forever."

A love I still wish would last forever. A love I don't want to give up on, but it very well might be out of my hands.

Unable to look her in the eyes, I ask, "Is that what you still want? To break this apart?"

"I didn't break anything, Ryot. So don't place that blame on me."

"No, I'm not," I quickly say. "I didn't mean it like that. I just meant . . . do you still want the divorce?"

When I glance up at her, she looks me dead in the eyes, and without skipping a beat, she says, "Yes, I do."

I rub my lips together and nod. "Can I ask why? Why you don't think we can fix this?"

"Because I'm just so hurt. I feel so alone. The damage has already been done. I feel so resentful toward you, Ryot, a feeling I never thought I'd feel. I've only felt resentful toward two other people in my life, my mom and dad. I haven't, nor will I ever be able to get over those feelings."

"I'm nothing like your mom," I say, the comparison slicing me open to my very core. I have never, ever raised a hand to her in anger. *I could never do that.*

"I know you've never hurt me physically, Ryot. I know you'd never do that." *Thank fuck.*

"So how am I——"

"Because of how you've ignored me. When Mom wasn't hurting me, wasn't . . . pushing me into walls or into tables, she was cold and distant. And all I can remember was feeling so, so alone. Vulnerable. And then there was my dad. What he did . . . I felt so . . . abandoned. That is what I've been feeling for months. With you." She takes a deep breath. I can barely stand, knowing I've hurt her so deeply. "It's hard to realize as a wife that you come second, that your opinion doesn't matter, that you will and can be forgotten. Something I knew a lot about growing up in a military family. I never had a say, and I hate that I married into that same situation. They say you marry your father, and it looks like I did. He broke me first. But you . . ." She sighs. "I'm not in a good mental space, Ryot. I don't like being here. I want to be near Nichole . . ." Her eyes well up, and her teeth roll over her bottom lip, cluing me into something.

"Is . . . is something going on with Nichole?" I ask.

She dabs at her eyes and says, "The cancer might be back. She hasn't told me. But I never wanted to leave Chicago——not my job, and not her. And I don't feel good here. I don't feel wanted. I don't feel like myself, and if I stay in this space any longer, I know I'll lose all the hard work I've put into making myself mentally healthier. I can't go back, Ryot. I won't."

And I don't want her to go back to that dark headspace either. I know how hard she's worked to be happy, to find what works for her. What a fuckup I am for not considering that.

Fuck.

I rub my hand across my forehead as I stare at her, the one single human I've ever truly loved to my core. How could I just let her go without a fight? Without trying to fix things?

Because, I caused them.

*It's hard to realize as a wife that you come second, that your opinion doesn't matter, that you will and can be forgotten. I never had a say, and I hate that I married into that same situation.*

I think the answer is clear.

I can *only* let her go because I love her, which means I want better for her.

And even though it's painful, I don't think that's me.

*That sensation of being so . . . abandoned is what I've been feeling for months. With you.*

I hate that I have caused her to feel so alone and abandoned. There's only one way I can fix that, it seems.

"Okay," I say.

Confused, she asks, "Okay, what?"

But I don't answer her. Instead, I go up to my room and retrieve the divorce papers from my nightstand. I pick up the pen, and with a tight throat and a broken heart, I sign my name.

I take the papers back down to her bedroom, where she's now sitting on her bed, looking confused.

"Here." I hand her the papers. "I want you to be happy, Myla, and I should have realized that earlier before putting my feelings ahead of yours and making us go through these three weeks of hell. It's done no good, and I want you to know there are no hard feelings. I know what I've done, I know the damage I've created, and I just hope . . ." My voice catches in my throat as my eyes start to water. "I just hope that one day, when you've created the life you deserve, and that beautiful smile has returned to your face, you can forgive me."

Her eyes fall to my signature. "Ryot . . . I'm . . . I'm sorry."

"Don't be sorry," I say. "There's no reason for you to be sorry. You did nothing wrong. You fought for us when I was too blind. Thank you for putting up with me." I take a step back and stick my hands in my pockets. "And about tomorrow and Napa, don't worry about it. I'll just tell everyone that you had to be with a friend. Go visit Nichole. Be with her."

"Ryot, I can go. It's not a big deal."

I shake my head. "It's best you don't." And then with that, I head upstairs, where I lie flat, unmoving, staring at the ceiling, wishing like hell I could turn back time.

Her truth, the reason we're getting a divorce is because of me.

I'm the one who fucked this up.

I'm the one who pushed her to the side for my own ambitions.

I'm the one who forgot about our plans for after baseball.

I steamrolled her.

I pulled her from her comfort.

And I'm the one who broke us.

I don't deserve to be with her, not after the way I treated her. Marriage is about compromise, supporting each other, and helping each other live out their dreams. This marriage has been completely one-sided, and that's because of me.

What a selfish fucking prick.

It's good I let her go. She deserves to be set free.

She deserves to find her own happiness, happiness that I know doesn't include me.

I spend the rest of my night allowing her words to slice me with every breath I take.

I replay the past couple of months over and over in my head.

And I think about how I could have possibly let our marriage—Myla—slip through my fingers.

Not that it needs an excuse because there is no excuse for treating my wife that way, but I was consumed. When I retired early, I had a shitty batting average, I wasn't on top of my game, and because my arm was wrecked, the media devoured me with relentless, disparaging commentary. It ate me alive at night, to the point that I felt the need to prove to everyone, all the naysayers, that I didn't need baseball to be successful. Myla is right. I did whatever it took to prove that. And I left her in the dust.

I took her away from her friends, Nichole in particular. I forgot about our promises for post-baseball life. I completely ignored her needs and desires. *Her life.* But knowing she felt so utterly abandoned, a deep trauma she's tried to heal from? That is not what a loving husband should ever do. *I* made her suffer. It's unforgivable. *You fucked up, Bisley.*

It makes me physically ill, because I've watched her grow. I saw her fight through her negative thoughts and finally realize her worth, and therefore, exploited the chance she took on me. It was beautiful to see her grow in such a positive way. To know that I forced her to experience the ugly side of her upbringing again is inexcusable.

I need to apologize again.

I need her to know how sorry I am.

I pull out a paper and pen from my nightstand.

⊏⊐

MYLA

MYLA: *He signed the papers.*
  ***Nichole:*** *Wait . . . what? Just now?*

**Myla:** *Yes.*
**Nichole:** *How do you feel?*
**Myla:** *Awful.*

My phone rings almost immediately, and I suck back my tears as I bury my head into my pillow and put my phone on speaker. "Hey." I sniff.

"Are you crying?"

"Yes," I answer.

"Okay, walk me through everything."

"Well, we finally combusted. He came charging into my room because he didn't think I'd packed for Napa, yelled at me—"

"Which is a given after all of the battery stealing."

"Yes, I knew it was going to happen, but it was the worst timing ever because I was finishing up my paper, that he knew nothing about, and well . . . it all came out. He asked for the truth, so I gave it to him." I dab at my eyes. "You should have seen the look on his face. He was completely destroyed, Nichole."

"I'm sure he was. Ryot has always wanted you to feel treasured, and I think seeing that you haven't felt that way would break him."

"It did. It's why I didn't want to tell him the truth because I knew it would hurt him. He apologized. He told me he loved me and that he didn't want to hurt me anymore, so he signed the papers. It wasn't out of spite or out of anger. He was defeated, genuine, and wants me to move on."

"He let you go," Nichole says softly.

"He did."

"And you don't know how you feel about it."

"I feel lost," I say right before I let out a large sob. "I know this is what I wanted, but now that it's over, I . . . I don't—"

*Knock. Knock.*

My eyes flash to the door.

"Myla, you in there?" Ryot asks.

"One second, Nichole," I whisper.

I set the phone down and go to the door. I quickly wipe at my tears and open it. Ryot is on the other side, holding a folded piece of paper in his hand. When his eyes meet mine, he looks tortured.

"You're crying," he says.

I wipe at my eyes again. "It's fine."

He shifts on his feet and says, "I know I said I would leave you alone, and I will, but I need to give you this." He hands me the paper. "I don't want you to think this is my way of changing your mind or making things up to you." He presses his hand to the letter. "I know it's too late for that. But before I walk away, I need you to hear these words. This is asking a lot from someone who owes me nothing, but promise me you'll read it when you're ready."

I stare down at the note and then back up at him.

"Please, Myla."

I nod as my tears fall again, unable to tamp down my emotions.

He lifts his hand and swipes at my tears with the pad of his thumb. "I'm sorry, Myla. I'm sorry for all the pain I've caused you. I'm sorry for these past two weeks. I'm sorry for not listening to you, and I'm sorry for not being there for you when I should have been." He lowers his hand and takes a step away. "If you need anything from me, let me know. And if Nichole needs anything, let me know." Another step back. "I hope you find peace and what you're looking for back in Chicago."

With the saddest smile I've ever seen, he turns around and walks back up the stairs as I slowly shut the door, more tears streaming down my face. When I pick up the phone, I say, "That was him."

"I heard. What does the note say?"

"I'm afraid to read it."

"Read it out loud. I'm here for you."

I take a deep breath and unfold the note to reveal his handwriting—slightly slanted, not too neat but not messy either. I wet my lips and then read. "'Dear Myla, I remember the first day I met you like it was yesterday. You were wearing a skintight red dress that should have pulled my attention away from the shitty game I'd had, but at that time, I was too blind to realize the woman eating my grapes and drinking a Capri Sun was going to be the one person in my life I needed the most.'" My voice catches on a sob.

"Take your time," Nichole encourages.

I swipe at my eyes and continue. "'It's funny how life works, right? There you were, a complete stranger on my couch, yet you held the key to my happiness without me even knowing. And I took that key for granted. I got comfortable. I grew complacent. And I became a man I don't even recognize now. You speak of a guy who is neglectful, a bully at times, a selfish prick, and I can't sit here and deny any of it. I can only nod in agreement. Because you're right.'"

I let that sink in as more tears fall.

"You okay?" Nichole asks.

"Yes," I answer and then continue. "'I forgot who I was. I forgot the journey. I forgot the future. I was thinking of myself and my ego, that's it. Nothing more. And because of that, I lost you. I made you feel forgettable, like you didn't matter. But Myla, you are the single most important thing in my life.'" I choke on a sob and take a deep breath. "'And until my dying day, I know losing you will go down as my biggest regret.'"

"Oh God," Nichole mumbles.

"'This letter is not to sway you to give me another chance because I know that ship has sailed. This letter is to offer you some semblance of peace, to let you know that your choice is justified, validated, and that if anyone was ever in the wrong in this relationship, it was me. You know I love you. I will love you forever, but I want you to be happy. No, I NEED you to be happy. If that means walking away so you can find your joy again, then I will. I have.'" I wipe at my tears. "'I truly hope you find what you're looking for, that you find someone who can make you smile again, who can put you first, and who can treat you the way you deserve to be treated. Like you are a priceless treasure—because you are. I'm sorry that I got so lost, that I forgot my number-one priority: bringing joy and love to our marriage. I love you, Myla. Thank you for everything. Yours, Ryot.'"

I set the paper down and lean back on my bed as sobs wrack my body.

"Well, that was unexpected," Nichole says. "From the sound of your crying, I'm going to guess you weren't expecting that either."

"No, I wasn't." I sniff. "I feel like . . . I feel like I made a mistake, Nichole."

"Because you still love him?"

"I do."

"Because his letter makes you think there's a chance change could be made?"

"I do." Because I just heard from the man I married. The thoughtful, selfless, loving man I said yes to all those years ago.

"So then find out."

"What do you mean?" I ask.

"See if there is any way you can salvage it. You have a week with him in Napa, so that's the perfect time to figure it all out."

"He told me not to go," I say.

I can hear the smile in her voice as she says, "When has that ever stopped you?"

# Chapter Fourteen

RYOT

*Seven years ago . . .*

"What are you going to wear for your first official date?"
Banner asks as he flops onto my bed.

"Uh, what I'm wearing now," I answer, looking down at
my jeans and T-shirt.

He winces. "Oh, really?"

"It's a casual date, you fuck."

"Still, your jeans could be nicer."

"These are my nicest jeans. What the hell is wrong with
them?"

"Those are it?" he asks. "Dude, you're paid millions.
Spring for a nicer pair."

"Fuck off." I move out of my room and toward the living
room.

Banner and I now live together in a posh apartment that overlooks Lake Michigan. It has been the one and only splurge we've made since we moved to Chicago. Banner has sold another app for a whopping seven hundred fifty thousand dollars, an app that took him a week to create. The man is an absolute genius. He's been conjuring up the next greatest deal while watching whatever he deems worthy on TV, and of course, bothering me whenever I get home.

From the console in the entryway, I pocket my wallet, my keys, and then slip on my shoes.

"Are you nervous?" Banner asks from the kitchen where he's opened a bag of pretzels. A new bag I just bought—well, ordered. We have groceries delivered now.

"No, I'm not nervous and don't eat all of those."

He shoves a handful in his mouth. Through crushed-up pretzels, he says, "Well, if you want the apartment to yourself, I'm going over to Kerry's place tonight."

"Who is Kerry?" I ask.

"Some girl I met at a bar last week. Hit it off. She's pretty cool."

"What about Nichole?"

"What about her?" He plops another pretzel in his mouth.

"I thought you were into her."

"I mean, she's cool and a fucking titan in bed, but she doesn't want anything serious, and neither do I, so I'm not attached to that."

I pocket my phone and ask, "Do you think you'll ever settle down?"

"Maybe, if the right girl comes along. But for now, I like having fun. Don't worry about me, bro. I'm good. You should be worried about yourself. What are your plans?"

"Going to pick her up and then take her to the rooftop."

"The rooftop? As in a few floors up from us? That rooftop?"

"Yes, that rooftop. Rented it for the night. I wanted somewhere peaceful where it could just be us."

"Get food catered?"

"Tacos. Her choice, and then vanilla cake for dessert."

"Vanilla cake?" He chuckles. "Her choice, I'm assuming as well."

"Yeah, I was caught off guard at first, but then again, this is Myla. She's never been like other girls. I ordered a vanilla cake with chocolate frosting from the grocery store and dumped rainbow sprinkles on the top. It's upstairs with the tacos."

"Well, sounds like you have it all planned out. Let me know if you need help with anything. I know how hard you've worked to get to this point. Can't let a boy down."

I laugh. "Thanks, Banner. I will. Hopefully, everything goes smoothly. Enjoy your night."

"You too." He waggles his eyebrows and pops some more pretzels in his mouth.

I'll be buying a new bag tomorrow.

⸺

HOLDING MY HAND TIGHTLY, Myla smiles up at me as we travel to the rooftop of my apartment building. She looks absolutely gorgeous tonight. Not that she doesn't look gorgeous all the time, but that smile on her face brings out the sparkle in her eyes. Plus she chose to wear a pair of dark blue lace shorts and a white crop top that shows off a few inches of her stomach and accentuates the curve in her hips. With her hair half up and half down, as well as minimal makeup, she's so fucking beautiful. During the entire drive over, I kept thinking how lucky I am that she gave me a chance.

"You smell good," she says, leaning her body into mine.

"Thanks," I say as I tip her chin up just as the elevator slows to a stop and the doors open.

I don't want to be biased or anything, but I've seen my fair share of rooftops in the city, and I have to say, ours is the best. Six-foot glass walls surround the perimeter to maintain the beautiful view, but you're not about to fall off into the street below you. Along the building are potted vines that have grown into the brick wall, creating a feel of nature in a city of concrete. There are a few short buildings in front of us and then endless views of the lake. Scattered around the space are cushioned couches, chairs, two firepits, and a secluded area blocked off by a reclaimed wood partition. Behind the partition is a plush couch and low table, where everything is set up. The lake is the only thing you see, giving you complete privacy from the city around you. And because it's Chicago, there's a roof over the partitioned area with strings of twinkling lights.

"Ummm . . . wow," she says as she takes in the space. "I knew you could possibly romance my shorts right off me, but this is too much. Look at that view." She steps up to the glass wall, and I step up behind her, placing my hands on her hips. "I can't believe you live here."

"I love it here. One of the only things besides a car that we've spent money on."

"Well spent." She moves around the space and runs her fingers over the tops of the couches and chairs, walks by the lit firepits, and then turns to face me. "I'm so making out with you tonight."

I chuckle. "Don't make promises you can't keep."

She walks up to me and drags her finger over my stomach in passing. "Trust me, I will keep this one. Now show me where these tacos are. I can't make out on an empty stomach."

I lead her behind the partition and pull out her chair for her. My hand caresses her back as she takes a seat, and I watch her roll into my touch as she glances over her shoulder and smirks at me. That one look says it all. We will definitely be making out tonight.

"This is a convenient secluded space," she says as she drapes her napkin over her lap. "And that couch over there is pretty deep, almost like mattress deep."

"Really? Haven't noticed." I carry over two covered plates and set one in front of her and then one in front of me.

"Such a liar." She chuckles.

Yup, I'm a giant liar because when I chose this space, I knew exactly the kind of atmosphere I was looking for . . . a place where we could be cut off from the world and fool around if we wanted to.

I lift the dome from her plate, revealing two barbacoa tacos with a side of lime, cilantro rice, and black beans. Chips and salsa are already on the table, and the cake is behind me, ready to be devoured.

"Ooo, this smells good. You said this is from your favorite taco place?"

"Yeah, it's around the corner. Banner and I can't get enough of it."

She picks up a taco and takes a big bite. Sauce drips over her lips and down her chin as she chews, causing me to smile. I love that she doesn't care. She doesn't even seem to notice that sauce is dripping down her face on a first date. It's endearing, charming, and relatable. She has no filters and hides nothing. I really like that about her, amongst other things.

"Okay, you have to tell me where this place is because these are phenomenal. Wow." She sets her taco down, reaches for a chip, and pats her mouth with her napkin. "You sure know how to work a rooftop. Sure the view is spectacular, and the company is hot as shit, but these tacos, they take the cake."

"Speaking of cake . . . your request is over there on the table."

She swallows and then gently presses her hand to her chest. "Ryot Bisley, you very well might be the man of my dreams."

"Things I love to hear."

———

"THIS SHIRT WAS MADE for your body," Myla says as we relax on the couch.

Together, we devoured our dinners and then had a small slice of cake because Myla said she didn't want to feel too bloaty. But watching her lick frosting off her fork wouldn't have stopped me if she was bloaty. She was intentional with her tongue and how she made eye contact with me. She even caught me staring at one point and joked about it. How could I not stare? She was treating that fork like it was my dick, and she was showing me exactly what she could do.

I glance down at my shirt and then back up at her. "Yeah, you think so?"

She's curled into my side, turned toward me so one arm is on the back of the couch and the other is on my chest. "Yes. I love how tight it is. Shows off your amazing pecs."

I smirk. "Laying down the compliments, are we?"

"Yeah, why not? I've never heard my mom compliment my dad by telling him how attractive he is or how she likes what he wears. There's never been open communication like that. I saw this clip on Instagram a while ago, a relationship expert. He said it's all right to gas up your partner and make them feel wanted, sexy. And that resonated with me because I never heard something seem so easy, actually done. So yeah, I'm giving you a compliment because I think you're extremely hot, and I want you to know that."

"That's a great way to see things, actually. So how about this? Moving forward, we make a valiant effort to, as you put it, gas each other up."

"I like that." Her fingers dance over my chest. "Seriously, though, you might have the sexiest arms I've ever seen. I know

I make fun of you for your weightlifting videos, but Ryot, they're so enticing."

I smirk as I tug a strand of her hair and start twirling it around my finger. "Well, then. That means I need to make more."

"More wouldn't hurt. Let all the women marvel at the wonder that is your biceps."

"There's only one woman's opinion that I care about, and it's yours."

With the hand draped behind me, she plays with the short strands of hair on the back of my neck. "Good answer, not that I needed it. I understand your loyalty."

"I'm glad because dating a professional baseball player isn't going to be easy. My schedule is demanding. Normally, I'd have a night game, and I wouldn't be up on a rooftop with you."

"I might not know a lot about baseball, but I do know that schedules are tricky for everyone. Also, I was there when you were called up, remember? I know how important it is to be where you are right now in your career and how hard you've worked. I'm not going to get in the way of that." She smirks. "But when you have some free time, I better at least know you're thinking about me."

"Myla, I can honestly tell you I've been thinking about you for the past four years."

"Been longing, have you?"

"Just a touch," I say, holding up my fingers.

Her other hand smooths up my chest and along my neck to join the other as she shifts so she's straddling my lap. I place my hands on her hips, holding her in place as I lean against the back of the couch.

"I've been longing too."

"Yeah?" I ask, feeling drunk with lust because fuck, have I pictured this moment when Myla gives herself freely to me.

When she makes the first move . . . when she's comfortable enough to straddle me.

"Yes, longing for more stories about you." She grins.

"As you sit on my lap?"

"Yes, this is clearly more comfortable. So tell me more about Maine. I've never been. Is it as cold as it looks?"

Seeing where she's going with this and not wanting to pressure her—she's in control—I answer, "Freezing. And I don't care what my parents, Nola, or Banner say. There is no way you get used to that kind of cold. Absolutely no way."

"As cold as it is here, in Chicago?"

"Colder. Although the wind here doesn't help. I just think it's more frigid up there. But the summers are gorgeous, and when I wasn't playing baseball, which was rare, I loved hiking with Banner and our occasional camping trips. One time actually, we set up camp, and we were supposed to be out there for three days. Our trip got cut short because we'd propped our tents right next to poison ivy and were itchy disasters after."

"Oh, no. Did you get it anywhere . . . special?"

"Thankfully, just on our hands and necks and faces, nothing below the belt."

"Penis poison ivy seems insufferable."

"Yeah, not something I wanted to get wrapped up in."

She presses both hands to my pecs as she asks, "Did you ever do s'mores or anything like that?"

"Every time. It's what we lived on. We didn't take much to eat but had plenty of chocolate, graham crackers, and marsh-mallows."

"You know, I've never had a s'more." She glances down, almost as if she's ashamed about it.

"Wait, seriously?" I ask.

She nods. "Yeah, seriously. It wouldn't have been something I did with my family because we didn't do much together. And it's not something my mom would have thought to do with me as a special bonding moment. She always thought I carried too much weight, so she kept my sweets to a minimum. So yeah, I've never had one."

How can someone go through their childhood without having s'mores? That's just . . . fuck, that hurts my heart. But it makes sense from what she told me about her mom and her childhood.

"Well, that's going to change," I say. "I'll be damned if you go through another summer without a s'more. Actually . . ."

I pull out my phone and shoot a text to Banner, letting him know I need him to get s'mores materials to me ASAP.

"Actually, what?" she asks.

"Actually . . . tonight is your lucky night."

—————

"YOU SERIOUSLY HAD your brother deliver ingredients to make s'mores?" she asks as I move her over to one of the firepits. It's U-shaped with blue crystal rocks along the fire and a comfortable couch across from it.

"Yes, I did." We sit on the couch as I say, "I can't have you wandering around this earth not knowing what a s'more tastes like."

I hand her a roasting stick and put a marshmallow on it. "Okay, so I just, roast this now?" She sticks the marshmallow directly in the fire, setting it on fire immediately.

"What are you doing?"

"I don't know. I haven't done this before. Is this wrong?"

I pull her stick up, bring the flaming ball of sugar toward me and blow it out.

"Oh, that's, uh, that doesn't look appetizing."

I chuckle. "Some people like it this way, but I personally don't. Let's try again, but this time, we'll do it together." With a napkin, I remove the burnt marshmallow and set it to the side. I load her up again and then move her to my lap so she rests comfortably on me. I hold the stick with her, and instead of sticking it directly into the flames, I show her how to hover above. Talking softly into her ear, I say, "This is the perfect placement, not too close so you burn the hell out of it, and not too far away that it will take ages to heat. This will grant you the perfect toast."

I feel her relax into my chest as my free arm wraps around her waist. "Thank you for teaching me. No one has ever taken the time to show me the ways."

I kiss her shoulder and say, "If you need help with anything else, I'm your man."

"You're my man either way," she says as she cuddles in closely.

Smiling to myself, I twist the roasting stick gently and say, "Now the success of a good marshmallow is to rotate the stick carefully so you get all sides toasted. See how it's puffing up?"

"Yeah."

"You have to be careful because it's separating from its gooey center, and there's a chance the marshmallow will fall off. So tip the stick up just a bit to prevent that."

"Like this?" she asks.

"Yes, perfect, babe."

She turns toward me and smiles genuinely. "You just called me babe. You did before, but this feels different."

"You okay with that?"

"It's cute."

"You're cute."

She rolls her eyes and nudges my shoulder. "Don't be corny."

"Just stating the facts. Oh hey, watch your marshmallow, you're getting close to the fire."

"Oops." She lifts the stick. "Close one."

I reach to the side and open the chocolate and the graham crackers and put together the pieces for her. "Okay, I think it's ready. Pull it out carefully, and then place the marshmallow on the chocolate." I hold it in front of her, and she does as instructed. "Then you take the graham cracker top and use it to pull the marshmallow off." I show her just how to do it.

"Ooo, smooth."

I take the roasting stick and set it to the side. "Now, take a bite."

She smirks at me and brings the s'more to her mouth, where she takes a bite out of the corner. The marshmallow and melted chocolate squeeze out on all sides, creating an ooey gooey mess. As she chews, a drop of chocolate lands on the corner of her mouth, so I scrape it off and then bring my thumb to my mouth.

Her eyes narrow in on the movement before she brings the s'more up to my mouth. I take a bite as well.

Once we both swallow, I ask, "What do you think?"

"You know . . ." She pauses. "I really thought I was going to like this, but it's, I don't know . . . not that great."

"What?" I ask, laughing. "Seriously? You don't like it?"

She grins. "No, just kidding. I love it. It might be my new favorite thing of all time." She then takes another bite. This time, she gets marshmallow on her lips, and I lean in and lick it off for her. When she finishes chewing, she shifts on my lap so she's straddling me again and feeds me the last bite of the s'more.

I chew.

Swallow.

And then watch as she brings her marshmallow and chocolate-coated fingers to my mouth. Eyes on hers, I suck on her index finger, rolling my tongue over the tip and sucking hard. As she watches me, her mouth parts slightly and her breathing picks up. With each finger I clean, she offers me one more until nothing is left on them.

When she pulls her last finger out of my mouth, I say, "Was it good?"

She wets her lips. "So good."

And then she grips the back of my neck and pulls me in close where our mouths meet, and she kisses me. Deeply. Like her life depends on it.

Her fingers dig into the back of my neck, her mouth parts open, and her tongue tangles with mine. There is nothing sweet about this kiss. It's feral, animalistic, greedy. And it's everything.

I slip my fingers under her crop top.

Her fingers tangle into my hair.

I release her mouth and kiss the side of her jaw.

She tilts her head back, giving me access to her beautiful neck.

I move my hand up to the clasp of her bra.

She mutters, "Please."

I don't need much more than that before I undo the clasp. She shifts around, taking her bra off and then dropping it on the couch next to us. Then with both hands, she grips my jaw and kisses me on the mouth as she rocks her hips over mine.

A low moan passes through me as I grow hard in seconds. Hell, when I was licking her fingers, I was getting hard, but now, with her rocking on top of me, it's a done deal. I'm lost, and I want her. I want her so bad.

"Touch me," she whispers.

"Not here," I say as I lift from the couch. While she's still straddling me, I walk us over to the partitioned area. The entire time, she's pressing kisses across my jaw.

"I want you, Ryot."

I sit on the deep couch, resting against the back, giving us more space. She makes herself comfortable on top of me. Her beaded nipples press against the fabric of her white shirt, enticing me, showing me that she's more than ready for my touch, so I slide my hand up her front, just below her breast.

A low hiss falls past her lips as she tugs on the hem of my shirt. "I want this off."

"Then take it off," I say right before she pulls on my shirt until it's all the way off.

She lets out a large sigh before her hands explore my pecs. "Your body is incredible, Ryot."

I cup her breast gently, letting the weight rest in my palm before I graze my thumb over the little nub. Her tits aren't too big but not small either, the perfect size for her body. Perfect for me.

Wanting more, I pull her shirt up and over her head, revealing her naked chest.

"Jesus," I mutter as I stare at her. "Myla, you're . . . you're so fucking beautiful."

And then her lips are on mine again. I don't get a chance to touch her breasts again before she's gripping my pecs tightly, peppering kisses along my jaw, down my neck, and then to my chest, where she nibbles along my muscles.

"Claim me," I say through clenched teeth as her hand finds my erection in my jeans and starts rubbing me. "Mark me, Myla."

She does just that. She drags her nails over my chest, past my nipples, bites along my pecs, sucks, and then licks all the way down my abs, taking a moment to mark them as well. It's so fucking sexy that my cock is straining to be released. When she reaches the button of my jeans and starts to undo it, I feel my cock jump against the fabric.

She undoes my jeans, pulls them down with my boxer briefs to release me, and pulls my length out.

"Oh yes," she says as she watches my cock stretch up against my stomach. And then, without a pause, she licks the entire length until she reaches the tip.

"Fuck," I groan.

"I want to suck you, Ryot. So bad. I need this dick in my mouth." She opens her mouth wide and sucks me in, all the way down to the root, deep-throating me in one smooth stroke. I nearly fly off the couch from the feel of her warm, tight throat taking me in.

"Fucking hell, Myla."

Her eyes water as she stares up at me, but she continues to take me deep, over and over and over again until a light sheen of sweat falls over my skin and my balls start to tighten.

"Babe. I don't want to come in your mouth, and that's what you're going to make me do."

She pulls off and then slides her shorts off, leaving her only in a thin, pink thong, then straddles me again, her spread legs allowing my length to slide against her . . . fuck, her wet fabric.

Wanting more of her, I slide my hands up her sides until I reach her breasts and then grip them both tightly before leaning forward and taking one in my mouth.

"Yes, Ryot," she hums as her fingers dig into my scalp and her hips rotate against me.

Sucking hard, I play with her nipple, tugging and nipping at it, finding out what she likes with how intensely she grips me, with her sighs, her moans, the drive of her hips over mine.

She loves when I nibble, when I release her nipple and nip at her breasts, marking her just like she marked me.

"God, I want you," she says, pulling on my hair so my head falls back and her mouth clashes against mine. I thread my fingers under the strings of her thong to her ass where I grip hard, encouraging her to work over my cock faster, harder.

"I want this off," I say, tugging on her thong.

She lifts, removes her thong, and then places her arousal directly on my length. At the same time, we both let out a loud, drawn-out moan as she slides her clit up and down my erection.

I dig my fingers into her ass and move her faster and faster.

"So . . . good, so long," she mutters as her mouth finds

mine again and our tongues tangle. "I'm going to come, Ryot." Her hips move even faster, creating hot friction between us, her arousal dripping around my cock as she pumps hard until her body tightens. She lets out a loud moan as she convulses over me, my name falling off her tongue.

I watch in awe as she takes what she wants without even asking. It's the sexiest thing I've ever seen.

And when she's done drawing out her orgasm, her beautiful eyes match up with mine as a smile falls over her lips.

"I need you inside me now."

Yeah, I'm going to need the same thing.

"There's a condom in my wallet."

Sliding down in her naked glory, she pulls my shoes, socks, jeans, and boxers off as I lie there, lightly stroking myself, watching her tits bounce with every movement.

She fishes through my wallet, grabs the three condoms I brought, and then places two on the table in front of us. With one tear, she has the condom out, and she kneels between my legs, removing my hand and replacing it with her mouth, where she takes me deep in her throat again. I press my hand to her cheek, amazed I could convince this girl to be with me.

After she sucks me in a few more times, she replaces her mouth with the condom and then asks, "How do you want me?"

"You tell me what you want."

Smiling, she says, "Lie back." I turn on the couch so I'm fully reclined, and then she straddles me, lifts my cock, and positions me at her entrance. "I love your abs. I can tell you work really hard." She drags her finger over the mounds. "I want to watch them contract when you pump into me, but maybe later. Right now, I want you to bottom out inside me."

And with that, she sits all the way down.

No inching my way in.

No taking it slow.

No, I'm at the hilt, swarmed in her warmth, in her tight

pussy. I groan so loud that I think the people in the apartment below us can hear exactly what's going on.

"Fuck." I breathe heavily. "Christ, Myla, I wasn't . . . fuck, I wasn't ready for that."

Her nipples are erect, her body hunched over as she takes deep breaths as well. When her eyes meet mine, she says, "You're so big. I've never felt this full. I'm going to come fast."

"Good . . . me too." I wet my lips. "Now give me that pussy, make me fucking lose control."

With her hands on my chest, she rotates her hips and undulates up and down as I reach out and play with her nipples.

She hisses.

I bring my thumb to her clit.

She falls back, placing her hands on my thighs.

I rub her out, applying pressure as I feel her contract around me.

"Oh God . . . it's . . . it's too much."

"It's not. Now fuck me, Myla."

She shakes her head as she loses her breath. "You . . . you fuck me."

That's all it takes. I pull her off me, have her sit up on all fours, and then I position myself behind her and drive inside her. With my hands on her hips, I piston in and out of her, our bodies slapping together, my balls tapping her with every thrust, my cock growing larger with every stroke, her pussy clenching with every moan that falls past her seductive lips.

She rests her forearms on the couch in front of her, angling her ass up, and I take the new position, going even deeper.

"Oh my God!" she cries out. "Oh fuck, Ryot. I'm right there."

"Take me, show me how much you want me."

She lets out a loud cry. I give her ass a slap. And then she's coming violently, her body convulsing around my cock, sucking so hard on my length that it takes two seconds before my body seizes. My muscles become useless as the blood in my body gathers in one spot. My cock expands, and then with one more thrust, white-hot euphoria rips through me like I'm fucking floating. The pleasure is so goddamn good that I know at this moment nothing will ever be better. Ever.

Our moans mix.

Our sweat is slick.

And when we finally finish drawing everything out, I collapse on top of her and kiss her neck as I nuzzle close.

"Oh . . . my God," she says breathlessly.

"Babe, your pussy. Fuck me. It's so good."

She chuckles and attempts to spin around to face me. I pull out of her and help her until she's facing me. She slides her hands up my chest and to my neck. "I can't believe I waited so long to be with you. What is my problem?"

I laugh and kiss the tip of her nose. "Have some regrets, do you?"

"Yes, many. I know there's something to be said about delayed gratification, but there is also stupidity. I should have been with you many years ago. Not just because of what just occurred between us, but because of everything that happened prior to that." Her thumb drags over my cheek. "You're so patient with me, Ryot. You never once pressured me. And despite constantly turning you away, you have never once made me doubt your intentions or your loyalty. You're . . . you're a good one. Thank you."

I bend down again and press a kiss to her lips. "You don't need to thank me, babe. Just keep giving me a chance."

"No need for a chance," she says. "You have me for as long as you want me." *I have a feeling that might be forever.*

---

RYOT: *Morning, babe.*

**Myla:** *Mmmmmmm . . . good morning. Why aren't you in my bed again?*

**Ryot:** *Early morning. I didn't want to wake you up.*

**Myla:** *I wouldn't have minded.*

**Ryot:** *I would have. How are you feeling?*

**Myla:** *Sore. There is beard burn all over my inner thighs. I have hickeys all over my boobs, from what I can see, and I'm more than satisfied.*

**Ryot:** *Good, when you walk around today, you'll remember who you belong to.*

**Myla:** *God, say more things like that.*

**Ryot:** *I woke up to a painted chest of your teeth marks.*

**Myla:** *Please tell me you took a picture for me.*

**Ryot:** *Only for you, a true thirst trap. [picture]*

**Myla:** *There are bruises all over you, and is that a scratch mark along your pecs?*

**Ryot:** *Sure is, and I fucking love it.*

**Myla:** *You realize we might have a problem, right? Because I felt a high last night I've never felt before. I believe I'll be chasing it for the rest of my life.*

**Ryot:** *At least we'll be chasing it together.*

---

MYLA: *When is your game?*

**Ryot:** *Around six. I'm just hanging out in the locker room now.*

**Myla:** *Want a boob pic?*

**Ryot:** *Do you even have to ask?*

**Myla:** *[picture] Look what you claimed.*

**Ryot:** *Those tits, they're mine. Fuck, they're so beautiful.*

**Myla:** *Now your turn to send a dick pic.*

**Ryot:** *LOL! Yeah, not sure I can do that in the locker room. How about I sneak into your place later tonight, after the game?*

**Myla:** *I have a late shift, and I won't be home until after midnight. I'm working the bar.*

**Ryot:** *Well . . . fuck. I leave for an away trip tomorrow.*
**Myla:** *Then I guess after my shift, I'm just going to have to come up to your place.*
**Ryot:** *It won't be too late?*
**Myla:** *Never.*

---

## **MYLA**

"HOW WAS WORK?" Ryot asks me as his fingers tangle with mine while guiding me to his bedroom.

"Boring, torturous, as all I could think about was you." That is the absolute truth because with every step I took today, I felt him between my legs. I remembered the moans erupting from his throat when I did something he liked or the feel of his teeth all over my sensitive skin.

I've been counting down the moments until I could see him again, feel him again, listen to his deep voice tell me how beautiful and sexy I am. And now that I'm here with him, I'm not going to let anything get in my way of taking exactly what I want.

When we reach his room, he opens the door, spins me around against the wall, and then closes the door behind us. He presses his body against mine and takes my mouth with his. Just one touch lights a spark in me, and I hop up and loop my legs around his waist, only for him to prop me against the wall, pressing his mouth to mine.

"This skirt is hot on you." It's short, black, and tight and now up around my waist. He glides his hand over my leg, feeling my thigh-high leggings. "And these are sexy as shit."

"I wore them just for you," I say as I tilt my head to the side, letting him run his tongue down my neck. When I got ready for work, I picked out my outfit specifically with him in mind. And my lingerie.

While he peppers open-mouthed kisses along my neck, I undo the buttons of my shirt and shuck it off.

He doesn't pause as he moves his mouth to my chest and pulls on one of the bra cups, bringing my nipple into his mouth.

"Yes, Ryot," I say as I feel his unmatched dick already hard and pressing against me. "I've wanted this all day. Wanted you all day."

He pulls down the other cup of my bra and sucks in that nipple while I weave my fingers through his hair.

"You taste so good," he mumbles against my skin.

"Then eat me," I say, which causes his head to pull back with a smirk. And then I say, "In the shower."

That makes his smile grow even larger as he walks me through his bedroom to his bathroom where he sets me on the floor. "Get naked, now."

I strip down while he goes over to the shower. The beautiful, black-tiled shower with a wraparound bench, rain showerhead, and what looks to be multiple jets. After turning it on, he also goes to a towel heater and sets two towels on it before turning toward me and slipping his shorts off, revealing his beautiful dick.

My mouth waters.

"You're not naked yet."

"You're distracting me with that erection."

"Hurry up, and I'll let you play with it."

I strip out of the rest of my clothes. As I approach him, he holds out his hand, and I take it just before he opens the shower door for me and lets me in. The steamy water falls over my already heated body just as he moves up to me and wets my hair.

I take his length in my palm and start pumping him.

"Fuck, that feels good," he murmurs as he moves closer

and trails kisses down my shoulder. "But that's not what I want, and you know it."

He moves me back to the bench and forces me to sit. He then grabs the showerhead attachment, turns it on, and kneels in front of me.

With our gazes locked, he says, "Spread your legs and hold them open."

I do exactly what he says as he runs the scruffiness of his cheek along my inner thigh.

"You're going to drive me crazy, aren't you?"

"I'm going to do what I damn well please." He kisses my thigh as he brings the showerhead between my legs and changes the spray so it darts out. I swear that setting was made for this reason and this reason alone because when he moves it over my clit, I nearly slide off the bench. He props me up, holding me in place, and starts applying the water pressure again.

I bite my bottom lip as I hold in my moans.

He brings his cheek to my other thigh and rubs against it, kissing, teasing, making me squirm.

And when I think he's not going to give me what I want, he lowers his mouth in front of my clit and brings the showerhead to my entrance, where it pulses inside me, giving me a new sensation as his tongue crashes down on me.

"Oh . . . shit," I say, my eyes nearly popping out of their sockets. "Ryot."

"Who does this pretty little pussy belong to?"

"You," I answer. "Oh my God, you."

He removes his mouth and replaces it with the showerhead, letting the pulsing massage my clit to the point that my body begins to tremble, my legs shake, and my stomach bottoms out.

"Close," I squeak out.

He brings the showerhead back to my hole, lets it pulse,

and then he flicks me with the tip of his tongue, edging me out, never applying sufficient pressure for me to fall over.

"Ryot. Let me come."

"You want more, babe?"

"Yes. Jesus . . . yes."

I feel his smile as he flattens his tongue and strokes me long and hard, quickening his pace as my legs close in on him. My body convulses until everything fades to black, and my body hits a peak of total bliss.

"Fuck . . . oh fuck, Ryot."

Trembling.

Shivering.

Pulsing.

My body experiences every sensation as my orgasm rips through me, and he never stops. He never gives in. He keeps giving and giving until I feel tears form in my eyes.

"Please, I can't take anymore."

That's when he stops and then gently kisses my pussy before working his way back up to my face, where he presses his lips to my cheeks.

"You okay?"

"Yes." I sigh heavily. "That was just intense."

"Good." He stands, his cock level with my mouth. I don't let him go but grip his hips, bringing him to my lips. He shifts my hair behind my ear, and with a gentle tone, he says, "Take me deep. I want to claim your throat."

And I let him.

RYOT: *I hated leaving you this morning. Did you get home okay?*

**Myla:** *I did. And the note you left was adorable.*

**Ryot:** *Just wanted you to know how much I like you. Remember, I'm yours. You have nothing to worry about while I'm gone.*

**Myla:** *I trust you, Ryot. I'm not worried in the slightest. You don't need to worry about that.*

**Ryot:** *Just want to remind you. In the past, I haven't had the same trust from women, despite proving I can be trusted.*

**Myla:** *That's on them, not you. I know where you stand with me and where I stand with you. Committed and that's all that matters. Plus, I know you'll never find anyone who can make you come the way I can.*

**Ryot:** *Facts. Anyone other than you would be a waste of my time. Once you've had the finest steak, you can't go back to meat from the grocery store.*

**Myla:** *LOL. I don't know if I should be offended that you compared me to steak or pleased.*

**Ryot:** *Maybe a little of both.*

**Myla:** *I can accept that. What are these road trips going to be like? Tell me what to expect.*

**Ryot:** *Since you work at night, probably phone calls in the morning, an afternoon FaceTime where you shimmy your perfect tits in front of the screen, and then we both get off, followed by texts after the game so when you get off work, you know I've been thinking about you.*

**Myla:** *Sounds intriguing. I can get into tit shimmy.*

**Ryot:** *Don't make me fucking hard right now.*

**Ryot:** *I'm going to miss you, Myla. I don't think you have any idea how incredible I think you are.*

**Myla:** *I'm going to miss you too, Bisley. Is that too soon? Too crazy?*

**Ryot:** *No idea. I've never felt so close to someone so quickly. I think it's all you.*

**Myla:** *Maybe . . .*

**Ryot:** *LOL. Smart-ass.*

**Myla:** *Honestly, I've never felt so seen before, Ryot. Never felt treasured.*

**Ryot:** *That's a tragedy. I need you to know that I will always treasure you as I know how rare you are.*

**Myla:** *You've made my day.*

**Ryot:** *You've made my year.*

# Chapter Fifteen

RYOT

*Present day . . .*

"Dude, where's Myla?" Banner asks as I adjust my tucked-in button-up shirt.

"Not here," I say quietly.

"What the hell happened?"

"Can't get into it now or I'll have a goddamn mental breakdown." I'm on the verge of losing it. I woke up this morning, red-eyed and devastated because last night . . . last night, I said goodbye to the love of my life. The feeling pumping through me is utter dread. Dread to move on, to take a step away from her, to allow this to happen despite me not wanting to let go. I swallow hard and say, "The excuse we're using for her absence is that she's visiting Nichole, who might be sick again."

"Hold up." Banner grips my shoulder, forcing me to look at him. "Seriously?"

"Yeah," I answer. "That's not the reason she's not here, but Nichole might be sick, so I told Myla to be with her."

"Well . . . fuck. Should I call her?"

"No, Jesus. Then she'll know we've been talking about her, and you know how much Nichole hates that."

"Right." He sticks his hands in his pockets and stares at the floor.

"I thought things weren't serious with you guys."

"They're not, and I truly mean that. They're not at all. But she has been a part of my life on and off for years. She's also my sister-in-law's best friend, so there's that."

"Ex-sister-in-law," I say. "As of last night."

"What?" Banner says just as JP and Kelsey walk up to us in the lobby.

And fuck do they look happy.

Smiles are plastered across their faces, there isn't but an inch of space between them, and love is just radiating around them. True happiness. True joy. It reminds me of how it used to be with Myla. How we would spend every free hour we had texting, talking, and being with each other. How even though we had to maneuver around busy schedules, we were each other's number-one priority.

I wish I could go back to that time when I wasn't fucking up, when I wasn't tormenting myself with having to prove something. I wish I could go back to a simpler time when holding my girl's hand was all I needed to be happy. When we went out on dates for the simple fun of it. When *I* prioritized my marriage.

Despite how morose I feel, I plaster on a smile for the bride and groom.

"Hey, there they are," I say in a greeting that sounds far too obnoxious, thanks to my overcompensating. "How are the soon-to-be bride and groom?" From the corner of my eye, I see Banner giving me a *what the hell kind of joy just shot up your ass* look.

"Good. Right, babe?"

Kelsey nods and pulls JP in closer, looping her arms around his waist. Jealousy rocks through me. Yearning flips my stomach into knots. "I just want to be married. I tried to convince him to have a quick ceremony tonight, but he was not happy about that idea."

"I'm worth the wait," JP says with a laugh. "Did you fly up?"

I tamp down my emotions that are so close to the surface from the sight of a couple in love. "Yeah, this morning. Banner drove up yesterday."

"Visited with a buddy who lives in San Jose. And then made the rest of the way up this morning. Longer drive than I expected." Banner chuckles. "With traffic, it was eight hours altogether."

"Brutal," JP says and then glances around. "Where's Myla?"

I knew the question would be asked, as it's natural to wonder where another person's significant other is. That doesn't mean that the truth isn't rocking me to my very core.

I could tell them the truth, that I fucked up royally and, because I was so blind and determined to prove I could exist without baseball, that I neglected her. Or I can tell them the statement I prepared for this exact moment, a statement that will still make it seem like everything is okay but also not make JP and Kelsey feel like they are second-best to other plans.

It would be freeing to just tell the truth and sulk in my hotel room until the wedding, but I know that's not an option. I might be in pain, but I'm not going to ruin this week for everyone else.

"Myla—"

"Hey, Bisley," I hear just as an arm is looped around my waist. Stunned, I glance down to find Myla standing next to me, holding me, looking fucking gorgeous in an off-the-shoulder maxi dress.

What the hell?

My heart trips and tumbles around as I blink, attempting to make sure I'm not dreaming. She's here, actually here. But why?

Then to my surprise, she lifts and presses a kiss on my lips. But not just any kiss, a kiss that sends a shock of lust all the way down to my goddamn toes. A kiss that flashes over a decade of my life through my eyes. A kiss that breaks me, shatters me, and creates a sense of severe longing that I might collapse right here.

My hand rests on her lower back, and I open my mouth just as she does, turning our kiss into something longer, hungrier than before. I soak it up. I lean on this moment. I let myself fall into the trap of hope as my tongue glides across hers.

But unfortunately, the kiss lasts a second.

One fucking second before she pulls away, rests her hand on my chest, and says, "JP, Kelsey, oh my gosh, you guys look so good, so happy." And then she gives them both a hug. "So excited to be here."

"Glad you could make it." JP glances over his shoulder. "Okay, transportation has arrived. Some of the party has already arrived at the winery, so I think we're the last to leave." He nods toward the front of the hotel, where a few cars are waiting to drive us over.

Myla takes my hand in hers, and together, we follow everyone while I feel Banner's eyes on me. I gently shake my head, mentally communicating not to say a goddamn thing, and thankfully, he doesn't. When we get to the cars, he picks up on my need to be alone with Myla and asks JP if he can ride with them because he needs to be educated about wine.

JP, of course, welcomes the tutorial with open arms and takes Banner with him, leaving me with Myla.

Thank God, because I'm going to need a second after that whirlwind. Her showing up, the kiss, her happy, smiling face. I feel like I'm in some sort of twilight zone.

I open the door for Myla, and she gets in, only for me to follow. Once we're buckled up and the driver pulls away from the hotel, I talk quietly. "What are you doing here?"

Matching the pitch of my voice, she answers, "A deal was a deal, Ryot."

"It was stupid of me to ask you that. Selfish. I was going to handle it. You don't have to be here. I know you don't want to be, and I'm absolutely okay with that." *I miss you so much, and I'm already so lost without you.*

She turns toward me and looks me in the eyes, those bright blue irises shining brightly. "I'm not about to create drama around someone else's wedding, okay? So let's just do this wedding thing and then move on."

The way she says it . . . it's different.

There's no malice.

There's no anger.

It's almost as if she's given up, surrendered, and now she's simply going through the motions.

I don't want to make her mad, go into detail about how she's feeling, or ask how she came to this conclusion because I know it won't get me anywhere. So instead, I reach over to her, take her hand in mine, and give it a squeeze.

"Thank you, Myla. This means a lot to me. I know I don't deserve it, but I appreciate it."

She doesn't say anything.

She just looks out the window.

So I do the same.

"DUDE, what the hell is going on?" Banner asks as he meets me in the bathroom.

Yup, guys gather in the bathroom too. It's not just women.

"I don't know." I push my hand through my hair as I lean against the wallpapered wall of the most elaborate men's bathroom I think I've ever seen. And I've been to my fair share of nice places. "She said a deal was a deal but, fuck, man, that kiss." I shake my head. "I felt it to my very soul."

"It looked real as shit."

"It was," I say as Banner walks up to me. "It felt so goddamn real, like nothing has changed between us. Absolutely nothing."

"So what did change?" he asks, and this is where I hang my head low.

"Me," I answer. "I'm the thing that changed and not for the better."

"What do you mean?" he asks, folding his arms.

"I really fucked up, man. I was so focused on what I was going to do to make myself feel better about retiring early that I didn't think about what I was supposed to be doing when I retired. It was supposed to be about Myla and me. I stepped all over that. *We* had plans for my retirement, and I completely neglected her by making decisions for myself. Not for us."

"Wait, you didn't talk to your wife about what you planned on doing?"

"I mean, I did, but I didn't talk about it, talk about it. Just skimmed. It wasn't up for discussion, and I can see now how that was a huge fucking mistake."

"Well, shit, I could have told you that was dumb."

"Yeah, thanks for the input." I push off the wall.

"Well, what now?"

"I have no fucking clue. I'm still reeling from that kiss. A part of me wants to see if something is still there, but I already signed the papers, I apologized, and I told her she could be free, which I know is what she wants. I don't want to get in the way of her happiness because I'm too scared to let go."

"You signed the papers?"

I nod. "It was the only way I knew how to make things better, to give her a sliver of relief from the hell I've put her through. She wanted out, man. I could see it all over her face and how she spoke the truth to me. I didn't want to stand in the way anymore. Holding this wedding over her was stupid, and trying to win her back was stupid. I should have let her go when she first asked."

"But you still love her."

"Doesn't matter. Love isn't enough in this situation," I mutter. "And now, fuck, now she's here, doing me a goddamn favor, and I'm not sure I'll be able to hold it together. I'm already a mess."

"Yeah, I've noticed, but you know, I didn't want to say anything."

"Wow, thanks."

"Do you think there's a chance you can still salvage this?"

I shake my head. "No, I don't think so." Although that kiss felt so fucking real, even though it was probably all for show.

"I don't think you're right. I think there could be a chance." He grips my shoulder. "Can I ask you one thing?"

"Yeah."

Looking me in the eyes, he asks, "Are you two sharing a hotel room?"

I swallow hard and nod. "We are."

Lips pressed together, he nods. "Yeah, I very well think there might be a chance."

⸻

TONIGHT, we're supposed to mingle, taste wine, eat some meats and cheeses, and just enjoy being in the presence of love.

I wish that were the case because it's not for me. I can't be too sure about Myla. She seems so relaxed, it's throwing me off. Maybe she's not that uptight or tense because I signed the papers. Maybe she does feel free, and that's why this charade is so easy for her. She knows that after this, she's done. *"I'm not about to create drama around someone else's wedding, okay? So let's just do this wedding thing and then move on."* Move on. That's her heart's desire.

Whereas I know this is the last time I will be holding her, touching her, kissing her. Even if it is all for show. It's the last time.

The last time I'll say good night to her.

The last time I'll see her all cuddly and adorable in the morning.

The last time I'll get to tell her how beautiful she looks, even if it is in the privacy of our hotel room. After these next couple of days, it's all over.

"Here you go," Myla says, walking up to me with another glass of wine. Our fourth of the night.

"Thank you," I answer.

"You know, when I was getting the wine, Kelsey came up to me and asked why you looked so sad. I told her it was because you had a hard time getting it up this morning and can't get over it."

I nearly spit out my wine as I turn toward her. "What?"

Chuckling, she brings her glass of wine to her lips and says, "Not really, but I'm glad you're no longer pouting."

"I wasn't . . . Jesus, I wasn't pouting."

"Please, you were pouting."

Banner walks up to us while holding a plate of meats in his hand and says, "Heard you couldn't get it up this morning."

I shoot a glare at Myla, who is now smirking—a genuine smirk—and I honestly can't fucking remember the last time I saw her do that. "I might have said that to Banner because I was uncomfortable. Given our situation, I just said the first thing that came to mind."

"It happens to all of us, man," Banner says, gripping my shoulder. "No need to be ashamed."

"I'm not ashamed. I'm just wondering why the hell that's something we're talking about when you didn't even see me this morning." I direct my attention toward Myla.

She taps the side of her head. "Don't need to see you to know that cosmic shift in the air when you can't get it up. It's like a cloud of humidity surrounds us, a dull throb roaring through the moist air. He didn't get it up. He didn't get it up."

I stare at her, truly fucking stare because color me confused. This is the fucking Myla I fell in love with. This is the girl whom I couldn't get enough of. This is whom I thought I would spend the rest of my life with. Where has she been hiding?

Behind me.

Behind my dreams.

Behind my aspirations. *Because of my fucked-up sense of entitlement.*

I miss this girl so fucking much.

Banner's laughter breaks through my thoughts. "He is moodier when he doesn't come, isn't he?"

Looking between them, feeling more confused than ever, I say, "I think you've both had too much wine. Not sure flaccid dick should be a topic of conversation in a place like this."

"You're right." Myla squeezes my arm. "Flaccid dick should be saved for a place that at least serves shots."

"So right," Banner says while offering a high five, and she takes it.

What the fuck is going on?

"AREN'T you going to ask me to dance?" Myla asks as she sets her wineglass down.

"Do you want to dance?" I ask her.

She taps her chin for a moment. "I'm not sure. The last time we danced, you stepped all over my feet."

"The last time we danced was at our wedding," I say.

"Yes, and I recall scuff marks all over my shoes because of you."

"I don't think you're recalling correctly."

"I always recall correctly," she says as she takes my hand and leads me to the dance floor.

I rest my hand on her lower back while she rests hers on my chest. Gentle guitar strings play in the background as we dance under the stringed lights with other couples.

Under normal circumstances, I'd tease her, whispering to her what I was going to do to her when we got back to our hotel room, possibly even tickle her when she'd least expect it, causing her to squirm.

But instead, I'm holding my breath so I don't get myself worked up as I try to navigate the flood of emotions I'm dealing with.

"Are you wearing a new cologne?" she asks. "You smell different."

"New detergent," I answer. "I couldn't find the stuff you get, so I grabbed something else. It's been throwing me off all day."

"It smells good."

"Thanks, you, uh . . . you smell nice too."

"You don't have to say things just to say them, Ryot."

"I know, sorry." I bite my tongue, wanting to ask her how she's acting so cool about this. I know it was my idea, but now that we're here, I'm having a really hard time pretending that I'm not fucking screaming in my head for a second chance.

After another two minutes of dancing, the music ends, and JP and Kelsey go to the front of the room. With their arms around each other, JP says, "Thank you so much for joining us for the next couple of days. I promise, this is the only scheduled event other than the actual wedding, so don't feel like you need to hang out with us every second of every day. We just wanted to bring some of our favorite people up to this beautiful winery for some peace and relaxation. Please feel free to test more wines, check out the pools, take some hikes, or just hang out in your room. We're just glad you're here to join us."

Kelsey kisses his jaw, and together, we all raise a toast to a fun week.

When the night concludes, I press my hand to the small of Myla's back and guide her out to the cars that will take us back to the hotel part of the vineyard. Since we're alone, I drop my hand and shift on my heels.

"Nice night out," I say awkwardly.

"You don't have to make small talk, Ryot."

"Got it," I answer, and for the rest of the short trip back to the hotel, up the elevator, and down the hall to our room, we don't say another word.

---

## MYLA

"THIS WAS NOT A GOOD IDEA," I say to Nichole as I crouch in the corner of the room while Ryot takes a shower.

"Yes, it was. You need this time with him. You need this closure, or else you'll never move on, and you know that."

"I know, but . . . being here with him, acting like everything is okay, it's . . . it's making me feel weird. Like maybe I'm making a mistake."

"Maybe you are," Nichole says. "But you'll never know until you try to find closure."

"But what about you? I should be in Chicago with you. That's where he told me to be."

"And that's great and all, but I don't need you here. I need you to be okay with your decision. Mentally. I know what he said to you before he signed the papers rocked you. I know that letter cut you to shreds. You cried for such a long time that night. This is your chance to close that chapter, so to speak, and I won't allow you to skip that."

Nichole is right. What he said that night hit me harder than I expected.

*I want you to be happy. I just hope that one day, when you've created the life you deserve, and that beautiful smile has returned to your face, you can forgive me.*

Forgive him. That's what's been sticking in my mind ever since he said it.

How can I forgive him? That's what I kept asking Nichole over and over again.

How can I move on from this purgatory I've been living in?

How can I say goodbye to the one man in my life who has been patient, who has cared for me, and who has made me feel like I matter? *Until six months ago.*

And that's when she told me I had to attend the wedding, that I would never be able to move on if I didn't give myself a chance to forgive him.

She's right.

It doesn't mean it isn't hard as I sit here, in the corner, staring at the king-sized bed we'll have to share tonight.

"I'm scared, Nichole."

"I know. Facing adversity is never easy, but trust me when I say, living your life to the fullest, knowing you've done everything not to hold back feelings, not to trap toxic thoughts inside you, it's the only way to live. And you know this because you've done so much work over the years to recover from your mom's malicious actions. Take these days to forgive his mistreatment of you and how that made you feel. To remember him as the man who you once fell in love with, and when the moment is right, release the anger, the tension, the hate that you've carried for the past few months so when it is time to leave, you can do it with a clear head and clear heart."

I let out a deep breath. "You're right."

"I know I am. Now, stop calling me and let me go so I can get some sleep."

"Okay. Love you."

"Love you, too."

I hang up just as the bathroom door opens. I quickly stand from the corner, adjust my nighttime shorts and tank top, and catch Ryot walking into the bedroom wearing only a pair of boxer briefs.

"I, uh, I didn't bring anything decent for nighttime because I thought I was going to be alone."

I smile softly. "Ryot, I don't think a pair of boxer briefs will make me clutch my pearls."

"Guess not." He scratches his bare chest, the way I love— like he isn't sure what to do other than scratch an itch that isn't there. It's adorable. "Can I ask you a question without you getting mad at me?" he asks.

"That's one way to put someone on alert."

"I know, I'm sorry," he says. "I just want to be honest, and my question might upset you, and I don't want it to come off that way."

"Well, thanks for the precursor. What's your question?"

He takes a seat on the edge of the bed and clasps his hands in front of him. "Why are you really here, Myla? I know you said it was because a deal was a deal, but I told you, you didn't need to come. So there must be some other reason."

It would be easy to lie at this moment. To tell him that what I said was the truth, but that would only cause problems with what I'm trying to accomplish while I'm here. So I go with the truth instead.

"I don't want to resent you."

His wet hair falls over his forehead as he looks up at me. "What do you mean?"

"We've been through a lot, Ryot. I would never say our romance had a fairy-tale feel to it because there were a lot of ups and downs, created mainly by me at the beginning, both of us in the middle, and you in the end. And the end of this marriage is clouding my ability to remember all the great things. I don't want to walk away from you feeling anger, or hatred, or resentment. It's not something I want to live with, and I don't want you to live with that either. So I'm looking for forgiveness. I'm looking for . . . for healthy closure."

He stares down at his clasped hands and nods solemnly. "Can't say I love hearing that." He lifts his gaze. "But I get it, Myla. I don't want you to resent me either. I hate what I've done to you, hate myself for it, so the last thing I want is for you to hate me too."

"I know the last thing you want is for us to be friends because I don't think that's possible, not with the heavy feelings we have for each other. But if we could at least, I don't know, find a way to part without bad feelings, it might help both of us move on."

He nods. "Yeah, I think you're right. I'd rather part knowing that you don't resent me than not have these next few days with you." He lets out a sigh and then stands from the bed. "It's late. We should get to bed."

"Probably."

I switch off the light in the entryway of the hotel room, then make my way over to the bed, where I plug my phone into my charger on the nightstand. He pulls down the sheets, and together, we climb in. But whereas I normally would have slithered over to his side, probably naked, and clung to him all night, it feels like at least three feet of cold, empty mattress is between us.

And even though we're attempting to ease out the tension and bitterness, we don't say good night to each other or roll over to face one another. *I've never felt more alone.*

━━━

# RYOT

RYOT: *For those of you not here, Myla came with me to Napa. We talked last night, and the reason she's here is that she doesn't want to leave our marriage feeling resentful.*

**Banner:** *I guess that's smart. I wouldn't want to do that either after everything you've been through.*

**Nola:** *Wow, she's stronger than I was. When Caleb and I broke up, I wished he fell in a well and never resurfaced again.*

**Penn:** *Remind me to never cross you.*

**Banner:** *She's cutthroat. Myla, on the other hand, no matter how many times she's tried to let you go, she's always come back. I can see why she doesn't want to feel bitterness toward you.*

**Ryot:** *I spent the entire night thinking about what she said. She doesn't want to resent me. She knows being friends isn't possible with the feelings we have for each other, but she at least wants to be in a headspace where there isn't any bitterness or resentment. I don't want there to be bitterness either, I want to work on this. I want to work on us. So . . . that's why I'm going to win her back.*

**Penn:** *Oh God.*

**Nola:** *\*\*winces\*\**

**Banner:** *Dude, is that the best idea?*

**Ryot:** *It's the obvious choice.*

**Penn:** *Or are we reading a little desperate?*

**Nola:** *I don't like agreeing with Penn, but you might be in a good spot to end things amicably rather than in a dumpster fire.*

**Banner:** *Yeah, after last night, I don't think trying to win her back is the right choice.*

**Nola:** *What happened last night?*

**Penn:** *Yeah, clue us in.*

**Banner:** *Well, after the kiss that nearly turned me on just watching it . . .*

**Nola:** *YOU KISSED?*

**Banner:** *I would like to clarify: Myla and Ryot kissed. Proceed.*

**Penn:** *I didn't think you (Banner) and Ryot kissed, although some-times brotherly love can go a bit far.*

**Nola:** *What the hell is wrong with you?*

**Penn:** *Can't say.*

**Banner:** *The kiss shook the hotel because he wasn't expecting it, and then after that, she was all light and breezy and fun. The Myla we all know and love. It was fucking strange. And he was eating it up. I think you're going to get your hopes up, man. She's in a different headspace than you, and I don't want you even more hurt and disappointed.*

**Nola:** *He's right. It's hard to try to get someone to fall for you when they're intent on letting you go.*

**Penn:** *If I'm looking at this right, I'm going to have to agree with them. It doesn't seem intelligent.*

**Ryot:** *Maybe not, but what did you say, Banner? She always comes back to me? Well, this is one of those instances. I admit that I drove her away, but I know how to fix it. I know how to make this right, and I will regret it for the rest of my life if I don't at least try.*

**Nola:** *You know I love you, but this is all very cringy.*

**Penn:** *Cringe factor is about a ten out of ten on this one.*

**Banner:** *I'd say eight out of ten. Ten out of ten would be if he proposed at the end and asked her to re-marry him.*

**Nola:** *Ooof, that made me shiver.*

**Penn:** *Please don't do that, man.*

**Ryot:** *I'm sorry, but I thought you all were my friends and family. You're supposed to be helpful.*

**Nola:** *We are. We don't think it's the right move.*

**Ryot:** *Well, I do. You didn't hear her last night when we were in the hotel alone. You didn't see the way she looked at me. Something is still there, and if I have to take the next few days to win her back the way I initially did, through friendship and trust, then I fucking will. I'm not giving up on her. She's had enough people give up on her in her lifetime. I won't be one of them.*

**Banner:** *Okay, that got me a little hard.*

**Penn:** *Nipples erect.*

**Nola:** *Please remove me from this thread.*

# Chapter Sixteen

## MYLA

### *Six years ago . . .*

"Ryot, you don't have to do this," I say, turning toward him as we sit in the car outside my parents' house. "We can go to the lake instead, or possibly go on a food tour. We haven't done that. It might be fun. Or maybe—"

"Babe, shhhh." He presses his finger over my lips. "Your dad said he wanted to meet me. Therefore, I'm going to meet him. We've been dating for a year, so I think it's time."

"I know." Panic trips around in my chest. "It's just . . . my mom. She's, she's going—"

"I'll handle her."

"I know you can, but she's going to put me down and tell you shitty things about me. She never likes it when I'm happy, and she knows how happy I am with you." She hasn't physically hurt me since I fought back when I was a teen. But I've learned that her tongue is capable of even more savagery. *Especially if I'm happy.*

"Then let her be jealous, babe."

He picks up my hand and kisses my knuckles. "Nothing, and I mean nothing, will change my mind on how I feel about you. Okay?"

"Okay." I let out a deep breath. "Let's get this over with."

We both exit the car, and when we meet on the sidewalk, he takes my hand in his. "I'm right here, Myla. The whole time."

Together, we head up to a house I didn't grow up in, just a house I've visited. There is no room dedicated to me. There aren't many pictures of me hanging up, nor is there an ounce of my childhood present. It's just a house. A house with no meaning to me.

I ring the doorbell and clutch Ryot's hand tightly as we wait for the door to open. From the other side, you hear my mom bellowing to my dad to answer the "goddamn" door while my dad's heavy feet shuffle along the hardwood floors.

Here we go.

The door unlocks, and he pushes the screen door open before smiling brightly.

Bald with a full white mustache, he's intimidating with his bushy eyebrows and hard lines on his forehead. Wearing his classic Air Force polo and blue jeans, he hasn't changed much other than his weathered-looking face. *He's aged.*

"Hey, Dad," I say as he smiles.

"My Myla Bean," he says, pulling me into a hug. "How are you?"

"Good," I answer. "I'd like you to meet Ryot, my boyfriend."

"Well, it's about time I've met someone special in your life." Dad reaches out and grips Ryot by the shoulder. "You know she's never brought anyone home before."

"I guess that makes me special, doesn't it, Mr. Moore?"

He takes Ryot's hand and gives him a stiff shake. "Very special. Now come in. Verna has been in the kitchen heating up the place with her chicken and biscuits."

Dad holds open the door, and we squeeze in. Whispering to Ryot, I say, "Take off your shoes and stack them neatly right there." I point at the shoe rack my mom is adamant about people using.

He does as he's told, and then we move into the quaint ranch house. My mom isn't into decorating, and neither is my dad. They've settled for a very minimalistic approach when it comes to their house. It's one of the reasons I love decorating my own place because I've been raised in such bland dwellings.

Two pictures are hanging in the living room, both Air Force-related. The carpet is brown, the furniture is brown, and the walls are a shade of brown. Not a pop of color, not an ounce of joy. Another reason I hate it here.

The only good thing about their house is the giant oak tree in the backyard. It's where I go to sit when I've had too much of my mom. My dad always joins me and tells me that my mom does love me but that she's just stressed. You know, all the excuses that are supposed to make me feel better, but they never do.

"Verna, they're here," Dad calls out. "Ryot, can I get you anything to drink?"

"I'm good." He still clutches my hand. "I can wait until dinner."

"Myla Bean?" my dad asks.

"I'm fine, thanks, Dad. I can wait too."

"Well, then, have a seat." Dad sits in his recliner and then yells again. "Verna, I said they're here."

Mom shouts back, the tone of her voice causing me to shudder. "I heard you. I'll come say hello when I want to."

I try to awkwardly laugh it off, but it falls flat. Correct me if I'm wrong, but usually parents sprint to the door when their kids come to visit them. They gush and coo and thank the high heavens that their "babies" are visiting again. Not my mom. She'll say hi *when she wants to.*

"So how did you two meet?" Dad asks.

Ryot and I discussed this before we came over because we knew my dad would ask the question. Nichole was banging Banner and I refused to leave her alone, so I slept on Ryot's couch while using his flag as a blanket. That's how we met, but it doesn't quite scream the greatest meet-cute in the world. So we decided to go with something else.

"Trivia night," I answer. "Here in Chicago. Ryot and his brother, Banner, needed two more players on their team, and so did Nichole and I. Worked out."

"You good at trivia?" Dad asks Ryot.

"Not as good as your daughter, sir. I went into that night thinking I was going to own the scoreboard, but your daughter taught me a thing or two."

Pridefully, Dad says, "She got that from me."

"Dinner is ready," Mom yells from the kitchen, which means everyone has about two seconds to get into the dining room before we all get yelled at for disrespecting her and not showing up to the table quickly enough.

We all pop up from the couch and head into the dining room, where there are four place settings facing each other. Steamed broccoli is piled in a bowl while a bowl of biscuits is on one side, and Mom's chicken gravy is on the other side. Each place setting has a fork, a knife, a napkin, and a glass of milk. That's the only drink you get when Mom serves dinner.

And speaking of Mom . . .

She emerges from the kitchen wearing black slacks, a white blouse, and a hardened scowl. Her hair is short and peppered with gray. There are newly formed wrinkles around her lips, most likely from constantly pursing them with disdain.

"Hello," she says, offering Ryot a nod, not a handshake. "You must be Ryan."

"Ryot," he corrects, which only makes her scowl even more. "Pleasure to meet you, Mrs. Moore."

She scans Ryot up and down and then says, "Wish I could say the same." She then turns to me and says, "Myla, I see you're still carrying that extra weight in your thighs. It's about time you've come to visit us."

Trying not to wither under her stare or her insult, I answer, "Been busy."

"With that waitressing job, I presume. Still haven't decided to start a real career yet?"

"Why don't we all sit down and eat?" Dad suggests, breaking up the tension.

Thankfully, Mom listens, and she rounds the table to Dad's side.

Yup, no hug.

No *good to see you.*

Just judgment about my weight, my career, and never visiting.

I wonder why?

Ryot pulls out my chair and helps me scoot in before he takes a seat. The minute he's settled, his hand falls to my thigh, and he doesn't move it once.

"So Ryot, you play for a baseball team?" Dad asks.

"Yes, sir. The Chicago Bobbies."

"We don't watch baseball in this house," Mom says while she divvies up everyone's allotted serving of food. I've warned Ryot that whatever she gives you, you eat.

Of course, Dad and Ryot get normal portions, whereas I get half as much. According to my mom, my thighs are too large, my arms are too fat, and she's shocked I can fit my ass into my jeans.

"Shame," Ryot says. "It's a great sport."

"Ryot is the starting third baseman," I chime in for God knows what reason.

"I see." Mom plops three pieces of broccoli on my plate. "So you have a steady income then?"

Here we go.

"Yes, ma'am," Ryot answers.

"Is that why you're with him?" Mom asks me. "Because of his paycheck?"

"No," I answer. "I don't even know how much he makes."

"You're not that dumb, Myla. He's a professional athlete, a starter, no less. He's making more than you would ever see in a lifetime serving lemonades to people."

Clearing his throat, Dad says, "Have you done something different with your hair, Myla?"

I glance over at my mom and feel Ryot squeeze my leg, reminding me not to let her get to me. "Just curling it a lot lately."

"It looks nice."

"Thanks, Dad."

"Better than the time she thought she looked good with bangs." Mom picks up some chicken on her fork. "I was so embarrassed having her walk by my side with those things."

"My forehead was too short," I say, finding myself starting to turtle in.

"Or the time she permed her hair with Nichole. What a disaster. I don't think she's ever been uglier than with that perm."

I push my broccoli around. "We left the solution in too long."

Ryot squeezes my thigh again. "I bet you were adorable," he whispers.

"What has Myla told you about us?" Mom asks, clearly fishing for incriminating evidence.

"What has she told me about you two? Well, that you were both very successful in the Air Force. Mr. Moore was an engineer and you, Mrs. Moore, were a therapist. That you've moved around a lot. Uh . . . oh, and she'd never had s'mores, which I thought was kind of funny—"

"Because she was overweight as a child, and we didn't want to encourage her journey to obesity."

"Mom," I say, feeling so humiliated that my heart is nearly pounding out of my chest.

"Is it not true? Being a daughter of parents in the military, you'd think she'd have more control around a breadbasket."

"That's enough," Dad says, finally speaking up. "We're here to meet Ryot, not travel down memory lane."

I want to throw my dad an appreciative smile for changing the topic, but I also think he should have stepped in sooner. I'm his daughter, after all. He shouldn't let my mom sit there and berate me like that. He might not say anything, but his silence is just as bad. And that's more prevalent than ever as I sit here with Ryot. When I'm alone with them, I let the insults just roll off me because what am I really going to do? But now that someone else hears what my mom has to say to me, it's creating this overwhelming sense of deep-rooted anger that's been there for years. But because I have no voice where they're concerned, that anger rolls into a ball of humiliation for being unable to muster the confidence to stand up for myself.

After a few bouts of silence, Ryot says, "Dinner is very good, Mrs. Moore."

"Thank you," she says tersely, and I can only imagine the sort of wrath my dad is going to face when we leave.

"So where are you from?" Dad asks, trying to break the tension as well.

"Maine, a small town called Bright Harbor off the coast. Born and raised. I took Myla there over winter. It's my favorite time of the year because the town makes it their mission to put you in the Christmas spirit."

"Did you like it, Myla Bean?" Dad asks.

"It was beautiful. Like a town you'd find in a Lovemark movie."

"You mean those unrealistic movies where bumbling women focus on finding love?" Mom asks as she cuts into one of her biscuits.

No one responds, so Ryot says, "Actually, the town next to ours is Port Snow, which is famous for a shop at the end of the harbor called The Lobster Landing. Many Lovemark movies have been shot there. When we visited, I took Myla around and showed her all the different landmarks movies have featured."

"That must have been fun," Dad says.

"It was," I answer. "One of my favorite trips ever. Not to mention, the countryside during the winter was beautiful." And how when I walked into his parents' house, I was immediately enveloped in love.

"I'm sure," Dad replies and then looks at Ryot. "Does that mean you're a lobster man?"

Ryot chuckles. "It does. Until my dying day, I will always say that Maine lobster is the best lobster."

"Did you have some when you were there?" Dad asks me.

"I did." I smirk and glance at Ryot. "It was okay."

"Okay?" Ryot asks, feigning insult.

I chuckle. "I preferred the baked bean sandwich."

"What's that?" Dad asks.

"A New England specialty," I answer. "This one had baked beans, cheddar, apples, and mustard on it."

"Horrendous way to pack fat on your hips," Mom says as she stuffs a piece of broccoli in her mouth.

I glance away and dab my mouth with my napkin. Ryot smooths his hand over my thigh, reminding me that he's still here with me.

"Did you meet Ryot's family?" Dad asks.

"Yes," I answer, knowing this will open the door for Mom to make a fuss out of something that she doesn't need to make a fuss about. "I met his brother before going to Maine. Ryot and Banner share an apartment. But I met his sister, Nola, while we were in Bright Harbor as well as Mr. and Mrs. Bisley. Nola and I got along so well that I snagged her number before I left, and we've been keeping in touch."

"You have?" Ryot asks, surprised.

I smile at him. "Yes. We talk a lot actually."

"So you talk to Ryot's sister a lot but visit us once a year?" Mom asks, and there it is. Took her long enough.

I don't know what to say other than the truth, and the truth doesn't sit well on my tongue, so instead, I stay silent.

"Well, I'm glad we're here now," Ryot says, and then silence falls.

It's deathly quiet as forks clang against plates and glasses of milk are sipped. I can't imagine what Ryot must be thinking. What must be going through his mind? When visiting his family during winter, it was warm and welcoming. There were no fights, there were no awkward encounters, and his parents never disparaged him. No, they loved on him, hugged him, welcomed me into the family, and made me feel like I was one of them.

This here is war. *The same battlefield I grew up on.*

Finally, Mom clears her throat, sets her napkin down, and rests both of her wrists against the edge of the table. "You're an attractive man, Ryot. Clearly successful, with a large bank account." Oh no, where is this going? *Please . . . please don't break me even more.* "So I'm wondering what you're doing with someone like my daughter, who is average at best, has yet to pick a career path, and from my knowledge, still shares an apartment with her friend because she can't afford to live alone?" Mom stares at us. "It's pretty obvious why she's barking up your tree. I can't possibly see why you're interested in her."

Old wounds are split open.

The past floods my brain, and what minimal confidence I

had walking into this house is washed away as self-doubt and hate pulse up my spine.

And this is exactly what I feared about bringing Ryot here. This disdain my mother has for me. This hatred. It's coming through in such an evil, awful . . . humiliating way that I can barely look at him as I shrink into my chair.

What Ryot must be thinking of me right now.

"Verna," Dad chimes in. "Why don't we change the subject? Tell Myla about the knitting club you joined."

"I'd rather not. She won't be interested in it. She doesn't quite understand what it means to have a hobby, other than the hobby of following her friend around, looking for attention."

"She's the most unique person I've ever met," Ryot says, drawing attention back to himself. He sets his fork down and looks my mom in the eyes. "That's what first attracted me to her. Then it was her eyes, the color of the sky on the sunniest of days. After that, it was her voice, which has an edge to it, an edge that says she's been through a lot in her life, but she's persevered."

"Ryot," I say, tugging on his hand. "You don't have to—"

"Then it was her body, which I'm not ashamed to say, because she's sexy. The curves you describe as 'packing on weight' are my favorite parts of her body. She's a real woman, a woman I love touching, feeling, and worshipping. Easily, without a doubt, the sexiest woman I've ever been with. So sexy, Verna, that I can barely keep my hands off her." Oh God. I gulp. "She's everything I would want in a woman, and it took me so goddamn long to find her. And when I got to know her better, I realized just how funny she is. Smart. Kind. She would do anything for anyone if she knows what she does is appreciated. I'm jealous of her courage and her strength and wish I possessed even half of it." He rises from the table, and I look at him, shocked as he grabs my hand and pulls me up from my chair as well.

"What are you doing?" I whisper.

"Your daughter is special, and it's pathetic that, as her mother, you can't see that."

"How dare you?" my mom huffs as Dad stands from the table as well.

Addressing my dad, Ryot says, "Mr. Moore, I apologize for the outburst, but I can't sit here and listen to your wife denigrate Myla with every word she says. That's unpardonable and disgusting. I can't and *won't* remain silent when someone I care about is being torn to shreds. However, I hope you and I can share a meal in the future."

He then turns to my mom and says, "I have simply no idea how you were ever employed as a therapist when you are so capable of such monstrous and hateful words, knowing the ramifications. No. Idea. Thank God you weren't able to destroy this precious woman by my side, emotionally . . . *or* physically."

With that, he leads me to the entryway, where he picks up our shoes but doesn't even bother putting them on before we are out of the house and heading to his car. He doesn't say a word, just opens my door, helps me in, and then tosses my shoes in as well. When he opens his car door, he shoves his shoes to the back, buckles up, starts the car, and drives.

Nothing is said.

And as we drive through the suburbs of Chicago, all I can think about is what my mom said . . . what Ryot said. Did he really mean all those things? I want to say he did, and that's why he stuck up for me, but the little girl inside me, the one that's been abused repeatedly by her mother, mentally and physically, she's the one who is suffering the consequences. She's the one feeling the doubt. She's the one who wants to crawl into a hole and never be seen again.

I don't pay attention to where we're going until we're pulling into the private parking lot of Ryot's apartment building. He finds his spot, shuts off the engine, and then grabs his shoes from the back. He slips them on quickly and then exits the car. I slip my shoes on as well just as he opens my door and holds his hand out.

Unsure of what else to do, I take it and allow him to guide me up to his empty apartment. He doesn't bother turning on any lights as he brings me to his bedroom and shuts the door.

"Ryot," I finally say, my voice tight from holding back tears.

He doesn't look at me, just charges toward the bathroom, where I hear something crash to the floor. The sound startles me.

He's angry.

Very angry.

*What do I do?*

I peek around the corner and catch him leaning forward, gripping the counter while breathing heavily. When he notices me shift, he turns so his eyes are on me.

"Come here," he says in a menacing tone. When I don't move, he softens and says, "Myla, come here."

But I don't listen. Instead, I twist my hands in front of me and say, "I know what you must be thinking."

"Oh?" He moves so now he's in the archway of his bathroom door. "What is it that I'm thinking, Myla?"

"That you . . . uh, that you feel sorry for me, that you think my life is a total disaster and that I'm probably not worth sitting through another one of those attempts at a dinner." I glance away, unable to look him in the eyes. "I, I don't know what to say about my mom other than I hate her. I hate that she has power over me, that she makes me feel so weak, so unwanted, that some of the things she said were true—"

"I'm going to stop you right there. Everything your mom said tonight was a blatant jab to demean you. Crush you. She attempted to poke every single wound you have, and it was spineless. People like her love to control others. They will do everything they can to make sure they continue to hold that power."

"Well, she does, and now she's dragged you in. So I can understand if you just want to . . . I don't know, go our separate ways—"

"You're joking, right?" he asks, his eyes narrowing. "Are you really attempting to tell me I can break up with you?"

I toss my arms up in the sky. "I don't know what to do, Ryot. You're clearly angry, everything that she said was humiliating, and this was a total disaster. I wouldn't blame you if you wanted to walk away."

"I'm angry because I can't believe a mother can speak about her daughter like that. I'm angry because your dad barely interjected to stop her yet, you think he's the greatest thing that's walked this planet. I'm mad because instead of spending one of my nights off with my girl, I had to spend it with two people who can't see the goddamn beauty that I see in you every day. I'm not angry with *you*, Myla. I'm angry with the people who should be loving you, supporting you, defending you, and rooting for you."

"Oh," I say.

"And yes, was the night a total disaster? It was. But I brought you back to my apartment for a reason because I know you see it as a safe place. And that's where I want you to be, safe." He takes a step forward and then another, and then another until he's inches from my face. He grips my jaw, his thumb extending to tilt my chin up. "Everything I said, I fucking meant. You have captured me, Myla, in all the best ways. And despite what your mom might think, I feel like I'm the one who is out of *your* league. I feel like at any moment, you could walk away and find someone better, someone more suited for you. I know the disadvantage I have in this relationship. I know that your heart, your mind, and your wit far exceed what I have to offer."

I shake my head, but he holds me still.

"Yes, Myla. It's fucking true, and don't tell me otherwise, do you hear me? You are an amazing woman, and I am so damn lucky that you're mine."

Tears drip down my cheeks as I stare up at him. He's lucky?

He thinks he's the lucky one? He has that so backward. I'm standing in front of a man unmatched. He's unlike any man I've ever met . . . or will ever meet.

"Do you understand?" he asks me, and when I don't answer because I wasn't paying attention, he repeats himself. "You're mine, and no one is going to make you fucking feel any less perfect than what you are."

He's perfect.

He's everything I could ever have hoped for in a man, and as I'm staring up into his powerful eyes, a wave of emotion washes over me. A feeling so strong, so intense, that I realize this is the real thing. With Ryot.

We've been together for a year. It's been hard with his schedule, but we've made it work. And even though we've spent that year together, we've never truly expressed our emotions, not until tonight. Not until we were at my parents' house. Not until I saw what love was not. Love is not abusing a child. Making them feel weak. Love is not staying silent when that child needs a champion. Love is being ready to stand up for and protect the one who owns your heart. And just as Ryot defended me tonight, I know I will do everything in my power to do the same for him if he needs that.

Wiping at my eyes, I clear my tear-stained cheeks and then rest my hands on his chest. "Ryot?"

"Yeah, babe?" he asks.

"I need to tell you something."

"What is it?" He lowers to look me in the eyes.

This is it. I wet my lips, our gazes lock, and then I let the words pour out of me before I can stop them. "I love you, Ryot." My throat tightens, and I repeat, "I love you so much."

His eyes soften, and he gently cups my cheek as he tilts my mouth toward his. He doesn't answer. Instead, he molds his lips to mine.

Soft.

Possessive.

But sweet at the same time.

He backs me up to the bed and gently lays me down so he can hover above me and continue our kiss. It's like a drug, his mouth on mine, it gets me so crazy, so high like nothing could harm me when he's this close. And I won't stop chasing this high, because it's the best feeling.

After a few more kisses, he pulls away and connects our foreheads. His nose rubs against mine, and he quietly says, "I love you, too. You're my girl, Myla. My everything. I've loved you for so long but never wanted to tell you in fear you weren't ready." He smooths his nose over my cheek. "But I know you're ready now. Your heart is open."

"It's been open for a long time," I say. "I just don't think I knew how to express it, but after today, it was as if it just came out of me. I love you, Ryot. Thank you for loving me. For being patient with me. For making me feel like I matter. I've been made to feel like I add zero importance to this world, but you . . . you make me feel worthy of the air in my lungs."

"Baby," he says softly. "You are so fucking worthy, and don't ever second-guess that."

And then his mouth is on mine again.

His hands are running up my shirt and pulling down the cups of my bra, where he plays with my nipples.

I undo his pants.

He removes my shirt and lowers his mouth to my breasts. And that's where he stays for a while, lapping at my nipples with the flat of his tongue, pinching them with the tips of his fingers, and sucking on them with his swollen lips. He doesn't stop until I'm writhing under him, begging for him to give me release. That's when he releases me and pulls my pants off as well as my thong. I remove my bra, and while I do that, he strips down to nothing.

I crawl back on the bed, spread my legs, and say, "I want you inside me . . . bare."

He pauses. "Bare? Babe, you don't have to."

"I want to. I'm on birth control. I want nothing more than to feel all of you with nothing between us."

He rolls his teeth over his bottom lip as he crawls closer and then brings his mouth to mine. While our tongues tangle, he positions the head of his cock at my entrance, and then with one more kiss, he pushes into me, inch by delicious inch. It's torturous but so, so good because I'm feeling every bit of him.

"Fuck, so warm, so tight." His eyes squeeze shut. "Babe, I won't last."

"Well then, you better make love to me."

And he does.

Sweet, slow, tender.

The way he kisses me. Holds me close. Never lets me lose contact.

It's the best sex of my life.

The best night of my life.

Nothing will ever . . . ever top this.

---

## RYOT

"WHERE ARE YOU TAKING ME?" Banner asks, looking out the window. "This whole meetup has been evasive and uncomfortable. I would appreciate a little heads-up. Some backstory. Anything. Anything other than you just sitting there in silence. I mean . . . where the hell are we? We're in a back alleyway. That's weird, man. Are you going to kill me? Are you part of a mob? Do you owe a bookie money? Dude, don't be Pete Rose. Don't bet on the game."

I put the car in park and get out of the car. When Banner doesn't move, I say, "Get your ass out here."

"Out where? In the brick alleyway? Do you really think that's a safe place to be? I've been working out, but, dude, these muscles are all for show. I don't know how to use them."

"For fuck's sake, Banner, we're not going to get beaten up. Now if you don't get out of the goddamn car, I might kick your ass myself."

"Brutal," he mutters. "Can't fucking win either way." He hops out of the car, rounds the hood, and stands next to me. "Okay, what are we going to do now? Scale the wall like Spiderman?"

Rolling my eyes, I walk up to the brick building's metal door and give it a knock. When it opens, a man in a suit answers. "Name?"

"Babe Ruth."

He nods and then opens the door. "Follow the hall, first door on the right."

"Thanks," I say as Banner stands there, his mouth agape.

When I push at his shoulder to get him moving, he whispers, "Dude, you're part of a mob, aren't you? Listen, I knew I said I would follow you anywhere, but this is pushing it. I won't survive in jail, you know that."

"Will you just shut up?"

"Will you just tell me what we're doing?"

We reach the door on the right, and I check the handle. It's unlocked, so I push it open and smile broadly as the small room is lit up by cases and cases of rings, an attendant at each case.

"What the hell kind of secret jewelry heist is this?" Banner asks, eyeing the rings. "Listen, this is some black-market kind of shit, and I'm not interested."

Turning toward my brother, I grip his shoulders, look him in the eyes and say, "I'm going to propose to Myla."

Understanding hits him, and his eyes scour the rings again. "Dude," he says, eyes wide. "Like legit propose?"

"Yes, and I want your help to pick out the right ring."

"Holy shit. Does she know?"

I shake my head. "She has no fucking clue. That's why I came here because I'm a high-profile figure in the city. If someone saw me walking into a jewelry store, it would have been splashed across the news, and she would have found out. So that's why we're here."

Banner rubs his hands together and nods his head. "Black market rings."

"No," I say. "These are from a few custom high-profile jewelers from around the country. They've pulled their best and are showing them off. Nothing to do with the black market."

"Maybe not, but I'm going to believe that's what's happening. It's more fun like that in my head. Now, where do we start?"

———

"WHEN ARE you going to do it?" Banner asks as he takes a sip of his beer.

"After the season. I want to be able to spend time together once I do it. I don't want to propose and then take off for an away game."

It took us about an hour and a half to look over the rings closely and pick the perfect one. I had my eyes set on one, a round-cut pink diamond that screamed Myla, but Banner was all about examining each and every ring just to make sure. I brought the pink diamond around, comparing it to the others, and nothing beat it out.

Easiest purchase of my life.

Once the ring was put into a jewelry box, Banner demanded I take him out for dinner. He earned it.

"True, good point. Any ideas?"

"I was thinking about taking her to Bright Harbor in the fall. She loves it there, and I could get Nola to take pictures from a distance."

"That's a good idea. Have you told Nola?"

I shake my head. "You're the only one I've told. So don't be fucking saying anything to Nichole."

"Dude, I don't talk to her. I haven't seen her in a while. Nothing is going on there, I swear. And I'm not just saying that but mean something else. Seriously, nothing is going on."

"Okay, well, just don't say anything."

"Your secret is safe with me." He lifts his beer to his lips and says, "Still can't believe you're going to propose. I remember when she barely looked your way."

"Tell me about it." I lean back in my booth, keeping an eye on the door because Myla is supposed to meet us here. "But after the other night, when she told me she loved me, I knew she was ready."

"The same night you met her dad and Verna, the venereal disease?"

I chuckle. "Yeah, the same night." I let out a deep breath. "Fuck, that woman. She has got to be the single most, worst human I've ever met. I still can't get over the shit she said with Myla sitting right there. Practically called her obese and said she was stupid and not good enough for me. Could you imagine Mom or Dad ever saying that about us?"

"Yeah, you know that trend that's going around where people ask, 'what would you say to your family to let them know you've been captured, without letting them know you've been captured?' Well, Mom and Dad would say, 'good riddance; you three children are the biggest disappointments in our lives, and we hope you rot in hell for eternity.' That would confirm they're being kidnapped because never in a lifetime would they even think those thoughts. When it comes to our parents, they believe we walk on water."

"We kind of do," I say just as the door to the restaurant opens and in walks Myla.

She's pulled her long, brown hair back into a ponytail and has dressed up in a black jumpsuit with a jean jacket and black high heels. She looks so fucking good. And when she spots me, the largest grin spreads across her face as she approaches.

"From the heart beams coming out of your eyes, I'm going to guess Myla just got here."

"Yup," I answer as I stand from the booth just as she arrives. "Hey, you," I say as I move my hand around the back of her neck and give her a soft kiss. "How was your meeting?"

She smiles brightly and says, "It went really well."

"What meeting?" Banner asks.

I help Myla into the booth and hand her my beer before draping my arm over her shoulders and pulling her in close.

"I had a meeting with a non-profit. It's called Renovate Chicago. They're looking for volunteers to come in and help with renovating homes around the city. I've always been into interior design, and I've been looking to see where I could gather more experience. I was actually talking to Nola about it, and she said her friend got a lot of experience working with a non-profit. So that's what I decided to do. I found Renovate Chicago, I just had a meeting with them, and they're going to find a place to fit me in."

"Babe, that's amazing."

Her smile is so big that I take a mental picture. It took a fucking second for her to recover from the dinner with her parents, and I've tried to speak positivity into her life as much as possible. I've reminded her that her mom is the one who's spineless, worthless, and not Myla. She won't unhear her mother's words overnight, but I'm hoping she's putting more effort into healing rather than stewing on the shit her mom piled on her.

"I know. I'm really excited. I was hoping to go to the office supply store tonight and grab some things so I could start some planning."

"Yeah?" I ask. "Well, I can take you now."

"No, I can wait. I don't want to blow off Banner."

Banner takes a long pull from his beer. "Actually, it would be best if you two left. There's a blonde by the bar that I'm itching to talk to, and this third-wheel shit is making me look pathetic."

"Are you sure?" Myla asks. "Because we can stay, and you know . . . talk."

He chuckles. "Yeah, you sound so convincing that you want to be here with me. Seriously, go get your office supplies, maybe grab a late-night hot dog, and let me do my thing with that blonde over there."

"You sure?" Myla asks, wincing.

"Positive," he says. "Now get out of here. The longer you stay, the harder chance I'll have at getting her to talk with me."

"Doubtful," Myla says as she sets my beer down.

I reach for my wallet, but Banner holds up his hand. "Jesus Christ, don't even think about giving me any money."

"Okay, just checking."

And then we're out of the booth, hand in hand with quick goodbyes to Banner. We head out of the restaurant, I get stopped a few times by fans, which Myla is used to by now, and then we're on the street, walking toward the office supply store.

"I'm really glad the meeting went well," I say to her as I drape my arm over her shoulders and hold her close. "I love seeing that smile and excitement on your face. It makes me happy."

"You know, Ryot, I feel for the first time in my life that I know what I'm supposed to be doing. I have direction and purpose. I know that might sound silly, especially to someone like you—"

"Don't put yourself down. Everyone is on their own path. It doesn't matter the timeline."

"You're right, sorry."

"And I understand your excitement, I truly do, because I know what it feels like to be lost. When I was in the minors and not getting called up as quickly as I expected, I truly felt like I possibly wasn't doing what I was supposed to be doing, but then, when I was called up, I saw the vision. The plan. And I knew I was doing what I was meant to be doing."

"That's how I feel."

"I'm glad, babe. So does this mean I get to buy my girl all the office supplies her little heart desires?"

"You don't have to buy me anything. You just need to haul it around for me."

I chuckle. "I'll do both."

"Ryot," she complains, and I stop her immediately.

"A present from me, okay? Just take it and say thank you."

She lets out a deep sigh. "Thank you."

"You're welcome." I kiss the top of her head.

And as we turn the corner, she says, "It feels like everything is going so great right now. I'm just waiting for the other shoe to drop, you know?"

"What do you mean?"

She shrugs and grips me tighter. "I just haven't had the best of luck in this life of mine. And I didn't think it was possible to feel this happy. I swear something will go wrong."

"Or maybe everything is going right because you're where you're supposed to be, with whom you're supposed to be with, and heading in a direction that you were supposed to be headed. Sometimes it isn't about being lucky or feeling like you're lucky. It's about connecting all the puzzle pieces in life. Babe, you're connecting them."

She glances up at me, her smile wicked. "Oh Bisley, you

are so going to get the best blow job of your life tonight after that heart-stopping statement."

I chuckle. "I have more where that came from. What happens if I give you two more?"

"Hmm." She taps her chin just as her phone rings in her purse. "Hold that thought." She fishes into her purse, pulls out her phone, and frowns.

"What?" I ask.

"It's my mom. She never calls me."

"Maybe she's calling to apologize about the other night."

Myla snorts. "Yeah, when pigs fly." Then she answers it. "Hey, Mom, what's going on?" The store is just down the street, so I keep us walking in that direction when suddenly, Myla stops in the middle of the sidewalk.

"What?" she asks, her eyes welling up with tears. "How? When?"

"What's going on?" I ask, turning toward her now.

She lowers the phone and looks up at me, an emptiness casting over her expression as she says, "It's my dad." She takes a shallow breath. "He's dead."

# Chapter Seventeen

RYOT

*Present day . . .*

"Morning," I say as Myla slowly rolls to her back, her hair fanning over her face.

"Who? What now? Where am I?" She thrashes around and then stiffens as if she was just pulled up by a string. "What's going on? Is there a fire?"

"What?" I ask. "Jesus, Myla, you're just in a hotel room."

She moves her hair out of her face and stares back at me. She takes a moment to take in my swim trunks, sandals, and bare chest before her eyes meet mine. "Are you going scuba diving?"

"Does it look like I am?" I ask.

"I don't know what you do partially nude." She flops back down on the bed and sinks into the pillow. "What time is it?"

"Ten in the morning. You missed breakfast."

"Ten?" She sits back up. "How is it ten?"

"That's what the clocks say."

"Well, Jesus, you shouldn't let a girl sleep in until ten. That's just irresponsible." She flings the sheets off her, stands, and one of her boobs is completely hanging out of her tank top. She glances down, and then back at me. "Uh, under normal circumstances, I wouldn't care about the wild beasts that are boobs in a tank top at night, but I'm just going to tuck this right back in." She shifts her boob and covers it up, but not before I got a good eyeful. *I've missed those girls.*

"Okay, yeah, well, I'm going to head down to the pool."

"Ah, hence the bathing suit." She moves by me and to the bathroom. "I'll go with you."

"You don't have to."

"Won't it be weird if I don't?"

I pull on the back of my neck. "Yeah, probably."

"Okay, so give me a second, and I'll be ready. Just going to brush my teeth, pee, wash my face, and throw my hair up into a ponytail."

"Okay," I answer as she grabs a suit from her suitcase and slips into the bathroom.

I take a seat on the chair in the corner of the room and let out a deep breath. Today is day one of convincing Myla that we belong together. That we're better together than apart. And even though we're talking to each other and not trying to steal batteries or any of that bullshit, I know we have a long way to go. I need to gain back her trust first. I need to make some lifestyle changes and remember what's most important in my life. And that's her.

After a few minutes, the bathroom door opens, and she walks out in a navy-blue bikini that leaves nothing, and I mean absolutely nothing, to the imagination. The strings on her bottoms cut high on her hips, leaving only a small triangle between her legs. And the top matches the triangle between her legs, small and barely covering enough.

I swallow hard and watch as her full hips shift, her breasts sway, her stomach contracts with every step she takes. Fuck, she's gorgeous.

If we were in a different place, I would be peeling that swimsuit off right now and not letting her leave this hotel room until I felt like I'd fully claimed her, marked her so the world knew who she belongs to.

But now, I just need to keep my lips sealed as she walks around, getting ready for our trip to the pool.

"Okay, I think I have everything I need." She plops sunglasses over her eyes.

I move to the dresser where I placed a yogurt parfait. I hand it to her and say, "Picked up some breakfast for you in case you were hungry."

"Oh, thank you." She glances up at me and then back at the parfait. "That was kind of you."

I just shrug. "Not a big deal."

"Okay, well . . . are you ready?"

"Yeah. Towels are by the pool."

"Great." She tosses on a cover-up, and then, with parfait in hand, we head out of the hotel room together, keeping our distance from each other. Thankfully, the resort is for adults only, meaning when Myla takes off that cover-up, she won't be having a nip slip in front of children, just me. Then again, we've already had one today.

"What did you have for breakfast?" she asks, probably trying to fill in the awkward silence.

"I went for a run this morning. Picked up a protein shake on the way up here."

"Should have guessed. Although, I thought that you would drop the regimen for a day and enjoy a donut."

I pause and wonder if that bothers her, that I'm always keeping up with my workouts, that I haven't really changed since I retired. I guess in that respect, I haven't slowed down on keeping fit. And I think a part of that is because I'm not ready to let go of that part of my life. If I stop caring so much, tracking all my nutrients, then that means I'm letting go of something that has been so constant in my life for so long.

"Maybe I will tomorrow. The waffles in the restaurant smelled amazing as I passed."

She chuckles. "You eat a waffle? That would be a day to celebrate. I don't think I've ever seen you eat any sort of carb in the morning."

"Well, there's always time for change," I say, making a mental note to show her I can change. I can listen. I can try new things. Like waffles first thing in the morning.

"Well, if it isn't the Bisleys," Banner says from behind us. "Headed to the pool, I see?"

When I look over my shoulder at Banner, he has a massive grin on his face. I can only imagine what's rolling around in his head at the moment. "We are. Where are you off to?"

He motions to his jeans and T-shirt. "Going on a tour of the vineyard."

"By yourself?" I ask.

He grins even wider. "No. I'm escorting Kelsey's cousin, Kenzie. She's a marine biologist."

"Are we interested in Kenzie?" I ask him as we reach the elevator.

"I'm always interested. But yeah, she's pretty cool. Really shy, hence why I'm escorting her on the tour. She's not very good at making friends. At least that's what Kelsey told me last night."

Silent, Myla hits the down button, and as the doors close, I say, "Well, let us know how the tour is. Maybe we'll go on it later."

"I bet you will," he says. "By the way, love seeing you two together." His smirk becomes genuine. "Makes me happy."

"We're not together," I tell him, hoping to redirect any

assumptions Myla might have. I don't want her thinking that I've told Banner we're together because that will freak her out, no doubt.

"Together, as in not biting each other's heads off, stealing batteries, or switching records around."

Myla spins toward me. "I told you, you did it."

I roll my eyes. "Yeah, and who else would have?"

In a sad impersonation of me, she replies, "The little fairies that keep taking the batteries."

When the elevator doors part, Banner holds up his thumb and says, "Your Ryot impersonation is spot on."

"Thank you."

And then we part, Banner heading toward the front of the hotel while Myla and I head toward the back.

Curious as to what she thinks about Banner, I ask, "Do you feel weird when he goes out with other people? Or flirts or talks about them?"

"Why would that make me feel weird?" she asks as I push open a door for her. When she walks past me, her shoulder brushes my chest, and even though it's a mistaken touch, it still excites me.

"Well, because of Nichole," I answer.

"Oh . . . no, not at all. I know where Nichole stands. She doesn't want a relationship. Never has and probably never will. Banner is just a boy toy she likes to have fun with on occasion. I could see him settling down at some point, but not Nichole. She will always be a free spirit."

"You think Banner will settle?" I ask as we walk side by side on the paved path that leads to the pool. Well-manicured gardens flank either side of us while mature trees drape over the path together, forming a tunnel of greenery. It's very romantic.

"I think the Bisley boys were born to settle. Banner might act like he's not interested in anything serious, but you can see it in his eyes when he measures up a new partner. I think he's always on the lookout, but no one has struck him the right way. He hasn't met his match yet."

"You said the Bisley boys. Do you think I was born to settle?"

We make it to the pool, which is empty, and I grab two towels while Myla looks around for a lounge that suits her.

"Were you born to settle? I don't know, Ryot, what do you think? You spent years trying to get me to go out on a date with you. Pretty sure 'settle' is supposed to be your middle name."

I chuckle. "Yeah, because the right girl struck me."

She takes the towel from me and says, "The right girl at the moment."

And I know the meaning behind that. Despite the easygoing conversation, there's still an elephant in the room. We're bound to be divorced once the papers are processed, and even though I think she's the right girl for me—for life—it's not forever. No one will be better. No one will match her.

But I don't push to prove her wrong. That's not what I need to do right now. If Myla has shown me something over the past week or so, it's that I've been blind to who she is and what she wants in life. My goal is to show her that I'm in her corner, that I'm sorry I ever left, and that if I could, I'd be her everything once more.

"Are you going to dip into the pool or just lie out?"

She eyes me and says, "When have I ever just laid out?"

The answer is never.

Myla is the girl doing cannonballs in the pool on vacation and tossing random items into the deep end so she can impress you by retrieving them within seconds of hitting bottom. She's not one to lie out by the pool, drink froufrou drinks, and dip her toe in the water momentarily.

Nope, she's all in.

"Wasn't sure if you were going to try something new."

"Never," she says as she lifts her cover-up over her head

and deposits it on the lounger. And then she walks up to the pool, turns around, and with a salute, she falls backward, right into the water, making me laugh.

When she pops up, she wipes the water out of her eyes and says, "Never a lounger, never will be one."

"You getting in there with your wife?" I hear a voice ask. I turn just in time to see Huxley and Lottie approach, hand in hand.

"Uh, yeah," I answer. "Can't let her swim alone."

Immediately, I'm doused back into reality where Myla isn't really my wife. But I have to pretend that she is. Therefore, I line up on the edge of the pool, give Huxley a wink, and then backflip into the water. When I surface, I hear Myla behind me whisper, "Show-off."

I push my wet hair back and turn toward her. "You could have been more creative with your entrance. You chose what you chose. Don't hate on me for being more theatrical."

"Do I need to jump into this pool again?"

"Up to you," I say as I float next to her.

She glances over her shoulder and smiles, then looks back at me. Whispering, she says, "If they didn't just park their asses next to our loungers, you can bet your tight ass that I would be reinventing the wheel when it came to pool theatrics, but I'll have to settle with knowing in my heart of hearts, I would show you up."

"Okay, keep believing that," I say.

"Oh awesome, you guys here for the class too?" JP says as he walks up with Kelsey.

"She dragged me to it," Huxley replies.

"Looks like Ryot and Myla are ahead of us."

"What class?" Myla whispers.

"Hell if I know," I reply just as a few more couples make their way into the pool. Glancing around, I ask, "What's happening?"

"I don't know, but they're surrounding us," Myla says.

Kelsey dips daintily into the pool while JP dunks his head in first and then flops the rest of the way. Huxley and Lottie enter by the stairs, taking it slow while holding hands.

"I've heard nothing but great things about these classes," Kelsey says while JP swoops his arm around her waist.

"Yeah, me too," I say, eliciting a pinch from Myla. "What?" I whisper. "Have to make conversation."

"Oh, here is the instructor now," JP says as a lady wearing leggings and a sports bra walks up with a Bluetooth speaker.

"Hey, couples," she says in a cheery voice. "Thank you for joining me this morning. If you would so kindly pick a portion of the pool for yourselves where you can find privacy, I'm going to set up and be right with you."

"What's happening?" Myla asks.

"I have no fucking clue, but I just want you to know, whatever it is, I didn't know this was happening. Please believe me." Panic laces my voice because it seems like whatever we're going to do will be intimate.

"I believe you, Ryot," she says. "I'm not mad."

"I know, I just . . . I don't know what's happening, and I don't want you thinking I planned this."

"I know," she says. "But it seems like we're in this now, so I guess we need to find a spot in the pool that's more private. How about over here?" She motions to a curve in the pool, where a low-hanging palm offers some privacy.

"Yeah, that works." We head over there, and then both lean against the pool wall as I watch the other couples find spots while clinging tightly to each other.

"My name is Mel, and I'm going to be your guide this morning," the instructor says as she sits on a yoga mat at the edge of the pool and switches on her light, instrumental music. "We're here to reconnect with our partners. I'm going to be quiet most of the time, just giving you emotional cues when necessary."

"Oh shit," I whisper, my muscles tensing. "Uh . . . Myla, we can leave."

"No, we can't," she says.

"Yes, I can make an excuse. I'll tell them that I forgot I have a meeting."

"You're going to lie about a meeting when you're in business with these guys? You don't think they aren't going to ask you what the meeting is about?"

"Could be about sponsorship stuff."

"Okay, everyone, take in a deep breath and then get comfortable with your partner," Mel says in a quiet tone.

Panic races up my spine. "Here, we can just sneak out right here, and I'll explain later."

"It's fine, Ryot," she says. "Maybe she can't see us over here, and we can just——"

"Behind the palm over there, are you guys able to hear me?"

"Uh, yeah," I say and then clear my throat. "Actually, we——"

"We're just trying to figure out how to get comfortable," Myla says over me.

"Oh, well, just wrap your arms and legs around your partner and face him. Whatever works for you."

"Thanks." Myla turns toward me and says, "Lean against the pool wall."

"Myla, seriously, we don't——"

"It might be good for us," she says, her eyes meeting mine. "Who knows, maybe we'll find some mutual ground."

Or I might get hard as shit with my fine-as-hell, soon-to-be ex-wife straddling me.

Before I can say anything, she slips her arms around my neck, presses her body to mine, and wraps her legs around my waist.

Fuck.

Me.

"This okay?" she asks softly.

No.

Not even a little.

*Because I miss you. Because I fucked up, and I want nothing more than to keep you like this, in my arms, and never let go.*

"Yeah, I think so," I answer through a tight throat.

"Once everyone is comfortable," Mel says, "I'd like you to tell your partner three things you appreciate about them."

What is this class?

I'm all for growth in relationships, but I'm having a really hard time understanding how Huxley Cane is in this class. Sure, I could possibly see JP doing this, but Huxley? I don't think he understands what emotion is. Crazy what love can do to you.

"Do you want to go first?" Myla asks. "Or do you want me to go first?"

"We don't have to. She can't hear us from here."

Myla's expression falls, and it surprises me.

Wait . . . did she want to do this?

"Yeah, she probably can't. We can probably just float like this until it's over." She glances away, and I feel like I did something wrong.

Hell, I know I did something wrong. This is a moment where I could offer her that change. I can show her a part of me that might have been lost in the past few months.

"Hey," I say while trying to gain her eyes. "Did you want to do the exercise?"

"No, it's fine."

"Myla, don't lie to me."

She sighs heavily. "I don't know, Ryot. It just seemed like something we could at least say to each other. Three things we appreciate? I told you I want to move on, and moving on by saying something nice rather than mean all the time might be better."

I don't even have to think about it to know that she's right, so I say, "Okay, then let's do this. You go first."

"Are you sure?" she asks.

"Yeah, I'm sure," I say as I move my hands to her lower back, holding her closer.

"Okay. Well, three things I appreciate about you would be that you have always, from the day we first met, been patient with me. I think it takes a lot of strength, especially in your heart to be patient with someone like me, and you've exemplified that often." Her finger rubs against my neck. "Even with the batteries."

I chuckle. "So we're no longer in denial about that?"

She shakes her head. "No, it might be healthy to come clean." Continuing, she adds, "I also appreciate your humor. You've always understood me in that way. Never judged me."

"You're funny. What's not to understand?"

She softly smiles. "And lastly, I appreciate your heart. You took a chance on me when I didn't think I deserved a chance. You helped me see that through the bruised and battered heart I grew up with, that I was able to open myself up to love."

"It's easy to love you, Myla," I say before I can stop myself.

"It's easy to love you, Ryot."

Any other human in my situation would say, *then why are you asking for a divorce, why are you trying to break away from me?*

But I know why.

Because I broke her trust. I broke our vows.

I've thought a lot about this over the past twenty-four hours. I've never verbally abused Myla. I've never flaunted her flaws or tried to make her feel small. But I'm seeing that in taking away her choices, moving her without any consultation or—let's be perfectly honest—*any thought* about her needs, I've treated her with the same level of disrespect as her parents. She's an intelligent, driven woman, and in many ways, I belittled that. I knew she loved her work with Renovate Chicago, and I'm now sickened by my disloyalty to her. My actions spoke loudly and negatively into her fragile self-esteem, much like her mother's words and her father's inaction did. I made her feel unvalued and inconsequential. *So she ran from me.* Because that's safer than confronting the bully, as she learned from her mother's abuse. God, I fucked up.

Clearing my throat, I say, "Well, I guess it's my turn." I move my hands down her back, repositioning myself as her legs grow tighter around me. "I appreciate your strength. You've been through hell and back, Myla, and even though there were times when you didn't think you could recover, you never broke. I appreciate everything you put into our marriage, especially when I was playing baseball. You made it easier on me, for me, and you tried to keep us from breaking, and I will always love you for that." She glances away because I know that's a touchy subject. She put her life on hold so I could pursue my dreams.

What have I done for her?

"And I appreciate your smile, which sounds lame, but that smile? It's turned some of my shittiest days into better ones. There were times when I would come home after some of the worst games of my life, and you would greet me with that welcoming smile and remind me that it was just a game. It was all just a game, and that what I have with you is so much better than any batting average I might ever achieve."

"Even during the strikeout streak we don't talk about?" she asks, clearly trying to lighten the mood.

"You mean the streak when I struck out every up at bat for three games in a row?"

She nods. "Now those were difficult times."

I chuckle just as Mel chimes in. "Okay, now I'd like you to confess something to your partner. It could be small, it could be grand, but if you're the one who is listening, I need you to understand, the key to a good marriage is listening, acceptance, and forgiveness. So please, don't use this confession against your partner. Use it as a base to grow. Remember the three things you appreciate about each other while you're listening."

"Confession . . ." Myla taps her chin. "It was me who was tilting the pictures."

I feign shock. "No, that was you?"

She chuckles. "Guilty."

"I had no idea. Wow, color me stunned," I say as I move my hands to her side and up her ribs.

"It's shocking, I know, you might have to settle yourself before your confession."

Funny thing is, I could either match the ridiculousness of her confession, keep it light after such a heavy moment, or I can bring it right back to being serious and confess something that has been sitting heavy on my chest.

My hands grip her tightly, my thumbs bobbing close to the sides of her breasts. I'm not sure I'll have another chance to say what I need to say. I have to say it. I have to get this off my chest.

"Myla?"

"Yes?" she says.

"My confession . . . well, it's not so funny and more God's honest truth."

"Okay," she says, sounding skeptical.

"I will live with two regrets for the rest of my life. One being that even though you were trying to talk to me, trying to tell me that I was hurting you, I didn't listen. I realize the damage it has done. I'm sorry. And my second regret is signing those divorce papers because, even though you deserved to be let go to live your life your way after the way I treated you, the love I have for you will never fade. And losing you will always be my biggest mistake. Not sure I'll ever forgive myself."

"Oh," she says as silence falls between us.

"Yeah . . . oh," I repeat right before dipping my head back to the edge of the pool.

———

## MYLA

"DID you hear anything from the doctors?" I ask Nichole as I pace the end of the hallway of the floor our room is on.

"That's really the first thing you're going to say to me when I answer the phone?"

"Yes, I want to make sure you're keeping me up to date."

"Trust me, you'll be my first call, so stop asking. Unless I tell you something, there is no news."

"Okay. Sorry."

"Now, what's the real reason you're calling? Wait, let me guess. You're freaking out because Ryot did something today that made you think, maybe, just maybe, you did the wrong thing by asking him for a divorce?"

I'm silent because . . . well, because she's slightly right.

"Tell me I'm not telling the truth."

"It was just a tough day today, well, tough morning. The day isn't even over. I have dinner with him shortly, and I'm just feeling weird, okay? I need to talk it out."

"Tell me what happened."

I explain the class to her, how we both didn't know what to expect, but when the moment came down to it, I thought that maybe it would be nice to see what he had to say about me.

"This is Ryot, Myla. Of course he's going to say sweet things. He always has. What did you think he was going to say? That you're a rotten bitch, and he hopes you burn in flames?"

"No, I just . . . ugh, I don't know. What he appreciated

about me was really sweet, but it was his confession that destroyed me, and the way he held on to me, like if he loosened his grip even a little, that I might float away." I let out a sigh and press my hand to my forehead. "Remind me why I asked for a divorce."

"Hey, I was never a super supporter of the idea, but if you need to know, it was because after he retired from baseball, you were supposed to spend your life together, accomplishing goals together, and having a life post sports. Then he started a business, ignored everything you said, moved you to California, and made your life miserable—even after you tried talking to him multiple times and he ignored you. One-track mind really kind of blew up your marriage."

"Wow, thanks, Nichole."

"You asked. Is there any way you could see yourself changing your mind?"

"I mean, possibly, but that doesn't change the fact that we're in a place in our lives where we want different things. He's so attached to The Jock Report and everything it represents that I couldn't imagine him ever giving it up. And I don't want to be in California. I don't want to be away from you."

"I'm not the reason you are breaking up your marriage. Stop bringing me into it."

"I'm not using you as an excuse, Nichole."

"You better not be, because who knows what's going to happen to me and where I will be a year or five from now? You need to want to move back to Chicago because that's where you want to be, not because of me."

"I do believe it's where I want to be."

"Why?" Nichole asks. "If I was out of the picture, why do you want to be in Chicago?"

"Because . . ." I say softly. It's where I had a purpose. I had a job, a role in Ryot's life that I loved. Dates were difficult because of his popularity in Chicago, but not impossible. He made time for me. Our downtime was spent relaxing, watching movies, catching up with friends, and having fun. We talked. We argued. We made up. He heard me. It's where I felt seen by Ryot. "Because it's where I have my best memories. It's the one and only place I've ever truly felt like I was home."

"Do you know why?" Nichole asks. "Because you were with Ryot out here. You have your best memories in Chicago because of Ryot. Not because of me, not because of your job, and not because you love the weather—which remember, you hate. You have the best memories here because of Ryot. So do you think you would still like it here if Ryot wasn't with you?"

I ponder on that for a second as I stare at the carpet. "I . . . I don't know."

Just then, Ryot pokes his head out of the hotel room and glances down the hallway.

"Oh, I think I have to go. He's looking for me."

"Okay, well, think about what I said, okay? And whatever happens, just keep pushing yourself to understand more, to put all the pieces together, because if I know one thing for certain, it's that Ryot Bisley might have lost your trust and broken your heart, but he very much could be the only one who could put it back together. Love you, girl."

"Love you," I say as I hang up the phone. I stand from the carpet and head toward the door.

"Sorry," he says. "I didn't mean to interrupt. I just wanted to give you a twenty-minute warning. I can head down, though, if you want, tell everyone you have a headache or something."

God, he's annoyingly sweet . . . and handsome. So freaking handsome. He's wearing a pair of gray Chino pants and a light blue shirt along with the watch I got him two Christmases ago, and his hair is still dewy from his shower but styled in that cute messy way that he always has. And oh my God, does he smell like a dream.

"No, you don't need to fake anything for me. I'm starving, and I could use some wine after today."

"Same." He rocks back on his heels. "So you want me to wait?" God, this is awkward, no thanks to the events in the pool from earlier.

"Yeah, just give me a second to change, and I'll be right out."

I move toward the closet where I hung up my clothes and choose a black peekaboo back, strapless romper that I know will pair well with my black heels. I wasn't sure what the events were for this wedding week, so I chose outfits I could dress up or dress down. Based on what Ryot is wearing, I'm going to assume this is a dressing-up dinner.

I slip into my romper, tie it tightly behind my back, and then check myself in the mirror. Looks pretty decent. I've gained a few pounds since I last wore this, so I wasn't sure if it would work or not, but it seems fine. I brush my hair out and slick it down into a low, tight bun at the nape of my neck, put on my gold Marin Knot earrings, and then do a five-minute face of makeup. My focus is on evening out my complexion and then tons of mascara to make my eyes pop.

I look in the mirror and smile. Not too bad for a few minutes to get ready. I slip on my strappy black heels, and I'm about to head out into the bedroom where Ryot is waiting when I consider Nichole's question. Is she right? Did I only love Chicago because of being with Ryot? Because if that's the case, then it would suggest that I'm happiest when I'm with him. Wherever we are, as long as it's together. *But I hate California.* Do I? Or do I simply hate what it represents? Now isn't the time to dive into this, but her question was a valid one, and something I need to give more consideration. I hated feeling unheard, invalidated, and irrelevant. Ryot's choices were selfish. *But am I wanting to flee the man I love or flee the feelings of inadequacy and unworthiness that his decisions triggered?*

I take a deep breath and head toward Ryot, who is sitting on the edge of the bed.

When he looks up, I watch his expression morph from neutral to appreciative while his eyes roam up my body.

"Wow," he says as he stands. "You look amazing, Myla."

This, this right here, is one of the reasons I fell in love with him because, with a simple comment, he can make me feel like I'm the most beautiful woman in the world. He's always made me feel like that, even over the past few months. He might not have paid as much attention, but when he did, he made me feel divine.

"Thank you," I answer as I brush my hand down my clothes. "Are you ready?"

"I am." His hand falls to my lower back, and the smooth touch sends a chill up my spine as his thumb grazes over my exposed skin. It's subtle, but it still reminds me of our bond and the strong pull we have toward each other. Such an undeniable attraction. But if I've honestly learned one thing lately, it's that I need more than just physical attraction in our marriage. I need respect and consideration.

He guides me out into the hall, shuts our door, and we head down to the elevator together.

Silence meets us, and I bite down on my cheek, wishing it wasn't like this. Wishing we could talk about what we just went through and the truth of it all.

Finally, he asks, "Everything good with Nichole?"

"Yeah, no news yet. She told me to stop asking, and if she hears anything, she'll let me know."

"I can understand that. I'm sure it's very nerve-wracking for her."

"I think I'm more freaked out than she is." When we reach the elevator, he pushes the down button and then turns toward me.

"I don't know if this is stepping out of bounds or offering too much, but if something, God forbid, is wrong with Nichole, I want you to know, even though we're divorced, I will one hundred percent be there for you both. Okay? I don't want you thinking that you can't come to me once this trip is over."

The elevator dings, the doors part, and we both get on.

When he pushes the lobby level button, I say, "I appreciate that, Ryot, but don't you think that will be hard? Seeing each other?" It's hard enough as it is, being next to him now.

"Yes, it will. But what would be harder is going through something difficult alone. So if there is something going on with Nichole, you need to contact me, got it?"

I nod. "I will."

"Good."

This is why it's hard to stop loving him because he does care. He might have forgotten the past few months, we might have pulled apart, and a foundation of resentment formed, but when it comes down to it, he loves me, and he will always care for me. He stated that in his letter, he stated that in the pool, and this right here shows that.

It's . . . it's confusing, and before I know what I'm doing, once the elevator doors part, I pull Ryot off to the side, out of sight of the group that is just up ahead in the lobby.

"What's going on?" he asks.

My nerves turn in my stomach as I stare up at him, knowing that I won't be able to get through the night if I don't at least say what's on my mind. "That was weird."

"What was weird?" he asks, glancing over his shoulder.

"The pool. That was a weird thing we did."

"Oh." He pulls on the back of his neck. "Yeah, that was sort of strange. Sorry if I made it awkward with what I said."

I shake my head. "You didn't. You were speaking your truth, and that's what you've always done. But I feel like you're tiptoeing around me, and it's making things even weirder."

"I don't know how to act around you at the moment," he admits. "I'd be lying if I said being near you, pretending like everything's okay isn't hard, because it is. I still love you, Myla, and it's going to take me a second to figure this all out and navigate through the process of letting you go."

I wet my lips and stare at the ground. "I feel the same way." When I lift my gaze to his, I continue, "These past few weeks, these past few months have been awful. And the other night, when you signed the papers, it was even more confusing, even harder because I saw the finality of it all. The culmination of our rough time coming to an end. It's been hard trying to let go as well."

"Thank you for admitting that," he says softly. The somberness of his voice nearly breaks me.

"This will continue to be weird if we keep . . . I don't know, thinking about what we lost. You know?"

"Yeah, I don't think anyone wants to see a grown man cry at a dinner table, but that's how I feel."

I bite down on my lip and try to lighten the mood. "It might be entertaining. You do have quite the ugly cry face."

He smirks and then pushes a loose piece of hair behind my ear. "Not as hideous as yours."

I laugh and then let out a deep breath. "How about this? Instead of focusing on what we lost, how about we celebrate what we had? Because what we did have was great."

"Some might call it . . . exceptional." He takes my hand in his, and we twist our fingers together.

"It was exceptional." I smile as I feel my heartbeat pick up with every stroke of his thumb over my knuckles. "So how about we just have fun? When people are around, we act like the exceptional married couple we once were, and when they're not, we just . . . take it easy, stop being awkward. Think you can do that with me?"

"Yeah." He smiles softly. "I can."

"Good." And just like that, hand in hand, we head toward the group.

Once we arrive, the group is directed by a guide down to the wine cellar where dinner has been set up for us. Old stone walls surround the dimly lit space as well as barrels and barrels of wine stacked one right on top of the other. A long table stretches out in the middle of the room with ten place settings beautifully set up with multiple wineglasses rimmed in gold, sage serviettes, and cream napkins. Twigs, eucalyptus, and votive candles decorate the length of the table while bulbed lights are strung from the curved tunnel-like ceiling.

It's breathtaking.

Name cards have been set at every place setting, so Ryot and I find ours at the end of the table, right next to Banner and Breaker—JP and Huxley's younger brother. Ryot pulls my chair out for me and then gently helps me scoot in.

When he takes a seat next to me, his hand falls to my thigh, like it did the night JP and Huxley came to visit our house. But this time, he's sitting much closer so our shoulders are brushing together.

"Comfortable?" he asks me.

"Yeah," I answer softly.

His mouth is right next to my ear as he says, "Having fun, right?"

"Right," I whisper.

His hand slides toward my inner thigh. "All the fucking fun."

An unexpected giggle pops out of me as I whisper back, "Not too much fun."

He grumbles but doesn't remove his hand. Rather, he just grips me tightly, claiming me like he used to before things started to change between us. It feels like he's marking me all over again.

This is my girl, no one else's.

Trying to distract myself from the feel of his warm palm on my thigh, I ask, "Who are some of these people?"

"I think the couple at the end is Kelsey and Lottie's mom and stepdad."

"Oh yeah, that makes sense." I glance around the room. "This is really nice. Like, I almost feel not dressed up enough."

He leans in close, his mouth nearly kissing my ear as he says, "You look perfect, Myla."

"Are you sure?" I ask, feeling incredibly insecure for some reason.

Probably because I know that this is only temporary, and I'm trying to fit into a crowd that I really don't belong in.

"Positive, babe," he says, the nickname slipping with ease past his lips.

Across the table, Lottie leans forward. "Myla, those earrings, I need to know where they're from because I'm in love."

Smiling, I touch the long, knotted strands and say, "Ryot got them for me for my birthday one year. You're going to have to take up your inquisition with him."

Lottie turns to Ryot. "Please tell me you remember."

Ryot smooths his hand toward my inner thigh, causing my muscles to twitch against the subtle touch. "A jeweler friend of mine. I'll send the info over to Huxley."

"You're a doll. I'm totally going to be that person who steals something you're wearing, and then wear it over and over again."

"Have at it," I say.

"So how did you guys like the pool exercise this morning?" Lottie asks. Huxley drapes his arm over the back of her chair, not saying anything at all, just observing his wife. From the way he carries himself and his possessive posture whenever Lottie is around, there is no doubt in my mind that their sex life is off the charts. I bet they get into some pretty kinky things.

"I thought it was very interesting," I answer. "Didn't know what to expect, but it was nice."

"Huxley hated every second of it." We all chuckle. "But I made sure to make up for it after." She winks, and yeah . . .

that says it all. Huxley's fingers smooth over Lottie's shoulder as he leans in and kisses her neck.

Okay . . . that's hot.

It might be the most subtle display of affection, but from here, I see the imprint he's leaving on her shoulder, marking her. I notice her quick intake of breath when his lips land on her skin and the briefest inhales in his chest as he pulls away like he can't get enough of her scent.

"From the way you two bolted from the pool, I'm going to guess you went straight to your room," Lottie says with a wink.

We did, but not for that reason. We were both sort of horrified.

"Sorry to interrupt," the server says from over my shoulder. "But could I interest you in a pinot noir to start you off? The bride and groom have chosen an array of delicious wines to try this evening."

"Yes, please, I would love to try whatever you have."

"Me too," Ryot says.

"Great, I'll bring you the tour of our tasting tonight."

"Thank you," I say as he walks away. I lean into Ryot and say, "Tour of our tasting, that sounds interesting."

"Sounds like a lot of wine."

"Think I might need it," I whisper back.

⊏⊐

"OKAY, is it me or is this cheese really good?" I ask, turning toward Ryot.

"It's really good," he says while picking up another piece off my plate.

"Hey, that's mine." I slap at his hand, making him laugh, but that doesn't stop him from taking a bite. "Ryot Bisley!" He chuckles some more and then lifts the remaining half to my lips. I part, and he slips the cheese into my mouth.

"There. Better?"

"No, I would have preferred the whole thing."

"What about this? You can have this piece of cheese for the one I took." He holds up a piece, and I sneer at him.

"That one tastes like the innards of your musty, old cleats. That in no way is a fair exchange."

"Musty, old cleats? Don't you think that's going a bit far?" he asks while finishing off his glass of wine.

That would be five glasses for each of us.

Five glasses that have been more delicious with each refill.

Five glasses that have turned us slightly giggly, very silly, and completely anti-social. Everyone else around us is engaging in conversation while I'm turned toward Ryot, and he has one arm draped over my chair.

On occasion, his hand will caress my shoulder.

Every once in a while, I'll press my hand to his thigh.

Gone is the mention of divorce, the awkwardness, the tension, and in its place, is just . . . friendship. Enjoyment. What feels like a distant memory of happiness I once felt but am truly feeling now.

"Then what would be an even trade?" he asks.

I glance down at his plate that he has torn apart. The cleat cheese, a cracker, and an olive are all that's left.

Not much to choose from.

"Your cracker. I want it."

"I was saving that cracker," he says, chin tilted in defiance.

"What were you saving it for?"

"I was going to dip it in my white wine."

"Dip the cracker into your wine?" I hiss whisper. "Ryot, you realize we're surrounded by the upper crust of people. They don't dip crackers in wine."

"They might."

"They don't," I reply.

"Maybe."

"Guaranteed, they don't." I reach for the cracker, but he slaps my hand away.

"Keep your sticky paws away from my cracker." And to my horror, he lifts his knife to his wineglass and clangs it against the surface, drawing everyone's attention.

He stands tall from his chair and says, "I would like to ask the room a question."

"Someone is enjoying his wine," Banner says, sitting back in his chair, nearly falling out. He grips the table and chuckles. "Whoa, maybe I am too."

Ryot lifts his cracker up and shows it off to the room. "Who here would dip this in their white wine?"

I tug on Ryot's pants and whisper, "You're drunk. Sit down."

"I would," JP says, rising from his chair.

"So would I," Breaker says, rising as well. All three of them holding up crackers.

"And so would Huxley," Lottie says, nudging him to stand.

"No, I wouldn't," he says back to her.

"Huxley, they're clearly enjoying some sort of man bond, so pull the stick out and get in there." Rolling his eyes, Huxley rises as well.

"I'll dip," Banner says.

"So will I," Kelsey's stepdad, Jeff, says.

"Then, men, we shall dip," Ryot says, lifting his cracker into the air.

Oh boy . . .

## Chapter Eighteen

MYLA

*Six years ago . . .*

"You are completely useless," my mom screams at me before she slams the door to the guest bedroom that I've been sleeping in since she called to tell me my dad had died.

Once she coldly delivered the news, Ryot rushed me to my mom's house, where she explained that he had a heart attack and never recovered. Three days *before* she called me.

Three!

I asked her why she didn't call me sooner, and she said because she didn't think I needed to know.

I didn't get to sit by his side in the hospital and tell him how much I loved him. I didn't get to say goodbye. I didn't get anything. I think she only told me he passed away because she needed help with the funeral arrangements.

I press my hand to my sore eye where Mom slapped me earlier for not answering the phone when she was expecting a call from the minister. When the machine picked up, it was a telemarketer. She didn't apologize.

I know there's a red mark, a bruise already forming. I don't need to look in the mirror to confirm because she packs a powerful slap. Even now, when she's looking fragile from her loss, her viciousness makes me feel like the little girl who was regularly abused by her mother—with no way out.

And that's how it feels. Like I'm drowning with no way out.

My phone dings with a text message, pulling me from my thoughts.

Ryot.

He's at an away game right now in Washington. He had to leave the day after I found out. And since they're currently only a handful of games away from the playoffs and fighting for a spot, he can't take any days off. But he checks in with me every chance he gets.

**Ryot:** *How's it going? How is everything? Can I do anything for you?*

I sigh and consider not texting back because I really don't have the energy, but I know that will just worry him.

**Myla:** *As best as it can be.*

My phone rings in my hand, and I see that he's trying to FaceTime me. I know if he sees my face, he'll be pissed, so I ignore the call and send him a text.

**Myla:** *Can't talk on the phone right now.*

**Ryot:** *Okay, sorry. Just haven't seen you in a bit. I want to make sure everything is okay. Seems like you're avoiding me, and I know I should be there with you, baby, but I'm strapped. I can't.*

**Myla:** *I know, Ryot. And I'm not avoiding you. Just trying to deal with all of this.*

**Ryot:** *Okay, because I love you and you know if I could, I'd be there for you.*

***Myla:*** *I know.*

"Verna, I swear to God, if you touch me, I am going to fucking scream. Now let me in." I hear Nichole yell from the entryway.

"How dare you," my mom yells back as I hear some bumbling around.

I shoot off my bed and out of my bedroom, where I run right into Nichole. "What's going on?" I ask.

"Your mom is trying to prevent me from seeing you." She lifts her hand to my eye and says, "And now I see why." She turns on her heel and heads straight for my mom.

Oh shit.

I quickly run up to Nichole and grab her by the waist before she can get any closer.

"What the hell do you think you're doing?" Nichole asks my mom. "Hitting her? Really? Don't you think you're a little old for that now? Didn't you beat her up enough when she was younger? Or did you not get enough hits in when she was living under your roof?"

"Nichole, stop," I say, pulling her back to my bedroom.

"You will not talk to me like that under my roof," my mom snaps.

"Really? I dare you to fight me. Go ahead, give me your best blow."

Mom doesn't move, doesn't say anything, just stares blankly.

"That's what I thought. You can hit the girl you terrorized for years, but you can't hit me. It's a shame you're not the one who died from a heart attack. Lord knows we need less of you in this world."

"Nichole, please," I beg, pulling her into the bedroom and finally shutting the door.

But she's not done. She pushes off the door and then forces me to look at her. "How many times did she hit you?"

"Does it matter?"

"It matters to me. And where the hell is Ryot? Why is he letting this happen?"

"He's at an away game in Washington."

"What?" Nichole shouts. "He just dumped you here with that monster and took off?"

"He can't get the time off, Nichole. They're close to the playoffs, and every game counts."

"Uh-huh." She nods and folds her arms over her chest. "You're telling me that baseball is more important than you?"

"No. It's just . . . it's not that easy."

"It could be, but he chose for it not to be. Unbelievable. Well, you're not staying here another night. I won't leave you here alone with her."

"Nichole, I can't leave her here. The funeral is in two days. Some things still need to be done."

"Who cares? Let her do everything on her own."

"I can't."

"Why not? She's obviously taking her anger out on you. How can you let her do that?"

I take a seat on my bed and sit there in silence.

"Myla, you're a grown woman. You're no longer the little girl who used to cower in the corner whenever she heard her mom's voice. You're stronger now."

"Yes, but she's hurting."

Nichole blinks a few times. "She's . . . hurting? Because she lost the husband she stopped loving years ago? Are you hearing yourself?"

I look away and quietly say, "Nichole, if you're not going to be supportive, then I'm going to have to ask you to leave."

"I *am* being supportive. This is called tough love, sweetheart. And it seems like I'm the only one who cares to give it to you. What is Ryot even doing to help?"

"Keep him out of it."

"Why? Because you're going to defend his passive behavior as well? Tell me you're okay with him not being here, that you're not miserable that he's in Washington while you're here, getting slapped around by your mom?"

I can't look her in the eyes, nor can I answer.

Because I'm struggling with the idea that something this important, this monumental in my life has happened, and he can't be there for me. Granted, he told me if we were married, this would be different, but there aren't exceptions for girlfriends.

Still, he's the one I need. He's my rock, my comfort, and the fact that I'm going through this without him is so painful, that it's almost impossible to comprehend.

"Nichole," I finally say, "I know you're trying to help, but you're not. I'm struggling with a lot, and I know you have your mama bear pants on, but I just need a shoulder."

She pauses, unmoving for what feels like minutes before she sighs and sits next to me on the bed. Her arm drapes over my shoulders, and she pulls me in tight. It's enough to break me. I spend the next few hours crying into her shoulder off and on.

I tell her how lonely I feel without Ryot. How empty my heart is and how bitter I feel. As someone who can step outside the situation and see what's going on, I know he can't be here. I get that, I truly do, but it doesn't make me any less bitter about the fact he's not.

That baseball is first.

Baseball will always be first.

I tell her that I've felt so lost, so confused, so wretched about losing my father, a man who I wish had stood up for me more but I know loved me with all of his soul.

I tell her that because of this empty feeling, mourning my father, and the bitterness, I've started to . . . to hate myself. I hate everything about myself. Why didn't I ask my dad those important questions? Why didn't I plead for him not to leave me alone with my mom? Why didn't I confront him later in life to clear the air?

Why didn't I beg Ryot to stay?

Why am I avoiding him now?

All of it has led to self-loathing, which has caused me to hole up in this house, this toxic, meaningless house that offers absolutely no value to my life. And, worst of all, it's led me to sink back into a world I never wanted to revisit, a world I thought I was too strong to ever see again.

Yet . . . I'm not.

I'm weak.

I'm defeated.

I'm lost.

And I'm not sure anything will help me get out of it.

"YOU WERE A DISAPPOINTMENT TO HIM, you know?" Mom whispers as I stare at the picture of Dad next to his gravesite.

The ceremony is over, everyone has retreated, and because my mom is such a cold-hearted bitch, she canceled the reception because she didn't think it was necessary. I heard rumblings that a lot of Dad's friends were meeting at his favorite pub, but I feel frozen, like stone, unable to move.

"Why did he let you do the things you did to me?" I ask, trying to find an answer from the wrong person.

"Are you playing the victim once again?" Mom asks. "You realize it's your father who died, not you."

I turn to her as I see Nichole in the distance, pulling up her car. "It's a simple question."

"I have no idea what you're talking about. And if your father wanted any say in the discipline that I was forced to serve on a constant basis because of your insubordination, then maybe he shouldn't have been tied to his second family."

"Wait . . . what?" I ask.

"Oh, sweetie, you didn't know?" Mom taunts in a condescending tone. "You thought he was away on work trips?" She tsks. "No, he was visiting his other family. His mistress and his two sons. Twins, actually."

"No." I shake my head. "You're lying. I don't believe you."

"Why would I lie to you?"

"Because you hate me, because you're cruel, and because you haven't taken enough of my childhood and want to take this away too."

"I have better things to do with my life than worry about taking away what pitiful life you have. You wonder why your dad and I fell out of love? Because he fell in love with someone else, that's why. And his mistress, she followed us around to every duty station. He would spend long nights and days with her, and when the boys were born, his time with us diminished even more."

"I don't believe it. Why didn't you divorce him, then?" I ask.

"Because I don't believe in divorce," she says with snobbery.

"You'd rather make your life and everyone else's around you miserable? Is that why you beat me as a child? Because you were mad at him, and you took it out on me?"

"I hit you because you were disobedient," she growls.

"So why do I have two black eyes now?" I ask, feeling the throbbing of where she hit me last night across the eye with a shoe. "I wasn't disobedient last night."

"You were late to dinner, and that's unacceptable."

"I was one second late. I was finishing a call."

"With that boyfriend of yours who is just like your father."

"No, he's not," I say.

"Oh, no? Then where is he? Playing baseball? Your father's work came first too, you know. I was pushed to the back. So were you. A man's job will always come first. Always. Best you realize that now before you're in too deep with the man."

"Are you ready?" Nichole calls out, approaching with a stern look on her face.

I glance over my shoulder and nod. But before I leave, I say, "I don't believe you about Dad. There is no way he had a second family."

She points to the right. "See those two men over there? Those are his sons. And the woman next to them, that's Miranda, his mistress. Don't believe me, just go ask."

I look over and see three people standing together, waiting for their last goodbyes.

"What is she talking about?" Nichole asks.

And I don't know what it is, maybe the pain slicing through me, or the need to clear the air, but I find myself walking over to them with purposeful strides. And as I draw closer and closer, I realize the men I'm walking toward have a very distinct look about them . . . those bushy eyebrows, the blue eyes, the tall, lanky stature.

My strides slow down, and when I'm a few feet away, I whisper, "Is it true?"

The men exchange glances, and before they can answer, the woman steps up. "You must be Myla."

Hands shaking, voice about to break, I ask, "And who the hell are you?"

Their expressions are sympathetic as the woman steps even closer. "I'm going to assume your mom just told you about us."

"No." I shake my head. "No, it's not fucking true. Tell me you're not my dad's other family."

"I'm sorry, Myla," Miranda says. "It wasn't . . . it wasn't supposed to be like this."

"Holy . . . fuck," I say as I move away from them, gripping my head in total confusion.

"Myla, please, let us talk."

"No . . . no." I continue to shake my head and then look up at the woman. I point and mutter, "Fuck you. Do you . . .

do you realize what you did to me? What my dad did to me? Who you *both* left me with? I grew up with a monster because you couldn't understand the fact that my dad was a married man. That he couldn't understand that he had a daughter who desperately needed him." I shake my head again. "No. There will be no talking. I want nothing to do with you. Fuck you, all of you."

And then I turn on my heel and head right into Nichole's arms.

"Want me to take you home?"

"Yes, get me the hell out of here."

⊏———⊐

"YOU KNOW I LOVE YOU, RIGHT?" Nichole asks as she brushes my hair away from my face.

When we got back to our shared townhome, she took me up to my room and let me cry on her lap until I fell asleep. When I woke up, it was morning, and I still hadn't moved.

"I know," I whisper, my throat feeling tight, hoarse from all the crying. "You might be the only one in my life who does."

"Have you spoken to Ryot?"

I shake my head. "No. And I don't want to."

"Why?" she asks.

"Because . . . what's the point? My mom was right. He's going to put baseball first. Every time. I can't compete with that."

"I hate to admit that your mom is right because that woman should truly be engulfed by hell at this point, but she is. This is his career. His passion. Someone who works that hard to get to that level isn't just going to give it up. They never will. And I hate to say this, but this was an example of that truth."

"I know," I say softly. "I love him, Nichole, but I'm not

sure he loves me enough and, after everything I've been through this past week, I don't think . . . I don't think I can handle the rejection."

"What are you going to do?" she asks just as the door to my bedroom opens and Ryot stands on the other side.

"Ryot," I say while sitting up. "What are you doing here?"

His eyes laser in on Nichole and then back to me. He looks . . . angry.

"We just got back. Myla, can I talk . . ." He pauses and then leans in, taking a closer look at me. "Jesus, fuck, what happened to you?"

"What do you think happened to her?" Nichole asks. "You left her with her mom."

Ryot's body tenses as his eyes flit back to mine. "Your mom did this?"

"Of course she did," Nichole says. "Myla was weak and vulnerable, and her mom took advantage. Several times. This is just a culmination of a week. Should have seen the slap mark from earlier on."

"Nichole. Please don't," I say.

"Is that why you wouldn't FaceTime me?" Ryot asks.

"That should have been clue number one," Nichole says. "But you were too busy with baseball to figure that out."

"Can I talk to my fucking girlfriend in private, please?" he asks, looking like he's about to lose his cool.

Nichole glances at me for permission, and I nod. She scoots off the bed and then says, "Remember what we talked about, okay? You do what's best for you." And then she walks out of the bedroom, but not before bumping Ryot in the shoulder.

When the door is closed, Ryot rushes over to the bed and sits next to me. "Myla, why didn't you fucking tell me?" He reaches out and gently caresses my cheek. "Have you pressed charges? Or are you going to press charges?"

I shake my head and try to find words to answer him. But

I can't say anything because the moment I try to open my mouth, a flood of tears hits me all at once.

⊏⊐

## RYOT

I SHOULD HAVE STAYED with her.

Not just because I had the worst series of my life, thanks to my inability to focus on anything but Myla, but because she clearly needed me so much more than I anticipated. If I had been with her, this would have never happened. Her mom would never have hit her . . . several times.

Fuck.

Bile rises to my throat from the thought of it. All I can picture is Myla, cowering as her mother lashed out. It's absolutely sickening.

"Myla, please talk to me."

She sucks in a deep breath, and when I think she's going to lean into me, she pulls away and scoots to the other side of the bed. "I think . . . I think you should go," she says, her voice wobbly.

"Go? Why?"

She doesn't answer.

She brings her legs up to her chest, hugging them close as she stares in front of her.

"Myla, what's going on?"

"I just think it's best if you leave."

"Are you mad at me?" I ask. "Baby, I told you, if I could have been here, I would have been."

"But you weren't," she says, her eyes snapping up to mine. "You weren't here, and no matter what happens, I know you won't be able to be there for me the way I need."

"I was there the best I could, but you weren't allowing me in. I tried calling. I texted. I sent things to let you know that even though I wasn't physically here, my presence was."

"I didn't need your gifts, Ryot. I needed you."

"And I told you, if I could have been here, I would have been. Do you think I like coming back here to see that your fucking mother has struck you? To hear that you've been going through hell? No. It pains me, Myla. It makes me fucking ill, and the fact that you wouldn't tell me, you wouldn't let me in, how can I be there for you if you don't let me?"

She looks away and hugs her legs closer.

"Myla, talk to me."

Tears roll down her cheeks, but she doesn't attempt to wipe them. "Just go, Ryot."

"I'm not leaving. You're my girlfriend, and I'll be damned—"

"Not anymore," she says, catching me off guard.

I rear back and ask, "What do you mean, not anymore?" When she doesn't answer, I continue, "Are you breaking up with me?"

"Let's not make a big deal about it, okay?" She swipes at her snotty nose. "It's obvious we were drifting apart."

"What the fuck are you talking about? We weren't drifting apart. We've been stronger than ever." She cowers into herself, almost like a turtle trying to hide, and I realize at this moment, observing her body language and watching how she can't make eye contact, that she's not in a good place mentally. And raising my voice, trying to get her to talk to me about this, will only fall on deaf ears.

She's not going to be receptive to what I have to say, and even though the last thing I want to do is leave this room knowing she's breaking up with me, being here will only make it worse.

"Okay," I say as I back away. "If you think we're drifting apart, then I'm not going to push you on the matter." More tears leak down her cheeks. "But I want you to know, Myla, that I fucking love you. More than anything. You are the love of my goddamn life, and I won't rest until you realize that, until you know for damn sure that you and I . . . we're never going to end. We are forever." I move toward the door, my anger simmering at the base of my spine.

I don't want to leave.

I don't want her to think I'm abandoning her.

I don't want her to think there is nothing left of us when I walk out this door.

But I've been with her long enough to understand the way she processes. She's been triggered, and she's in protection mode. I hurt her by not being here, so she's eliminating the things that hurt her to find a healthy frame of mind.

Does it hurt? Yes.

Do I understand her? Yes.

Will I fight? Abso-fucking-lutely.

I glance over my shoulder one more time and say, "I'll wait, Myla. I'll wait for as long as you need it. We're not over. I'm not giving up on you, baby. Never will." And then I walk out of her bedroom and down the stairs to the living room where Nichole is sitting, feet up on the coffee table.

I think about just slipping by her, but then, the anger that's been simmering comes to the surface, and I spin around and say, "What the fuck did you talk to her about?"

"That's none of your concern," she answers, her attention returning to her phone.

"It is my goddamn business when she decides to break up with me. So what did you talk to her about?"

Nichole sets her phone on her lap and glances up at me. "Just trying to help her see what's right and wrong in her life."

"Yeah, and who gave you the authority to do that?"

Pointing at her chest, she says, "I'm her best friend. I've known her longer than you, and I've seen the damage her mother has done. So that gives me the authority."

"Yeah, and weren't you just saying the other day how she was the happiest she's ever been? Do you know why?" I tap my chin sarcastically. "Hmm, I don't know. Maybe it has something to do with me?"

"Don't give yourself that much credit."

"You're kidding, right? She's told me I make her happy. She's told me that she loves me. That she wants to be with me, so what the hell changed between when I left and when I came back? What have you been saying to her?"

"Just what she's been thinking—that you weren't there for her when she needed you the most."

"I couldn't fucking leave!" I shout. "For fuck's sake, Nichole. I don't have a regular job like everyone else. I can't just decide when I want to show up and when I don't want to show up. I don't have vacation days that I can just use whenever the hell I want to. It doesn't work like that. And she knew that. She knew my schedule was brutal, but I told her I would be there for her in other ways. And I was until she started pushing me away. And it looks like you didn't help in that matter. It almost seems like you assisted in the pushing. Why?"

"She doesn't need you, Ryot."

I step back and stare at her, and that's when all the pieces start coming together. "You . . . you mean, she doesn't need *you* when I'm around. Am I right?"

She rolls her eyes. "Please, I'm not that petty."

"You're mad that she's been spending more time with me, aren't you? That she went to me for comfort."

"Grow up, Ryot." She picks up her phone again.

"Unbelievable," I say while shaking my head. "You know what, Nichole? If you were her true friend, someone who actually cared about her, not about yourself, you would put her happiness first. And you know damn well her happiness is with me." I move away from the living room and grow closer to the entryway. I spin around one more time and say, "I used to think you were on my side, that you wanted us to work out.

333

I don't know what has happened since, but it's disappointing. *You* are disappointing."

"Could say the same about you," she mutters but doesn't look up from her phone.

So . . . I leave.

———

RYOT: *I know you asked me to leave, and you think we're broken up, but I'm going to tell you again, over and over until you hear me. I'm not leaving your side, Myla. You matter to me. You must know that.*

**Ryot:** *Morning, baby. Wanted to tell you how much I love you. I'm sorry I couldn't be there for you the way you needed me, but I'm here. I'm always here with you. You just need to let me in.*

**Ryot:** *Remember the day you came to watch me play baseball? The first game ever? Do you remember our conversation in my car after the game? I told you I would always be honest with you. When I say you come first, you do. In my mind, you're always fucking first, and even though there are times when my job won't allow me to hold your hand or cradle you to my chest like I know you need, you are eating up the space in my head. That's because I love you. Always have, always will.*

**Ryot:** *I'm stopping by to drop off some of your favorite soup. I'll leave it outside so you don't have to face me if you're not ready. Love you, baby.*

**Ryot:** *I stopped by your restaurant tonight, after the game, in the hopes to at least catch sight of you, but they told me you don't work there anymore. Myla, I would love to just talk. Please, just let me in.*

**Ryot:** *We made the playoffs. The boys are off celebrating, but I didn't have it in me. I want to celebrate with you. Text me back. Maybe we can go grab some Drumsticks. Or some Cold Stone. You don't have to twist my arm to splurge on the good stuff for you.*

**Ryot:** *Off to Atlanta. I left a package on your doorstep. It's just some stuff in case you decide to watch the games. Some of your favorite popcorn, chocolates, and some Bobbies underwear. I'm not expecting you to* *wear it but, you know, if you did, I wouldn't be opposed. Love you, Myla.*

**Ryot:** *Getting ready for the game, and one of the guys walked in after a long night out, and I swear to Christ he smelled like you. He was wearing some girl's perfume, and it's what you wear. I was turned on and confused all at the same time. You're the only one I'm telling this to.*

**Ryot:** *Okay, I told Walker, and now he believes I'm in love with Charles, who was wearing the perfume. This is what happens when you consume my brain.*

**Ryot:** *I miss you, Myla. So much so that I looked through pictures of us tonight. Have I told you how much your smile lights up a room? Well, it does. I want to see that smile again. I want to see you happy. Please, Myla . . . please text me back. I love you.*

# Chapter Nineteen

RYOT

***Present day . . .***

"You're jealous," I mouth to Myla from across the room while the guys and I hover over a plate of crackers and two bottles of white wine that the waitstaff so kindly brought us.

The first dip was interesting. The second, third, and fourth were marvelous.

And as we stood over here, dipping crackers into glasses of wine to our heart's content, Myla and the girls sat at the table, drinking their red with the good cheese.

Yup, they were able to get more as well.

And sure, would I have preferred to sit at the cheese table? Yes. Clearly, that's the better table because that cheese melts in your mouth.

But the brothership by the crackers is unbreakable. A

once-in-a-lifetime bromance, something I would never give up for cheese.

Actually, that's a lie. I would give it up real quick.

Myla shakes her head and chuckles at me before plopping her last piece of cheese in her mouth.

Can we just take a second to fucking appreciate her?

When she walked out of the bathroom in that romper, I was taken back to a time when we first started dating, and she wore something similar. We didn't even go on our date because we didn't make it out of the bedroom. I desperately wanted a repeat but knew that wasn't an option. It pained me walking out of our hotel room with only a light touch to her lower back. Trust me, I wanted to do so much more.

And when we sat down at the table, my hand instinctively fell to her thigh. I wasn't doing it on purpose. It was a natural thing that I've done for years, so when she didn't shake me away, I didn't pull away. I didn't want to.

I wanted that connection.

I want . . . fuck, I want more.

Staring at her from across the room, I want so much more.

"Dude, you look like you're about to eat her alive," Banner says next to me.

"I love her, man," I say as I sip my wine, watching as she laughs with the girls.

"I know." He grips my shoulder just as the waitstaff comes out with plates of dessert.

The men flock back to the table, the cracker bromance quickly dissolved, and as I return, Myla turns into me and rests her hand on my leg as she leans in. "Guess what?" she asks, a lightness in her voice.

Yeah, we're both feeling the wine. That much is obvious.

"What?" I ask as a chocolate mousse is placed in front of us.

She leans in closer, her breast pressing against my shoulder as she says, "The girls said it looks like you want to eat me."

When she pulls away, I stare down at her lips and then back up at her eyes. "Because I do," I answer without even thinking.

She smirks and then whispers in my ear, "Remember the time I surprised you in Atlanta? I was naked in your hotel room, and you spent half an hour torturing me with your tongue."

"Baby, that memory lives rent-free in my brain forever. As well as the way you tasted."

She turns to her plate, carves out a piece of the mousse, and brings it to my mouth. I open and she feeds me. My lips pull over the spoon right before she takes it away.

"I always loved your mouth," she confesses. "I love your smile, your teeth, and your tongue. The tiny scars above your lip where you were clipped with a cleat by that guy sliding into third." She smooths her finger over my lips, and I open and nibble her finger, causing her to laugh.

Then it's my turn to feed her, so I scoop up some of the chocolate and place the spoon in front of her mouth. Keeping her eyes on mine, she opens and allows the spoon to slide over her tongue in the most seductive way I've ever seen. When she releases the spoon, she licks her lips and whispers, "So good," in a tone I've only heard in the bedroom.

"You two are making me hot," Lottie says from across the table. She then turns to Huxley and says, "Can we leave?"

He doesn't answer. All he does is stand and offer a wave to the table before gripping Lottie's hand tightly and walking off with her.

"We're going to take off too," JP says, holding Kelsey's hand. "Thanks, everyone, for coming."

And they're gone.

One by one, people get up and leave until Myla and I are the only ones left.

"They didn't even finish their dessert," she says as she feeds me another spoonful.

"Fools," I answer as Myla pours us another glass of wine, this one red. She hands me the glass and then holds hers up.

"To new beginnings," she says and then clinks my glass. Either I don't care or I'm drunk, but her toast does nothing for me, so I raise my glass.

"That toast was shit."

"Think you can do better?" she asks.

I nod. "Yup, cheers to the night when you played with my balls until I came."

She laughs. "Ooo, that was a good night." We both take a sip. "Or what about the time you let me spank you?"

I shake my head. "I didn't like that."

She laughs. "You're such a goddamn liar."

I place my finger against my mouth and shush her. "Don't tell anyone. Remember, that's a secret."

"Oh, right," she whispers. "Your dick was so hard that night."

"Because you were also wearing one of those demi bras I love so much."

"It was red and see-through, I remember. A Valentine's Day present."

"Best Valentine's Day of my life." I finish off my wine and then lean back in my chair. "Fuck, I think I'm drunk."

"Me too." She sways. "Want to walk it off with me?"

"Yeah, I do," I say and then stand. I reach out my hand, and she takes it.

"You know, no one is here. You don't have to hold my hand," she says.

"I'm afraid I might lose you to the wine if I let go."

She nods. "Good point."

After tripping over a few stairs, we make our way to the main lobby, then head out to the manicured lawns, past the pool—don't need any nighttime swims in our clothes.

"It's so beautiful here," she says. "Look at the moon. It's huge."

"So big, it feels like you can touch it." As I attempt to lift my hand, I stumble over a rock and plaster myself to the ground. I end up rolling down a short hill while Myla laughs her ass off the entire time.

She peeks down the hill and says, "You okay?"

Lying on my back, I stare up at her and say, "I fell."

She laughs some more. "I noticed."

I hold my arms out. "Baby, I need your help. I think . . . I think I fell on a rock, and I'm bleeding. I feel something moist on my back."

"Hold on, there are stairs right here." She walks down the stairs and carefully comes closer, balancing on her heels the whole time. When she reaches me, she reaches into my pocket.

"Oh yeah, a little to the left, babe."

She playfully swats my chest. "I'm looking for your phone." She pulls it from my pocket and then turns on the flashlight.

"I really think I got jabbed. I might need stitches," I say.

"You're ridiculous. You can get hit in the elbow by a ninety-five-mile-per-hour baseball and not even flinch, but a rock to the back has you crying for medical care."

"I have my strengths and weaknesses."

She shines the light on my back and then gasps before chuckling. "Oh . . . you landed on grapes. For a second, I thought it was blood."

"Are you sure?" I ask her.

"Positive."

I exhale. "Thank God, no stitches." And then I lie back on the grapes again and stare up at the night sky.

"What are you doing?" she asks.

"Enjoying the view."

She looks up at the sky and then back at me. "Aren't I the view?"

"If you were topless, yeah."

"Pervert," she mutters, causing me to laugh. And then I do something I probably shouldn't do, but hey, I'm drunk, so who cares? I lift her and pull her on top of me, placing her directly on my lap.

"My dear sir, what do you think you're doing?"

"Using you as a blanket. I'm chilly."

"Aw, you poor baby," she says as she pats my chest. "Let me see if your nipples are hard." She runs her hands over my pecs and glances to the side. "Hmm, can't quite tell. I'm going to need a closer look." She untucks my shirt from my pants and slips her hand against my warm skin. Her palm lights me up as her fingers caress my erect nipples. "Oh, look at that. They are hard."

"Yeah, something else is going to be hard in a second if you don't stop playing with my nipples."

She grins. "You always loved getting your nipples touched, licked . . . flicked."

I place my hands behind my head to prop myself up a bit more. "Yeah, what else did I like?"

"What didn't you like?" She rolls her eyes dramatically, the moon casting sufficient light so I can discern her facial expressions. "You were a champion of all things in the bed. You even let me strap that vibrator on you that one time." She leans forward and whispers, "Remember you came so hard, you got cum in your eye?"

"Yeah, and remember when I said that was to never be repeated again?"

She shrugs. "It's best you know that I've told Nichole that story at least three times."

"Is that why she calls me a pirate?"

Myla lets out a roar of a laugh and nods. "Yes." When I don't laugh with her, she drags her fingernails over my chest— another thing she knows I like. "Please, as if you've never told Banner anything embarrassing about me."

"Never," I reply.

"You're such a liar." Her nail passes over my nipple, and I let out a short hiss.

"Myla, I'm drunk, but not drunk enough to get hard, so stop it."

She chuckles again and then gets off my lap. She stands above me and holds her hand out, so I take it, and she helps me to my feet.

"Your shirt is all disheveled," she says.

"Want to tuck it back in for me?" I waggle my eyebrows at her.

"I'm okay. Thanks for the offer, though." She takes my hand, and we walk back up the hill, me supporting her as she does it in heels. When we reach the top, she says, "I need to get out of this romper and this strapless bra, or I might die."

"Want me to take it off for you right now?" I ask. "I don't mind."

"I'm sure you don't," she says from over her shoulder as she walks away, pulling my hand with her.

I really would.

So fucking bad.

I would also like to peel that romper off.

Find out what kind of underwear she's wearing only to peel that off as well.

"You're quiet," she says as we make it back to the hotel and the elevators. "Have you lost your voice?"

"Not even a little," I say. "Just thinking inappropriate things."

"Oh, are those things about me?"

"Always, babe," I answer, squeezing her hand.

"Such a charmer." She presses the up button and then twirls into me, her hand to my chest. "When we get in our room, I'm ripping these clothes off, so I hope you're ready."

"You are?" I ask, eyebrows up to my hairline. "What, uh, what do you plan on doing after you take your clothes off?"

"Snuggling into my pillow and passing out of course.

What did you think I was going to do?" The elevator dings, and she pulls me in with her.

"I don't know. I mean, if you need a massage or anything, just let me know. I'm your guy."

"I'm sure you are."

When we reach our floor, she drags me down the hall to our room where I drape my arm over her shoulder as she unlocks it. Once we're in our room, door shut, she reaches behind her and undoes her romper, letting it fall to the ground, just like she said, leaving her in a thong and a strapless bra.

Hell.

In a haze, I kick my shoes and socks off, then pull my shirt up and over my head and drop that on the floor as I work my way to the bathroom, where I find Myla completely naked.

"Myla," I groan as I turn back around. "Come on."

"What?" she asks through toothpaste gathered in her mouth. "You've seen me naked."

"Yeah, but you're hot as fuck, and I'm already struggling to keep my hands to myself, so you naked is not helping."

"Toss me one of your shirts then."

I grab one of my Bobbies shirts from my suitcase, then toss it into the bathroom.

"Thank you," she calls out. After a moment, I hear, "Okay, I'm decent."

I walk back into the bathroom and grab my toothbrush. I keep my eyes straight ahead so I'm not tempted to look at her as I prep my toothbrush and start brushing. It takes all but ten seconds before I glance her way and catch her staring at me.

"What?" I ask.

"You're sexier," she says. "Not that you weren't sexy before, but you're more muscular, more ripped. Your abs are more defined. What's that about?"

I glance down at my stomach and then back up. "I don't know," I answer and then spit out my toothpaste.

"Is this a revenge body or something?"

I chuckle. "No." I brush my tongue and then rinse my mouth. "Now get out of here. I have to go to the bathroom."

"Fine," she says, but as she walks by me, she drags her fingers along my back. When I glance over my shoulder at her, she just smiles and then heads into the bedroom.

I don't know what she's up to, but she has a look in her eyes, something devilish. Normally, I would be on high alert, but the wine has caused me to feel love drunk, and I couldn't care less what happens tonight.

Once I take care of my business and strip down to just my underwear, I go back into the bedroom where Myla is in bed, staring up at the ceiling. I flip off the light and go to my side, where I slip under the cool covers.

"It's chilly in here," I say.

"I know." She scoots in close. "Can I spoon you for some warmth?"

"If you want to," I answer, unfazed as I turn my back toward her and tuck my pillow under my head.

I feel her move closer until her body is plastered against mine. In seconds, the bed turns from chilly to boiling.

"Mmm, you're always so warm. I feel like you're my warming rock, and I'm a lizard."

I lift a brow, even though she can't see my face. "Not a fan of that analogy."

She chuckles and brings her arm around my waist, where she rests her hand against my stomach. "It's all I could think of." Her fingers move lightly across my abs, passing through the indents. It feels so goddamn good that I want to roll over and give her full access to my body, but we're not doing anything like that.

We're sleeping, and that's it.

We had fun.

We drank.

Now we're sleeping.

"I had fun with you tonight," she says softly as I feel her breath on my back.

"I had fun with you too," I reply just as her fingers travel along my skin. From the lightest touch, it sends my muscles into a bout of contractions, all bunching together while her fingers slowly, and I mean achingly slow, move down to the waistband of my briefs.

My chest fills with air as my cock twitches.

Fuck, I'm getting turned on, just like that. The smallest of touches is all it takes too.

"I feel like we've lost that fun along the way. I'm glad we decided to have fun tonight."

"Me too, babe," I answer right before she scoots in even closer. "The fun always brought us back together when we were going through tough times."

Her fingers now press against my skin, so close to the waistband of my boxer briefs that I grow hard. If only she'd slip her fingers past the waistband, feel my throbbing cock, and see how much she still makes me feel like the luckiest fucking man when she touches me.

"Because that's how we started, with just fun," she says. "Remember the night we had dinner together? Nachos and broccoli?"

"How could I forget? I stared at your tits for half the night."

She chuckles, and her breasts jiggle against my back. "I should have known then that you were going to spend most of our time together worshipping them." She slowly slides her index finger along the elastic of my waistband until it slips just under.

I clench down on my teeth, my body straining to remain in control.

"You have the best tits, babe. Hands down. I love sucking on them," I say, testing the waters, seeing what she has to say about that. When she doesn't tell me to stop, I add, "And your nipples. Fuck, when they're hard, nothing turns me on more."

I feel her chest rise and fall quickly as her fingers slip lower into my briefs.

Fuck.

She's getting close, so goddamn close, and because I have no self-control, I lightly twist, maybe an inch, to give her better access, in case she wants it.

"And then there was the first night we ever saw each other," she says, changing the subject. "When you walked in, I couldn't get over how hot you were."

"You didn't show it," I say as I give her another inch.

"Because I was annoyed you didn't have more snacks for me." Her fingers dip even lower and lightly stroke the sensitive skin right above my cock.

I gulp. "Well, I was annoyed because you decided to use my flag as a blanket."

She chuckles against my back and draws her fingers up and down, right above my pubic bone. My dick grows exponentially harder in seconds. "Well, if you gave me a blanket, I wouldn't have had to use your flag."

I suck in a sharp breath. "I . . . I didn't have a spare blanket."

"Liar," she says, her fingers moving an inch lower. I bite down on my lip, holding in my moan. "Everyone has a spare blanket somewhere, Ryot." Her voice is seductive now, enticing me, making me believe that maybe there's a chance she wants more.

I gulp, trying to contain my voice. "Not me," I answer while I twist a little bit more so I'm teetering between lying on my back and lying on my side.

From my movement, her fingers slide even farther south until they're right above the base of my cock. From how hard I am, I'm surprised she hasn't collided with my erection just yet.

"If you were a gentleman, you would have given me the blanket off your bed." Her fingers toy with my length, just a touch, but that's all I need.

I twist so I'm all the way on my back now, and she lifts slightly so I can look her in the eyes.

"You already took my snacks. Why would I give you my blanket?"

"Because you thought I was hot and wanted to please me."

She releases her hand from my briefs, and I nearly whimper from the loss, but then she reaches for the waistband and drags my briefs all the way down my legs. Without a word, I help her until I'm completely free of them. Satisfied, she returns her hand to my cock, which is now stretched up my stomach, and drags her fingernails over the length.

Fuck . . . yes.

Christ, I'm a goner.

I feel my eyes roll to the back of my head from the gentle, exquisite touch. Somewhere in the muddiness of all the wine, I can feel myself trying to communicate that maybe I shouldn't be doing this, maybe I should stop us and focus on fixing things. But hell . . . there is no way I'm going to be able to make sense of it all, not with her touching me the way she is.

"I was in a bad fucking mood that night, and there was no way I was going to be able to get out of it, even for the hottest girl I'd ever seen." I wrap my arm around her and drag her shirt up so her bare ass is exposed, and I gently stroke it with my fingers as she strokes me.

"Is that why you followed me on Instagram the next day?"

"Yeah, hopeful that I could stare at your picture on Instagram. But to my dismay, you only posted pictures of drinks."

She chuckles and presses her palm to my dick before dragging it down to my balls, where she cups them.

"Fuck," I let out in a desperate tone. That's it. I can't

avoid what's happening anymore. "Baby, please don't tease me."

"Who's saying I'm going to tease you?" she asks as she sits up on her knees and faces me. She pushes the blankets, exposing me, and then with her hand that isn't playing with my balls, she drags it up my torso to my pec, where she starts playing with my nipple.

"Myla," I groan while I press my hand against her ass.

"I've always loved playing around with you, seeing what gets you the hardest. Teasing has been one of them. You love the little touches. You love when I play with the seam of your balls like this." I groan even louder as I feel my cock stretch again. "And you love when I pinch your nipple. Not many men love that, but you do." She takes my nipple between her fingers and does exactly what I like.

"Fuck . . . me," I say as I drape my arm over my eyes, my pelvis lifting to the sky, searching out relief.

"Mmm, I love it when you surrender to me like this. When you hand me the reins for a moment. I know how much you like control in the bedroom, how much you feel the need to control me. When you give in to my touch, it gets me so horny, so wet."

"You wet right now?"

"You tell me." She spreads her legs, and I slip my hand under her and feel how soaking she is.

"Myla, fuck, that's hot."

"Do you know what's even hotter?" she asks and then hops off the bed.

"Where . . . where are you going?" I ask her as she fishes through her suitcase and then holds up a bottle of lube. My eyes zero in on it. "Baby . . ." I say softly as she comes closer and removes her shirt, leaving her naked. "Why do you have that?"

"Found it in my suitcase from our last vacation." She

returns to the position she was just in and says, "Spread your legs."

I know exactly what she wants to do, and I don't even put up a goddamn fight. I spread my legs and then place my hands behind my head. Smiling, she lubes up her finger and then lifts my cock with her non-lubed hand. She sucks me in past her delicious lips, slips her finger past my balls to my ass, and inserts it slowly.

I moan so loudly that I swear everyone in the hotel can hear me. Her other hand goes back to my nipple, and I'm completely at her mercy. Like a well-oiled machine, she presses up into me while sucking me hard at the same time and twisting my nipple.

Immediately, sweat breaks out over my body as an intense wave of pleasure starts to roar through me.

"Take my cock," I say. "Take me deep, baby. I want to hear you gag."

She dips her head down, her hair crashing all around her face, only for her to pull back up to the tip and flick at the underside.

"Jesus Christ," I mutter. "Again."

She listens. She lets me feel the back of her throat. She lets me feel her gag reflex, only to pull back up.

"Fuck me, babe. Again."

Another time, she pushes inside me, twists my nipple, and gags.

Crazy fucking lust shoots through every vein, every muscle in my body as she does it again, and again, and again, until this fog falls over me. Euphoria takes over, and from the depths of my being, an orgasm so strong, so forceful climbs up from my toes, past my thighs to my balls and, with one final suck, my body stills, my cock swells, and I come violently in her mouth.

She sucks up every drop and licks my length. When she releases me, I fall back lifelessly on the bed, attempting to catch my breath. I hear her go to the bathroom, rinse, and then she brings a warm washcloth to my cock and cleans me up. When I'm finally able to look her in the eyes, I say, "Jesus fucking Christ."

She chuckles and then lies back on the bed, spreads her legs so I can see how wet she is, and she fingers herself right in front of me.

"How does that feel?" I ask her.

"Would be better if it was you."

"I agree." I twist her so she's lying flat on her stomach. I drag my hand from her shoulders and down her spine, all the way to her ass. "You have the sexiest body, Myla. I love these curves. I don't know if you realize how much they turn me on."

"I have an idea." I hear the smile in her voice.

I take a few pillows and stack them under her pelvis until she's lifted in the air to where I need her.

"The anticipation is killing me," she says. "I think one touch, and I'm going to come."

"You throbbing, baby?"

"Desperately. I love watching you come. I love everything about it. The way your body tenses, the muscles, the veins firing off. Your sound. Your taste. Everything. Nothing makes me more turned on, more ready, than watching you combust."

"Then let's see," I say as I spread her legs, exposing her completely. I gently drag my finger down her center and get lost in her slickness. "Jesus, Myla."

"I told you." She sighs. "Nothing, and I mean nothing, will ever make me feel this way. Only you, Ryot."

"Better be only me," I say, even though in the back of my head, I realize that might not be the truth. "What do you want?"

"I want you to fill me up." And then she tosses me the lube, and I know exactly what she needs.

I lube up as well, and then slowly insert myself into both of her holes with my fingers.

"Yes," she cries out. "Oh my God, Ryot."

Pleased with her response, I lower my head to her slick clit and say, "No matter what happens to us, Myla, this cunt, it will always be mine. Do you hear me?"

"Yes," she groans right before I press my tongue against her and take a long, languid stroke. "Oh . . . my . . . God."

As I work my hand in and out of her, I continue to press the flat of my tongue against her clit, pulling out every moan, every pleasure in her body, and I revel in it. I revel in her taste, in the spasms that wrack her, and in the way she begs and pleads for me to go faster.

"Ryot, fuck . . . just . . . just fuck me hard. I need to be fucked. Please."

The sound of her pleas, the throatiness in her voice, it has me hardening, and I give myself a few more seconds of fucking her with my fingers before I feel fully ready and then bring my cock to her entrance. Her hands grip the comforter beneath her, and she yells out in pleasure as I enter her.

Hands on her hips, I move in and out at a relentless pace. *Oh my fucking God. I have missed this. Her. The feel of her.*

Emotions evade me as I realize what the hell I'm doing. This woman, the love of my life, I'm giving her what she wants, what she needs. I know I signed those papers, I know I told her I would let her walk away, but fuck . . . I'm not sure that's possible. I'm not sure I can let go of this, of her. Not when everything feels so right. Not when I feel like I could get lost in her forever. This, us, we're supposed to be with each other. There's no mistaking it.

So how do I keep her?

How do I make sure I always have her in my life?

This feeling, how do I hold on to it forever?

"Ryot, God, you feel so good. You always make me feel so good." I move my hand around the front of her and slide it between her legs, where I play with her clit. She moans even louder and thrusts her hips up, offering me a different angle, an angle so deep that I don't think there is an end. "Yes, oh fuck me, Ryot. Take me."

I grunt as I pulse harder and harder, both of our orgasms building, both of us moaning and twisting and pulsing, reaching for that impossible feeling until she convulses around me, tightening to the point that everything around me goes black. She's the first to erupt, her body writhing with euphoria. And then I follow right behind, everything tightening as I come inside her.

Our moans mix and our heartbeats slow together until we're completely listless on the bed. I collapse to the side of her, my arm draping over her back while her chest heaves, looking for any air she can suck in.

After a few minutes, she says, "Ryot?"

"Hmm?" I ask, my head buried in the sheets.

"I want to do that again."

I chuckle and murmur, "Give me a second, baby."

She twists and turns toward me. She loops her leg around mine and pulls me in close. When I look in her direction, she grips my cheek and pulls me into a kiss. Shock registers before my mouth melts into hers, and I kiss her back, our tongues tangling, the heat of our bodies colliding.

I don't know what the fuck is happening, but I'm not going to say a damn thing. I'm going to take everything she will give me.

Every goddamn thing.

THE SUN BEATS down on me while I feel the weight of another human on my body. I rub my palm against my eye and slowly open them to find Myla sleeping on top of my

Untying the Knot

chest. Her cheek is pressed against my right pec, her body lined up with mine, her cute-as-shit butt fully exposed.

A warm, comforting feeling fills me as I slowly run my fingers up and down her spine. This is heaven.

This right here.

My girl in my arms.

Fully satisfied after a night of sex with my favorite person. With my love.

And now, as I lie here, her on top of me, I start to wonder how long this is going to last, what this will bring. What will she say? Will she regret it?

We were clearly both drunk last night, and that's the main reason we crossed that line, but now what?

Should I even ask?

So many questions pass through my mind as panic sears my chest. I don't want to lose this feeling. I don't want her to wake up and regret everything that happened. Because I don't regret it. Not one second.

My fear is that she'll wake up, realize what we did, and ask me to just ignore it, to chalk it up to a drunk night, and we go back to being practical strangers again.

I'm not sure my heart could take that.

She starts to stir. Her arms clutch me, and then I hear a light groan as she picks her head up to look me in the eyes. Her hair has fallen over her forehead, so I push it behind her ear, and when her eyes connect with mine, I hold my breath, waiting for her to pull away, waiting for her to freak out.

But instead, the warmest smile passes over her lips before she drops back down on my chest and kisses my skin.

A wave of butterflies erupts in my stomach as I continue to drag my fingers up and down her back.

"Mmm," she murmurs. "Can I stay here all day?"

You can stay there forever for all I care.

"Whatever you want," I say. "I can order breakfast if you

353

want and have it brought up here. Or if that's too clingy and pathetic, I can take a shower and get out of your hair."

Her laughter rumbles against my chest, and she kisses my pec and then laps at my nipple. I grow hard beneath her. And that fucking knowing look that passes over her beautiful face drives me nuts as she slides down my body and between my legs.

"Or I can just . . . play with you for a bit." And before I can answer, she lowers her mouth over my erection and rolls her tongue around the top.

"Baby . . ." I say softly. "You . . . aw fuck, you don't have to do that."

"I know," she says as she kisses down my length and to my balls. She laps at them with her tongue and spreads my legs farther before taking my balls gently in her mouth.

"Hell," I whisper as I shut my eyes.

And that's how I start my morning, with my girl sucking my cock, only for me to turn her around and return the favor to her clit.

---

"GO AHEAD, SAY IT." Myla wiggles her eyebrows, causing me to laugh.

I lean back on the headboard and let out a deep sigh. "Fine. Waffles are by far a superior breakfast meal."

"Over any protein bar or protein shake?"

"Yes, waffles beat out any sort of protein-enriched breakfast."

She smiles, satisfied, and then picks up my fork and feeds me the last bite of my waffle. "Does this mean you're going to ditch the protein bars?"

If it means I get to keep you, then yes.

"I think it means I'll be opening up my variety of breakfast meals."

"And people say you can't teach an old dog new tricks." She gathers our plates and carries them to the cart that was wheeled in. My eyes don't stray from her, or the way she looks in my Bobbies shirt, or her mussed-up hair from where I dug my fingers through it, or the evident beard burn on her legs.

It reminds me of what life used to be like.

So carefree.

Makes me yearn for her even more.

I rest my hands on my lap and say, "So . . . did you get a grade on your paper yet?"

She pauses and glances over her shoulder. Her look of shock should be cute, but it's just a reminder that I've neglected this part of her life.

"Uh, no, that's going to take a few weeks."

"Ah, well, what was it about?"

Now her brow creases as she stands tall and faces me. I can see her wanting to respond with a sarcastic comment since it's in her nature. Probably something along the lines of "why would you care?" But she surprises me as she makes her way back to the bed and takes a seat on her knees.

"It was a design for a lobby of a major office building. The idea was to turn an old lobby from the eighties and make it modern while reusing the building materials so there wasn't much waste. I was given a concrete-style lobby that didn't have much to work with, so I decided to use stains and paint to update the space, divide it into sections, and then with the minimal budget that I did have, I added a slat board front to the lobby desk that was twelve feet long, stained it black, and added as many plants as I could to bring nature into the concrete jungle. And they had a bunch of old computers lying around, so I had those taken apart and then mounted on the wall to give this blast-from-the-past feel of where technology originated. The computer was my favorite because upcycling those made the space feel modern but also authentic to its original glory."

I sit there . . . stunned.

Absolutely fucking stunned.

I knew she was good and that she had an eye for design. I knew that from what she did with our house in Chicago, but this . . . this feels like next level.

"That sounds fucking amazing, Myla. Do you have any pictures?"

Her cheeks redden as she says, "I actually have my computer with me if you want to see."

"I do."

Smiling brightly, she hops off the bed and pulls her computer out of its bag and then brings it over to me. She sits with her back against the headboard, her shoulder bumping into mine. I loop my arm around her shoulder, and she snuggles in close. *Fuck, I've missed this. How long has it been since we simply snuggled in bed and shared something about our lives?* The fact that I don't know shows what an utter asshole I am.

She turns on her computer as she says, "I just have mockups since this is a fake project, but the cool thing is, the building is real. It's in downtown LA, so I got to go view it and plan it out. I took pictures of my own and could play off those in my design program."

"That's really cool, babe."

"And our teacher said that she's going to submit the top five to the building owner and see if they're interested in any of them. If they are, there's a possibility to be hired out."

"Holy shit, really?" I ask. "That's awesome, Myla."

"I know it's a long shot." She taps around on her computer. "But it would be pretty cool." She opens a screen and shows me a picture of a plain concrete lobby. Expansive windows reach up to the ceiling, but that's about it when it comes to any architectural appeal. "So this is what it looked like before. The best thing about it was the sunlight coming in." She clicks around and pulls up a picture. "And this is what it would look like with my special touch."

The lobby is transformed from a bleak, cold space to a bright and modern aesthetic with her slat board lobby desk, potted, leafy ficus plants, and then paint accents that make the concrete feel oddly warm.

"Wow, Myla." I take the computer from her to get a closer look. "This is . . . this is incredible. I like the natural colors you used. Pulling in that sage color warms the place up and makes it not so cold and dreary. The desk is clearly the focal point, and the computers on the wall behind it are really fucking cool."

"Thank you. I really love it. And like I said, I know it would be a long shot to get picked, but it's something cool to place in my portfolio that I've been building for a bit now."

"You have more?" I ask.

"Yeah."

"Can I see them?"

She glances at me and says, "Are you sure this isn't boring you?"

I shake my head. "No, babe, not at all. I really want to see them."

Her smile stretches from ear to ear, filling me with joy because that's the smile I fell in love with. It's utterly beautiful. Relaxed. Carefree. My Myla's. "Okay, let me pull them up."

⊂⊐

"HOLD ON, WHERE DID YOU GO?" I ask Myla as we sit across from each other at dinner. We opted to have dinner together, just the two of us, in the balcony restaurant that overlooks the vineyard. Not sure how I scored the table, but it seems like someone was watching over me.

We spent most of the day looking over her portfolio with her explaining everything that went into them. I listened. I asked questions, and I was fucking amazed. She's brilliant. When it came to lunch, we both decided to take a walk to the pool, where we ate poolside and hung out with Huxley and Lottie while JP and Kelsey went over last-minute wedding preparations.

After lunch, we walked the vineyards hand in hand and talked about the night of the steak and shriveled potatoes. I admitted that it tasted like absolute garbage, and she admitted that she took extra long eating hers so she could rub it in my face.

We both laughed.

And when we got back to the hotel room, I asked her if she wanted to take a nap since we barely got any sleep the night before. She said yes, and she cuddled into me the entire time.

It's been . . . fuck, it's been eye-opening. I can't remember the last time we had a day like this, where it was just us, nothing going on but doing what we felt like. I've been so focused on making sure that I prove myself to . . . fuck, who knows, that I've forgotten how to relax. Not to mention, I'd forgotten how perfect Myla is for me. How spending time with her used to be my solace. My joy. *How did I lose sight of that? Of her?*

Myla picks up her wineglass and looks at me mischievously. "While you were in Atlanta a few years back, it was . . . God, you had that big toe injury that you kept bitching about."

I chuckle. "It hurt!"

"Oh my God, it was your big toe. Get over it." She takes a sip of her wine. "Anyway, I couldn't take your moaning anymore, so when you went to Atlanta for the start of your away trip, Nichole and I went to Hawaii."

I shake my head, unable to believe it. "But I spoke to you. We did FaceTime, and I saw our bedroom."

"Nichole brought a green screen."

"No, she didn't." I lean back in my chair in disbelief.

Myla nods. "Yup. We thought we were being so sneaky.

We did a green screen and made sure to practice before you called. Oh yeah, we really pulled the wool over your eyes."

I tap my fingers on the table and say, "You realize if you told me you went to Hawaii, I wouldn't have cared. I would have encouraged it."

"Yes, but this was out of spite because of all your toe complaining. Plus, it was fun to see if we could get away with it. You know how we love the adventure."

"Yeah, I do." I lightly chuckle. "Was that the only time you did that?"

"Yes. Because it was the only time you pushed me over the edge with the complaining about your big toe."

"Babe, that shit hurts. It's a legitimate injury."

She smiles and lifts her wineglass up. "Okay. So would you compare your pain to something like . . . I don't know, menstrual cramps?"

"Oh no, you don't." I shake my head. "I'm not going to fall for that. Nothing, and I mean nothing, is as bad as menstrual cramps."

"You're only saying that because when we did the simulator, you clocked out at level six."

I lean forward and whisper, "Babe, I thought my balls were about to explode."

She tilts her head back and lets out a roar of a laugh. Clutching her chest, she says, "The image of you ripping the pads off your genitals will live rent-free in my mind forever."

"Fantastic." I chuckle. "Any other memories that live rent-free in your head?"

She twists the stem of her wineglass on the table as she stares at me. The sunset behind her is casting a picturesque glow around her, so I pull my phone out of my pocket and say, "Smile." *I need to capture this moment. She's so goddamned beautiful.*

She offers me one of her closed-mouth smiles that just barely tilts up the corners of her mouth.

I snap the picture and then sigh as I look at it. "Sorry, but the way the light is hitting you from behind, and the sunset . . . you're stunning, Myla." I show her the picture, and she just smirks.

"Rent-free memories? Well, obviously, when we first met, the look of confusion on your face is one of my favorite moments. The rooftop, where we were intimate for the first time." She wets her lips and stares down at her wine. "The day you went with me to the reading of my dad's will after he passed away, the way you told my mother off. Probably will never forget that."

"Me either," I say quietly.

She quiets as well when she says, "You realize that was single-handedly the best moment of my life? And sure, when you proposed was beautiful and our wedding was the best day of my life, but when you stood up for me, when you promised my mom that she would never, ever hold her strength over me ever again, I felt free. Free for the first time, like you released me from this dreary life I was living under."

"I told you I'd protect you until my dying day." I move my fork across my plate and say, "I might have lost sight of that for a second, but even when we go our separate ways, I will always protect you, Myla. Always."

"You never stopped protecting me, Ryot." The air between us grows thick, and I don't know what to say, what to do other than wish and hope that after this time in Napa is over . . . we're not over.

"I messed up, Myla."

"You did," she replies. "But you never stopped protecting me."

Guilt consumes me as I think about her words that night.

*"When you retired early from baseball, it was as if this cloud cast over you, and you turned into a different man. You looked straight ahead, plowed forward, and you walked over everyone to prove yourself . . . including me."*

How can she say I never stopped protecting her?

"You might not have needed protection from the outside world, but you needed protection from me." I let out a deep sigh and then look up at the ceiling. "Shit, I just turned a good time into a morose one."

"I think it was needed," she says, pulling my attention back to her. She nibbles on the corner of her lip before saying, "I think getting this out, hearing it all, I think that's what we needed." Her eyes connect with mine. "You haven't been the man I married for the past few months. Why, Ryot? Did retiring early really hurt you that much?"

My eyes dart to the side as my chest tightens.

"Look at me, Ryot." I take a moment, but when I finally look her way, she says, "Were you hurt mentally?"

After a few seconds, I say, "I felt meaningless." She sets her wineglass down and then rises from her chair before moving it right next to mine. When she sits back down, she places her hand on my thigh. "My entire life has been base-ball. Nothing else. I spent so many fucking years chasing the dream that when I made it, I spent the rest of that time making sure I earned that spot and didn't miss a training or a practice because I was terrified of becoming a has-been." I shake my head. "When I hurt my rotator cuff, I knew deep down that that was it. It was the end. I was too old to make a full recovery, and there were younger and cheaper guys waiting to take my position. It happened so fast, like one giant nightmare. One day I was living my dream—with you at my side—and the next, it was all over." And although she was at my side, I no longer saw anything but the disap-pointment.

"You felt like it was stolen from you."

"Yes," I answer. "I felt like I needed to demonstrate that *I* wasn't meaningless by finding success elsewhere. I kept chasing after something that validated me. Nothing I've done has really taken away the hurt. The utter disbelief that the life I loved was finished was all I could see. Looking at it now, it's so clear how ridiculous that was. At that point, I still had you. So, I actually had everything I needed."

When our eyes meet, I cup her cheek and softly say, "But by the time I lifted my head to see the world around me, I was too blind to realize that I neglected the one thing that mattered the most to me."

"How come you never told me how you were really feeling? It seems like you were spiraling, Ryot."

"I was . . . I am," I answer honestly before pressing my palm to my eye. "I didn't want to say anything because I didn't want to believe it. But listening to you, looking in on myself, and spending these past few days with you, as if . . . as if we are the same couple from six years ago, it's made me realize that I haven't been happy these past few months. I've just been pretending."

"Why?"

I press my hand to hers and whisper, "Because I'm supposed to be the strong one, Myla. I'm the one who is supposed to do the protecting. I'm the one who is supposed to take care of you. Not the other way around."

"What are you talking about?" she asks and then presses her fingers to my chin so I'm forced to face my problems head-on. "Ryot, a marriage is about being in a partnership. It's never one-sided. You aren't the only one in our marriage who was supposed to be strong."

"I realize that now," I say and then leave it at that. I don't know what else to say. I don't want to get into this in a restaurant, or really get into it at all because it just hit me like a ton of bricks.

My career.

My feelings.

My inability to lean on Myla when I should have.

I pushed her away, ignored her, and tried my hardest to show that I wasn't hurting.

I put on a show for the world to let whoever was watching

know that I was happy, successful, and pleased with the new chapter in my life, but in reality, I haven't been.

"Are you okay? You went quiet on me," Myla says.

"Yeah," I answer while I smooth my hand over my leg. "You know, I'm getting pretty tired. Want to head back to the room?"

She studies me for a moment, and I feel her wanting to press more, to dive deep into my confession, but thankfully, she doesn't. "Sure."

I pay the bill, and then we both rise from the table, and I take her hand in mine. Together, we head back to our hotel room.

⊏══⊐

## MYLA

I STARE at my reflection in the mirror while I finish brushing my teeth. Ryot already finished getting ready and is in bed, but I've taken longer because I've needed to stop and think.

I've been thinking about tonight, about the past few months, about missing the cues that Ryot might be depressed or hurting. Feeling like he didn't want to show me weakness because he assumes I'm the weak one in the relationship . . .

That last one is giving me a second. I know he didn't say it, but he didn't really have to. It was written all over his face. And I don't know how I feel about it.

I'm not mad.

I'm not really upset either.

Because how could I blame him? After everything we've been through, he's been the protector. He's been the one who shielded me—our marriage from the press, from my mom, from the world—and he's cherished that role and me up until a few months ago.

I spit out my toothpaste and rinse my mouth before drying off.

I stare at my reflection again. God, I'm so confused, yet I still want to be near him. I don't want this day to end with an awkward beat between us. That's why I find myself slipping off my bra and underwear and slipping on one of his shirts.

When I open the bathroom door, I spot him resting in bed, one hand behind his head while the other rests at the edge of the sheets that barely reach his waistline, leaving his impressive chest on full display. The contours of his muscles are highlighted even more by the dim lighting. The casted shadows play with the divots and curves along his pecs and abdomen, showing off his brute, carved strength. And then there's the way he looks at me. His eyes roam from my legs all the way up to my face in an appreciative, starving perusal. But he doesn't move, and he doesn't shift. He just stares at me like a hungry man, ready to devour his meal.

It's how he's always looked at me. He's always made me feel like the sexiest woman in the room, despite how I might have felt about my body in the past, thanks to my mom. He's loved my curves, he hasn't batted an eyelash when I've gained some weight, and he's never once turned me away, always worshipping.

Always.

"Hey, baby." He wets his lips.

"Hey," I say softly and go to my side of the bed, where I slip under the covers.

As I turn toward him, he turns as well and props his head up as his hand falls to my side. "I'm sorry for ruining the end of our night."

"You didn't ruin it."

His hand grips me tighter as he says, "I did. We were having a great time, and I brought down the evening."

"You were being honest, Ryot. That's not bringing down the evening."

He attempts a smile, but it doesn't come close to reaching his normal one. "Well, either way, I'm sorry."

"Ryot, you don't need to—"

"Myla, can I ask you something?"

I pause, confused, and say, "Sure. Of course."

His eyes fall to my lips and then back up to my eyes as he says, "I don't want to be that guy, but . . . today kind of rocked me, and I just need to know where you stand when it comes to me."

I open my mouth to answer, but he continues, "I don't want to put pressure on you. Trust me, that's the furthest thing from my mind, but I also need to know if you see this time we're spending together as some sort of goodbye tour, one last hurrah kind of thing. And if it is, then that's fine, but I need to know because I don't want to get my hopes up that what we're doing could be something else. But if this feeling, this electricity, these conversations are repairing what we used to have, please tell me. I want to work things out with you."

Well, I was not expecting him to want to talk about that. I assumed that it would be more about how he had to leave baseball, but then again, that conversation seems to be paused. I think it was paused at the restaurant. As much as I love to believe that he's been completely open with me, I can sense that he's still hiding things, feelings he's keeping to himself. I'm not sure if it's because he doesn't fully feel them yet, or if he's hiding them for a reason.

This question might be the reason.

He's protecting himself.

I'm protecting myself.

And I'm not sure either one of us knows how to navigate this.

The only option at this moment is to be as honest as possible, even if it might not be what he wants to hear. "Will you hate me if I say I'm not entirely sure what this is?"

His voice softens as he says, "Myla, I could never hate you. There might be times when I'm frustrated or angry, but I never feel hate toward you. Ever."

And I know that's the truth. We've been through so much, and even in the end, he's always shown me love. Even now, after he signed the papers, he's showing me love. I just wish . . . I wish we hadn't stumbled . . . or drifted apart during those last few months.

I drag my finger over the divot between his pecs and say, "I've missed you, Ryot. This trip, well, it's been fun, and I feel like we haven't had fun in a while."

"We haven't," he replies. "And that's my fault, I know—"

"There's no reason to point fingers and assign blame. That's not going to do anything other than continue the bitter awkwardness between us, and I don't want that."

"I don't want that either," he says as his hand moves to the hem of my shirt.

"So let's just have a conversation then." I wet my lips and say, "The past few days have felt like we transported to six years ago, hell, even six months ago, before everything with The Jock Report exploded. And maybe I've gotten lost in this . . . this bubble where we've tried to find healing and perhaps got lost in it all. I've missed it. I've missed you."

"I feel like there's a but that follows that sentence," he replies while his hand slips under the hem of my shirt and his warm palm presses against my hip.

I take a deep breath and say, "I don't want to hurt you, Ryot. And I know you want clarity, you want to know what all of this is, what it means, but I don't have a fair answer for you." I speak softly, clearly. "I can't go back to the way we were living. It was demoralizing, not having my husband inter- ested in my life, only hyper-focused on his. And I know this seems easy now, you and me, but that's because we're not living real life. Outside of this Napa Valley bubble, you still have your responsibilities, I still don't matter, and we can't seem to find a neutral space."

"Myla, you matter. I might not have shown that over the past few months, and that's something I have to live with, but I need you to know, you do matter."

"I appreciate that," I say. "But I just . . . I don't know, Ryot." I waver between wanting him and being scared while having to protect my scars and my mental health. "I want to believe everything between us could magically just . . . go back. They could change, we could grow, but I'm just not sure."

He nods in understanding, and I hold my breath, waiting for him to get mad, to show an ounce of anger, because frankly, he has to be frustrated. We both are. But he doesn't.

"How about this?" His hand slides up my side, to my ribs, dragging my shirt with him. "Instead of trying to pick a direction for which way we'll be going, why don't we just take this one day at a time, one hour if you want? Just continue to connect, be honest, and see what happens?"

I can see it in those sparkling eyes of his that he doesn't want to let go. Even though he said he would before we left for Napa. To my face, in his letter.

And I told Nichole . . . I wasn't sure if I could let go either. Yet I'm not sure I can stay.

My silence must worry him because he adds, "Just one moment at a time, Myla."

My eyes meet his, and I ask, "That won't give you hope?"

"No." He shakes his head, but I don't fully believe him. "I just want to spend some time with you. Even if it's a farewell, at least I get to remember this time with you and part ways wishing you joy and happiness."

Something about the desperation in his voice, and the compromising just to keep talking to me, makes me feel so fucking guilty. I know he's not trying to make me feel that way, but we're both in a tough spot, and I know I'm waffling. I should have a clear-cut answer for him, but I don't.

"I'm sorry, Ryot."

Panic envelops his irises as his eyes bounce back and forth, looking at me.

Looking for answers.

He swallows hard and says, "Why are you sorry?"

"Because, instead of being a mentally strong person, you must deal with my past trauma, which doesn't allow me to give you a straight answer. I wish I could, but I'm scared. Damaged. Afraid." Terrified of feeling so utterly abandoned by the man who swore he'd never leave me. My dad's true life blindsided me at the funeral, but I'm still unable to fully forgive him for leaving me with Mom when he did. He must have known what she did to me. He heard all the things she said and didn't defend me. *His silence felt like abandonment. And Ryot's silence triggered that.*

"Listen to me," he says with such strength that it impresses me. I wish I could be as strong as he is. "From the very beginning, I told you I'd help carry your baggage, that you didn't have to walk alone. And I meant that. I understand what you've gone through, and I know how that affects your everyday life. I'm not blind to that, and I knew that going into this relationship. I'm the one who lost sight of it all."

"You shouldn't have to babysit me," I say, feeling ashamed by my past.

"I never babysat you, Myla," he says. "Marriage is a partnership. We both carry each other in separate ways like you said at dinner. You gave just as much to this relationship as I have. We've patched up each other's wounds, we've guided each other through the dark and through the comfort, and when it came down to it, we were each other's number ones. That's what falling in love is for, Myla, the give and the take, the partnership, the knowledge that no matter the circumstances, you don't have to walk alone."

Tears spring to my eyes, and I let them fall down my cheeks with one blink.

"Baby, why are you crying?" he asks, tugging me closer so we're only a few inches apart.

"It's just so much," I say. "All of it. Everything you're saying right now makes me believe that things could be okay between us, but you . . . you hurt me, Ryot."

He presses his lips together as his legs tangle with mine. I can tell he's drawing closer because he doesn't want to lose me. "I know. And sorry just isn't good enough, but I'm sorry."

"I don't know how to get over that hurt." My tears hit my pillow. "But I don't know how to let go either. You're the one person who can break me, but also the one person who can put me back together."

He slides his hand higher and says, "If you let me, I'll put you back together, Myla, and swear to never break you again. Put *us* back together. You're right about the Napa bubble, and when we get back, let's sit down and talk about *our* future. How to incorporate *our* dreams. I want to do it right. With you."

"I want to believe you, Ryot. I really do." I drag my hand over his chest. He's literally just spoken the very words I should have heard so many months ago. *"Let's sit down and talk about our future. How to incorporate our dreams. I want to do it right. With you."* And it's not that I feel they've come too late. It's more that I'm not confident they will come to fruition. So, instead of dashing his heart here, I'll be leaning toward the compromise and hoping he doesn't realize I'm ignoring this option. "Okay. So maybe . . . maybe we do just take this one moment at a time."

I can see the hope spring to his eyes. "Yeah? One moment at a time?"

It's scary to think that I'm even considering this, but it's scarier to believe that this might be the last time I see him, so I nod. "Yes, one moment at a time."

His shoulders deflate as if he's been holding his breath this entire time, and he pulls me in even closer so our bodies line up. "One moment, baby. I'll take it." And then he closes the rest of the space between us and kisses me lightly. Our lips barely mold together before he moves me so I'm on my back, and he hovers above me, his strong, muscular body trapping me into a warm cocoon.

And as his mouth descends upon mine, his lips trailing along my jaw, my neck, and down between my legs, I hope and pray the entire time . . . please don't let him hurt me again. *Please show up. And then please stay present.*

# Chapter Twenty

## *MYLA

### *Six years ago . . .*

"You don't need to text him. You can do this," Nichole says through the phone. She's currently in New York City on a work trip.

"I can't," I say as I rock back and forth on my couch. "He texted me this morning, telling me about his day, and that if I'm free, he'd love to see me."

"He's texted you every day since you broke up with him, multiple times a day. Today is no different."

"Today is different," I say. "Today is the only day my dad's executor can meet up with Mom and me. She's already made comments to me about Ryot. About how he's lucky that he got away when he could, something she assumed since he didn't show up to the funeral. She's been so cruel, Nichole. And this is awful, but I just want to prove her wrong. I want to show her that everything is okay."

"You are strong, Myla. You don't need to pretend."

I shake my head even though she can't see me. "No, I'm not strong." My hands tremble as I think about having to be in the same room as my mom. "I wish I was. I wish I could show up unattached and act like whatever she's going to say to me won't hurt, but I'm too raw. With just the right insult, just the right shitty comment, I know I won't survive it."

It's been a week since the funeral and since I broke up with Ryot. And it's been the hardest week of my life. Dealing with losing my father, being shaken to my core about his second life, reeling from the backhand of my mother, and shutting out Ryot, I'm at a breaking point.

"You're stronger than you think you are," Nichole says.

"Nichole," I say softly as tears spring to my eyes. "I am so scared, so terrified to be in the same room as her, that I have thrown up twice now. I want to believe in my heart that I can do this, but I know, deep down in my soul, that I can't. I think I need to text him."

"You're going to confuse him. Plus, I thought you were moving on. I didn't think you wanted to be attached to him. Not to mention, I don't want to see him hurt you again."

"I don't know if he hurt me, or if I hurt myself," I say, the confession slipping off my tongue since I've been thinking about it the past couple of days.

"He wasn't there for you."

"He was," I answer as tears stream down my face. "Just in a different way, and I think that's something I need to come to terms with."

"He's going to hurt you."

"No, Nichole. You're the one who's hurting me right now. I'm telling you that I need him for support. I need him to pretend to be with me to make it through a few hours with my mother, and you shouldn't be making me feel bad about that."

"I'm not trying to make you feel bad. I'm just trying to put things in perspective for you. You're hurt right now and—"

"Nichole, this isn't up for debate. I'm meeting my mom in an hour. I don't even know if he's free. I can't physically get off the couch right now because I'm shaking like a leaf. If you were here, I would take you, but you aren't. That leaves him."

She's silent for a second and then finally, "Okay, if you think you need him, I don't want you to do this alone. But just be careful, okay?"

"I will." I say my goodbyes and then stare down at my phone.

I hover over Ryot's name and debate if I should do this or not. I know that if I don't show up, my mom will believe she's won. And I don't want that. If I show up alone, she's going to think the same thing, that she won, that I'm such a disappointment in life, that *I can't even keep a boyfriend.*

Any option is a loss for me.

I might as well call him.

On a deep breath, I tap his name and bring the phone to my ear. After the second ring, his voice comes through. "Myla, hey, is everything okay?"

Just hearing his voice makes my nausea roar to life, because I missed it. I missed him.

"Umm . . . Ryot?" I say, my voice tight. "Can I ask you a favor?"

"Anything, baby. Ask me anything."

With that simple word, baby, I burst into tears.

⸻

"THANK YOU FOR PICKING ME UP," I say as I get into Ryot's SUV.

"Of course." He turns toward me and those soulful eyes of his split my heart in two. I've missed them. Missed his fresh

373

soap smell, his smile, his touch, his voice. Everything. "Are you okay?"

I dab at my eyes with the tissue that's crumbled in my hand and nod. "Yeah, just lots of emotional stuff is all. I don't want to bore you with it."

"You never bore me, Myla."

I try to smile, but it falls flat.

He clears his throat and turns back toward the steering wheel. "We're going to your mom's?"

I shake my head. "No, a legal office, which is actually ten minutes away. I plugged it into my phone for you." I hand him my phone, and he sets it on his lap.

"Okay." He puts the car in drive and once he gets on the road, he says, "So what's the plan?"

I clench my hands together and answer, "Um, to act like we're still together. I know that's asking a lot from you, and I really shouldn't be asking since, well, you know, since how things went down. But I can't show up alone. She'll make a comment about how I'm unlovable, and I just don't think I can go through the mental anguish of dealing with her today, not alone."

"Babe," he says softly, placing his hand on my leg. "You know I'd do anything for you. I wouldn't want you to do this alone either."

"Thank you, Ryot."

I stay quiet for the rest of the drive, unsure what else to say to him. But when we arrive and he parks, he tells me to wait in the car as he gets out. I watch him round the hood and then come to my door where he opens it for me. He holds his hand out like a gentleman and whispers, "Hold on to me for as long and as tight as you need. Okay?"

I press my lips together and nod as he helps me out of the car.

And I hold his hand. I hold it all the way into the building, up the elevator, down the hall, and when we reach the law offices, I grip him even tighter when I see my rigid mother sitting in one of the chairs, hands in her lap, waiting for the meeting to start.

"I got you," Ryot whispers close to my ear.

My mom looks up and with a scowl so fierce, she says, "About time you showed up." We are right on time, but anything but twenty minutes early isn't acceptable to my mother. "We can start now." She stands from her chair and walks up to reception. "The rest of the party is here." She glances over her shoulder at me and Ryot and says, "Although, he'll have to stay out here and wait for you."

I grip him tighter, and he steps in before I can say anything. "Myla has made it quite clear that she will not be left alone with you. If you have a problem with that, we can speak to the authorities about how you used your fists and other objects to beat her after her father passed away." Ryot's voice is harsh, threatening, and thankfully, it works, because my mom turns her nose up and says to the receptionist, "Just show us to the conference room."

Looking confused, the receptionist stands from her chair, offers us some drinks, and then leads us to a conference room in the middle of the law office. My mom sits on one side while Ryot and I sit across from her. When we are informed that Mr. Tarkin will be with us shortly and the door is shut, Mom wastes no time in starting to harp on me.

On us.

"Surprised you're even here, Ryan."

"It's Ryot, but I understand your pathetic need to show dominance. Please, continue with whatever pointless drivel you need to feel a minuscule amount of importance."

I nearly choke on the water I'm drinking as I set my bottle down and glance over at Ryot. His jaw is clenched, the veins in his neck are popping, and his gaze is unwavering as he stares my mom down. He resembles a wild beast, ready to take down anything and everything that crosses his path.

Mom's eyes narrow, and a response is on the tip of her tongue, but before she can reply, the conference door opens and Mr. Tarkin walks in with a folder tucked inside his arm.

My mother might thrive on playing mental fuckery with people, but when in public, she holds herself to a higher standard. She just waits until we're alone.

"Good afternoon. So sorry about the delay on all of this." Mr. Tarkin takes a seat.

"I'm just a little confused," Mom says. "Not sure why we have to meet at all. After all, this was my husband."

Mr. Tarkin shifts uncomfortably and unfolds his folder. "Yes, well there were some alterations and stipulations made to Mr. Moore's will a year ago."

"Excuse me?" Mom proclaims as she sits taller. "What sort of alterations and stipulations?"

Mr. Tarkin flips over a piece of paper and says, "It will be easier if I read his letter out loud." He clears his throat and says, "'From the desk of Edward Moore. Myla, depending on when I pass, I may not have told you about Miranda and the boys. If that's the case, forgive my cowardice in life. Sadly, I'm sure your mother would waste no time in telling you about them. It would be in her nature to do so. The older you've become, the more I've wanted to sit you down and tell you the truth. To meet with you one on one and be honest. I'm sorry I was too much of a coward to tell you myself, but I need you to know, you weren't the reason I split my time. It had everything to do with your mother. I pleaded, begged her for a divorce, told her I would take you with me and set her free to do what she wanted to do—focus on her career. But instead, she decided to make our lives miserable. I wasn't the father I was supposed to be for you and for that, I am sorry. But my biggest regret is never pulling you out of a situation that you should have been pulled from.'" Tears spring to my eyes, and Ryot notices immediately and hands me a tissue from the center of the table before wrapping his arm around me. "'You deserved better. So much better, and I just hope that you find someone in your life that will bring you joy. That you find peace. And that you spend the rest of your days searching out your very own happiness.'" Mr. Tarkin clears his throat and moves the paper he was reading to the back.

"Was that it?" Mom asks, her voice and expression remaining stoic.

"No, there's more." Mr. Tarkin shifts again, and from his body language, I can see that he doesn't want to read what's next. "'Verna, you have made every person's life who lived under my roof miserable, and I only wish that you were the one in the grave, not me.'" My eyes widen in shock. Dad wrote that? No way.

"How dare he," Mom mutters.

Mr. Tarkin continues. "'Therefore, I hereby bequeath my retirement, life insurance, survivor benefit plan, and my personal savings to my daughter, Myla. The house that is under my name, I have given to Miranda and the boys to do what they would like with it.'"

"What?" Mom shouts, as my jaw hits the table.

"'And as for my possessions, I request they are donated to goodwill. My art collection to the Veteran's League of Chicago is to be sold at value or to be used for decoration. I hope this is a lesson to whoever is in this room: treat those close to you with kindness, don't be a coward like me, and never let anyone or anything hold you back from what you truly want in life.'"

Mr. Tarkin removes his glasses and pinches his nose, clearly relieved that he got through that.

"This is preposterous. How do I know that letter wasn't forged?"

"We have a record of two witnesses watching him write it as well as the document being notarized. It's truly from him." He glances down at his watch. "And I'm sorry to have to run, but I was told to deliver this message and leave. Myla, any questions you might have regarding your father's estate, please feel free to contact me, but this is all you will need." He slides me a thick envelope. "Mrs. Moore, I am sorry to say, but you have thirty days to vacate the premises. Any damages to the property before leaving must be fixed by you or an outside contractor. If you would like to dispute this, please feel free to find your own attorney, but I will say this, you will not win in court. Good luck to both of you."

And then Mr. Tarkin is out of his chair and out of the conference room, shutting the door behind him.

The moment the door clicks shut, Mom turns her fury on me. "You made him do this, didn't you?"

"What? No." I shake my head.

"He changed this a year ago? That's just around the time that you started visiting us again. This is your way of getting back at me. This is how you treat the one constant in your life? I always knew you were a selfish whore, but—"

"Enough," Ryot says, slamming his fist on the table, startling us both. His back tense, muscles in his arms firing as he leans his hands on the table and stares my mother down. "Once again, I will not sit here and listen to you berate my girlfriend because it makes you feel better. It's time to come to terms with the facts, Verna, and the fact of the matter is, you're an absolute piece of shit. You have convinced yourself that you are the victim in your life when in reality, you're the monster. This woman, sitting right next to me, the woman I love, she's not a product of you, nor your late husband. She's a product of what not to be. She is proof that good can come from evil. She has a heart, she has a soul, and she has several caring bones in her body. And despite the uphill climb her childhood was, she has prevailed, and I will be damned if I ever see you near her again." Ryot takes my hand and pulls me up from the chair. "If I hear at any point that you contact her, or even go near her, you will have me to answer to, as well as the cops. Assault and battery won't look good on that

378

precious, squeaky-clean image you attempt to portray. Oh, and we have witnesses and pictures. Stay the fuck away from my girl."

And with that, he guides me toward the door and out of the office, leaving me and my mom in an absolute state of shock.

When we reach the elevator, I feel his entire body shaking, trembling, ready to fire.

"Ryot."

"Not right now," he says, but it's not in an angry tone. It's quieter. He hears me, but he doesn't want to discuss anything yet.

We walk hand in hand to his car where he opens the door for me, helps me in, and then retreats to his side. The entire time, my heart is beating a mile a minute, and my palms are sweaty. It doesn't feel like I can suck enough air into my lungs because . . . oh my God, I can't believe Ryot did that.

I can't believe he put my mom in her place.

He . . . defended me.

Protected me.

Made sure that she will never, ever interfere with my life again.

I'm . . . I'm speechless.

I'm grateful.

I'm overwhelmed because I feel like this is what I've been waiting for my entire life, this . . . freedom. She's not going to bother me. She's not going to ever touch me again. And that is the most liberating thing I've ever felt.

And it's all because of him.

Ryot climbs into his seat and grips the steering wheel tightly before letting out a deep breath. "Fuck, Myla, I'm sorry." He's sorry? What could he possibly be sorry for? He changed everything. In a matter of seconds, this weight that has been heavy on my shoulders, chipped and tarnished from my childhood, was lifted and shattered into the ground. He always said he would help me carry my baggage, but this right here, this was him unloading it forever, and I'm so grateful. He grips the steering wheel tighter. "I wasn't thinking, but I wasn't going to sit there and let that piece of shit—"

I swoop across the console, grip both of his cheeks, swivel his head toward me, and kiss him. Hard.

He's stunned at first, but then when he realizes what's going on, he slips his hand under my curtain of hair and to the back of my head where he holds me in place.

Tears stream down my cheeks as our mouths clash and collide. His soft lips part and our tongues dance together, reminding me how much I love this man, how much I've missed him.

How much I need him.

I part from him, only slightly though. I press my forehead against his and say, "I love you, Ryot. And I'm so sorry for how I treated you this past week."

"Stop," he says as his thumb drags over my bottom lip. "I know what can happen when your mind takes over, and you've been through a lot." He cups my cheek. "You've been through more than you deserve."

I grip his hand and hold it close to my cheek, leaning in for support. "It doesn't excuse treating you the way I did."

"Myla," he says, forcing my eyes to match his. "I hear your apology, and I thank you, but I'm telling you right now that I understood where you were coming from. When you're out of control and it feels like there's nothing you can do about it, you try to control other things around you. You could control our relationship and, because you didn't want to be hurt or disappointed again, you stepped back. Found an excuse to end things."

"Yes." More tears cascade down my cheeks, but these he swipes away with his thumb. "But don't you see how shitty that is?"

"I saw the woman I love struggling to find her footing. It's why I didn't give up on you, why I showed you that I was going to be a constant in your life. I was waiting for you, Myla. I will fucking wait for you forever."

"I don't deserve you."

"You deserve so much more. I'm just the lucky son of a bitch you chose." His fingers tilt my mouth up and then he's kissing me all over again. Possessively.

His grip is tight.

His mouth demanding.

And when his tongue meets mine, I'm lost.

## RYOT

"DO YOU WANT TO . . . hang out, maybe stay over?" Myla asks as she walks me up to her place after the most intense make-out session of my life.

Right there, in the parking lot of the law office. We couldn't get enough of each other, and we didn't stop until it felt like an hour had passed and I was so fucking horny that I was going to burst if we didn't leave.

Before we went back to her place, we found a food truck and ate some chicken wraps while she looked into the envelope Mr. Tarkin gave her. Inside were documents about her dad's estate and basically . . . her inheritance. Over two million dollars. Color us both shocked. She'd had no clue, but he had a solid life insurance plan. I'm pretty sure she's in shock over the whole thing.

"Do I want to come back to your place, uh yeah, babe, I do." She chuckles as we entwine our fingers and make our way through the front door of her townhome where Nichole is sitting on the edge of the couch.

Myla stumbles to a stop and says, "Nichole, what are you doing here?" From what Myla told me, Nichole has been out of town, and it's the one reason she asked me to come with her today.

Her eyes fall to our connected hands and then back up at us. "I felt bad being away when I knew you needed me, so my boss sent me home on his private jet. Although, it looks like everything went well," she says while folding her arms across her chest.

"It . . . it did," Myla says nervously. "Uh, we were actually going to—"

"Hey, babe, can I speak with Nichole separately?" I ask. I think that's what needs to be done right now. Things won't be weird between Myla and Nichole, but things are most definitely awkward between me and Nichole.

"Oh, I don't think that's necessary," Myla says.

"No, I think it is," Nichole says. "Meet me in the kitchen, Ryot." And then she takes off.

When she's out of earshot, Myla turns toward me. "I don't like this. I know she's not a fan of yours, and I don't want her to say anything that will hurt you."

I grip her chin and say, "Whatever she says to me will not deter me from the fact that I'm in love with you, and nothing is going to change that. Nothing, Myla." I lean down and press a very light kiss to her lips. "But I need to talk to her because she needs to know where I stand with you."

"Okay."

"Now go upstairs, get naked, and I'll meet you up there soon."

A smile spreads across her lips. "You want me naked?"

"Baby, I always want you naked." I spin her around and give her glorious ass a smack. "Now get up there."

She chuckles and takes off, glancing over her shoulder twice as I watch her. When she's all the way up the stairs, I head to the kitchen where Nichole is sitting on the kitchen island, one leg crossed over the other, her hands gripping the edge.

"I'm assuming you two are back together," she says as I lean against the counter across from her.

"We are," I answer. "Is that going to be okay with you?"

She picks up her phone and looks through it, stopping on a text message. She then glances up at me and says, "I got a text from Myla. She told me that you told off her mom in the conference room. That you said you'd get the cops involved if she came near Myla. Is that true?"

"It is," I answer. "I wasn't about to listen to that sorry excuse of a parent demoralize Myla again. And I made damn sure she wouldn't be bothering her in the future either."

Nichole slowly nods. "Well, thank you."

"I didn't do it for your approval."

"I know you didn't, but I'm still saying thank you."

Not wanting to say you're welcome, because I owe her nothing after what she did, trying to break Myla and me up, I push off the counter and say, "Is that all?"

"No," she replies, keeping her hands locked on the counter so her shoulders rise to her ears. "What are your intentions with her? Because she needs to matter in your life. You need to put her first. She needs to be the most important thing to you."

"She is," I answer. "But I can't throw away my career for her either, Nichole. That wouldn't be smart because then I wouldn't be able to provide for her in the way that she deserves. Something you need to learn is that I can still care for her without having to be in the same room. She knew what my life would be like going into this relationship. She knew the demand of my job, and she didn't need you convincing her that it was detrimental. If we were married, this would have been a different situation. And I plan on fucking marrying her, but we hit a bit of a speedbump these past couple weeks."

"Wait . . . what?" she asks, her eyes widening. "You're going to propose?"

"Yes. I have a ring and everything. But her dad's passing put everything on pause. I have no intention of letting her go, Nichole. She's the love of my life, and I will be damned if anyone or anything gets between that. So you can either be on our side and cheer for us, or you can make your life a living hell and try to break us up. But news flash, I'm not going to let that happen. I'm not going anywhere."

She slowly nods and then lets out a gentle sigh. "Okay, then prove me wrong, Ryot. Prove to me that you're going to be there for her and make her happy."

"I don't have to prove a goddamn thing to you, because I've already proven to Myla that I deserve her. That I will protect her. That she never has to worry about another day in her life when she's with me. And I will be cordial with you. Hell, maybe in the future, we might even become friends again, but that's because I love Myla so much and I know how much you mean to her, not because I want to make things work out between you and me."

"Don't you think that's a little counterintuitive?"

I shake my head. "No, because I tried to be nice to you, and look where that got me. So you can come to terms with the fact that I'm not going anywhere, and maybe over time, we'll grow to appreciate each other. Until then, I plan on asking her to marry me, and I truly hope that's something you can accept. Either way, I'm going through with it."

She runs her tongue over the front of her teeth as she says, "You know, normally the boyfriend would try to make the best friend like them."

"Normally the boyfriend doesn't have to deal with the best friend trying to create discord."

"Just looking out for my girl." She hops off the counter. "But I can see that she's happy with you, and I do appreciate that you protected her from her mom. It means a lot to me actually." Her expression turns soft. "Not that you need it or want it, but you have my blessing to marry her. And like you said, over time, maybe we'll grow to be friends."

"Maybe," I say and take a step toward the living room where the stairs are. "But don't fuck with me again, Nichole."

And then I'm out of the kitchen and walking up the stairs, relief in my shoulders as I reach Myla's room and open the door to find her lying on her bed, under the covers. From the amount of skin I can see of her shoulders, I know she did exactly what I wanted.

Keeping my eyes on her, I reach behind my head and pull my shirt off. I also remove my shoes and socks, and as my hands float to the waistband of my jeans, I watch her lick her lips, hunger in those sultry eyes of hers.

"Everything okay with Nichole?" she asks.

I tug on the blankets to reveal her perfect tits, and I nod as I stare. "Yeah. Everything is good."

I shuck my jeans and then remove my briefs as well and then grip my half-hard erection. "Remove the blankets completely, baby."

She does, leaving her stark naked.

"Beautiful," I say. "Now, spread your legs and finger yourself. I want to see you try to make yourself come."

⊏⊐

## MYLA

"LOVE YOU," I say as I kiss Ryot one last time. His hand on my robe-covered ass squeezes me hard before he drops his forehead to mine and sighs.

"Fuck, I don't want to leave."

"I don't want you to leave either, but you have to." I run

my hand over his thick pec. "But after the game, you're coming over here?"

"Or, you can just be at my place waiting," he says as he reaches into his pocket and pulls out a key.

"You're giving me a key?"

"Yeah." He grips my cheek with his warm palm. "I want you there, babe. Come and go whenever you want."

"Okay, well, then I'll see you at your place tonight."

"Naked?"

I chuckle and push at his chest. "No, wrapped up in a Bobbies flag. I have to bring this thing full circle, after all."

He lets out a hearty laugh. "Sounds sexy, babe. And you're going into the restaurant today to quit?"

I nod. Once I receive my dad's inheritance, Ryot and I decided that it would be the perfect time for me to quit waitressing, focus on Renovate Chicago, and work out where I want to go from there. "Yup, can't wait to tell them thank you for the time, but I'm done."

"Good. Okay. I'll see you tonight." He gives me a chaste kiss and then opens the door and starts jogging down the front steps. "I love you, Myla."

"I love you," I say back as he gets into his car and leaves.

When I shut the door, I walk over to the kitchen where Nichole is hovering over a cup of coffee.

"You had quite the night," she says.

"Did you hear us?"

"Myla, the dogs three blocks away heard you."

I wince. "I'm sorry. I hope I didn't keep you up."

She shrugs. "No, I put my earplugs in, took some melatonin, and passed out."

"You know, you didn't have to come back last night. I feel bad that you did and then we didn't even talk."

She shakes her head. "Don't even worry about it. I think I need to apologize to you."

"For what?" I ask.

"For the way I acted when your dad died." She leans against the counter and clutches her cup of coffee with both hands. "You know I'm not interested in a relationship at all. It's just not something I want or need, but I see how much you need it in your life. I see how you lean on him, how you depend on him, and I think I got a little jealous. And when he wasn't there for you the way I thought he should have been, I gave you some bad advice."

"Nichole, emotions were high for everyone. There is no need to apologize, but I do need you to know that no matter what, I will always need you. I'm not replacing you."

"I know." She takes a sip of her coffee. "We're growing up, and I think that's tough for me because it's clear we want different things. You're ready to settle down and be with someone, and I'm not."

"Yes, things are different, but Ryot is still out of town a lot during the season, which gives us plenty of time to catch up. I know the winter was tough because I hung out a lot with Ryot, but I'll be better at making sure to make time for you."

"You don't have to do that. I'm not so pathetic that I need you all the time. I just . . ." She smirks and shakes her head. "God, I'm going to miss my wing-woman. It's not like I can take you to random men's houses anymore and have you wait for me."

I cringe. "Doubtful Ryot would be happy about that."

"He'd be furious." She sets down her mug and puts her arms around me. "I'm happy for you."

"You are?" I ask, returning the hug.

"Yes. He loves you, cares for you, and is willing to cut people for you. That's all we could ask for, right?"

I chuckle. "Especially the cutting."

She releases me and says, "What's the point of dating anyone if they're not willing to slash some things on your behalf?"

"No point at all."

# Chapter Twenty-One

## MYLA

### *Present day . . .*

**Nichole:** *How's it going?*

I stare down at where Ryot's head is resting on my lap, and I stroke his hair before texting Nichole back.

**Myla:** *Currently poolside, under a rented cabana, and lounging on one of those oversized loungers while Ryot takes a nap on my lap. So . . . pretty good and, before you get all crazy with questions, we're just taking it one moment at a time.*

**Nichole:** *One moment at a time. I think that's smart, but set that aside and tell me how you really feel.*

Of course, Nichole wouldn't let me get away with an answer like that. It was worth the try, though.

**Myla:** *I'm just enjoying being near him again, the Ryot I fell in love with many years ago. We've had some intense conversations. They haven't* *fixed anything, but they've helped us open up, and I think that's what we've been missing.*

**Nichole:** *From what I've seen, it's easy to become complacent and skip over those hard conversations, even in friendships like ours. I'm glad you're getting time to talk to him.*

I drag my hand over his hair and sigh. I feel the need to keep him close, to keep touching him, because, at the end of this, I'm not sure what will happen. I can only hope that I'm not hurt again.

**Myla:** *Tomorrow is the wedding, and then after that, we leave, so it's only two more days. I'm getting nervous.*

**Nichole:** *Do you know what you're going to do?*

**Myla:** *No idea, but I'm sort of leaning toward working things out with him.*

**Nichole:** *Good.*

**Myla:** *Good? You make it seem like this is what you want.*

**Nichole:** *I do want this for you. I've never forgotten how fiercely Ryot fought for you. He fought your mom. He fought me. That's not someone you let go of. And . . . I want someone to be there for you.*

I stare down at her text, slightly confused, my anxiety gearing up. When I decided to file for divorce, she said she'd be there for me, that she'd bring me back to Chicago and figure everything out. So why is she glad that we might work things out now?

**Myla:** *You're not telling me something.*

**Nichole:** *You just have fun and figure this out. Okay?*

Now I sit up taller, disturbing Ryot from his slumber. I pull up her number and call her, but she doesn't answer. I get her voicemail, so I try calling again. When I'm sent straight to voicemail, I get a text from her.

**Nichole:** *Calm down. No news. I'm just . . . covering all my bases in case something comes back not in my favor.*

**Myla:** *Don't talk like that.*

**Nichole:** *Being realistic. But I must get to this meeting. Love you.*

*Don't focus on me. Focus on yourself, and when I hear something, I promise I'll let you know.*

**Myla:** *Okay. Love you.*

"Everything okay?" Ryot asks, still lying on my lap.

I set my phone down, and I stroke his cheek, his scruff feeling like sandpaper on my finger. "Yeah, just had a scare from Nichole for a second. She's fine. No news yet."

"Okay." He turns his body to face me and then slips his hand against the underpart of my legs. "Thank you for letting me take a nap."

I smile down at him. "It was nice. It reminded me of the time we went to Hawaii and spent most of it sleeping."

"Sleeping . . . and fucking." He waggles his eyebrows, and it makes me smile.

"Seems like we've sort of done the same thing here."

"With the addition of talking, going on walks, and drinking more wine than humanly possible."

"The wine . . . so much wine."

He kisses my thigh and then smiles up at me. "What do you want to do for dinner? The rehearsal dinner is tonight, but they're doing a close family thing, so it's just you and me. Well, and Banner if you want to invite him."

"Hmm, dinner alone with you or dinner with you and Banner? Well, the clear choice is inviting the third wheel."

He chuckles just as I hear, "Third wheel? I hope you're not talking about me." JP comes up to our lounger along with Huxley. They're both dressed in nice pants and button-up shirts. They look fresh from the shower with styled hair and both smell so freaking good. Not sure what kind of cologne they wear, but I shamelessly want to get it for Ryot. Maybe I'll ask the girls.

"Hey, man," Ryot says as he sits up. "You guys heading over to rehearsal soon?"

JP smiles sheepishly. "Actually, I have a special guest

coming, and I'm meeting up with him in a few to take some pictures."

"A special friend?" Ryot asks.

Kelsey comes up and loops her arm through JP's. "Don't let him fool you. He's talking about a pigeon."

"What?" I ask with a snort. A pigeon? I never in a million years would have imagined JP taking pictures with a pigeon.

"He has some sick obsession with saving the pigeons." Kelsey rolls her eyes. "Kazoo is practically his best friend."

"First of all," JP starts, "pigeons need love too. They are highly underrated creatures. Do I need to show you the PowerPoint again?"

"God, no. That might jeopardize our marriage," Kelsey says.

"And second of all, Kazoo is a best friend, and if I had it my way, he'd deliver our rings on our wedding day, but you vetoed that idea."

"Because the last time we saw him, he pooped on my head and then nearly clipped me in the eye with his wing."

"He could sense the hostility and jealousy you had toward him."

"Dear God," Kelsey mutters and then turns toward me. "While these two go hang out with Kazoo, think you can grab a glass of wine with me? I have something I want to talk to you about."

"Oh, sure," I answer.

"Good, meet you for drinks over at the wine tasting?"

"Sure. Should I go shower and change first?"

Kelsey waves her hand at me. "No, not at all. I'll grab a table outside and a flight of wine. Lord knows I'll need it once JP is done talking with a pigeon."

"You're so lucky you're marrying me," JP says, while squeezing her tightly.

"Very." She kisses his jaw and then takes off. The boys say bye, and when we're all alone, I turn toward Ryot.

"What do you think that's all about?" I ask.

"Nothing bad, I assume," Ryot says.

"Oh, I don't think it's bad. I'm just curious is all. I haven't spent any alone time with them."

"Maybe that's why she wants to hang before the wedding." He tucks a strand of hair behind my ear. "She wants to get to know you better."

"Maybe." I scoot off the lounger. "I'm going to run up to the room and change. I don't feel comfortable going in a bathing suit and cover-up."

"I'll come with you."

"No, don't leave because I am. Maybe sleep some more."

"Not as comfortable as being with you." He stands from the lounger and helps me pack things up. "I might take a shower and order some dinner. How do you feel about ordering room service tonight?"

"That sounds perfect."

He takes my hand in his, and we walk back to the hotel room together.

I go straight to the bathroom, where I take the quickest shower of my life. I quickly lotion up and then throw on a touch of mascara and put my hair in a tight bun. I walk out into the bedroom with a towel wrapped around my body that barely covers me.

"Are you trying to get me to tie you up so you don't leave this room?"

I glance over at him as I pluck a dress from the closet. "Don't even think about it."

He laces his hands behind his head and leans against the headboard. "Can I entice you in some way?"

"You can, easily, but you shouldn't." I drop my towel, revealing my naked body and causing him to groan.

"Baby, noooo." He covers his eyes. "Come on."

I chuckle and slip the dress over my body, sans bra and underwear. "No time for modesty." I adjust the straps of the maxi dress and say, "Do my boobs look okay? Like not too saggy or anything?"

"Saggy?" Ryot's eyes nearly pop out of their sockets. "Myla, your tits are anything but saggy."

"Are you sure? Should I wear a bra?" I play around with my boobs.

"You should wear a bra."

"Really?" I ask when I look up at him, and I notice the scowl between his eyes.

"Yes, because I don't want some guy getting a good look at those hard nipples against that thin fabric."

I roll my eyes and pick up my phone and clutch. I stick a key card inside and then walk over to the bed, where I rest my hand on his bare chest and plant a kiss on his jaw. "Let's get some nachos tonight."

"Text me when you're done, and I'll order them."

"Okay." I push off his chest to leave, but he snags my wrist and pulls me down on the bed on top of him. "Ryot." I giggle as his lips find my neck. "I have to go."

"Or you can just stay here and FaceTime in. I'll be quiet."

I laugh some more then grip his head so he's forced to look at me. "Order the nachos, and then I'll eat them off you."

His eyes brighten. "Or . . . I'll order some queso, and you can lick it off me."

"Whatever your heart desires." I pat his cheek, and then he helps me up. "See you in a bit."

"Hurry up, I'm hungry." When I glance over my shoulder, he adds, "For you."

I roll my eyes. "Work on your lines while I'm gone, Bisley."

He lets out a roar of a laugh just as I leave the hotel room.

It doesn't take me very long to walk down to the lobby and then to the restaurant where I spot Kelsey and Lottie on the patio with a flight of wine for each of us.

"Hey," I say, feeling nervous for some reason. "Sorry about

the wait, I wanted to change, and then Ryot was being clingy."

"Oh, don't worry, we know all about our men being clingy," Kelsey says as she pushes my chair out for me. "You didn't have to change by the way."

"I was not about to sit here with you two in these nice dresses while I was in a bathing suit." I take a seat and Lottie pushes a flight of wine toward me.

"We got this for you. Hope that's okay."

"That's great." I look between the two sisters. "Although, is there a reason you're trying to get me drunk?"

Kelsey laughs and shakes her head. "Not at all. We just wanted to talk to you without Ryot. Get to know you better. We have time before the rehearsal tonight."

"Oh, well, if that's the case"—I hold up a wineglass—"cheers."

━━

"WOW, you really did use his flag as a blanket," Lottie says as she stares at the Instagram picture Ryot took of the flag many years ago.

"That's what happens when you mess with the wrong girl." I finish off my fourth glass just as another flight of wine shows up.

"You are my hero," Lottie says while handing me my phone back. "And I love that your love story has a strange beginning. I don't feel so alone."

"How did yours start?" I ask, realizing I haven't spent enough time with these two girls.

Lottie dismissively waves her hand at me. "Oh, you know, just the old classic story of having to pretend to be his fiancée for a business deal."

"What?" I ask with a laugh. "Seriously?"

"Yeah. We met on the corner of the street—not in a prostitute kind of way—and I was lost. He was stomping around trying to figure out his life, and we ran into each other. I needed help, he needed help, we struck a deal, and then, well . . . the rest is history."

"Wow, that's way better than how Ryot and I met."

Lottie shakes her head. "No, I like your story, acting as a wing-woman for your girl and then ending up constantly bumping into this guy who never gave up on you. It's adorable."

"It really is," Kelsey chimes in. "True love at its finest."

"Yeah, true love," I say with a smile, even though in the back of my mind, I feel like I'm betraying them, given what is really going on. But I'm not about to open up to them, not with Kelsey's wedding tomorrow.

"How was it being married to a Major League baseball player?" Lottie asks. "Was it crazy? I can only imagine all the attention he would get, especially from women trying to claw their way into his life."

"It was crazy, but also . . . fun," I say, thinking back to when he was playing. "Since he was regularly gone on away trips during the season, we'd get creative to spend time with each other, which meant constant FaceTime dates and virtual sex."

"Why is that so appealing to me?" Lottie asks.

"Because it's a different type of intimacy. People who can make their partner come just through their voice truly understand what they need. Ryot was . . . God, he was so good at it. He wouldn't have to do much, just say certain things to make it seem like I was there with him. And when it came to women . . . well, there was never a doubt in my mind who he belonged to. He let that be known very quickly. I was his. That's it."

"That's so hot," Lottie says.

"And Ryot seems like the best guy. Very outgoing and

sweet, but driven. Huxley and JP are always saying the best things about him. They love working with him," Kelsey says.

"He likes working with them as well." A smatter of guilt hits me because he is a good guy. The best, actually. And I've never had to doubt where his love for me stood. It's always been in my hands along with his heart.

"Are you liking California? Big adjustment from Chicago, I'm sure," Kelsey says.

Maybe it's the wine, or I'm feeling more comfortable with them, but I don't curb the truth. "It's not my favorite."

"Really?" Kelsey asks, eyes wide.

"The traffic is the absolute pits," Lottie says.

"Yeah, I guess I just wasn't quite mentally prepared for the move, and my best friend is in Chicago. I was settled on living there. It was the first place that felt like home since my parents were both in the Air Force, and we moved around a lot."

"Oh, I can see how that would be difficult," Kelsey says in an understanding tone. "I wish the boys would have said something about you not fully loving California because we could have given you a good introduction. Have you been anywhere yet?"

"Not really," I say. "With Ryot hitting the ground running as soon as he got here, it's been hard to have any time to explore together." As the words come out of my mouth, I realize that's been one of the problems since we've moved. I've been stuck in the house, not really doing much, while he's been running around. That's one of the reasons I've had a hard time since we moved.

"Well, that's the problem," Lottie says as she sips from her wineglass. "You haven't done the proper exploring. You need to stick with us, girl, and we'll show you all the fun things California has to offer. For instance, we like to go for hikes on Saturday mornings. It's in the hills, and we've found this secret path that leads to a clearing that overlooks this mansion with one of the nicest pools I've ever seen. And the owner, he loves walking around naked." Lottie leans forward. "The penis on that man is exquisite. Granted, not as nice as Huxley's, but it's nice."

"The staring at the penis thing was not my idea," Kelsey says. "That was all Lottie."

"Nothing wrong with some window-shopping, you know, in case Huxley ever crosses me."

"He seems obsessed with you," I say. "I doubt he'd ever cross you."

"True." Lottie smiles over the rim of her wineglass. "He is quite obsessed. Possessive. I love it."

"Is that how Ryot is with you?" Kelsey asks. "It seems like he always needs to be touching you."

I nod. "Yes. He is. Very protective. I didn't have the best childhood, and he knows all about it, so I think he's made it his mission to make sure nothing ever harms me again." My body warms from the thought of how protective he has truly been. He's protected me from me, from my thoughts and fears, from my past, from my mom, and from the media . . . *Oh my God.* "The Jock Report," I say, trying to make sense of it all in my head, not easy after five glasses of wine. "He created that with Penn, to tell a true story, I just . . . wow." I shake my head. "I just remembered when I was blasted all over social media once during his last season. Ryot was the angriest I've ever seen. He went around to all his social media accounts and posted about our love story and then told me how he wished he could control the narrative and not rely on the algorithm to show his posts." Is that where The Jock Report stemmed from? I know he said it was to tell Penn's and his story . . . but was it also because of me?

"If you don't want to talk about it, that's okay, but what were people saying about you?" Lottie asks.

"Oh, that I was not skinny enough to be with someone like Ryot."

"What?" Kelsey asks with such galled outrage that it makes me chuckle.

"It stung for sure. I've dealt with body issues my whole life, thanks to my mom, so yeah, it took a toll on me. But Ryot has made me feel sexy . . . always. He loves my body."

"As he should, you're hot," Lottie says. "Your boobs alone are what dreams are made from."

I chuckle and then nod at her. "Speak for yourself."

She shimmies her boobs at me. "Huxley can't get enough of them."

―――

"UGH, WE HAVE TO GET GOING," Kelsey says. "The rehearsal is in a few minutes."

"No," Lottie groans as she rests her head on the table. "I don't want to leave. I like our new friend."

"I like her too," Kelsey says. "But JP won't be happy if we aren't at the rehearsal."

"Have him walk down with the pigeon. You know Kazoo is who he really wants to marry anyway."

"Kazoo?" I ask right before I hiccup. I cover my mouth, and we all laugh as I set down my finished wineglass. Yup, it's official, I'm drunk.

"Kazoo is a pigeon JP is in love with," Kelsey says while rolling her eyes. "The pigeon is great and all, but"—she leans forward—"I don't see what the big deal is."

"What are you ladies talking about?" JP asks as he walks up to Kelsey and presses a kiss to her neck. Her eyes widen right before she sinks into his touch.

"Nothing worth mentioning," Kelsey says as she turns to face him. "Mmm, let's get you out of your clothes."

JP's brow shoots up as he takes in his fiancée and all the empty glasses on the table. "Are you drunk?"

"No, are you?" Kelsey asks right before giggling.

"Wine is yummy," Lottie says as she clings to a rigid Huxley. "I want to lick it off you."

I watch as Huxley leans close to Lottie and grips her jaw while whispering something in her ear. She melts right in her chair, and immediately, just like that, I'm turned on. I can't possibly sit here and watch these men command their women without getting jealous, without knowing there's a man back in my hotel room waiting for me.

"You girls are in trouble," JP says as he grips Kelsey by the waist. "How are we supposed to go through rehearsal?"

"Carry us down the aisle," Kelsey says with a grin.

JP just shakes his head and kisses her.

"Well, I guess I'll be letting you guys get to it," I say as I slip off my tall chair and nearly hit the ground from my unsteady wine legs.

JP catches my arm right before I tumble all the way down. "Whoa, you okay?"

"Yup." I stand tall. "Just a little wobbly."

"Want me to call Ryot down here?" he asks.

"No need," I hear Ryot say as he comes up to me and loops his arm around my waist.

"Oh my God, you came to my rescue," I say as I wrap my arms around his neck.

He smiles and asks, "Enjoy your wine?"

"Yeah, and we had girl talk."

"Awwwww," Kelsey whines. "We didn't talk about you coming to work with me on some building designs."

"What?" I ask. "You want me to work with you?"

"Yes, we heard you're amazing, and I need help." Kelsey clutches her hands together. "Please think about it. I don't know what you have going on, but I would love you to help me."

"Oh wow, yeah." I blink. "I'll think about it."

"Hear that?" Kelsey says to Lottie. "She's going to think about it."

"Well, at least we know for certain she'll be looking at the peen on Saturdays with us."

"What peen?" Huxley asks, a scowl deep on his forehead.

"Yeah, what peen?" Ryot asks me.

"I'll tell you about it later." I pat his chest.

"Oh good, you're all here," Banner says as he jogs up to us. He temporarily catches his breath. "Jesus, fuck, I need to do more cardio." He rests his hands on his hips and then says, "Dude, you'll never believe who I just got off the phone with."

"Who?" I ask, confused as to why he's huffing and puffing and so excited.

"Well, I haven't told you guys this yet, because I wasn't sure it was going to pan out, but I just heard back from a guy I know over at ESPN. I told them about The Jock Report. Of course, he's heard of it and uses it, and he talked to his boss, and they want to feature The Jock Report as a regular segment, hosted by . . . Ryot."

"Wait, what?" Ryot's grip on me grows tighter. "ESPN wants me to host a segment?"

Banner nods as JP and Huxley both congratulate him.

"That's incredible," JP says. "This could be huge for the app. It takes the company more mainstream, which is exactly what we need."

"Could not agree more," Huxley adds. "This is exactly what the app needed. Good work, Banner."

I glance at Banner, who is beaming with pride. "Thanks, and sorry to barge in on whatever you're doing, but I had to tell you."

"Wow." Ryot pulls on the back of his neck and then glances down at me. "Well, I guess, uh . . . I guess it's something to discuss when we get back into town."

"I'll be on my honeymoon," JP says. "But I'm sure you three can handle it along with Penn." JP lends his hand out to Ryot and gives him a firm shake. "Congrats, this is amazing."

"Thanks," Ryot says and then looks over at Banner. "Didn't know you had this planned out."

Banner smirks. "Well, thought I would try to pull some strings. Glad it all worked out, but they were most excited about doing it because you'd be the face of it all."

"Yeah, I guess so." Ryot lets out a long breath.

"Okay, we've got to go, Kelsey," JP says, pulling her away from everyone. "Come on, Huxley. Rehearsal time, now."

Huxley gives Ryot and Banner a handshake and then takes off with Lottie clutching his hand.

"Sorry for interrupting, but I had to tell you." Banner pats Ryot's chest. "Dude, isn't this amazing?"

"Yeah," he says, but his voice doesn't sound excited at all.

"I have to go send out some emails, but fuck, I'm excited." Banner glances at me and then tilts his head. "You have your drunk smile on. Have you been drinking?"

"Wine," I say while lifting my hand. "Yummy!"

Banner chuckles. "Okay, well, you two have fun." And then he's out of here just as quickly as he arrived.

Now Ryot turns toward me and says, "I didn't know that Banner was contacting ESPN."

I wave him off. "Let's not talk about that." I move my hand up his chest. "Unless you want to, but I'm going to tell you right now, I am horny and needy, and I want you to take me back to the hotel room."

The furrow in his brow smooths out as he grips me tighter. "You're horny?"

"Very."

"And you're sure you don't want to talk about this ESPN thing?"

I shake my head. "Not much to talk about. What an opportunity." I lift on my toes and kiss his jaw. "Now take me back to our room."

# RYOT

"CAN I go to the bathroom and freshen up for a second?" Myla asks as we reach our room.

I hold the door open for her and say, "Do whatever you need, babe."

She winks and then walks over to the bathroom, looking free and . . . tipsy.

Once the bathroom door shuts, I quickly pull my phone out of my pocket and shoot a text to Banner.

**Ryot:** *What the fuck, man? I wish you would have talked to me about the ESPN thing.*

I kick my shoes off and move over to the bed.

**Banner:** *Uh . . . are you angry about this? You heard JP and Huxley. This is huge!*

**Ryot:** *Yeah, huge for you guys. Fuck, Banner, you know I'm struggling with Myla right now. This news doesn't help my case.*

**Banner:** *Oh shit, I didn't even think about that.*

**Ryot:** *Yeah, that much is obvious.*

**Banner:** *But this . . . this is the dream, Ryot. Slipping you into mainstream media with the business name slapped onto a segment will solidify our spot in communications. This was what we were aiming for.*

**Ryot:** *I understand that, and any other time, I would be jumping up and down, but I have no idea what's going on with Myla. And having a spot on ESPN like that would mean a huge commitment, and one I'm not sure I'm able to take right now. I need to fix my marriage.*

**Banner:** *Not to be a shithead in the moment, but . . . aren't you getting a divorce? I know you've been trying to fix things, but at the end of the day, do you really think you'll be able to do that?*

I stare down at his text, my mind trying to process what he's saying. Sure, I've been trying, and it's been great since we've been here, in this little Napa Valley bubble, but what will life be like when we leave? That question has been in the back of my head ever since Myla arrived, and it's slowly eating me alive.

Now with this new opportunity looming, I'm worried that it will turn her away even more.

**Ryot:** *I don't know, man. I have no fucking clue what's going to happen, but if I have a chance at saving my marriage, then I'll pick that chance, even if it means passing up this opportunity. I'm sorry.*

**Banner:** *Don't apologize. I get it. I know how much Myla means to you, and if you get the chance, I want you to work it out. We have time to think about all of this. Just focus on her for now.*

**Ryot:** *Okay, thanks, and I'm sorry for not being excited with you.*

**Banner:** *I understand more than you know.*

The bathroom door opens, and when I glance up from where I'm sitting on the bed, Myla appears wearing absolutely nothing.

Fuck.

Me.

With a wicked gleam in her eyes, she walks up to me and says, "Move to the head of the bed and take your shirt off."

Even though my stomach is twisting with worry, it doesn't stop me from enjoying this moment with Myla and giving her what she wants. I would give her anything. So I move to the head of the bed while taking my shirt off.

"You're so sexy, Ryot," she says, so confident in her skin that I grow hard from the way she struts toward me. "Your body is insane." She straddles my legs as her hands go to the waistband of my jeans and undoes them. She slips her hands into my briefs and jeans and then pulls them off along with my socks, leaving me stark naked. She wets her lips as her eyes fall to my erection. "And you're hard. Do you know how much that makes me feel like the sexiest woman on earth?"

"That's because you are," I say as my hand falls to my cock, and I start stroking myself.

"No touching," she says as she moves my hand away. "I want to be the one who makes you come."

"Then tell me what you want," I say.

She spreads my legs and then pushes them up so my feet are flat on the bed. "Hold your legs," she says. I grip my knees and keep myself in place as she goes to the nightstand and pulls out the lube.

"Babe," I moan quietly.

"Hmm?" she asks with a devilish grin.

"You're going to make me come in your mouth, aren't you?"

"Is there a problem with that?"

"There is when I want to fuck you into this mattress."

A smile graces those beautiful lips of hers. "Then you're just going to have to control yourself, aren't you?" She pops open the lube and spreads it over her fingers before positioning herself between my legs.

Excitement spikes up my spine as she lowers her mouth to the head of my cock and swirls her tongue around it.

"Fuck," I drawl as my head presses against the headboard.

She swirls around and around, her slick tongue hot on my tightening skin. It feels so fucking good. The only thing better than her mouth is her pussy. Nothing, and I mean nothing, can beat that.

Her mouth drags up my length and back down, running along the veins and paying particularly close attention to the underside of my head, where it's the most sensitive. I squirm beneath her touch, looking for some pressure, but she continues to tease me with her tongue, and it's sweet fucking torture.

"Babe, give me more."

"Why would I do that when I'm perfectly content just tasting you with my tongue?" she asks as she moves her tongue to my inner thighs now, kissing and licking along the sensitive flesh. She crosses over, dragging her mouth over my cock and then back to my other leg as she positions her fingers behind my balls.

"Christ, Myla." I slouch a little more, giving her a better angle right before she slips her fingers inside me. My eyes squeeze shut, and I groan as her mouth descends over my cock at the same time, taking me all the way to the back of her throat. "Baby," I groan.

She pulls off my cock and drags her fingers until they're almost all the way out. I suck in a heavy breath, my lungs trying to consume air, but my breaths fall short.

And then she pushes her fingers in and swallows my cock all the way until she gags and then quickly pulls out.

She repeats this process over and over again until my legs start to shake, and a light sheen of sweat crawls over my body.

"Myla, it's . . . it's so fucking good." I slouch some more, unable to hold myself up, and she positions herself so her fingers tease me even deeper, creating such a dynamic, evasive pressure that my cock surges in her mouth against her teeth, where she lightly clamps them over my length and drags up. "Mother . . . fuck," I groan as my legs start to slip from my sweaty palms. "Babe, I'm right there."

"Mmmmm," she hums, making my eyes nearly roll to the back of my head. And then she pops her mouth off and goes back to lightly licking while her fingers curl up in a "come hither" motion that has the room around me turning black.

A euphoric feeling spreads through my veins, wraps around my muscles, and sinks into my bones as everything turns hot, uncontrolled, and wild. The need for pressure is so fucking overwhelming that I feel like I could scream, beg, plead for more.

"Baby, suck me off."

"You want to come in my mouth?"

I growl. "Fuck . . . no . . . I mean . . . yes. Fuck, I don't know. I need something."

She chuckles and then starts circling her finger around, and the loudest moan of my life falls past my lips as I release my legs and cover my face with my hands.

"Fuck . . . fuck. Myla, give me something, anything."

I feel her smile along my cock as she very lightly licks along my length, still teasing and never giving me what I want. And I'm seconds from moving her to the side until she opens her mouth wide and sucks me all the way to the back of her throat.

"Yes, take me all the way in. Own my cock."

She swallows while my dick is touching her throat, and my knees jack up from the sensation as sweat drips down the back of my neck. She continues to swallow and dip over my length over and over again until I'm seconds—fucking seconds— from coming.

"Right there, baby. I'm going to—"

She pulls off me but keeps her fingers inside and holds them still.

"What . . . are you doing?" I ask, catching my breath as my cock jolts against my stomach.

"Playing with you."

"I don't need you playing. I need you fucking me."

"Oh, okay," she says with another evil grin. She removes her fingers, drags me down so I'm lying flat, and then she straddles my cock, her wet center rubbing against my erection. "Feels so good, Ryot." Her hands filter through her hair as she rocks over my length, never inserting herself, just rubbing her slit along my ridge.

"Baby, I'm going to need more than this."

"This is perfect," she says as a painful sweat breaks out along my skin from my cock being so hard but not getting what it needs.

"It's not," I answer as I flip her off me and onto her stomach. I push my hand against her back but then prop up her hips, only to spank her ass hard enough to leave a red handprint.

"Oh fuck!" she screams right before melting into the comforter.

"I don't appreciate you teasing me," I say as I spank her again, causing her to moan. I then flip her to her back and hover above her, bringing my mouth to her neck. Her hands press into my hair to hold me still, but I continue to move down to her breasts, where I pull one into my mouth and nibble tightly on her nipple.

"Ah," she yells just as she sinks into my grasp. "You're being rough."

I pull away just enough to ask, "You okay?"

"More than okay," she answers with a smile. "I want more. Fuck me hard, Ryot."

I groan out of desperation, move her legs farther apart, and then bring the head of my cock to her entrance.

"Yes," she whispers while I clamp down on her nipple again.

My body is thrumming to be inside her, throbbing, pulsating with so much need that I feel like I could combust. I slip inside but take it achingly slow to repay her with the sweet torture she made me go through.

With every inch, it feels like she grows tighter and tighter until it feels next to impossible to slide into her.

"Baby, relax."

She shakes her head. "I can't. I'm already so close."

I bring my mouth back up her body until I meet her lips. I wet them with my tongue and then open her mouth with mine, kissing her deeply. My body breaks out in tingles from the connection as her hand filters into my hair, tugging on the short strands as she kisses me, our tongues tangling, our moans mixing. Slowly, as she falls into the kiss, I enter her to the hilt. That's when we both groan together.

But I don't let up. I continue to kiss her, take everything she's giving me, while I move my hand down her stomach to the spot right above her pubic bone. With my palm, I apply a bit of pressure by pressing down while I pulse inside her.

"Oh fuck," she yells as her fingers dig into my scalp. "Ryot . . . oh my God."

I smile against her mouth and continue to press down as I pulse in, creating a rhythm that is so dangerously intensifying that my impending orgasm climbs up the back of my legs to the base of my balls.

Her legs wrap around me, her heels digging into my ass, giving her leverage to lift her pelvis, adding to the pressure.

"Shit, Myla, I want you to come. I want to feel that sweet cunt throbbing around my cock."

Her mouth clashes with mine. She forces me to pick up the pace from the digging of her heels, and I listen. I prop my hand on the bed for leverage, push down on her stomach, and then rapidly pulse into her.

Our moans collide together, our desperation tangles, and our need for release peaks.

"Yes, Ryot. Fuck me. Fuck . . . me."

I slam into her, one slap after another, so hard that I feel the bed slamming into the wall with my movement, but I don't care. I keep going.

I forget that we're in a hotel.

I forget about the divorce.

I forget about the troubles we've been having.

And I live in this moment, where she's mine, where I have control over her pleasure, where nothing could stop me from making this woman come all over my cock.

"Oh God. Yes, Ryot. Yes," she screams just as her pussy clenches around my cock and her orgasm pulses through her.

"Fuck, Myla. Fuck, I love you," I announce just as my cock swells and I explode inside her, letting her pussy clench around my length until there's nothing left inside me. "Jesus Christ," I mumble as I slow my hips and attempt to catch my breath.

Myla does the same, but while her chest rises and falls, she grips my jaw and forces me to look her in the eyes. "You love me," she says, almost in amazement.

I lean into her hand. "I do."

Her eyes well up right before she wraps her arms around my neck and pulls me into a hug. I circle my arms around her and hold her close. I pepper light kisses on her neck and then kiss her lips.

"I love you more than anything, Myla. I need you to know that." I lift and kiss her eyes, her nose, her mouth again. "And I'm so sorry. I'm so sorry I hurt you."

Her hand strokes the back of my head as she says, "I know."

And then she kisses me again, and I can feel her passion all the way to the tips of my toes, but even though she's here in my arms, holding me tightly, I can't help but think about how I told her I love her . . . and she didn't say it back.

# Chapter Twenty-Two

MYLA

***Present day . . .***

I stretch my arms in the air, my back aching as well as the spot between my legs. "Urgh," I groan as I roll over to the side, my face landing right on Ryot's chest.

His arm snags me around the waist, and he drags me on top of him so our naked bodies are pressed together, his morning erection nudging my stomach.

"Morning," he whispers as his fingers glide up and down my back.

I snuggle into his chest. "Good morning."

"Do you feel okay?"

"Yeah, why?" I ask.

"You had a lot of wine last night. We were kind of . . .

animalistic, especially when I was fucking you against the wall. I want to make sure you're okay."

"I'm perfect," I say just as there's a knock on the door.

"Ugh, fuck," Ryot says while he tries to get up.

"You have a massive erection. Let me get it." Laughing, I get up, grab my robe from a chair, and wrap it around my body.

I go to the door, where I find an employee with a cart on the other side. "Breakfast courtesy of Mr. JP Cane."

"Oh, thank you." I step aside and allow the man to wheel it in. "Smells amazing."

"Eggs, bacon, fresh croissants, fruit, coffee, and tea, as well as crispy breakfast potatoes with an assortment of spreads. Enjoy."

"Thank you. Here, let me grab you a tip."

He waves his hand. "No, no. Mr. Cane has already generously provided that. You just enjoy and call us when you want the cart removed."

"Okay. Thank you." I see the man out and then shut the door behind him. When I return to the cart, I notice a letter. "Ooo, from the bride and groom. Shouldn't we be sending them things on their wedding day, not the other way around?" I ask as I pluck the card from the table.

Ryot sits up and scrubs his hand over his face. "You'd think so. What does it say?"

I lift the envelope flap and pull out the card. "'Ryot and Myla. Just wanted to say congrats again on the huge ESPN news.'" I pause . . . oh yeah. I sort of forgot about that. "'Wish we could do more, but here is breakfast on us.'" I look up at Ryot, who has a panicked look in his eyes. When I set the card down, I casually say, "Well, that was nice of them."

I move the covers off the plates and release the built-up steam as I try to wrap my head around what happened last night.

Too much wine.

Lots of appreciation for Ryot.

When Ryot started thinking about The Jock Report.

Banner's news . . .

"Myla," Ryot says, and immediately, that elephant in the room has reappeared, and there's uncomfortable tension. "I . . . I don't know . . . I mean, I had nothing to do with that. The ESPN stuff."

"Why are you freaking out?" I ask, remaining as casual as I can while I put some eggs, fruit, and bacon on a plate for him. "It's a big opportunity for you."

"It is," he says, a crease forming on his brow. "But I'm not worried about that right now. I'm worried about you and me." He moves off the bed and puts on a pair of athletic shorts, his erection nowhere to be found now. "Tonight, well . . . tonight is the last night before we return to reality. And it's still unclear what's going on between us."

"Yes, so, instead of worrying, how about we just focus on enjoying the rest of our time here?" I hand him the plate I just piled food on. He takes it but sets it down.

"Myla, maybe we should talk."

"I don't want to," I say. "I want to just enjoy today. We can talk tomorrow. Okay?"

His Adam's apple bobs, and there's indecision heavy in his pupils. He wets his lips and then finally turns away. "Yeah, we can talk tomorrow."

And just like that, the easy, flirty bubble we've lived in is popped by a fresh dose of reality.

Our marriage is uncertain.

Our future is hard to predict. I'm floating between loving this man to the end of time and fearful that the moment I take him back and ask for a second chance at love, he'll retreat into himself again. Leaving me very much alone.

This new opportunity is a direct example of that. It would solidify our time in California because I'm sure he'd have to be close to a studio. There'd be no chance we'd return to

Chicago. I wouldn't be near Nichole, and I would still probably be miserable.

I'm not sure I could suffer through that again.

But when he looks at me, when he holds me, when he's so
deep inside me I feel like he's touching my soul, I know there's
no way I'll ever be able to let him go because I love him more
than anything. And I'm not sure anything will change that.

I pick up a croissant, spread some jam on it, and instead
of sitting next to him on the bed, I opt for a chair across the
room. I pull my legs up into my chest and munch on my
croissant.

And we both sit in silence, him eating his breakfast while I
munch on mine.

———

MYLA: *Nichole, I don't know what to do.*

**Nichole:** *What's going on?*

**Myla:** *Today is the wedding, and it feels like this impending bomb
is about to explode. Like I need to decide by the stroke of midnight, and I
. . . I don't know what's going on in my head, or in my heart. It's all so
confusing. And then Ryot got some news yesterday that has really put a
damper on things.*

**Nichole:** *What kind of news?*

**Myla:** *He got a segment on ESPN titled The Jock Report, where
he brings in stories from the app. It's a pretty huge deal because it puts
them in the mainstream media.*

**Nichole:** *Wow, that's huge. He must be thrilled.*

**Myla:** *That's the thing, he's not. He's worried about me. He's
apologized about the news, told me he didn't know. Have I made him that
paranoid?*

**Nichole:** *From what I know of him and the situation, I'd say he's
probably worried that you're thinking . . . "wow, another thing The Jock
Report will take." And this is all happening when he's trying to figure
things out with you. It probably scared him more than anything.*

**Myla:** *I guess I didn't look at it that way. That makes me sad because he should be happy about this. Despite everything that's gone down, this is a big accomplishment.*

**Nichole:** *Have you told him that?*

**Myla:** *No. I brushed him off until tomorrow because I wanted to enjoy this last day. But it's ruined anyway. I'm down by the pool, and he's across the patio talking to Banner. They've been there all morning.*

**Nichole:** *Ignoring it is making it worse. Seems like you need to at least tell him that you're proud of him because, if anything, you are . . . right? Despite what you went through for him to accomplish this, you're still proud?*

**Myla:** *There's resentment there, but if I push past that, I am proud of him. He's one of the hardest workers I know, and even though he forgot about our promises to each other to create something of this magnitude, I am proud.*

**Nichole:** *It might help if you say that. I'm not saying you need to go crazy and congratulate him with a celebration, but I think if you two are going to move on—apart or together—you have to at least acknowledge that the smattering of promises wasn't in vain.*

**Myla:** *You're right. And maybe if I say that, he won't be so awkward. We had such a good night last night, and I feel like it's getting muddied by this new thing.*

**Nichole:** *Can I ask where your head is at when it comes to him?*

**Myla:** *I don't know. I'm so terrified to let go, but I'm also still upset. Although, I was having drinks with Kelsey and Lottie last night and something crossed my mind. Remember when those Internet trolls attacked me for my body size and how I didn't deserve someone like Ryot?*

**Nichole:** *Yes, don't get me started on that because I will fume all over again.*

**Myla:** *Well, I remember him saying that he wished there was a place where he didn't have to rely on an algorithm to get his word out, that he could tell the truth through something like . . . a text. That's where that part of the app was developed. I always thought The Jock Report was started because of the way Ryot retired and how Penn was being slan-*

*dered by the media, but I think . . . I think it was created after that incident.*

**Nichole:** *Oh, I remember that conversation. He was livid.*

**Myla:** *Just made me think differently, you know? And then Kelsey said she really wants me to work with her on designing interiors.*

**Nichole:** *That's pretty fucking cool. What did you say?*

**Myla:** *Not much. I mean, I don't want to stay here, Nichole. I want to be back in Chicago.*

**Nichole:** *You don't. There is nothing here for you.*

**Myla:** *That's not true. You're there. My life was there.*

**Nichole:** *Your life is with Ryot.*

"Hey, babe." I glance up from my phone to where Ryot is standing at the end of my lounger. "We should get ready for the wedding. It starts in an hour."

"Oh, okay," I say as I stuff my phone in my bag, Nichole's words ringing through my ears.

*Your life is with Ryot.*

Is she right? At one point, I thought it was. I thought my life revolved around him, and his life revolved around me, but then, he retired, and everything changed. Could it be that if we worked hard enough, we could get back to where it used to be?

"Everything okay?" he asks as he grabs my bag from me and then takes my hand. When he starts to move, I stop him and tug on his hand so he's facing me.

"Ryot?"

"Yeah?" he asks, a crease of concern on his brow.

"I'm proud of you," I say, the words feeling like a sense of relief as they slip off my tongue. "Really proud of you."

"What? Why?"

I place my hand on his chest, and I quietly say, "The Jock Report. You've worked so hard to create something that helps others. And I know that it's damaged a part of us, but I want you to know that what you've created, it's huge, and you should be proud of yourself. Because I am."

His eyes soften, and he lowers his forehead to mine. Quietly, he whispers, "Thank you."

I move my lips up to his and gently kiss him before pulling away. "You're welcome. And this new opportunity with ESPN? It's amazing, Ryot. It truly is. You're perfect for the segment. Charming, handsome, knowledgeable, and you care, which matters the most."

"Myla, we don't have to talk about that."

"No, but I need you to know I'm proud of you. I don't want you to hide your accomplishments from me, ever."

He sighs heavily as he brings our linked hands up to his mouth and presses a kiss to my knuckles. "That means more to me than you know." His voice is strained, and it makes me sad because I know in other circumstances, he wouldn't be so concerned about me, but rather, we'd be celebrating this great news.

"Okay," I say, gripping his hand tighter. "Let's go get ready."

We make our way through the hotel and to our room. We don't say much other than how our mornings were, simple things like that, but I'm not sure there's much to talk about after the conversation we just had, so I'm grateful for the uncomplicated chat.

When we're in the room, Ryot sets my bag down while I walk over to the bathroom. Since my hair is already in a bun, I turn on the shower and strip down to nothing just as Ryot walks in and leans against the bathroom doorway. His eyes peruse me, hunger tainting them as he wets his lips with his tongue.

"You're so fucking fine," he says as his eyes reach up to mine. He removes his shirt and pushes down his shorts.

I smirk. *I do love naked Ryot.* "Speak for yourself."

I move into the shower and wet down my body as Ryot opens the door and slips in as well.

"What do you think you're doing?"

"Showering with the hottest girl I know."

"I can't get my hair wet."

"Can you get other things wet?" he asks with a waggle of his brow.

"Do you expect cheesy lines like that to turn me on?"

He chuckles, then turns me around and covers my back with his large body. His hands smooth up my sides to my breasts, where he cups them. I feel his erection grow against my backside as he toys with my nipples.

"Do we have time for this?"

"Probably not," he whispers. "But I want you, Myla. All of you. Forever." Then he bends me forward so my hands rest on the built-in bench in front of me, and he positions his cock at my entrance. "I need this. I need you."

He slowly enters me, and I squeeze my eyes shut, enjoying every pleasurable inch of him. All I can think about is how much I need him as well.

RYOT

"SHE LOOKS HOT," Banner says as he holds a glass of whiskey. "And I say that with all the respect in the world for your wife. But that dress."

Yeah.

I know.

That dress.

She's not wearing a bra or underwear. I know this because I watched her slip the silky sage-green fabric over her curvy body. The back of the dress dips to just above the arc of her ass. The thin straps barely press into her delicate shoulders as her breasts sit high on her chest, shown off by the thin fabric. She styled her hair into a bun on the top of her head and placed baby's breath around the thick bun. Her makeup is minimal because we didn't have much time after I fucked her in the shower. But it works for her. I've always liked minimal makeup on her, just enough to make her eyes stand out even more than they already do.

"Besides the bride, I feel like every fucking guy in here is staring at her," I say as I watch her speak animatedly to Kelsey and Lottie.

The wedding was beautiful of course, besides the moment when a pigeon was wheeled down the aisle in a special cart made just for him, the rings next to him in boxes. Not quite sure what that was about, but the pigeon did have a tuxedo on, so that was pretty legit.

The entire time when JP and Kelsey were reading their vows, I held on to Myla's hand, remembering the day we shared our vows. We eloped. She hadn't wanted to deal with a big wedding when she had just lost her dad and disconnected from her mom, so we took Banner and Nichole with us, had them FaceTime the rest of the family, and got married on the edge of a cliff in the Grand Canyon. It was intimate and perfect, everything we'd ever dreamed of.

I wondered if she was thinking of the same thing.

Honestly, I have no clue what she's thinking at this point. When she told me she was proud of me, I was . . . hell, I was blown away. I was not expecting that at all. Given our situation and where the trouble started, I never would have assumed that she was proud of me. So hearing that nearly broke me.

Made me feel guilty.

Made me feel proud.

Made me love her so much more.

"I'm guessing since I saw you two dancing together earlier that things have changed since this morning?" Banner asks.

"I don't know if *changed* is the right word. I think things just shifted." I lift my drink to my lips before saying, "She told me she was proud of me this morning. Proud of the ESPN segment and what we've accomplished."

"Oh shit, really?" he asks. "That's unexpected."

"Tell me about it," I say as I lean my elbow against the bar-height table we're standing at. "And I can't decide if she was telling me everything was going to be okay or if she was closing the chapter, you know? Like letting me know she forgives me."

Banner rubs the side of his jaw. "Yeah, that's a tough one. I have no fucking clue. It seems like you two have been getting along so well, though."

"Yeah, I know. And that's what terrifies me because I think we could make this work. I hurt her deeply by ignoring her needs. Her dreams. Her. Fuck, I hate that I did that to her. And I need to rectify that. I need to make changes that show her that I love her more than anything else in my life. And then hopefully . . . hopefully, she'll want to stay married to me."

"Sounds wise, brother," Banner says. "I guess enjoy this day with her, and when you get to talk to her, tell her how you feel. How you need to make changes."

"She doesn't want to stay in California. That poses a huge problem, especially with this new opportunity."

Banner shifts and says, "Yeah, that sort of does." He's quiet for a second. "Do you think you're going to take it?" When he looks up at me, I see it in his eyes, the realization that there is a possibility that I might not, which means destroying his dreams and the hard work we've put forward on this project.

Banner isn't a particularly emotional person. He's easygoing. But he does take his work seriously, and this project has been an enormous undertaking. He's worked so damn hard at it. To just neglect that hard work is like a slap in the face to my brother. *But isn't that what I did to Myla by moving us here without her input?*

I rub my hand across my forehead. "Fuck, I don't know, man. It's like a lose-lose for me. If I take it, then there's a great possibility that I'm going to lose her. But if I don't take it, I'm letting down every single person who's had a hand in this business. It's so fucked up."

He's silent for a moment and then says, "You know, sometimes we have to consider that there's more to life than what we accomplish and the goals we check off." He sets his drink on the table and turns toward me. "There's a reason the human body is conditioned to love, and it's so we don't have to walk around this planet alone. So we don't have to face the trials and tribulations of our journey in the dark, but rather in the light from the guidance of the ones we love. Goals and dreams come and go, but love, that lasts forever. Don't lose it because you're too worried about what might happen to your goals."

I shake my head. "Banner, I can't fucking disappoint you."

"You won't," he says.

"But—"

"But nothing. You won't disappoint me. Keep the business and me out of the picture along with everyone else attached to it. If those factors weren't part of the issue, tell me, would you move back to Chicago to make her happy?"

"I'd do just about anything to keep her in my life and make her happy." And if that means packing up and heading back to Chicago, then . . . I guess I would.

"Then I think you have your answer." He drains the rest of his whiskey before setting the empty glass back on the table. "I love you, man, and I know you're not happy, not without her. I don't want to watch you lose her, so do what it takes."

I grip the edge of the table and look over at her. Her head falls back as a laugh flies out of her mouth. Her hand grips Lottie's arm while she nods. I can see it. I can see her living here, loving it here. I can see her becoming great friends with Kelsey and Lottie. I can see her working with Kelsey, finding great joy in creating spaces that portray her style and Kelsey's models of sustainability. I can see us finding a home we love and creating a life around it. But just because I can see it doesn't mean that she can. It doesn't mean she'll forgive me and no longer resent me for hurting her in the first place.

"Like I said," Banner adds, breaking into my thoughts. "Don't worry about it now. Think about it later."

"What are you two talking about?" Penn asks, walking up to us, wearing a large smile. "If you tell me the divorce, I'm going to be pissed because we're at a wedding."

"Sort of," I answer.

"Ugh, come on, man. Look at your girl over there." He gestures toward Myla. "She's having a hell of a good time. Go join her. Show her that you're not some morose platypus over here, just counting down the minutes until you leave Napa."

"Platypus?" I ask.

He thins his lips and makes them look like a platypus bill. "A platypus."

"Oddly, that does resemble a platypus," Banner says with a smirk.

"Shut the fuck up. I don't look like that."

Penn nods. "Yeah, you do. I smelled platypus pout from a mile away. Now knock it off and go dance with your girl. For fuck's sake." Penn pushes me toward her, and I have no choice but to walk up to Myla and interrupt her conversation with Kelsey and Lottie.

"Hey, babe," I say as I hold my hand out. "Care to dance?"

She looks over her shoulder and smirks. "Took you long enough to ask." She slips her hand in mine, and I pull her out onto the dance floor under the bulb string lights. A cover band plays a slow version of *Wicked Game*. I place my hand on her bare back and pull her in close before I start moving.

With my lips right next to her ear, I whisper, "Everyone who isn't staring at the bride is staring at you."

Her free hand roams up to the back of my neck. "I only care about one set of eyes staring at me."

Her gaze meets mine as we slowly move across the dance floor. "I can't seem to take my eyes off you, Myla. You're stunning."

"Thank you," she says. "I don't know if I mentioned this, but you look really good in this suit." Her hand toys with the collar of my jacket.

"How good?" I ask, making her chuckle.

"So good that I think it might look better on the floor of the hotel room later tonight."

"Mmm," I hum into her ear. "That must be really good then."

"Very good."

"You know"—I slide my hand a few more inches down her back so my pinky nearly touches her crack—"if we weren't at a wedding and in front of a bunch of people, I'd do some pretty wicked things to you in this dress."

"That's my hope for later," she says as she rests her head against my chest.

Our position immediately brings me back to our wedding day, when we danced beneath the setting sun, the sky lit in hues of orange, pink, and yellow.

"This reminds me of our wedding, dancing with you this close."

"That was one of my favorite days," she replies. "It was so simple, yet so special."

"Would you do it all over again?" I ask her.

"Marry you?" She looks me in the eyes. "Easily," she answers, making my heart twist in my chest with possible hope. "Marrying you was one of the greatest decisions I've ever made."

"Asking you out on a date was one of my best decisions. Pursuing you after that was my greatest."

"What do you miss the most from those early days?" she asks.

"The Instagram messages. Opening Instagram now doesn't hold as much appeal as it did back then because I always hoped for a message from you. I looked forward to them."

"I did too."

"What about you? What do you miss the most?"

"You looking for me in the stands. Once we started dating and I was going to more games, I loved watching you try to spot me because the moment you would, the biggest smile would spread across your face. That image lives rent-free in my mind."

"I loved seeing you in my jersey, cheering for me."

"I remember when the person next to me found out I was your wife. She was going off about her favorite players and how she couldn't believe you were married . . . especially to me."

My grip on her grows tight. "Little did that woman know how infatuated I am with you."

Her fingers dance across the short hairs on the back of my neck. "Can I ask you something?"

I pull away just enough so I can look her in the eyes. "You can ask me anything."

"And you'll be truthful?"

"Yes," I answer.

"Well, you remember when all that gossip went around about you and me? About how some fans believed I wasn't fit enough to be with someone like you? Is that where The Jock Report originated? You always said it was because of Penn and your retirement, but it almost seems like that was the moment it became an idea in your head."

I press my lips together and let out a heavy sigh. "Yes, that's where The Jock Report originated."

"How come you never told me that?"

"Because you were really sensitive about that situation, and I didn't want you thinking I was riding in on my white horse trying to save the day. Hell, you didn't even like talking about how it all went down, and you suffered so much. I didn't want to remind you or take you back to that moment. It sounded far too close to the things your mom used to say, and I couldn't bear you hurting."

"Oh . . ."

"Are you mad?" I ask her.

Her eyes meet mine, and she shakes her head. "Not even a little." And then she kisses me lightly on the mouth.

---

"WHAT ARE YOU THINKING ABOUT?" I ask Myla as I join her on the balcony of our hotel.

We left the wedding not long after the bride and groom took off, which was right after the cake was served. We spent a good portion of the night dancing, talking, and then fed each other cake at a table by ourselves. We spoke to Penn and Banner on occasion, but for the most part, we spent the evening alone, and I loved every goddamn second of it.

And now that we're back in our hotel room, looking out over the vineyard, I keep thinking about how I let things between us go so awry. How could I go through my daily life not paying attention to her, not listening, not focusing? I can't believe I took this woman for granted, and now that she's slowly slipping from my grasp, I'm attempting anything and everything to keep her from leaving me.

"I'm thinking about what a great time I had with you here," she answers as I slowly move the strap of her dress off her shoulder.

She tilts her head to the side, giving me a better angle at her neck, so I take advantage of it and pepper kisses along her skin.

"How I don't want it to end," she adds.

I want to tell her it doesn't have to.

That we can stay here as long as she wants, that we can continue this back at our house.

That I will do just about anything to prolong this feeling of being able to hold her in my arms.

I slip the strap off her shoulder as I move my other hand past the open back of her dress, under the fabric to the front, where I grip her breast and play with her hard nipple.

"I love this, Ryot," she says, and I notice that she said this, not you. And that hope that was blooming takes a hit. Is this a farewell for her? Is she treating this night as one glorified send-off?

I'm not sure my heart could handle it. Actually, I know it couldn't.

I turn her around and press her against the balcony wall as I lift her chin so her lips are inches away. "I love you," I say to her, my voice sounding strangled, shredded from the emotional turmoil we've been through. Her hand clasps mine as I repeat, "I love you so fucking much, Myla. And I know you don't want to talk about this right now, but I need you to know how much—"

*Ring. Ring. Ring.*

Myla stiffens, and she glances over my shoulder.

"What's that?" I ask.

"Nichole's ringtone." She pushes past me and goes into the room as she fixes the strap of her dress. I follow closely. She locates her phone and answers, her voice in a panic. "Nichole? Everything okay?"

I walk up to her, close enough to hear both sides of the conversation.

"Myla, I'm . . . I'm sorry."

"Sorry about what?" Myla asks, her body starting to shake.

"I wasn't telling you the truth."

"What do you mean?" Myla asks.

"I'm sick," she says softly. "The cancer is back, and I didn't want to tell you until you worked out things in your head, but I just passed out in my house, knocked my head on the counter, and now I'm in the emergency room, and I had no one else to call."

"I'm coming," Myla says through chattering teeth. "I'll be there as quickly as I can."

"Thank you," I hear Nichole say through tears.

Before Myla can say anything, I'm dialing Huxley's number on my phone. It rings a few times before he picks up. "Ryot?"

"Hux, man, I need a favor."

"Name it," he says.

"Your plane, can I borrow it?"

"I'll make arrangements now. Where and when do you need to leave?"

"Now and we have to go to Chicago."

"Say no more. Be down in the lobby in ten minutes. I'll have everything arranged."

"Thank you so much."

"You're more than welcome. I'm assuming something is wrong?"

"I'll fill you in later." I thank him again and then hang up the phone as Myla still talks to Nichole on the phone.

I race around the room, packing us, shoving clothes and toiletries in our bags. I then strip out of my suit and into a pair of shorts and a T-shirt. I grab a set of leggings for Myla and one of my shirts and help her change while she stays on the phone with Nichole, reassuring her the entire time that everything will be okay. Once I have everything packed, I help her into a pair of sandals and say, "Got a plane. We need to head to the lobby where a car is waiting."

Gratefulness passes over her eyes as I guide her out of the hotel room with our bags in hand. When we make it to the lobby, there's a black SUV waiting for us. I hand off the bags and then help Myla into the car. Tears are streaming down her face. Once buckled up, I shoot off a text to Banner, asking him to grab Myla's dress and my suit from the hotel room and anything I might have left behind and let him know I'll be in Chicago for the foreseeable future.

Then I put away my phone as Myla hangs up. When she turns toward me, she falls into my arms and bawls.

I don't ask questions.

I don't say anything.

I just hold her and hope it's not as serious as it sounds.

# Chapter Twenty-Three

MYLA

***Present day* . . .**

Tears clouding my eyes, I push through door 210 and find Nichole lying in bed, hooked up to a bunch of machines, her head wrapped in gauze.

Her balding head.

When I was on the phone with her, she told me that her doctor found cancer in her liver, not her breasts, but her liver. They came up with a plan of attack, and she's been going through chemo . . . alone. She said she was doing fine up until this last round. She felt so nauseous, and so weak that she passed out in her kitchen and hit her head. She woke up to a puddle of blood and immediately called emergency services to get her.

The thought of Nichole lying unconscious on the floor makes my stomach twist in knots.

The worst part of it all, though? She has stage 4 liver cancer. These treatments are, as she called it, a last-ditch effort.

I can't even consider what that means, not at this point.

I run up to her and quickly take her hand in mine as I lean against the bed. "Nichole," I say through a shaky breath. "I can't . . . I can't believe this happened. I just saw you two weeks ago. How could this have become so grave since I last saw you?"

Her lashes flutter open, revealing a pair of bloodshot eyes. The minute she sees me, they fill up with tears. "Chemo, it happens fast. I started my first treatment the week before I came to visit."

"And you didn't tell me?" I nearly yell but hold back, knowing she doesn't need that right now. I take in her bandage and rest of her body. "How are you feeling?"

"Banged up. Exhausted. Not myself." She glances around and asks, "Where's Ryot?"

"Out in the waiting room, as he wanted to give us some privacy." I now take a seat on her bed and very softly say, "I really wish you'd told me."

"I know." More tears fall from her eyes. "I'm sorry," she says right before I wrap my arms around her and pull her into a hug.

"Sorry, I shouldn't make you cry, I'm just . . . fuck, Nichole, I'm trying to wrap my head around this, and none of it is making sense."

"I'm still trying to wrap my head around it too, and clearly not doing a good job."

"Why didn't you tell me?"

"I should have. But when I found out, you were just going through so much that I knew this news would tip you over the edge and force you to make a one-sided decision to leave Ryot, and I didn't want that to happen."

"I wouldn't have," I say, even though in the back of my mind, I know for certain that I would have dropped everything to be with Nichole and take care of her.

Through tears, she says, "I love you, but you and I both know that's a lie. You would have used any excuse to leave California."

"It doesn't matter because I'm here now, and we're going to get you better." I pat her hand, my positivity feeling pitiful in my own ears.

And Nichole's too as she looks away, unable to look me in the eyes. After a few seconds of silence, she says, "I'm sick, Myla. The prognosis isn't looking good."

My throat grows tight, and I try not to let that sink in.

Stage 4 liver cancer. You can imagine the type of searching I did on my phone all the way to Chicago. I did so much that my eyes turned blurry, and all I saw was that it was bad. Really bad.

"Hey." I try to smile. "We're going to do this together, okay? I know it might be scary now, but you have me, and we get through everything together. Don't worry, I'm moving into your apartment, and I'll take you to your appointments. I'm going to ensure you have everything you need to get well. And hey, I saw that we can do some juicing to help. I can go to that farmers market we love so much and get some fresh fruit and veggies to juice. I can cook you any meal that you want, we can binge-watch shows together like we used to, and if you're ever feeling bad, I can——"

"Myla, stop," Nichole says, sounding tired.

"Stop what? I'm just trying to——"

"You're trying to over plan and keep yourself busy so you don't have to focus on the tough things happening around you." She turns her head and looks me in the eyes. "Myla, I'm dying. It's as simple as that."

"No." I shake my head. "You're not."

"I am. I'm doing the chemo because I feel like I should. But I know what's going on in my body, and what's happening doesn't feel right."

I wipe away my tears and move in closer. "It feels weird now, but it will get better. It will, Nichole."

She clasps my hand tightly and says, "I need you to not worry about me. I know I called you here, but that's because I truly believe you deserve to know the truth about everything, but I don't want you changing your life for this."

"I'm not," I say. "I was going to move here in a couple of days anyway."

"Were you?" she asks with a raise of her brow. "Because last we chatted, you were leaning toward staying with Ryot and giving him another chance."

"No" is on the tip of my tongue. I want to tell her that's not the truth, that I was just saying goodbye to him over the past few days and was always going to move back to Chicago. But that would be a lie.

Because if I were truly honest with myself, I was planning to have a conversation with Nichole about how I was going to stay in California.

But now that she's sick, that fleeting thought has changed.

"I was thinking about it," I answer her. "But it wasn't set in stone, and now that I know what's going on with you, that has solidified my choice."

"Myla, you love him."

I swallow hard and look away because I know it's the truth. Even though I've held back from admitting it to him, I do love him, so much. And these past few days have proved that. He's paid attention to me. Listened. Learned. The awe in his voice as he looked over my designs still brings tears to my eyes. I felt so united with him at that moment. And I also saw changes within him that I *never* thought could change. Simple things like eating waffles for breakfast. And the fact that his reaction to the ESPN opportunity wasn't a solid yes without talking to me about it. *I haven't felt as alone as I had been feeling.*

Just then, there's a knock on the door, and I look up to see Ryot standing to the side, hands in his pockets. The entire flight here, he never once released my hand. He kept whispering that everything was going to be okay, that he was there for me. And when we arrived here, before he took off for the waiting room, he gave me the softest kiss.

"Sorry to interrupt, but the nurse said she was going to kick us out soon since visiting hours are actually over."

"I'm not going anywhere. I'm staying with her," I say, but Nichole grips my hand tight.

"Myla, I'll be fine. Go get some rest and then come back tomorrow morning."

"No, I'm not leaving you."

With a heavy sigh, Nichole says, "Don't make me call security on you. You know I would, and it won't end well."

"But you need someone here with you."

"I need someone who has a clear head, and the only way that can happen is if you get some rest. Now please, go with Ryot, and I'll see you in the morning. Maybe you can bring me some Frankie donuts tomorrow."

"I'll bring you whatever you want."

Nichole smiles. "Then bring me a pistachio, red velvet, and that blueberry crumble goodness." She squeezes my hand. "Seriously, go. And get some sleep. What time is it now?"

"Two in the morning," Ryot says. "But that's midnight for us, given we're operating on Pacific Time."

"After a big day. Don't come back here until at least ten. Understood?"

"Nichole—"

"I'm serious, Myla. Don't come back here until then."

I sigh heavily. I don't want to leave her, but I also know Nichole always gets what she wants, so if she wants me out of here to get some sleep, then that's what I'm going to do. Doubtful I'll get any rest, though.

"Okay." I lean down and press a kiss on her bandaged head. "I'll see you tomorrow at ten."

"With donuts."

"With donuts," I say, and then I walk over to Ryot, who offers his hand, and I take it.

"Let us know if you need anything else, Nichole," he says before we exit the room.

Together, we head toward the elevator and then out of the hospital in silence, where a car is waiting for us—different from the one that collected us from the airport. Ryot opens the door for me and helps me buckle up before he goes to his side and slides in toward the middle, where he loops his arm around me and pulls me in tight.

That's when I break down again.

Through sobs, I hear him whisper about how much he's here for me. How he loves me. How he will take care of me.

But none of it sinks in because all I can think about is how my best friend is dying, and I can't do anything about it.

RYOT

"HELLO?" I whisper into the phone as I step into the penthouse living room. I booked the place as soon as I knew we were going to Chicago.

"Hey, man, how's everything going?" Banner asks.

"Not good," I answer quietly. "Stage 4 liver cancer. Not sure she's going to make it."

He's silent and then, "Fuck, are you serious?"

"Yeah." I blow out a heavy breath. "Dude, I don't know

what to fucking do. I can see that Myla is spiraling, and Nichole looks sick. It's all too fucking much."

"I'm coming. I'll book a flight today and be out there so I can help in any way needed."

"Okay." I drag my hand over my face. "I know this will be a really selfish thing to say given the circumstances, but dude, I think she's going to pull away. I can feel it deep in my goddamn bones. This is our undoing."

"You can't think that way."

"She was already acting weird after hearing about the ESPN thing, despite her saying she was proud of me, but this . . . this is it."

"Let's just focus on one thing at a time, okay?"

"Yeah, okay."

"I'll let you know about my flight, and then I'll meet you out there. Keep me posted."

"I will."

We say our goodbyes, and when I turn around, I find Myla standing in the bedroom doorway, her eyes sunken and bloodshot, her hair in a tangled mess, and her clothes askew.

Fuck, did she hear what I said?

"Hey, good morning," I say, trying to act casual. "How are you feeling?"

"Who were you talking to?" she asks.

Yup . . . she heard.

"Banner," I say.

She nods and folds her arms over her chest. "So you think this is it for us? That's really what you're thinking about right now? Our marriage?"

Fuck!

"No, Myla, that's not . . . I mean, I'm worried about that, yes. But I'm also worried about you, about Nichole navigating all of this."

"Or are you worried about yourself?"

I can see it in her eyes. She's distancing and pulling away.

She's becoming emotionless and frigid because she doesn't know how else to deal with her feelings. And whatever happens next, I know it's because she's having a hard time processing what's going on with Nichole. Losing another person in her life is not something she'll handle in a healthy way.

"I'm worried about *you*, Myla." I take a step forward, moving slowly. "I'm worried about how you feel and how you're dealing with everything."

Her eyes well up, and she shakes her head. "How do you think I'm doing?"

My palms start to sweat. "Hurt. Scared. Fearful. Uncertain."

"To name a few." She glances away.

"How can I help?" I ask her.

"You can't." She stares out the window of the penthouse. "So maybe it's best if you just . . . go."

And there it is. I knew it was coming, but it still doesn't mean it doesn't sting. Now the question is, how do I handle this?

"Myla, I know you're hurting, baby, but I'm not going to leave, not when you need someone to lean on. So why don't we just take a shower, get ready, grab the donuts, and go see Nichole?"

"I don't need you holding my hand," she says. "I can do this by myself. You don't even like Nichole, so why do you even care?"

"I like Nichole," I say. "We've had our differences, but that doesn't mean I don't feel something for her. And you're, well . . . you're special to me." I was about to call her my wife, but I think we all know sidestepping that was a smart choice. "And I don't like to see you hurting. It's important to me to be there for you."

"Oh, so now you care?"

I grind my molars together and try to hold back my tongue.

I know she's attempting to keep me at arm's length. It's so obvious, and even though I know she's doing it on purpose to protect herself, it doesn't mean I'm not hurt or annoyed by it.

"I don't want to argue with you. Let's just get ready for the day, okay? We can talk about the semantics of everything later. I just want to get you to Nichole so you can be with her."

I'm ready for her to tell me to fuck off or to keep arguing, but instead, she lightly nods and then moves toward the bedroom and into the bathroom.

I let out a deep exhale.

Fuck, this is going to be harder than I expected.

---

## MYLA

"WHERE'S RYOT?" Nichole asks as she shakily lifts her donut to her mouth and takes a bite.

I shrug. "Somewhere in the hospital."

"Why? Shouldn't he be in here?"

"No. Why would he be in here?"

Nichole gives me a look. "What's going on?"

"Nothing you need to worry about. Now let's talk about something else, like your treatment."

"Do you really think that's something I want to talk about?"

"It's something I want to talk about. I need the details of everything so we can beat this."

She sighs and leans back in her bed. "Myla, I'm not beating this. I would rather talk about your future and what you're going to do."

"Stop saying you're not going to beat this. Have you

gotten a second opinion yet? Sure, you started treatment, but there must be something else we can do, someone else we can talk to. Aren't there experimental drugs we can try? We need to think outside of the box."

"I know this is hard for you because you're just now hearing about it—"

"You're damn right this is hard for me," I shout as I stand and push my hand through my hair. "Jesus Christ, Nichole, you should have told me. You had more than enough opportunities to tell me."

"As you're going through a divorce? Do you really think you could have handled all of that?" *Why does everyone else believe they know what I can and can't handle?*

"The divorce could have been put on hold. All of that could have been put on hold."

"So you could push him away?" Nichole asks. "Like you're doing now?"

"No," I answer, even though I know it's a lie. "I'm not pushing him away."

"Uh-huh. So call him, bring him in here."

"Nichole, stop. This isn't about him."

"No, this is about us," she snaps. "And as much as you might hate to admit it, Ryot is a part of us. He has been for a while. So call him up and ask him to come in here if everything is fine."

I twist my mouth to the side, and despite it all, I reach for my phone and start to text him, but she stops me and says, "No, call him. I don't want you sending him any kind of code."

I roll my eyes and press his name to call him. It rings once before he answers.

"Hey, baby, everything okay?"

Just from hearing his voice, an overwhelming need to cry rockets through me.

Working through a tight throat, I say, "Can you come to Nichole's room? She wants to talk to you."

"Of course. Be right there."

I hang up and smile at Nichole. "He's coming."

"Good." She has a challenging look in her sunken eyes. "Is this really necessary?"

"It is because I know how you're feeling right now. You're going through multiple stages of grief simultaneously, starting with denial and anger. Those two combined are not going to do you any good."

"Denial? No, I just need the facts, Nichole. And you're not giving them to me. And anger, well, yeah. My best friend, my . . . my sister has been sick for God knows how long, and I'm just finding out about it. So yeah, I'm angry."

"You're just going to be angry with me then? Is that what's happening? Which, knowing you, will result in pushing people away, curling in on yourself, and not letting anyone in."

"I don't need you psychoanalyzing me right now. You're not even giving me a goddamn second to process this. That's not fair. You've known about this for what did you say? Five weeks? I haven't. I have the right to be angry, and I have the right to believe that none of this is happening."

"You do, but not at the expense of your marriage," Nichole says just as Ryot walks in.

He pauses in the doorway of her room and glances between us. "Uh, would you like me to leave again?"

"Yes," I answer.

"No," Nichole says. "I need you to come in here and talk to me."

"Nichole," I say with a warning tone, but she completely ignores me.

Ryot—looking as unsure as ever—walks into the room and leans against the wall, keeping a good distance from us both.

"You know, I think he looks hotter. Have you grown more muscles?" Nichole asks.

"Protein bars," he mumbles, knowing he's in the crossfire of Nichole and me. It wouldn't be the first time he's witnessed such an event, and he's returning to old behaviors. Say as little as possible.

"Well, I'm sure my dear friend Myla over here has been taking advantage of the hard work of those protein bars, hasn't she?"

"Nichole, just stop," I say in an annoyed tone.

"Why?" she asks. "You said everything was fine between you two, so why can't I ask?"

Ryot glances at me, and I look away because I know he has the truth on the tip of his tongue. The only question is, will he say anything?

"Anyone going to fill me in on how married life is? Any news? I mean, I know he signed the divorce papers, but I know you haven't, Myla."

I wince as Ryot's head snaps toward me. "You haven't signed them?" he asks.

"It slipped by me," I say.

"It's because she still loves you," Nichole says.

"Nichole," I snap at her.

"What?" she asks. "Why wouldn't you tell the man you love that you have an undying affection for him? Isn't that what love is all about? Unless . . . oh, I see, you're trying to push him away because you're scared of abandonment, right?" Her sarcastic tone is starting to really grate on me. "If *I* leave you, that means he's the last one left, and you wouldn't be able to take that kind of heartache, right? You might as well cut ties with him now. Might as well move back here like you planned all along and leave him in California so you don't have to suffer through the possibility of losing him too."

"You know what? Fuck you, Nichole," I say as I start to head toward the exit, but Ryot steps in my way. "Ryot, move."

"No," he says in a stern voice. "I'm not going to let you just walk out because you're not happy about what's going on." He lifts my chin so I'm forced to look him in the eyes. "Tell me, were you planning on moving to Chicago this whole time?" My eyes flit away, but he tugs on my chin, bringing me back to him. "Tell me the truth, Myla."

"I . . . don't know," I say as tears well up in my eyes. "Yes, that's where I was headed, but then everything in Napa happened, and I just . . . I don't fucking know. Okay?"

"But you still love him," Nichole says.

"Do you?" he asks, his voice soft. I expect him to be angry and ready to fly off the deep end from what Nichole has been saying. Instead, he's steady, even-keeled, and I think that's more nerve-wracking than anything.

I wet my lips and look away again.

"Look at me when you answer," he says, controlled.

I take a deep breath, and I meet his gaze. "Of course I still love you, Ryot."

"But are you in love with me?" he asks. It feels like the beeping of the machines quiet, and the hustle around us settles as he waits on an answer.

"Don't lie to him," Nichole says from her bed.

I roll my teeth over the corner of my mouth as my heart beats wildly. And because of his grip on my jaw and chin, I can't look away. All I can rely on are my bubbling emotions as tears cloud my eyes.

"Yes," I answer. "I'm in love with you." His shoulders visibly relax as he lets go of my chin. "But that doesn't mean anything," I add.

His brow furrows. "What do you mean that doesn't mean anything? It means everything."

"No, it doesn't. We're going in different directions, Ryot."

"Myla, don't be stupid," Nichole says from the bed. "You're not moving here."

"Yes, I am," I say while stepping away from Ryot. "I'm not leaving you alone here. As much as I might be mad at you, that doesn't mean I'm going to leave you to fend for yourself.

For fuck's sake, Nichole, you passed out and had no one to help you. I refuse to let you do this by yourself. You're only going to become weaker and weaker, and you'll need someone to drive you to appointments. Not to mention"—I motion toward Ryot—"you're starting a new job with ESPN that requires you to be in California. So yeah, I might love you, but that means nothing."

"I'm not taking the job," Ryot says.

"Ryot, stop," I say. "Of course you're taking the job. This is a huge opportunity that everyone is counting on. You don't have a choice in the matter. You're taking the job."

"I'm not," he says. "I already told Banner." He takes a step toward me. "I told him there was no way I could take it because things were up in the air with you, and I will do anything, and I mean fucking anything, to keep you in my life, Myla." Another step forward as the air ceases to filter into my lungs. "I'm resigning from The Jock Report and setting that part of my life to the side because what we have, Myla, it's way more important than anything else in my life. I'll be damned if I let it slip through my fingers again."

My jaw shivers as tears descend my cheeks. "You . . . you can't do that. You worked too hard."

"At the expense of losing you," he says, now only a foot away from me. "Do you know how fucking ashamed I am for being so blind to how I was treating you? Treating our marriage? It eats me alive at night, Myla." He closes the rest of the space between us and moves his hand to the back of my neck, right at the nape. "You are what I care about. You are my goals. You are my dreams. You are my future."

I shake my head. "No, you . . . you can't."

"Can't what? Put you first? Because I am. I'm putting you first, I'm putting us first, and if you think I'm going to let you just slink away, drive a wedge between us because you're scared, then you're absolutely fucked. That's not going to happen. I didn't let it happen when your dad passed away and

I won't let it happen now." His thumb rubs over my cheek, wiping away my tears. "I know I have a lot to make up to you, and I know that getting back to a new normal will take some time, but it's time worth spending because you are my life."

My lip trembles, and before I can stop it, a sob escapes, and my legs give out on me. Ryot pulls me into his chest, wrapping his strong arms around me and holding me tight. He scoops me up and carries me over to a chair where I sit on his lap and cry into his shoulder. He clutches me tightly, his hand soothing my back as he whispers to me.

"I'm here for you, baby, and I'm not leaving you. As much as you want to push, I'm not leaving." He kisses the side of my head. "I'm loving you for the rest of my goddamn life. There will never be another woman, another human as important to me as you." I break out into another sob as I clutch his shirt, holding on for dear life so I don't feel like I'm drowning.

"I need you, Ryot."

"I know, baby."

I lift from his shoulder to look him in the eyes. He wipes the tears away, and from Nichole's bed, where she's been watching the entire thing, she says, "Can you kiss her, please? I'm dying over here."

It's a small moment of levity.

But just enough to tip the corner of my lips up as I lean my forehead against Ryot's and move my nose along his. He lifts my chin, and my lips connect with his in a soul-searing kiss that steals my breath and fills me with a chance of hope.

His mouth parts, and so does mine as my grip on him grows tighter and my need even stronger than before. I don't need him to give up his job for me, especially now that I understand where his idea for The Jock Report stemmed from. Me. His love for me, his desire to protect me. *He never gave up protecting me.* And he's been showing me that for years. He's shown me that I'm worth loving for years too. He signed the divorce papers because he thought that would make me happy. Who does that? This precious, loving, kind man.

I pull away and stare him in the eyes. "I appreciate you wanting to resign from The Jock Report, but I can't let you do that."

"And I can't let you leave Nichole, so it looks like we need to figure something out."

"Myla, can I please have a conversation with Ryot, alone?" Nichole asks from her bed.

"Why?" I ask.

"Because I said so," Nichole says in such a mom voice that it makes me smile.

Turning back to Ryot, I smooth my hand up his chest to his cheek, where I cling to him. "I'm sorry," I whisper.

"For what?" he says quietly.

"Everything," I answer. "For doubting, for pushing you away, for acting like you weren't worth trying for, even though you have shown me that I'm worth the effort."

"Myla." He dips his head to get a better look at me. "When I took my vows, I said that you would come first in my mind, always. And I broke that promise. You have nothing to apologize for. If anything, I need to thank you for the wake-up call, for the second chance, because I'm not sure I would have snapped out of it unless you did something drastic." He presses a sweet kiss to my forehead. "You have nothing to apologize for. All I ask is that you keep giving me and us a chance. Keep loving me, and we'll figure this out. Okay?"

I nod and then press my lips to his one more time before I stand from his lap. Just as I start to move away, Banner knocks on the door.

"Hey," he says, looking shy and awkward in a pair of sweatpants and a T-shirt, his hair completely disheveled. When his eyes travel over to Nichole, I notice the shock in them.

"Banner, what the hell are you doing here?" Nichole asks in a teasing tone.

"Uh . . . I heard you fell."

"I've fallen many times, but you've never come to see me before."

He pulls on the back of his neck. "Yeah, well, this is different."

She rolls her eyes and then shifts on her bed. "Banner and Ryot, line up at my bedside. Myla, can you please go find me some apple juice? And don't come back until I tell you, you can. I need to talk to these men."

"Why can't I listen in?"

"Because I love you very much, but I need your comfort, not your decision-making. Now go on."

Sighing—because I know she's right—I go back to Ryot and whisper, "Can I borrow your wallet? I don't have my purse with me."

He pulls it from his pocket and hands it to me right before pressing a kiss on my lips.

I turn back to Nichole and ask, "Do you need anything else?"

"Just for these guys to take their shirts off. I'm sick after all. The least they could do is give me a good show."

I chuckle as more tears come to my eyes because this is my girl. Positive, funny, loving Nichole.

I can't fucking lose her.

# Chapter Twenty-Four

RYOT

***Present day . . .***

"Do you really want our shirts off?" Banner asks as he grips the collar of his T-shirt.

Nichole smiles and shakes her head. "No, but pull up a chair because I need to speak to you two."

With Myla on the hunt for apple juice, Banner and I pull up chairs to Nichole's bed. I sit closest to her while Banner sits just to my left.

She looks at Banner. "I hope you're not here to express some undying love to me. Please tell me that's not the case because I am not in the mood to turn a man down."

He chuckles and shakes his head. "Here as a friend. Here for support. Here for anything that anyone might need."

"Okay, because we've had that conversation. You're hot, but also not my type."

He laughs some more. "Best orgasm of your life is not your type? Not sure how that works, but okay."

"My type is noncommittal, and you and I both know that deep down, you want to commit. You just need to find the right person first. Which by the way . . . how was Kenzie?"

I turn toward Banner. "Who the hell is Kenzie?"

"Kelsey and Lottie's cousin." He sighs. "And nothing happened there. That's why I don't tell you shit."

"Wait, you two talk?" I motion between them.

"Sort of," Banner answers. "We'll talk about random things. I saw a wine that reminded me of the night we had in my car when she was visiting two weeks ago, which by the way, thanks for the fucking memo on your cancer."

She just casually shrugs. "It would have ruined the moment. I needed to get some good dick in before the chemo really started to hit me." Leave it to Nichole to tell you like it is.

"That was some good dick." Banner winks. "But yeah, I texted her about a bottle of wine, she asked what I was doing, and I told her I was waiting around for Kenzie, who I thought would stand me up. She was twenty minutes late, so I was texting Nichole how annoyed I was about it."

Nichole turns to me. "I think your brother likes her. And when I say think, I mean, I know he likes her. And he thinks she's a virgin."

"Can you not discuss that stuff? I thought we were going to talk about you," Banner says.

"Why would I talk about me when clearly getting you riled up about Kenzie is more fun?" Speaking to me again, she says, "She's a total wallflower. Loves knitting, right? And can barely even look him in the eyes. Also, he told me she smells like a book. This hungry beast wants her."

Even though I know what Nichole is doing—deflecting—I

join in because the girl probably wants a break from talking about serious issues for a moment. Hell, if I were in her position, I'd want the same thing.

"Funny, you never mentioned that to me," I say to Banner, who is now rubbing his hands over his thighs.

"Because there's nothing really to talk about. She's, you know, shy and whatnot. Quiet—"

"Beautiful, and really funny when she finally opens up. Smart, quick-witted, and what did you say to me, some of the greatest tits you've ever seen?" Nichole adds. "Besides mine of course."

"You saw her tits?" I ask.

"No," Banner says quickly. "Just, you know, when she bends over and her shirt opens up a bit. They just look plump and nice."

"She wasn't wearing a bra at the reception, and he could practically hang a *just married* sign off her hard nipples."

"Nichole," Banner chastises, which makes her laugh even more.

"Dude, why didn't you say anything?"

"First of all, there's not much to say, and second of all, you've been going through something with Myla."

"But you think she's a virgin? That's something you would have said to me."

Banner rolls his eyes. "I don't know for sure, okay? But she just gives off those vibes."

"Or maybe she's a total freak in the bed, as sometimes the quiet ones are the ones you have to look out for."

"Can we stop talking about Kenzie? Nothing is going on there."

"But you wish there was," Nichole says with a smirk. "Don't lie to me. You were interested."

"Sure, whatever. Maybe there was some interest, but she blew me off completely, so clearly, she's not interested in me, and I'm not about to chase."

Nichole lets out the biggest guffaw. "Oh, Banner. It's cute how you think that. But you, my friend, were born to chase, especially after the girl who grabs your attention the most. And she has grabbed your attention."

He leans back in his chair and clenches his hands together. "Is this why you wanted to talk to us?"

"When I saw you walk through that door, yes, that was immediately put on the list," Nichole answers. "But also, we need to talk about Myla." The jovial mood Nichole was just in vanishes completely as she says, "I couldn't tell you how much time I have left, if I have time at all, or if I have some months to spare. My doctor doesn't think it looks good, but if Myla wants me to try to fight, then I will. I can make some more calls, do some more research."

"I can help," Banner says. "I met some leading hepatologists from Johns Hopkins when I was working on a medical app a few years back. I'll call them and see if they recommend any oncologists whose specialty includes liver cancer."

"Normally, I'd say I don't need help because I like to do things on my own, but I think I'll accept help with a phone call."

"Consider it done," Banner says.

"Okay, back to Myla. She's going to want to focus on my health and make sure I have everything I need, but I think we all know at this point, she can get lost in that. She doesn't handle stressful situations well. She won't let me focus on her, so I'm going to need you two to focus on her health, and her mental capacity for taking care of me. And I'm saying this because I need to know that if and when I leave this earth, she will be taken care of." I go to speak, but she lifts her hand. "I know you will do that, Ryot. You've proven yourself from day one. And I know we've had our ups and downs throughout your relationship with Myla, but looking back at it all, you've always loved her—loved her more than any other man in her life. But you did fuck up."

"I know. I fucked up, hard."

"We all have our moments," Nichole says. "I'm no angel. I think we know that after what happened when Myla's dad passed."

"Water under the bridge," I say.

"Yeah . . . I know," she says with a smirk, causing me to chuckle. "But I'm glad you've realized where your focus has been and that you're bringing it back to our girl, but I need you to know that's not where I want all of your focus going. You still need to do the ESPN show."

"Nichole. I already told you, I'm not—"

"I know what you said, but your decision is completely reactionary. There is emotion behind it rather than an intelligent, well-thought-out decision."

"The only thing that matters to me is keeping Myla."

"That's the right answer. But let's say, five years from now, you gave up The Jock Report, something you and I both know started because of Myla, and you're feeling immense regret. How do you think that will hang over your marriage?"

"She's right, dude," Banner says. "As much as I want to believe that giving up The Jock Report is going to be easy, it won't in the long run, not when you've put your heart into it."

"Which is why you need to take the job with ESPN. It doesn't have to be one or the other, you can have both."

"Not when Myla wants to live here. I'm not going to let there be space between us. She'll let me go if I allow there to be separation."

"Which is why I am posing an idea." Nichole shifts and reaches for her water. I reach out and hand it to her. She takes a few sips and then says, "I would like to move to California."

"What?" I ask. "Seriously?"

"Yes, I would. I've always loved the beach. My job has offered me medical leave for as long as I need it, and Myla will be able to help with appointments. I'm not super attached to my doctor, so finding someone in California won't bother me, especially if I have Banner's help. Myla keeps saying she wants to live in Chicago again, but we both know she just wants to live in a place where she has good memories, memories shared with you, Ryot. Being here in Chicago without you won't be what she wants. She needs to realize that it's okay to form new memories in a new place. So here is what I'm thinking." She smiles. "Are you two going to take notes?"

Banner and I glance at each other and then fish out our phones from our pockets. Seems like we're going to be told exactly what to do.

⊏⊐

## MYLA

I ENTER the room with five apple juices in hand, a shirt that says F*ck Cancer—they were selling them in the gift shop—and two word searches with accompanying pens. "I didn't know how many juices you wanted."

Nichole chuckles and says, "The more, the better." I hand one to her and then set the rest down on the table next to Nichole's bed as well as the word searches and pens. "Why don't you sit on your husband's lap?"

"Am I still her husband?" Ryot asks. When I glance at him, I still see some insecurity, and that's natural, given everything we've been through in the past few weeks.

I walk up to him and sit on his lap. "I never signed the papers, so yeah, you are." He smirks as he wraps his arms around me and holds on to me tightly as he kisses the back of my neck.

"I love you," he whispers, only for me to turn toward him and kiss him on the lips.

"I love you," I whisper back. Saying those words out loud

is something I've truly missed, and I've missed the joy it brings him. Those words are like fuel to the flame, igniting me from the inside out.

Nichole clears her throat, so we turn toward her as she says, "I would like to start this conversation by first saying, there will be no protesting. The decisions have been made per my request. Therefore, you must all go along with it. Please nod your heads so I know that you agree."

"But what if—" I start, but Nichole holds up her hand.

"I'm going to stop you right there and tell you that all decisions were made in your best interest. Therefore, there will be no protesting. I'm serious, Myla. What's done is done. That's it. End of discussion."

"How is that fair?"

"Because you are far too emotional to be involved in this conversation. I've gone over everything with the boys, and they've deemed it worthy, so you can either leave or you can listen to what the plan is. You tell me."

"Babe, just listen. I promise you'll like it." Ryot grips me soothingly, which warms me and eases my tension.

"Okay, but I reserve the right to have an opinion at the end."

"Cute that you think that." Nichole clears her throat. "Now, first things first. Number one on my list is that Banner is required to ask Kenzie out on a date."

"Kenzie?" I ask as Banner sinks into his chair.

"Jesus Christ, Nichole."

"You know you want to," she says.

"What's going on with Kenzie?" I ask.

Ryot leans into my ear and coos, "Banner likes her."

"Oh, is that so?" I turn toward him as he motions to Nichole to keep going.

"Let's move on."

"Remember, there is no protesting, so Banner, you must do as you're told." Nichole smirks, and even though she looks unwell, there's still a glint in her eyes. "Next on the list. Ryot will be accepting the ESPN job as well as keeping his position with The Jock Report."

I turn toward him, and he just says, "Keep listening."

"Thirdly, Myla, you won't be moving to Chicago. You will be staying in California with your husband—"

"I'm not leaving you," I protest, even though I know I shouldn't.

"Babe, give her a second." Ryot smooths his hand over my arm.

With an evil glare, Nichole continues, "You *will* be staying in California with your husband. You're going to take that job with Kelsey because from what I understand, it's a fantastic opportunity and something you've been dreaming of. Not to mention you seem to get along with them very well, from what I've been told. And me, well, I'll be moving as well to a beach house in California."

"Wait . . . what?" I ask, perking up.

"So will you and Ryot. He spoke with Huxley, who has a friend out in Malibu who rents houses. There are two right by the ocean, two doors down from each other, which would work perfectly for us. Your dearest husband has demanded to help with the cost of the rent. Banner has some doctors he wants me to talk to, and I'll continue my treatments in California."

"Seriously?" My eyes well up with tears.

"Yes. Now, there are no promises as to where this will take me, or what treatments are available. But even if I'm afforded a year, that's one more year just sitting by the beach, reading all the books that I want to read, and enjoying the most beautiful sunsets while living near my best friend again."

Tears stream down my face as I walk over to Nichole. I sit on the edge of her bed and say, "Are you sure that's what you want to do?"

"I'm more than positive." Then she whispers and nods toward Ryot, "You sure you still want to stay married to him?"

I look over my shoulder at the most handsome, generous, and loving man I've ever met. "More than sure," I answer.

"Good, that was a test, and you passed."

"So this is happening. You're moving to California?"

Nichole nods. "Yup. There will be some transferring we have to do with my treatments, but Banner has already been in contact with some people. It might take a week or so, but Ryot said you two will stay out here as long as we need to and then move me out to be with you."

"Oh my God." I lean into Nichole and hold her tightly. "Thank you," I whisper.

Nichole rubs my back and says quietly, "I don't know what the future holds for me, but what I do know is that you will be taken care of. That you will continue to live the life you deserve, and that I won't have to worry about it when I do finally pass. The one thing I wish is for your happiness." She lifts away to look me in the eyes. "You are happiest with Ryot."

"Thank you for helping me see that."

"Anything for you. After all, you've so generously been my wing-woman for several years, landing me some of the best action of my life. It's the least I could do."

I chuckle and then hug her again.

Nichole is right, her future is uncertain, but at least with this plan, I'll feel comfortable knowing we've done everything we could to give her the best chance. And to give my marriage the best chance possible.

━━━

"ARE you sure you're not hungry?" Ryot asks as we enter the penthouse.

After a day of planning at the hospital, looking at the Malibu houses repeatedly, and hiring movers to help Nichole pack, she was completely toast and ready for some sleep. The doctor said she would be able to be discharged tomorrow. They just wanted to monitor her for another night before they signed her out. So of course, she kicked us out and sent us on our way.

Banner took a flight home so he could speak to some doctors for her and come up with an action plan. When I asked about Kenzie, he just ignored me and moved on. There is no doubt in my mind that Nichole will hold him to that date.

And now that we're back at the hotel, I'm exhausted and just want to lie down.

"I don't want to eat right now. Can we just go to bed?"

"Sure," he says as he takes my hand and leads me to the bedroom.

Together we get ready, taking turns using the bathroom, sharing the toothpaste, and splashing our faces with water. I change into one of his shirts, and he undresses down to his briefs. When we're both ready, he lifts the covers of the bed so I can get in first. When he slips in, he turns toward me and immediately places his hand on my hip, pulling me in close.

"You okay?" he asks.

I nod and draw my finger down his chest. "Can I talk to you for a second?"

"Of course."

I've been thinking about this all day, wanting to clear the air with him because we didn't start the day off well. We had to make up in front of other people, and now that we're here alone, I just want him to know how much he matters to me.

As much as I've been absolutely terrified thinking about Nichole's cancer, I've also been thinking about why I didn't try harder with Ryot. We did make vows, as I was reminded of when we danced at JP's wedding. Vows to stick together no matter what life threw us. To love each other with everything we have. Unlike my mom, who did everything in her power to devalue me and wreck me, Ryot has never offered me anything but praise and positivity. Opposed to my dad, who never stood up for me, who abandoned me when I needed him the most—*for his other family*—Ryot has been my protector. My champion. I am the luckiest woman in the world.

"I know you said I don't need to apologize, but I still want to. I'm sorry I put fear into your heart about where I stand when it comes to us. I need you to know that I never stopped loving you, Ryot. Never. Even when I handed you those divorce papers, I was still as much in love with you as I was the day we married. That has never changed. I just didn't think I had the mental capacity to stay with you after going through those few months with The Jock Report."

"I get it, baby. You don't need to explain anything."

"But I need you to know I was still very much in love with you."

He nods and then quietly says, "That means a lot to me, because when we were in Napa and you weren't saying I love you back, it nearly broke me."

"I thought I'd break if I did say the words. I was protecting my heart and my head. As I said, you are the one person who can break me, yet also the one person who can put me back together."

"I hope I'm putting you back together now."

"You are." I scoot in closer. "The way you handled everything today with Nichole, it means more to me than I think you'll ever know. You stepped up. You protected me once again. And instead of walking away like others would have done, you stuck by my side. Without criticism. It's the kind of man you are, one I will never find again in this lifetime. You are one of a kind, Ryot, and I am so freaking lucky to call you mine."

He leans his forehead against mine. "I'm the lucky one." His nose rubs against mine. "You create this sense of peace within me, Myla, and when I had to turn over those divorce papers, it was like the peace was snatched from my hands." He slides his palm up my side and under my shirt. "I was trying to give you your space, but desperately attempting to figure out a way to get that peace back." His hand slides past my stomach, past my breast, and lands right above my heart. "Your heartbeat is the cadence of my life, and without it in my palm, I'm an aimless wanderer. I don't ever want to feel that again. Ever. And I swear to you, at this moment, where it's just you and me, I will never take you for fucking granted again. You are everything to me, Myla. And I'm sorry that I lost sight of that."

"I promise to do the same because you are my everything too, Ryot. Nichole is right, you are my happiness, and I want to hold on to that until my last breath." I lean in and press my lips to his, feeling him suck in a deep breath as he rolls me to my back.

He doesn't say anything else. Instead, I get lost in the feel of his strength taking over my body. Through every kiss and every touch, he silently holds on to that promise and strengthens it so there is no way we're ever untying the knot that is our life together.

# Epilogue

## RYOT

***Myla:*** *At Nichole's. We have falafel and hummus.*

I chuckle, staring at Myla's text, and quickly remove my suit and change into a pair of shorts and a tank top. After a long day of shooting The Jock Report segment with ESPN, I'm ready to see my girl.

It's been a month since Nichole was in the hospital. We ended up staying a little over a week in Chicago before we could transfer her on a private jet to California. She met with her new doctors immediately, and they came up with a plan. We're not overly optimistic, but they have said there could be a chance of possible survival if they can reduce the tumor and stop the spread. We're taking it one day at a time.

Malibu has been the right move for us. Even though we're renting, Myla has made the beach house more of a home than our initial place. She's hung pictures of our wedding, created an inviting space with Caribbean tones—her words, not mine

—and added a touch of her own flair with color-blocking murals that she's started adding in the office building spaces.

Speaking of my girl, she just started working with Kelsey this week, and she's already designed some spaces that Kelsey is in love with. They had a design meeting yesterday, and from what Myla has told me, Kelsey was swooning. Myla is truly in her element, and I don't think I've seen her this happy. Makes me realize that, in fact, you can get wrapped up in your own head and forget to see the things around you. It's good to lift your head from the hole every once in a while and look around.

Ready to walk over, I send a quick text to Myla.

**Ryot:** *Need me to bring anything over?*

She texts back quickly.

**Myla:** *Just your sweet ass.*

Speaking of ass . . . Myla and I got a sex swing installed in the room, and last night, she swung on it while lying on her belly. That's all I'm going to say about that, but Jesus Christ, it was an experience still living in my brain.

I lock up the house and head on over. The walk is short since she's only two houses down, and the neighborhood is incredibly peaceful. I truly believe the fresh air and the sun are helping Nichole. And sure, I might be just telling myself that to make myself feel better, but every day, it seems like her smile's becoming more genuine.

I don't bother heading to the front door. Instead, I enter the pin to the keypad that keeps her side gate closed and then head to the back deck where I know they're sitting. It's where Nichole spends most of her time. As I approach, I hear their voices. I'm tempted to stop and listen to their conversation, but I'm also desperate to see my girl, so I round the corner and find them lounging together on one of the oversized loungers under a large black and white umbrella.

"Our cabana boy has arrived," Nichole says with a wink.

Over the past month, my relationship with Nichole has

grown to where we used to be before Myla's dad passed away. It didn't take much. We both found out we were rooting for one another after a serious conversation and, ever since, we've been a solid support for one another.

"I'll be your cabana boy, but not free of charge. You're going to have to tip me this time." I walk up to them and lean down to give Myla a kiss. "Hey, baby, I missed you."

"I missed you too." She smiles as I pull away.

"Enough with the heart eyes, can we please eat? I'm starving," Nichole says.

"Can't let the girl starve." I bring over the food that's in a take-out bag and set it on the lounger. While I divvy everything up, I ask, "How was your day, Nichole?"

"Good. Those binoculars you got me have been a godsend. I caught a couple behind some rocks today doing the old blow job. I learned a thing or two."

"How could you possibly have learned something?" I ask in a teasing tone.

"Ask your brother. Not the greatest at a blow job, not like my girl here."

I glance at Myla, who is smirking.

Yeah, she's fucking good.

Really good.

Having her mouth on my cock is probably one of the best feelings ever.

"My gag reflex is too strong, but this girl was doing all sorts of wizardry with her hands."

"Well, don't be opposed to sharing, you know . . . that's caring after all," I say. I hand Myla a plate of food and say, "What about you, babe?"

"Well, besides the fact that I just learned my friend is a total voyeur and that my husband believes there could be improvement made on my blow jobs—"

"What, no, I didn't say that," I backtrack. "Just you know,

if she ever wants to share information, that's all. Babe, you know you give me the best head."

She chuckles. "Wow, what an accomplishment. I should put that on my résumé. Gives best head."

I take a bite of falafel and say, "I'd hire you."

She rolls her eyes. "Anyway, while I was going over some designs with Kelsey today, I got an email from my professor. You know the design I did for my year-end project? Well, the company loved it so much that they want to use it. They're commissioning me to assist with the project."

"Holy shit. Really, babe?" I ask.

"Wait, seriously? You've been sitting on that information this whole time while I've told you about how I watched a seagull poop on someone today?" Nichole pushes Myla playfully.

"I wanted to wait to tell both of you. But yes, my design was chosen, and I'm freaking out. I asked Kelsey if I could do both, work for her and handle the project, and she said absolutely. She thinks it will be good for me to take on the job, as it would be great to have it in the portfolio when we approach other buildings."

"Baby, that's amazing," I say as I stand from the lounger and take her hand in mine, coercing her to stand so I can wrap my arms around her. I pull her into a hug and lean down to her ear, where I whisper, "I'm so proud of you. Jesus, babe, you're amazing."

"Thank you." When she pulls away and rests her hands on my chest, she says, "I know we don't talk about those few months when things were difficult between us, but there is something that I never told you. If it wasn't for those months when you were focusing on yourself, I don't know if I would have taken the time to focus on me and what I needed to be happy, separate from our marriage. I found myself, and I found you all over again."

I drag my hand over her cheek and whisper, "You amaze

me." Then I lean down and kiss her on the lips, reveling that everything feels so right, connected, and in tune with the universe.

Nichole's journey might be up in the air, but she's propelled us forward in ours, so weirdly, I think this was all meant to happen this way.

It's odd. When you feel like you're at your absolute worst, total rock bottom, it could be the universe letting you know that you need to build a new foundation, a stronger one—a foundation that will jumpstart the next chapter in your life.

Myla handing me those divorce papers was more like the universe giving me a shovel with a gentle nudge to encourage me to start digging.

"All right, enough with the lovey-dovey stuff," Nichole says. "I need you to tell me more about this design. And then when you're done, I have some tea to spill about Banner and Kenzie."

Myla's head snaps to the side, and she says, "Forget my design. Give us the tea."

Printed in Great Britain
by Amazon

39706503R00258